Acclaim for Greg Dinallo's

FINAL ANSWERS

Books by Greg Dinallo

Final Answers*
Purpose of Evasion
Rockets' Red Glare

*Published by POCKET BOOKS

GREG DINALLO

FINAL ANSWERS

POCKET BOOKS

New York   London   Toronto   Sydney   Tokyo   Singapore

This book is a work of fiction. Names, characters, places, and
incidents are either products of the author's imagination or are
used fictitiously. Any resemblance to actual events or locales or
persons, living or dead, is entirely coincidental.

POCKET BOOKS, a division of Simon & Schuster Inc.
1230 Avenue of the Americas, New York, NY 10020

ISBN: 0-671-73312-5

First Pocket Books paperback printing October 1993

10 9 8 7 6 5 4 3 2 1

POCKET and colophon are registered trademarks of
Simon & Schuster Inc.

Cover art by Lee MacLeod, stepback photo by A. Friedlander/
Superstock, Inc.

Printed in the U.S.A.

For those who are still unaccounted for,
and those who live with the uncertainty.

Acknowledgments

For technical information I am especially indebted to: Lt. Col. Johnie E. Webb, Jr., Commander of the Army's Central Identification Laboratory, as well as Sergeant Richard Huston and Thorn Helgesen of the CIL staff; and to John Vieira, friend, actuary, and Principal of Towers Perrin, and his associate Gordon Gould. I'd also like to thank: Betsy Cox and Kelly Murphy of the National League of Families; Paul Gray of the National Personnel Records Center; John Holman and Wanda Ruffin of the Friends of the Vietnam Veterans Memorial; Ray Moreau of Electronic Data System Corp., who designed the FVVM's "In Touch" computer system; Frank Johns, Major, USAF, retired; Shari Lawrence of U.S. Total Army Personnel Command; Major Ronald Fuchs USAF; Nora Alter and Loris Mirella of the University of Pennsylvania; and my colleagues in the screenwriting trade—Burton Armus and Joe Gunn, formerly of the NYPD and LAPD, respectively.

Final Answers

"—2,700,000 served,
    300,000 were wounded, 11%
    75,000 were disabled, 3%
    57,000 died, and more than 2%
    2,500 remain unaccounted for. .001
    They are not forgotten."

From the official program at the ground-breaking
ceremony for the Vietnam Veterans Memorial.

November 13, 1982

1

I TELL FORTUNES," I SAY MATTER-OF-FACTLY, KNOWING the woman will be intrigued. "And I'm good at it." That's what I always say at cocktail parties when I'm asked what I do for a living. Pressed further, I admit to being one of the guys who predicts the future for the power hitters of corporate America.

I can tell from her expression that the Capitol Hill matron who's latched on to me is having visions of risk taking and leveraged buyouts. But her eyes glaze when I reveal that I'm an insurance and pension plan actuary, which means I spend my day statistically predicting when people will die.

She forces a smile, finishes her champagne, and hurries off in search of a refill before I have a chance to tell her that the two most important words in my vocabulary are probability and death.

They usually hang in there until I explain that since my discharge from the Army more than twenty years ago, I've realized that the former—in the guise of a high draft number—is responsible for my current fascination with the latter. The specter of Vietnam never fails to send them scurrying for cover.

I didn't think much about death as a child. I wasn't one of those kids who squirted ants with lighter fluid. I was the bored, gifted type who cut classes and could be found at Fenway Park recalculating Ted Williams' batting average in my head, or at the movies watching *Double Indemnity* and rooting for the wiley claims investigator played by Edward G. Robinson, not Barbara Stanwyck and Fred Mac-Murray, the conspiring lovers who had murdered her husband

1

for his insurance. I was still in my teens when I came face-to-face with death in its most violent forms.

It seemed like a great idea at the time. Twelve years of Catholic education had taught me that the wrath of God was nothing compared to the threat of Communism. I breezed through basic training, volunteered for Ranger school, and ended up in Special Operations.

I arrived in Vietnam in 1967 during the first week of October. The monsoon season had just ended. Search and destroy operations were resuming. I was assigned to a counterintelligence unit and soon found myself in a Huey gunship heading to a landing zone about fifteen klicks inside Laos.

"A little OJT for the FNGs," my team leader said in his East Texas drawl as we streaked above the jungle. At twenty-two, he was a combat-weary three-striper with vacant eyes that concealed his disdain for the fucking new guys they kept sending him, one of whom, he had no doubt, would eventually fuck up and get him killed.

"Tags off, Bambi," he growled, glaring at me. "One piece of tin in each boot, like this." He removed the dog tags from his neck chain, then undid his laces, and tucked one behind the tongue of each boot, threading the lace through the hole in the dog tag before retying it. "These start playing 'Jingle Bells' in the bush, get you greased real quick."

When we reached the LZ, the helicopter circled it several times, then hovered above the clearing before touching down. A chubby Asian girl, no more than seven or eight years old, came out of the jungle and began running through the grass toward the chopper.

The sergeant crouched in the door, watching her. He waited until she was about twenty feet away, then calmly fired a burst from his M-16. The rounds tore into the child's chest. Her tiny body flew backward as if it had been hit by a truck; then it landed, and began twitching in grotesque spasms.

"Chrissakes!" I blurted, horrified. Despite all the training and Special Ops orientation lectures, I was still back in high school. "Chrissakes, that was a kid! A fucking kid!"

The sergeant nodded matter-of-factly, then leapt to the

ground as the slick settled down. The patrol piled out and followed. Three grunts approached the child's body that was lying motionless in the grass.

"Ain't no such thing in-country," the sergeant drawled as the rest of us fanned out and began setting up a perimeter around the LZ.

"No what?" I demanded, my voice ringing with anger.

"Fat little gook kids. Just ain't any. Y'all remember that."

I wasn't sure what he meant until a deafening explosion knocked us to the ground in a shower of bloody tissue. When we got to our feet, a smoking crater the size of a two-car garage was centered in the clearing. The girl's corpse had blown up, killing the three GIs who were defusing the twenty pounds of plastique taped to her scrawny torso. If she had made it to the chopper, she would have blown us all to bits.

The field was covered with body parts. We spent hours tagging and bagging them. By the time we finished, my tiger stripes were smeared with blood and dotted with bits of dried flesh. I tried peeling them off with my jungle knife, then used my fingernails like everyone else. I don't remember how many times I vomited.

Six months later, I was the hard-stripe with vacant eyes. I was the one who conducted the on-the-job training. I warned the FNGs, "If you're in the fucking jungle and a path looks inviting, don't take it. Never, *never,* go through a gate—climb the fucking fence instead. Enter a hutch through a window, never through a fucking door." And that was exactly what I did, and still damn near got killed.

The North Vietnamese had set up a series of relay stations along the Ho Chi Minh Trail, their main supply route through southern Laos, along which massive caches of arms, food, clothing, and equipment were concealed. These storage depots were brilliantly camouflaged and couldn't be located from the air.

My counterintelligence unit was choppered across the fence into Champasak Province to run search and destroy sweeps. We humped through the jungle for days before finding the main operations hutch just south of Thateng. Prior to entering any building, we'd always toss in a couple of grenades to take out gooks and detonate booby traps. But not this time. This time we had orders to take prisoners. I went around back and climbed through a window. My foot snagged a trip wire concealed in the thatch, detonating a Bouncing Betty buried in the floor. An explosion of steel fleshettes tore into my legs. The impact blew me back out the window into the bush. A couple of my buddies had just reached me when the North Vietnamese came out of the woodwork and all hell broke loose. GIs were going down everywhere.

I was lucky.

My guys got me to an LZ, where a medic worked on my wounds until a medevac chopper came in and got me out of there. I woke up in a field hospital, both legs wrapped in bandages. A week later, I was flown to a hospital in Saigon, then spent several months in rehab at Tripler in Hawaii before mustering out.

My luck continued to hold. The young woman I was madly in love with since high school had waited for me.

Nancy was bright, compassionate, and incredibly supportive. We married and headed for California, where Cal Tech beckoned. She held me together through the years of emotional turmoil that followed: the guilt at having survived—at what I'd done to survive—the disillusionment of having fought in an unpopular war, and the fire fights that haunted my nightmares, all the while teaching school to support us while I got my degree in economics. She handled the throes of developing a business and raising a family with the same spirit and good humor.

Now, decades later, our two daughters are away at college, and the empty nest syndrome is our biggest problem. They were home for Christmas, but before we knew it, they were gone again. We're really feeling the separation now.

I have to be in Washington, D.C., for a few days. Congress is formulating legislation that will revise the social security system. Over the years, my company has provided actuarial data for several federal pension and insurance programs, and I've been asked to appear before the committee as an expert witness. Fortunately, the trip coincided with

semester break, which meant Nancy, who teaches high
school, could accompany me.

It was late afternoon when our flight landed in a cold
drizzle at Dulles International. We took a cab to the Hay
Adams, which rivals the best hotels of London. Our suite
has high ceilings, fine antiques, and arched windows that
overlook Lafayette Square and the White House directly
beyond. After a shower and change of clothes, Nancy and
I ventured downstairs to the cocktail party, hosted by members of the committee, where the Capitol Hill matron
latched on to me. She turned out to be the high point of
the evening, and Nancy and I retired early.

We awaken at dawn to discover the rain has turned to
wet snow. I'm not scheduled to testify until after lunch, so
we bundle up and go sight-seeing, starting on the Mall with
the Washington Monument. Its pale shadow points the way
to Constitution Gardens, where the Vietnam Veterans Memorial is located.

Nancy leads the way.

It's an extremely long walk to the wall.

And my gut tightens with each step.

I wasn't one of the thousands of vets who flocked to
Washington in November of 1982 when it was dedicated.
I'd resolved my anger. I had a family and a successful
career. The healing was complete. I didn't want to relive
the pain. But over the years, I felt the wall's pull and did
some reading about it. I know it's the work of Maya Ying
Lin, a Yale architectural student whose design was selected
from thousands of submissions; that it created controversy
and political backbiting; that it was approved, funded, and
built in the face of formidable opposition and puzzling apathy; that it has moved men to tears and poetry; and that the
concrete foundation entombs a dead pilot's purple heart.

We come over a small rise where three bronze servicemen are standing in a thicket of bare trees. A mantle
of snow drapes incongruously across their tropical battle
gear, nestling in the folds of metal. Far below, the white
earth appears to have sheared on a V-shaped fault revealing
the granite wall. In the soft mound of snow that drifts
against it are flags, wreaths, flowers, snapshots, religious

articles, and military mementos left by visitors. We continue down a gentle slope to the cobblestone-lined path that parallels the wall. Soon the black granite is towering above us, the 58,176 names stretching as far as we can see in each direction.

"It's like descending into a tomb," Nancy whispers.

I nod solemnly, unable to reply. Nothing I've read or heard has come close to preparing me for this; neither for the sudden surge of emotion that comes from being in this sacred place, nor for how powerfully and eloquently it expresses the meaning of courage, sacrifice, and devotion to duty.

Large snowflakes are falling lazily around me as I read the names that are listed in chronological, not alphabetical, order. Those who died together are listed together. It doesn't take me long to find names I know: names of men I led in battle; names of men who died in my arms; men whom I came to love like brothers; and men who were killed before I ever got to know them. I run a fingertip over the wet granite, reflecting on the thrills and horrors we shared, when I see what seems to be another familiar name. I gently brush aside the snow that has stuck to the wall covering some of the letters, and am baffled by what I see. For a few moments, I just stand there trying to make sense out of something that makes no sense at all.

"Nancy? Nance, look at this," I finally call out, my voice cracking with emotion. "Nancy?" I repeat to no avail. Like the millions of visitors who come here, she has become lost in the names etched into the polished black granite, and in her feelings.

"Nance? Come here. Take a look at this, will you?" I call again.

"You know," she says, as she joins me. "The next time we're thinking about sending men into battle, the President should come here first; and then, if he still thinks it's a good idea—" She shrugs and lets the sentence trail off.

I nod, my teeth tugging at the inside of my lower lip, and gently touch the wall. "Look."

Nancy steps to where I'm pointing; and engraved in the granite, in the middle of panel 50E, she sees the name—A. CALVERT MORGAN—my name.

2

"SIXTY PERCENT OF ALL THE PEOPLE WHO HAVE EVER lived are alive today," the senator says, reading from the prepared testimony I've submitted to the committee. "Furthermore, as a result of highly improved medical care, diet, exercise habits, and health consciousness, and despite the impact of plagues, famines, wars, sex education, and modern methods of birth control, this number continues to rise steadily." He pauses, removes his glasses, and looks at me, soliciting a comment.

I stare at him blankly. I heard the words but have no idea what he said. The hearing room is neither hot nor stuffy; and as an expert witness, I've no reason to be distracted or unprepared; but between me and the dais stands an impenetrable wall of names carved in black granite. I can't get the incident at the Memorial out of my mind.

"This statistic," the senator prompts with the slightest hint of a drawl, "what does it have to do with social security legislation?"

"Well sir," I say, collecting my thoughts, "when it comes to probability analysis, past performance counts. It might be helpful to keep in mind that it's a lot like parimutuel handicapping."

A ripple of laughter comes from the dais and gallery. The senator's family has been breeding and racing Thoroughbreds for generations—a fact I noted in the packet of background profiles the committee routinely supplies to witnesses.

The senator's eyes flare with indignation. He holds up a document that could pass for a phone book and challenges,

7

"Mr. Morgan, am I to understand you're comparing this bill to a racing form?"

"To be brutally honest, Senator, I use the same computer program to analyze both."

He tries to hold back, but can't and laughs along with the others. "Picked a few winners in your day, have you?" he prompts knowingly.

"A few. Let me put it this way, Senator. Figuring the odds and beating them are what make actuaries tick. It's in our genes. Keeping that in mind," I continue, deciding to make the most of the moment, "the success of this legislation depends on how accurately we can predict human longevity. I think some of this data is way off the mark." In the ensuing exchanges I make a convincing argument that it needs to be revised.

"The committee thanks you for your time, Mr. Morgan," the senator says when I finish. "I assure you, your comments will be taken under advisement."

Taken under advisement? Isn't that what I say when my staff is pushing an idea I know is going nowhere? It's frustrating and distracting, and takes my mind off the Memorial for a while, but during the ride back to the hotel and all through dinner I keep drifting back to it.

"Come on," Nancy counsels, "there was probably more than one Cal Morgan who died in Vietnam."

"Not humping in my platoon. Those were my guys on there. The ones that went down in Thateng."

"Anything's possible," she says, her eyes taking on a mischievous glint that always means I'm about to be unmercifully zinged. "Hey, any actuary worth his salt knows the odds are about one in sixty thousand."

I smile, but that initial A. keeps nagging me. "Arlo? Archibald? Adlai?" Nancy teased when we were dating in high school. She finally hit on Angus, which I sheepishly admitted was the name of a great-grandfather in Scotland. We've been playing this word game ever since: A is for agreeable, abrasive, astonishing, alluring, angry.

We're back in our hotel room propped up in bed. Nancy has one eye on an old movie on television, the other on the term papers she's correcting. I'm doing some homework on my laptop.

The Compaq LTE is my favorite electronic toy: 386 processor running at 20 megahertz, 18 millisecond access time, 60 megabyte hard drive, VGA gas plasma screen, NiCad battery, internal modem, 8 pounds, about the size of a package of typing paper. It can handle spreadsheets, word processing, statistical analysis, a bridge program capable of match-level play, and can do some serious number crunching.

I'm running a longevity simulation when something occurs to me. "A is for absurd," I say, thinking aloud. "The name on the wall can't be mine."

"Why not?"

"Well, if it is, it means I was recorded as killed in action."

"I guess," she says, wondering where I'm headed.

"Wouldn't my parents have been notified?"

"Uh-huh, but they weren't."

I nod, then, after thinking about it for a moment, I hear myself saying, "Maybe they were."

"I don't follow you."

"Suppose I was listed as KIA, and they were so relieved when they found out it was a mistake, they never said anything? You know those old 'Southies' and their superstitions." I reach to the nightstand and lift the phone.

"You're going to call them?"

"Why not? I mean, if they were notified, it'd put an end to all this, wouldn't it?"

Nancy nods, and I start dialing.

"Dad, it's Cal." I hear the television in the background and picture him in the living room of his house in South Boston engrossed in a basketball game.

"Hi. You did pretty well today. Congratulations."

"Thanks. How do you know?"

"C-Span. I'd like to tell that committee a thing or two."

"Instead of complaining, why don't you—"

"Write my congressman? I did. You really think they pay attention to old farts like me who—"

"Dad? Dad, I have a question for you."

"Oh, sure. Sorry."

"I know this is going to sound weird, but when I was in

Vietnam, were you and Mom ever notified that I was killed in action?"

"Killed?" he says after a long pause. "No. God forbid."

"You're sure. The Army didn't make a mistake or anything?"

"Positive. That's not the sort of thing a parent would forget."

"I guess not."

"We were notified that you'd been wounded. That was more than enough to handle, believe me. What's this all about, anyway?"

"Nothing important, really." His voice has taken on an emotional timbre and I realize being forced to relive those moments has unsettled him. "By the way, you see that game Bird played yesterday?" I ask, purposely changing the subject. Dad gets right into it, and we spend the next ten minutes arguing the chances of the Celtics winning the playoffs.

"Sounds like he got upset," Nancy prompts when I hang up.

"A little. He'll be all right."

"What about you?"

"Number one, babe," I say. It's military slang for the best, terrific. Guys who went home alive were number one, and it became a little thing between us after my return from Vietnam.

Nancy smiles knowingly, realizing that what's really bothering me about my name being on the Vietnam Veterans Memorial is not being listed as dead, but that being listed is an honor I, fortunately, haven't earned.

"Cal," she says thoughtfully, adjusting her position in the bed to face me. "I think we should find out one way or the other, don't you?"

I let out a long breath at the thought of having to deal with the bureaucracy and nod. I go back to the laptop, exit the simulation, and pull up my schedule. "Jammed solid. I've got meetings all day tomorrow."

"I don't."

"What about Georgetown? I thought you were taking a tour?"

Nancy shrugs. "Maybe I'll have time to do both. If not, it'll still be here next time."

"Thanks," I reply softly, pleased she's taking it on. Over the years, I've realized that whoever said "If you need something done fast, ask a busy person to do it" had Nancy in mind. She's the most meticulously prepared and tenacious advocate, or adversary, as school boards, politicians, and charities in our community well know.

"Feeling better?" she prompts, hearing the relief in my voice.

"Sure am, babe." I roll over onto my stomach and begin nuzzling her. "Where you going to start?"

"With your serial number."

"Good idea," I say, slipping my fingers beneath her nightgown. "Somebody's got to have a list of them."

"You remember it?" she asks, pinning my hand against the smooth flesh of her abdomen so it can move neither up nor down.

"One one six three zero one seven four three," I recite, without missing a beat.

"Not bad." She releases her grip on my hand in reward. "It's either the same serial number as the name on the wall or it isn't."

"Uh-huh."

"And if it is?"

"Who cares?" I whisper with the false bravado that so often accompanies these moments.

3

ONE ONE SIX THREE ZERO ONE SEVEN FOUR THREE,"
Nancy says, as she pulls off her gloves and slides onto the
chair opposite me.

We're in Kramer's, a bookstore on Connecticut Avenue
just north of Dupont Circle. Some friends told us about the
place and we decided to meet here at the end of the day.
As it turns out Kramer's is a hangout for the District's
intellectuals; and on this below freezing afternoon, they
seem more interested in the steaming cups of espresso and
cappuccino served in the café than the broad selection of
printed matter on the stacks that tower over us.

"You're positive it was my serial number?"

Nancy nods solemnly. "I'm sorry, I was hoping to be
able to tell you it wasn't. I saw it on the computer next to
your name."

I let out a long breath, coping with the knowledge that
the name on the Vietnam Memorial is undoubtedly mine. I
drain my coffee, hoping it will forestall the hollow feeling
that's growing in the pit of my stomach, then flag a passing
waiter for a refill. Nancy orders a hot chocolate.

"Where?" I finally ask her. "Where'd you find this
out?"

"From the people who built the Memorial." She hands
me a pamphlet titled Friends of the Vietnam Veterans
Memorial.

An introductory paragraph explains the FVVM is an independent, nonprofit organization that helps veterans and the
families of deceased or missing vets find each other, and
raises funds that are used to maintain the Memorial.

"They were in the phone book," Nancy continues. "I figured if anyone had a list of the people on the wall, they would."

"How'd you know about them?"

"We get a fund-raising thing in the mail every year."

"We do?"

"Yes. I always send something."

I smile and shake my head in amazement. With characteristic resourcefulness, Nancy has managed to get the information without dealing with the government bureaucracy. "What'd they say when you told them it was a mistake?"

"Well, the clerk who was helping me didn't get rattled, if that's what you mean. Matter of fact—" Nancy pauses before delivering the punch line and removes a notebook from her briefcase—"he said you weren't alone."

"I'm not?" I ask, somewhat astonished.

She shakes her head no, opens the notebook, and hands it to me. At the bottom of a page of hastily written notes are three names: Robert Bedeker, Willard Craig, and Darrell Lausch.

"These guys are on the wall too?"

"Uh-huh."

"And they're all alive and well, and living in the U.S.A.?"

"That's what he said. He took it right off the computer. Evidently their data base includes every man who's listed on the wall."

"He say if he had any idea how this sort of thing could happen?"

"Yes. As far as he knew all three were data entry errors made in the field."

"You mean they were recorded as killed in action instead of wounded."

"Right. He said somebody probably wrote KIA instead of WIA."

"Hell, even just a guy with sloppy handwriting'd account for it."

"Yes, he was surprised that mistakes weren't made more often. He mentioned something about—I think he called them collection points. It wasn't clear. I got the feeling he didn't want to get into it."

Who could blame him? Collection points were jungle-based checkout counters where the price of war was tallied; the place where dead GIs were brought to be processed by graves registration personnel; where the rubberized canvas bags that contained their bodies were stacked like cords of firewood next to the portable refrigeration units that were always filled beyond capacity; where the stench of death, not cappuccino, hung in the air. I can smell it now; an acrid, stomach-turning odor that suddenly fills my head, unleashing a burst of lightning-fast flashbacks: the village, the hutch, the window, the explosion, the blinding pain, my guys dragging me through elephant grass, the voices of medics, the sting of needles, the shouts of "Chopper coming in, chopper coming in!" drowned out by the whomp of rotors and sharp chatter of machine-gun fire, enemy rounds whizzing past, punching holes in metal and flesh as frightened eighteen-year-olds lifted me into the hovering slick, and then—through a morphine haze—the earthy rhythms of "Dock of the Bay," and a white flash that I eventually realized was a smile.

"Looking good, soldier," a comely nurse at the field hospital said.

"This is the WLW?" I asked weakly, assuming the worst.

"No fucking way," she replied, assuring me that I wasn't in what we called the white lie ward, where hopeless cases were housed until they died. "I wouldn't plan on auditioning for the Rockettes," she joked, "but the guys in OR did a hell of a job patching up those gams."

"Buy them a couple of Party Packs for me, will you?" I asked. A Party Pack contained ten joints of high-grade Cambodian Red that were machine rolled just like cigarettes, filters and all. "Hell, shoot the works, make them hundreds." The hundreds were longer than a standard cigarette and had been soaked in opium. "Ten for ten," the Mommasans who sold them would call out, and worth every penny of it.

"Sure. Who should I say they're from?"

"Cal Morgan, Sergeant, G Company Rangers," I replied, reciting my serial number. "Why do you ask?"

"You came in without any ID; not even dog tags. Bet they were in your boots, right?"

"Uh-huh."

"Well, you didn't have them, either. Medics must've yanked 'em during triage before you were vacked out. One of these days they'll put the boots on the gurneys like they're supposed to." She gave me another shot of morphine, and suddenly everything was gone.

I'm staring numbly at the reflection of the overhead lighting grid in my espresso when Nancy's voice pulls me out of it.

"Cal, you okay?" she asks, seeing how my expression has darkened. "Cal, what is it?"

"My boots," I mutter in reply.

"Your boots? What do they have to do with a clerical mistake?"

"It wasn't a clerical mistake," I say, suddenly seeing it all very clearly.

"Why not?"

"Three reasons. For openers, after talking to Dad last night, we can be pretty sure that I wasn't listed as killed in action by mistake like these guys."

"And the other two?"

"My dog tags."

It's been twenty-four years since I told her about the incident at the field hospital, but I can tell from the way her eyes widen that she remembers it.

"I had leg wounds; they removed my boots and my pants. My tags and ID probably went with 'em."

"You think somebody else ended up with them?"

"Uh-huh. Only he wasn't lucky like me. He didn't make it."

"But what about his dog tags and ID? I mean, I remember your ID had your photograph. Wouldn't that have tipped them off?"

"Maybe, maybe not."

"I also remember you telling me dog tags weren't the only thing they used to make identifications."

"You mean fingerprints, dental charts?"

Nancy nods uncomfortably and tilts her head toward the

next table where a man seems to be eavesdropping on our conversation from behind a newspaper.

"When they could," I say in a detached tone that hasn't come out of me in years. "You know how many bodies I saw without hands, without heads? Every time a grunt tripped a VC booby trap, the guys who weren't blown to bits spent the next couple of hours collecting the body parts; then they got to decide which ones belonged to who, and bagged 'em. Finally, a chopper dumped 'em at a collection point where a graves registration guy, putting in fourteen-hour days, is slogging his way through a pile of body bags that never gets smaller. In one of 'em he finds a mangled torso, a couple of limbs, maybe a pulped hand, some bloody fatigues, and a loose pair of boots with dog tags dangling from the laces."

"I understand."

"If I'm right, whoever that poor bastard was—" I pause and swallow back the bile rising in my throat—"it's *his* name, not mine, that belongs on that wall."

4

NAMES. AN ENTIRE WALL OF DEAD GIs' NAMES.

I don't know a whole lot about the Vietnam Veterans Memorial, but I do know that Jan Scruggs, the veteran who started it all, was into the names. I remember reading that he woke up in the middle of the night terrified they'd all be forgotten. He tried to drown his fears in a bottle of whiskey, and when that didn't work, he decided he was going to put the name of every GI who was killed in Vietnam on a memorial to make sure they weren't. He pulled it off.

But one name is missing.

Now, the mystical force that was driving him seems to be driving me. It kept me up half the night.

The travel alarm reads 6:21.

Nancy is still sleeping. I slip out of bed and cross to the window of our hotel room. The Washington Monument is shrouded in mist, its red warning beacon winking eerily in the darkness. Below, a few people bundled against the cold are crossing Lafayette Square on two long paths that converge on the White House.

I can't help thinking about the decisions that were made there, decisions made by four Presidents to send young Americans into battle, decisions responsible for those fifty-eight thousand names and for my frustrating case of insomnia. I don't know how long I've been standing at the window when I feel Nancy beside me.

She wraps her arms around my waist and hugs me in silence. "It's really gotten hold of you again, hasn't it?" she finally whispers.

I let out a long breath and nod. "The guy died for his country, babe. His name should be on the Memorial. I just can't get it out of my head."

"I think you need to get home," she says, knowing that just being in the modern, light-filled house built on a hilltop in the Santa Monica Mountains above Malibu always brightens my mood.

"Maybe," I say with a solemn shrug. "I'm sorry, I just can't help wondering about him, you know? Was he an FNG, a lifer? Black, white, brown? Married? Did he have kids, a cat and a dog? Parents? The questions just keep coming. I mean, if my parents weren't notified, who was? What happened to his body? Who was it sent to for burial?"

"I don't know, Cal," Nancy says, almost mouthing the words. She has a look in her eyes that I haven't seen in years; a look of poignant sadness, bordering on fear, that tells me she's concerned I'm being dragged back into the past, into the ugliness I worked so hard to overcome. "Are you sure they're your questions to answer?"

"No. No, I'm not. But it's my name. So who else if not me?"

"Well, yesterday the clerk said he was going to report it to the Army. They made the mistake; maybe you should let them handle it."

"You're right. I probably should," I reply defensively. "Trouble is it doesn't have anything to do with what I'm feeling. I mean, I just have this . . . this . . . compulsion to find out who he was myself."

Though I don't have the answers, I don't have to run a probability analysis on my computer to know that if another soldier ended up with my dog tags, he was most likely killed on the same day and in the same province where I was wounded. In descending order of probability, he was a member of my squad, platoon, or company, or other units deployed in the area. It's a basic data analysis problem: assemble a complete roster of names, eliminate those on the wall and those who'd survived, narrowing the list to a few men, preferably one who somehow wasn't officially accounted for.

"You have the name of the clerk?" I ask, deciding the

Friends of the Vietnam Veterans Memorial data base would be as good a place as any to start.

"Our flight leaves at eleven," she cautions as she fetches her notebook.

It's our last day in Washington. I'd forgotten. It'll be hours before FVVM offices open. I spend the time entering Nancy's data into my laptop, then list as many names of GIs in my company as I can remember. At 8:45 I go downstairs to get a taxi. Nancy stays at the hotel to pack our things.

Friends of the Vietnam Veterans Memorial headquarters is on M St. NW about a mile and half east of the Hay Adams in a four-story brownstone converted into office space. The small staff works in simply furnished surroundings where an almost churchlike quiet prevails.

The clerk, a soft-spoken man in his early forties with thinning hair, seems uncomfortable at being face-to-face with the latest member of the group I've crudely nicknamed The Living Dead. I brief him on my time/place parameters and ask if he has any ideas how I might go about identifying the soldier.

"Well, I've notified the Army Casualty Office," he replies, confirming what he told Nancy. "By the way, in case you're wondering about having your name taken off the wall, we looked into it when we found out about the others. Must've been three, maybe four years ago. But nobody's been able to figure out a way to do it without defacing the Memorial or replacing the panels."

"I'm more interested in adding one," I say a little too sharply, shifting into management mode. "I need to find out which guys in my company were killed on a certain day and in a certain province, but I don't have very many names. Are you programmed to do multitarget searches?"

"Sure are. Company, date, and province is all I need. I can check every company that was in the province on that day, if you like."

"Yes, I like," I reply, my mood brightening as I rattle off the information—G Company, 18 April 1968, Champasak Province—and he begins entering it.

"It's a brand-new program," he explains while the computer does its work. "We put it together to help veterans, families, and friends keep in touch. That's what we call it, 'In Touch.' " He glances at the screen and types something, then looks up and says, "Spent some time in Laos, huh?"

"Yeah, creating traffic jams on the Trail. You?"

"Can Tho; that's way down south in the Delta. I was a gunner on a PBR."

"Riverine forces."

"Uh-huh. Haven't been on a boat since."

"I know what you mean."

We continue trading war stories until the printer interrupts us. There are approximately twenty-five to thirty names. Mine is one of them, as are the ones I saw on the wall. I keep my emotions in check, and slip the printout into my attaché. "Any idea where I go next?"

"Well, when we were compiling the names for the wall, we had a master list made up of casualty reports from all the service branches. It was raw data, loaded with mistakes, misspellings; so we had each entry checked by the NPRC. They've got the original personnel files for everybody who's ever been in the military."

"The NPRC?"

"National Personnel Records Center. If anybody can figure out who your man is, I'd say it'd be them."

"Thanks. I still have a little time before my flight. Where are they, the Pentagon?"

"Oh, no, they're in St. Louis."

"You mean as in Missouri?"

"Yes, sorry. It's a big building out by the airport. The guy who was in charge of the verification project was a Mr.—" he pauses, and spins the wheel of a Rolodex— "Collins. Jack Collins."

I can't believe it. I'm in the nation's capitol, surrounded by government buildings, and the records of all military personnel are stored in Missouri. I return to the hotel and ask Nancy how she feels about making a stop in St. Louis.

She sighs, overwhelmed. "I still haven't gotten through those term papers, I've got a staff meeting in the morning before classes start. I've got to get home and get my act together."

We decide she'll return to Los Angeles, and I'll go to St. Louis alone. I have no trouble getting on a flight but can't reach Mr. Collins. His secretary explains he's at a meeting outside the office and isn't expected back until after lunch. I make an appointment.

The flight to Lambert–St. Louis International is scheduled at two hours, seven minutes. I spend the time working my way through the alphabet in an effort to recall more of the men in my company.

It's a short taxi ride from the airport to the National Personnel Records Center on Page Boulevard. The five-story building is sheathed in horizontal bands of glass and concrete curtain wall. It isn't big, it's gargantuan, easily as long as three football fields, and surrounded by acres of cars.

A receptionist clips a visitor's tag to my jacket, then directs me to an institutional green office with government furniture and the obligatory portraits of the President and Joint Chiefs. A stocky man with the unflappable demeanor of someone who processes thousands of requests for information each day waves me in.

"Jack Collins," he says, latching on to my hand. He's genuinely intrigued when he hears why I'm there, and reveals there are more like fourteen mistakes on the Memorial, three of which have been publicly acknowledged; but he balks when I request information on the men in my company who came back from Vietnam. The rules are hard and fast: access to files other than my own requires permission in writing from Total Army Personnel Command in Virginia. Furthermore, it could take hours to retrieve my file from the archives. He suggests we look up my listing on the master casualty list first.

He fetches a horizontal format computer printout that's as thick as a dictionary. Labeled *A through M*, it contains the names of approximately half the men who died in Vietnam. Collins finds the section he wants. Morgans fill half of one page and all of the next. There must be at least a hundred of them.

"That's you," he says, pointing to an entry near the top between Abraham Bruce and Aubrey Donald. Each runs in a single line across the page. Mine reads:

```
A116301743 MORGAN A CALVERT
LAA289613SFCE512/05/68
BOSTONY2322/3/48BC621SM10*10/3/
6863IVBR19
```

I'm used to working with statistics condensed in this fashion, but each data log has its own code, and I'm as baffled as any layman. "You have the key handy, or do you know it by heart?"

"Not enough of it." Collins retrieves a binder that contains the data keys. The first divides the line of letters and numbers into columns—more than thirty in this case—and identifies them. The others are used to decipher the entries under each. "The first column's the service branch," he begins. "As you might imagine, A stands for Army; the column right after your name is the country of casualty. LA stands for Laos, not Los Angeles."

I force a smile.

"A2 means died from hostile wounds."

"Fits," I remark, referring to the soldier who died with my dog tags.

"Then there's case number, rank, pay grade, date of casualty: 12 May '68. Hometown, Boston; that Y means you enlisted; next is—"

"Hold it. You say 12 May?"

"Uh-huh."

"That's weird. I was wounded on 18 April. The way I figure it, the guy had to be killed on the same day in the same province.

"Yes, I'd think so," Collins muses, as he runs a finger along the line of data, then scans the key. "Province code's sixty-three. Sixty-three is Bolikhamsai Province."

"Bolikhamsai? That's *really* weird. You sure?"

"Uh-huh. Why?"

"I was wounded in Champasak." I can see the worn map of Laos I carried with me in the field as if it were yesterday. "Bolikhamsai's at least four, maybe five hundred miles north."

I'm baffled. How could somebody all the way up there have ended up with my dog tags, let alone three weeks after I was wounded? My theory didn't last a day. My time/place parameters and the list of KIAs in my attaché are useless.

"There's always a chance they're data encoding errors. You know, somebody checks a wrong box, hits a wrong key, and nobody catches it."

"That would mean there's no mistaken identity, and no other soldier," I say, torn between being spared the torment of reliving the past, and being cheated out of the satisfaction it's giving me.

"Could be. On the other hand, if it's all correct—your date, province, cause of casualty, wound—then I'd say somebody else died with your tags."

"Any way we can find out?"

"Sure, check your file. You'll have to fill out a one-eighty first." He takes a form from a drawer, makes a red X in the lower left corner, and slides it across the desk with a pen. "Make sure you sign it."

Form 180–106—REQUEST PERTAINING TO MILITARY RECORDS—has more blanks than the SATs. Collins makes phone calls while I work on it. "Is it really going to take hours to get this stuff?"

Collins nods then tilts his head, reconsidering, and copies some data from the computer screen onto a routing slip. "Let's go," he says, reading aloud as we leave the office. "Third floor, sector N–W, aisle twenty-six, rack eighty-four, shelf five, box two. I'll probably catch hell for doing this myself but—" he pushes the elevator button, then looks at me with sad eyes "—I lost a close friend over there."

We ride in silence. When the doors open, we exit into a narrow canyon of identical cardboard file boxes stacked on shelving units that tower over us. My head fills with the musty smell of paper and ink.

"In case you're wondering, this place holds over a hundred million individual military jackets in over two million cubic feet of storage space." He makes his way through the maze guided by signs that act as street names and house numbers. Finally he rolls a ladder in to position, then climbs up, removes one of the boxes, and carries it to a table beneath the windows.

My pulse quickens as he opens it and culls through the

jackets. He quickly finds—MORGAN A. CALVERT 116301743—and starts thumbing through the documents, which are several inches thick.

"What're you looking for?"

"The report filed by the medic who treated you in the field."

He finally slips a yellowing page from the jacket. The pertinent data blanks read: WIA 18/04/68 CP LA—wounded in action, 18 April 1968, Champasak Province, Laos. It's all correct.

We set the medic's report aside and examine all the other documents to see if one of them contains the incorrect data that's on the master casualty list.

"Pretty much settles it," Collins says, after we determine that isn't the case.

How I wish it did. "The date someone was killed in action came from a casualty report, right?"

"Right. If somebody in the field recovered a body, or even part of one, with your dog tags there's got to be a record of it."

"But you don't have them here," I say, knowingly.

"No. They're retained by Mortuary Affairs."

My shoulders sag in defeat.

Collins notices and studies me for a moment. "Better get used to it."

"That bad, huh?"

He nods gravely. "You have no idea what you're getting into, believe me."

"But getting copies of the mortuary records shouldn't be a problem. I mean, I'll be asking for information under my name and serial number."

"True. Of course on the other hand—" he shakes his head, dismayed by a thought that occurs to him "—there's no guarantee now that he was even Army."

"Hadn't thought of that," I say, feeling a little shell-shocked.

"That's exactly the sort of thing I'm talking about. I'd give serious consideration to forgetting about this, if I were you."

I shove my hands into my pockets and nod numbly.

"Anything else you want?"

I mull it over for a moment. "A copy of that medic's report, I guess."

"No problem."

As Collins heads for a nearby copying station, I stand amid the records of the countless millions who served in the military through four wars in this century alone, thinking that every new piece of information seems to be complicating the mystery instead of solving it. I still have no idea who the soldier is, just the slim chance that the answer lies somewhere in the files of the casualties that were processed by the military mortuaries in Vietnam—mine, or one of the other 58,176.

5

I'M TWENTY-EIGHT THOUSAND FEET ABOVE THE GRAND Canyon, spread out over two seats in the first-class cabin of a 767 working on my laptop. Undaunted by Collins' warning, I got the address and phone number for Army Mortuary Affairs at Fort Sam Houston in San Antonio, Texas, from him before leaving the NPRC; and as soon as my flight was in the air, I began writing a letter requesting copies of all data filed under my name and serial number.

Due to the three-hour difference in time, it's only 3:35 P.M. when I arrive in Los Angeles. Nancy picks me up from business trips whenever she can. It gives us a chance to talk before the clients, computers, and phones close in. Her Range Rover came with all the options, but she made sure a cellular phone wasn't one of them. Today, her flight from Washington arrived just a few hours before mine, so I've arranged for one of the company drivers to meet me instead.

Minutes after touchdown, I'm tucked in the backseat of a Lincoln Town Car heading north on the 405. At the first interchange, we take the Santa Monica west to the tunnel that channels all traffic onto Pacific Coast Highway. I drive through it every day on the way home from work. It's right out of *Star Trek*—a fleeting fifteen-second time warp that teleports me from a world of stress and urban sprawl to one of peace and natural beauty. The Lincoln is soon climbing Malibu Canyon Road into the mountains, where, bathed in golden light as our architect planned, a cluster of angular white structures hugs the rugged terrain. Nancy said I needed to get home and she's right.

I intend to go right to my den and print out the letter to Mortuary Affairs, but I don't. Instead, I take a refreshing swim in the pool, then spend some time in the spa with Nancy, watching the sunset. But as the last amber rays streak skyward from beneath the horizon, I start feeling restless again.

"Better go do it now," she says, knowingly.

"Do what, Nance?" I ask, as if I haven't the slightest idea what she's talking about.

"Whatever it is that's making you fidget. You'll be distracted all through dinner. Go."

I get into some comfortable clothes and head downstairs to the den. It's an electronics-packed sanctuary with a view guaranteed to make the most insecure executive feel invincible. I transfer the Mortuary Affairs letter from the laptop to my PC, which is tied in to the mainframe at the office, then print it out on the laser jet. I'm proofreading it when my mind wanders to the time/place discrepancy. I'm lost in thought when Nancy pokes her head in the doorway.

"You going to be much longer? Cal?"

"Oh, sorry, I was somewhere else."

"I don't need to ask where, do I?"

I smile and shake no. "I was thinking about helicopters."

"Well, I've been thinking about food. How does Geoffery's sound?" she asks, referring to a trendy restaurant perched on a bluff above the Pacific.

"Sounds okay," I reply halfheartedly. I turn off the computer, then come around the desk. "You know, according to the master casualty list, whoever died with my tags was killed three weeks after and four hundred miles north of where I was wounded."

"That's strange."

"Yes, it's been bugging me. I was just thinking the medevac chopper might account for it."

"What do you mean?"

"Well, they linked the fire bases to the hospitals and mortuaries. There's a chance my ID got lost in the chopper that took me to the field hospital."

"And you think it might've been reassigned to another area after that."

"Uh-huh," I reply as we start upstairs. "Weeks later the

same chopper's working this other province; goes into a hot LZ and hauls out a load of grunts: live, wounded, dead—happened all the time. My ID turns up, and some terrified kid figures it belongs to the pile of carnage next to him without tags.''

''That makes sense.''

''So what? No matter how I look at it, it still doesn't give me a thing.''

''That's because you haven't eaten. You know how your brain refuses to function without fuel.''

''Without protein. Forget the angel hair and shitake mushrooms. Let's go get some steaks.''

The next morning, Nancy is out of the house by 7:15. I spend a half hour on my rowing machine, working off a sixteen-ounce T-bone and sorting through the events in Washington and St. Louis. I have a feeling that something basic is wrong but can't put my finger on it. I shower, dress, and head for the office—an effortless drive in a Mercedes 560 sedan that seems to know the route by heart.

Morgan Management Consulting is located in one of the aluminum-clad towers in Century City. It's within striking distance of the corporate and financial center downtown, and the electronics and defense industry corridor on the west side.

I park in the underground garage, using one of those card keys to activate the gate arm, and take the elevator to the twenty-fourth floor, half of which my company occupies. In keeping with the management philosophy we preach, the decor and furnishings are minimalist in design, the artwork contemporary. I drop the letter to Mortuary Affairs in the mail chute and head for my office. I'm settling at my desk when my secretary informs me that Washington is on the line.

My words didn't fall on deaf ears. One of the senators's aides, faced with revising the legislation to reflect my data, needs help. It's too complex to cover over the phone, but could be handled in person by a subordinate. I assign it to a bright young woman who worked on my prepared testimony, then meet with one of our actuarial teams to review a troubled pension plan study.

It's obvious a poll used to gather raw data was poorly

designed. "Garbage in garbage out," I lecture. "We ask the wrong questions, we don't stand a chance in hell of getting the right answers. Now—" I pause. Something just clicked. I know what was bothering me at home this morning. I've been too driven by emotion and impulse. I haven't really defined the problem and developed an approach to solving it. I clear my office and call the National Personnel Records Center.

"You have it figured out already?" Collins prompts when he comes on the line.

"Not the way I was going at it."

"I'm not sure I follow you, Mr. Morgan."

"I've been asking the wrong question," I say, feeling a little guilty for chastising my staff. "I mean, the question I'm trying to answer is: Whose body was recovered with my dog tags? But when you really think about it, the one I should be asking is: How has the military accounted for this guy? John Doe's body or part of it was identified as mine, right? When Mr. Doe didn't turn up—dead or alive—what did they think happened to him? I may be wrong, but the way I see it, there are only two possibilities: They listed him as either missing in action or AWOL."

"You might be on to something there."

"Can you help me narrow the parameters?"

"Well, for openers, I'd say the chances that he's listed as AWOL are pretty slim."

"Why?"

"The circumstances. Bolikhamsai Province in Laos, or any battle zone for that matter, isn't where GIs go AWOL. In most of the records I've seen, and I've seen a lot of them in my day, guys who went AWOL in Vietnam were usually last seen somewhere in one of the big cities, Saigon, Bangkok, Chiang Mai."

"Heavily into women and drugs," I hear myself adding, which makes me acutely aware of just how selective my memory has become. I knew guys who went AWOL: for days, for weeks, forever. "It's been a long time, Mr. Collins, but that makes a lot of sense now that you mention it."

"Yes, when you get right down to it, odds are he's listed as MIA. Nothing else left."

"There any way to find out for sure?"

"Not without his name." He pauses briefly, then adds, "I don't know what this'll give us, but I'm kind of curious to see what the master list has under yours. Hold on."

After a short silence, I hear a muffled thud followed by the rustle of pages turning. "Yes, here it is," Collins says. "There's a category called Body State; the entry is BNR; that means body not recovered."

That's the last thing I expected. It really throws me. "I don't get it," I say, thinking aloud. "I mean, I assumed a body somehow ended up with my tags by mistake and my name ended up on the wall."

"So did I. That's why I didn't check it the other day. Was your family notified?"

"No. That's one of the first things I covered."

"Well, that fits the pattern. A body had to be fully processed by one of the mortuaries before a notification was triggered. No body, no notice."

"And no records," I add, realizing this latest twist means the letter I sent to Mortuary Affairs is a waste of time. "In any event, assuming it's not a data encoding error, chances are I'm looking for someone who's listed as missing in action."

"Yes, which narrows those parameters quite a bit. There are only about twenty-three hundred MIAs."

"Twenty-three hundred," I repeat, hearing pages turning again in the background.

"Twenty-two hundred and seventy-three at last count, to be exact," Collins corrects.

I quickly calculate that out of a total of 58,176, I've eliminated 96.093 percent of the possibilities. "I guess that's not exactly back to square one, but I haven't the slightest idea where to go next."

"I'd try the National League of Families," he suggests. "They're the authority on MIAs. If they can't help you, they'll know who can."

"Where are they? Alaska?"

"Washington, D.C.," he replies with an amused chuckle. "I warned you."

After ending the call, I track down the staff member to whom I gave the Senate committee assignment and suggest she cancel her travel plans. She isn't going to Washington next week. I am.

6

DESPITE NARROWING THE POSSIBILITIES TO 2,273 MEN, I've raised as many questions as I've answered. There's nothing in my personnel file that suggests a clerical error was made. All the entries—date, place, cause and type of wound—are correct. But my entry on the master casualty list contains conflicting information: all the basic data—the dog tag stuff—is mine; all the casualty-related data—the field stuff—is someone else's; which, as Collins pointed out, means another GI, who was killed in action, was identified as me by mistake. But the time/place parameters of that casualty aren't even close to when and where I was wounded. The tags-in-the-chopper theory I developed could account for it; but it also means that a body—with my ID attached—had to be *recovered* for my name to be on the wall. Yet the master casualty list indicates Body Not Recovered.

I spend most of my spare time building a computer model of all the possible intersections of time, place, and personnel. I've been working on it for almost a week and am no closer to an answer. Only one angle makes any sense: Whoever died with my tags had to be listed as missing in action. I'm counting on the National League of Families to help me sort it out.

The sun is sending long shafts of light across the Virginia countryside as I land at Dulles. I stumble off the red-eye with my two-suiter and attaché and take a taxi to Capitol Hill. Work sessions to revise the actuarial data in the Social Security bill have been scheduled over several mornings in the senator's offices in the Russell Building on Delaware Avenue.

"What're you doing here?" he says when he sees me. "I thought you were leaving the nuts and bolts to one of your staffers?"

"So did I," I confess, going on to explain about the National League of Families.

"Courageous group," he replies, his brows arching in tribute. "Took on the government and won. There was a lot of suspicion and mistrust in the beginning. Now, they're like this." He crosses his fingers tightly.

"I wasn't aware of that."

"Well, in the late sixties when the League was formed, the country was getting fed up with the war, and the government was keeping a very low profile on the POW/MIA issue. They wanted to get on with the fun stuff: relations with China, Watergate, Begin and Sadat, the SALT talks. But those wives and families wouldn't let go. They wrote letters, raised money, brought law suits, and held a lot of people's feet to the fire. They've come a long way. The League's even involved in policy-making now; an integral part of the IAG."

IAG? Like every infrastructure, mine is as rife with acronyms and insider jargon as the next, but I'm finding myself more and more on the outside. "I'm afraid I'm not familiar with that, Senator."

"Inter Agency Group: Defense, State, the JCs, DIA, NSC, and NLF are members. Every time we meet with a Southeast Asian government on this issue, the League's Executive Director is at the table; and every bit of new data on an MIA or POW is released to his family, regardless of its substance or reliability. The League fought long and hard for those rights, believe me."

When our first session comes to a close, the senator and his staff go to a committee meeting. I take a taxi to the National League of Families on Connecticut Avenue. Unlike the Friends of the Vietnam Veterans Memorial offices, where an almost eerie quiet prevailed, the League's cramped second-floor quarters are alive with ringing phones and harried staffers at long tables assembling packages of information, stuffing envelopes, working the phones. It reminds me of a telethon.

I make my way to a reception desk where a young woman who can't be much older than my daughters is fielding calls. There's a sense of righteousness and divine purpose about her. She's so preoccupied that I skip the preliminaries—my initial discovery at the wall and the ground I've covered since—and explain that I have information that, if it matches one of their profiles, might resolve the fate of an MIA.

"I'm sorry. We don't have that data computerized, Mr. Morgan," she explains, handing a stack of pink phone messages to a woman who passes behind me on the way to her office. "All we have are mailing lists for fund-raising and letter-writing campaigns. That's it."

"You people are the experts. It's hard to believe you don't have any data on the men who are missing."

"Oh, we are the experts, and we have tons of data." She gestures to a wall of file cabinets across the room. "Most of it's stuff the families send us. Letters, photos, clippings from local papers, personal mementos. Remember you're dealing with people here; with the families, not bureaucrats."

"I'll try to keep that in mind," I say, more amused than offended by her zeal. "Now, just to be certain, you're saying you don't have any loss data? I mean, I can give you very specific parameters: 12 May '68, Bolikhamsai Province, Laos."

"It's possible there's a match in our files," she says, jotting the information down with one hand and reaching for a ringing phone with the other. "But we have no way of finding it without a name."

"That's the only thing I don't have," I say, unable to conceal my frustration. "That's what I'm looking for."

She answers the phone on what must be the sixth ring, puts the caller on hold, then buzzes one of the offices on the intercom. "It's the General on two." She hangs up and turns back toward me. "I'm sorry it's so crazy around here today."

"What's going on?"

"Our annual meeting's next week. It's usually in July

but we changed it. Something to do with hotel accommodations. By the way, have you reported this to the Army Casualty Office?"

"Yes. I've also been to the FVVM, the NPRC, and now—" I pause, exasperated. "Frankly, I'm not getting the kind of feedback I expected. I thought you folks'd be thrilled to get some information that might—"

She pouts and lets out a long breath. "I'm sorry, but you have no idea how much we get. Most of it's useless, just a lot of DTRs."

"A lot of what?"

"Dog tag reports. This issue is exploited by a lot of people. They start rumors that we'll pay cash or resettle the finder for information. Then they make it up and sell it to desperate refugees who think it's their ticket to a new life. We get pictures of dog tags, information copied from dog tags, lost dog tags, fake dog tags, snapshots of GIs, letters. It's endless. The bottom line is, less than four percent has anything to do with a man that's missing."

"Well, this does," I say sharply, stabbing a finger at the pad where she's written the information. "Now is there any chance you might be able to tell me how many men are listed as missing in Laos?"

"Five hundred forty-seven," she replies somewhat contritely.

"Thank you," I say, calculating that I've just eliminated 1,726 out of 2,273 possibilities, or 75.93 percent. "That helps."

She studies me for a moment as if deciding something, then gets one of the women working at the tables to cover the phones.

"I shouldn't be doing this," she says in a confidential tone as she directs me aside. "I mean, we have a policy of not encouraging free-lancers, but one of our family members might be able to help you even more. Her husband was lost in Laos. When it came time for reparations, and their government didn't cooperate, she took it on herself to organize the families of all the men missing there. To make a long story short, they got Congress into it and the Laotian Government recently agreed to abide by repatriation agreements and give us access to crash sites."

"Sounds like somebody who gets things done."

"You bet. Her name's Kate Ackerman. You should talk to her."

"But—she's in Laos," I say, making, what I hope for my sake, is an attempt at levity.

She smiles. "Pennsylvania—" she corrects, letting the smile widen before she adds "—Avenue."

"She's in Washington?" I exclaim, thinking it's about time I had some luck.

"Well, she lives in Alexandria, but she's over at the Marriott this afternoon. That's where the meeting's going to be. Try the Grand Ballroom."

"The Marriott."

"It's on Fourteenth just the other side of Lafayette Square. You can walk it."

"Thanks," I say, with a little farewell wave. She escorts me to the door. I'm not sure whether she's being polite or making certain she's rid of me.

"I have a feeling you and Kate'll hit it off," she offers as we walk to the elevator.

"Oh?"

"She's sort of a loose cannon too."

7

A BLUSTERY WIND PUSHES ME SOUTH ON CONNECTICUT to 17th and on through Lafayette Square, where the cannons that flank the statue of Andrew Jackson are old and weathered and anything but loose. It's been years since young women thought of me in such terms, so I decide to take the remark as a compliment.

The J. W. Marriott is a block-long edifice of rust-colored brown brick and marble next to the National Theater. I enter from 14th Street and find myself on the top level of an atrium sheathed in mahogany, marble, brass, and plush oriental carpets, capped by a series of arched vaults. Its four balconies are joined by high-speed escalators that take me down to the ballroom level. I push through a set of massive wooden doors into a vast space of equally opulent decor.

"I just want to make sure I understand this," I hear a woman saying in a commanding tone. Rather tall and smartly dressed, she stands beneath one of the crystal chandeliers, surrounded by a group of young workmen. They all sport low-slung tool belts and T-shirts that advertise local sports teams and favorite beers. "So humor me and we'll go over it again from the beginning. Okay?"

The workmen nod in unison.

"The displays are on the truck, right?"

"That's right," the spokesman replies.

"Where's the truck?"

"At the loading dock."

"The one here or the one at the warehouse?"

"Here."

"Then why hasn't it been unloaded yet?"

"Because it's still in drayage."

"I thought you said it was here?"

The young men break up with laughter.

"It is here, ma'am," the spokesman explains as the others settle down. "Drayage is like—well, let's just say the truck hasn't cleared local customs yet."

"Ah. Now I get it. Okay, no problem. Here's what you do. Call your boss and tell him there's going to be a story in tomorrow's *Post* that his people are holding up the families of dead servicemen for a payoff."

Jaws drop.

She turns on a heel and walks away.

I'm standing off to the side concealed by one of the sliding partitions used to divide the room. "Mrs. Ackerman?" I call out, stepping into view.

She changes direction without breaking stride and comes toward me. She's polished and at ease with the way she looks. Her generous features are framed by long, dark brown hair swept back to accentuate her cheekbones, and intelligent amber eyes that have an alluring cant. After her run-in with the workers, I'm expecting they'll have a fiery glare, but there seems to be a sadness in them instead, a burnished cast that matches the copper MIA bracelet on her wrist.

"Who're you with?" she challenges. "Food, beverages, concessions?"

"Veterans," I reply, introducing myself. "You handled that pretty well."

"Thanks. It's a dirty job—" she pauses, then pleased with herself adds "—but I loved doing it."

"They had it coming. I'm told you're the League's unoffical expert on Laos."

"Yes," she says with a laugh. "They can't live with me and they can't live without me."

"That makes two of us."

"How so?"

"I'm trying to identify someone missing in Laos. I'd like to see his name added to the Memorial. They thought you might be able to help."

"My pleasure." Her eyes brighten as she says it, then

cloud in thought. "What makes you think he's not already on it?"

"Well, as I said, he's MIA."

"That doesn't mean his name isn't on the wall."

"It doesn't? I'm sorry, Mrs. Ackerman. I'm not sure I follow that."

"Obviously not," she says, shaking her head in dismay. "You're really out of touch, aren't you?"

"What do you mean by that?"

"I mean, you sound like one of those guys who made it back and then made believe it never happened."

"Yes, I put it behind me. Believe me it wasn't easy."

"Well, maybe you tried too hard."

"I didn't come here to be insulted, Mrs. Ackerman. Are you going to help me or not?"

She sweeps her eyes over me while she makes up her mind. "You have a half hour, Mr. Morgan?" she asks in an intriguing tone.

I nod curiously.

"There's something I want to show you."

We take the escalator to the hotel's underground parking garage. She leads the way to a Volvo Turbo sedan that emits a series of musical chirps when she deactivates the alarm. We get in and she drives off, tires squealing on the smooth concrete as she circles up the ramps, then exits onto 13th Street, making a left toward Constitution. She misses the light at the corner of E, reaches for the cellular phone tucked between the seats, and presses one of the buttons that automatically dials a prestored number.

"Hi, it's Kate. The Georgian in Kalorama—are we out of escrow yet? Shit. Better stay on top of it. Check on that listing in the *Post* for me too, will you? Thanks. Should be back by four-thirty the latest."

"You sell real estate?"

"Uh-huh. The market's soft. I'm holding my own."

"I can see that," I say, indicating the car.

"Really? I suppose now you're going to ask me why a member of the National League of Families didn't buy American, right?"

"Well, now that you mention it—"

"I almost did. Then I saw that commercial. You know

the one where the Volvo smashes head-on into the concrete wall without being totaled?'' She pauses dramatically, then adds, ''Well, my husband gave his life for his country, and I just decided that the Ackermans had already done more than their share.''

There's something about the way she says it that's tough, poignant, and funny all at the same time, and I want to laugh.

''Go ahead,'' she says, sensing I'm holding it in. ''Everybody breaks up when I say that. Anyway, I like real estate because my time is my own, and I can work League activities in around it.''

She makes a right onto Constitution, drives about six or seven blocks through heavy traffic, and swings into a parking area behind a huge limestone building. A sign warns: Tow Away—Authorized Parking Only.

''You sure you can park here?''

''I'm like the six-thousand-pound gorilla,'' she replies as she flips down the sun visor, revealing an official League insignia. ''I park anywhere I want.'' She gets out, activates the alarm, and starts crossing the street, threading her way between traffic.

I don't know the city very well, but I sense where we're going when I see the Washington Monument and reflecting pool in the distance.

''I love approaching it from here. It's such a surprise.'' She strides briskly across the grass, then stops at the edge of a sudden drop-off; and there directly below us is the Vietnam Veterans Memorial.

We are literally standing on the top of the wall, looking straight down at the visitors. We watch them for a few moments, then proceed to the far end where the path that parallels the Memorial begins its descent from ground level. The sun has fallen below a layer of threatening clouds, and as we walk past the panels of polished granite, rays of light catch in the recessed letters making each name seem illuminated from within.

She goes directly to one of the panels and, like a blind person reading braille, gently and lovingly runs her fingertips over one of the names.

JOHN W. ACKERMAN.

"Your husband."

She nods. "You see that?" she asks, pointing to the space between his name and the next.

I move closer to the wall and see a tiny cross engraved in the granite.

"You know what that means?"

"No, but I'm sure you'll tell me."

"Well, if you look around you'll notice that most of the names have a diamond engraved after them; but a few have one of these."

"I hadn't noticed," I admit warily, expecting to be chastised again.

Instead, as the rumble of distant thunder rises and darkening clouds move in front of the sun softening the light, she seems to have a change of heart and smiles. In an almost contrite tone, she says, "To tell you the truth, Mr. Morgan, most people don't. I'm afraid I overreacted before. I owe you an apology."

"It's okay," I say, returning her smile. "You were right. I guess I am a little out of touch." I step to the wall and run the edge of my thumb over the tiny cross, feeling the texture of the stone change. "This means he's missing in action, doesn't it?"

"That's right. The original group of MIAs, about twenty-five hundred in all, were included on the Memorial. Of those, thirteen hundred or so were declared dead due to the circumstances surrounding their loss."

"Killed in action, body not recovered," I say, reflecting on my meeting with Collins in St. Louis.

Kate nods. "They were lost in air crashes mostly. Flight crews, special forces guys, fighter jocks," she pauses reflectively, then adds. "A lot of them were pilots."

"Your husband a pilot?"

"Yes," she replies, her face suddenly coming alive. "He loved to fly; he loved danger more. That's what attracted me to him. We were such opposites."

"No Volvo for him, huh?"

She shakes her head no and breaks into a wistful smile. "You know, months after those men were declared dead by Congress somebody flying over a crash site saw one of their initials and date of loss burned into a field."

"You think the man's still alive?"

"No. Probably not. But there's always that little glimmer of hope. Of course, after twenty years, almost thirty for some, most families are realistic. I am."

A few drops of rain streak the granite next to us as we resume walking. She seems to be looking for something on the wall. We've gone a short distance when she finds it and points to a space between two names. "See this?"

The symbol she indicates is a combination of the other two; a cross with a diamond inscribed around it, connecting the four points.

"That means he's an MIA whose remains have been repatriated and identified . . ." Her voice breaks and she pauses briefly to regain her composure. "They added the diamond to signify that his fate's been resolved."

"That's all you want, isn't it?"

"That's what all the families want. To know what happened to their loved one beyond any doubt. To have that final answer and to have some part of him, however tiny or grotesque, to bury with honor and dignity."

Despite the painful longing in her eyes, her face has a serene strength that reminds me of Nancy; of how she looked when, by the sheer force of her will, she would rescue me from terrifying flashbacks of violence and human carnage. I can't help thinking, but for a lot of luck and the grace of God, that could easily be *my* wife standing there.

"What if one of them turns up alive," I wonder.

"Then a circle, not diamond, will be inscribed around the cross." She looks off for a moment, then adds, "I can't show you one of those."

A steady drizzle has begun falling. We're about to leave when an idea strikes me. "Just a minute. There's something I want to check," I say, curious to see how my name is marked. I walk along the wall until I find the panel. I've seen it before, but the sight of it sends a chill through me anyway. A cross, not a diamond, separates my name from the next.

"You okay?" she wonders, seeing I'm deep in thought.

"I'm fine. This is the problem," I reply, pointing to the cross. "It doesn't make any sense."

"What do you mean?"

"Well, like you said, a cross after a man's name means his body wasn't recovered, right?"

"Uh-huh."

"Which means somebody—one of his buddies, his commanding officer, a fellow pilot—either saw or deduced what happened and reported him missing in action."

"Yes. What's your point?"

"I was wounded. My guys got me out. I checked my personnel file. I even saw the reports the medics filled out. There weren't any mistakes. No one reported me missing."

"So, what do you think happened?"

"Well, I know for certain that I got separated from my tags and ID when I was wounded; I figure a KIA ended up with them by mistake."

"But that means his body would have to have been recovered for your name to be on the wall."

"Exactly. But it wasn't," I counter, indicating the cross. "That's the piece that doesn't fit."

"It probably never will," she says resignedly. Then her chin lifts with curiosity and she asks, "What do you do? I mean for a living?"

"I tell fortunes."

"Pardon me?"

"I do statistical analysis."

"A number cruncher?"

"Fair enough."

"You don't like that."

"Well, we're usually called actuaries, though there are those who think accountants without personalities is more like it. Why?"

"Oh," she says with a little laugh, "I was just wondering why you think things have to add up."

"Because they always do."

She smiles thinly and makes a gesture with her shoulders to indicate she disagrees. Then, with a glance to her watch, she announces, "I almost forgot. I've got a house on the brink of escrow."

"Go ahead. I'll grab a cab."

"You'll never get one in this," she says, turning a palm to the rain. "Where are you staying?"

"Hay Adams."

42

"It's on the way. Come on."

It starts pouring as we return to her car and drive north on 24th. We're approaching Washington Circle where traffic slows to a crawl when I realize I'd been so caught up in the details, I'd overlooked their significance. "If my guy is MIA, he's on the Memorial," I announce brightly.

Kate breaks into a knowing smile and nods.

"How many guys could be listed as missing on 12 May '68 in Bolikhamsai Province?"

"Something tells me you know how to find out."

I call the Friends of the Vietnam Veterans Memorial offices on Kate's car phone, give the clerk the time/place parameters, tell him my guy is MIA, and ask him to run a search.

Traffic has come to a complete standstill. The wipers move across the windshield like metronomes, each hypnotic sweep adding to my anticipation. We're just starting to inch forward when the clerk finally comes back on the line. I switch the phone to the hands-free mode so both Kate and I can hear him.

"I list twenty-three men missing in Bolikhamsai Province," he reports. "But none on that date. None at all in May as a matter of fact."

"None. You sure?"

"Far as I can tell."

"Far as I can tell? What do you mean by that?"

"Well, as I said, it's a new program. We're still working out some bugs. In an oddball case like yours, there's always a chance he slipped through the cracks. Wish I could be of more help."

"Thanks for trying," I say glumly, ending the call.

"Sorry," Kate says softly.

"You're sure all the MIAs are on the wall?"

"Positive. Have you given any thought to his being listed as AWOL?"

"Sort of."

"That would explain why his name isn't on the Memorial."

"I guess. I'm not real thrilled at the idea of this guy being a deserter."

"Maybe he isn't. I mean, being listed as AWOL doesn't

always mean a man deserted. There have been cases where GIs on leave were mugged by bandits, or murdered by enemy sympathizers, and their bodies disposed of. When they didn't return to their units, it looked like they went AWOL. It took years to clear their names."

"Never thought of that. Trouble is, this guy Collins at NPRC thinks the data works against his being AWOL, and I tend to agree. Maybe he did fall through the cracks."

"It's possible. I'm sure Mr. Collins knows his business, but, for what it's worth, when it comes to people who are unaccounted for, nobody's better than the CIL. That's where I'd go next, if I were you."

"The CIL?" I say, forcing a smile at the mention of yet another group. "Who's the CIL?"

"Central Identification Lab. They recover and identify remains of missing personnel. They have all the original files."

"Computerized?"

"Uh-huh. Cross-referenced every which way," she replies, maneuvering around a truck into a faster-moving lane. "The League works very closely with them. I know Colonel Webster, the commanding officer, and some of his people pretty well."

"And they are where?"

"Hawaii."

"I should've known."

"But they're all going to be here at the meeting next week."

"Unfortunately, I don't think I can take any more time away from my business."

"You could leave the information with me. I'd be more than happy to go over it with him."

"Thanks. I can always do it over the phone and fax it to him."

She nods, then tilts her head thoughtfully. "You know," she says, her voice taking on a more serious tone, "a lot of things'll be competing for the Colonel's attention after this meeting. It wouldn't hurt to be sponsored by the League's unofficial expert on Laos."

I mull it over for a moment, then nod. "Okay, Mrs. Ackerman, you're on."

"Was it my charm or my furrowed brow that convinced you?"

"Neither. I decided to practice what I preach to my clients, and delegate."

"Good. Now you can relax."

"I can?"

"Well, I'm sure the CIL will be able to track him down. It's only a matter of time now. This week, the next at the latest, you'll know who he is."

About twenty minutes later, she drops me at my hotel and drives off into the rain. I don't want to admit that it's been a burden, but as her car vanishes in the thickening traffic, I suddenly feel a tremendous sense of relief. Despite it, I can't help thinking about the tiny cross. Whether my guy was listed as MIA, AWOL, or just fell through the cracks, it's virtually impossible for my name to be on the wall unless a body was recovered, but the cross and the documents I've unearthed leave no doubt that one wasn't. Kate Ackerman's right. It doesn't add up, and it's bothering me.

8

THE RAIN HAS TURNED INTO A RAGING THUNDERSTORM. I have dinner at the hotel and spend the evening in my room working on the laptop. It takes me several hours to boil down the information in my data base to a few manageable pages.

The next morning, while I'm meeting with the senator's staff, one of his secretaries is good enough to make printouts and fax them to the real estate office in nearby Alexandria, where Kate Ackerman works. I finish the revisions to the Social Security bill, and catch an early afternoon flight to Los Angeles. Nancy picks me up at the airport in the Range Rover. As she maneuvers through traffic to the freeway, I fill her in on the progress I've made.

"Good," she replies with a grin when I finish. "Now you have no excuse for being distracted."

"Why? What's going on anyway?"

"Couple of things. For openers, I got the tickets for *Phantom*. We're going two weeks from Thursday. I already confirmed with the Grants."

"Great. How much were they? Or shouldn't I ask?"

She grins and holds up two fingers.

"Hundred?"

She nods.

"Apiece?"

She nods again. "Best seats in the house. Front row center, dress circle."

"Well, Gil's an important client."

We're on the coast highway when I detect a muted rotational clicking. "It's still making that noise, isn't it?"

Nancy nods contritely.

46

"I thought you were getting this tank serviced while I was away, because you'd have the Mercedes."

"I know. School's been a little crazy and I just haven't had a chance. I mean, I haven't even had time to touch up my roots."

"Nance!" I exclaim, feigning shock as I muss her fashionably short-cropped bob. "I thought this was really you."

She laughs. "Well, every girl has her secrets."

"I missed you, babe."

"Me too."

A short time later, we're heading up the canyon into the mountains. It's been a hellish week. Nancy insists I need to unwind and arranges for us to spend the weekend sailing with some friends. On Monday, Kate Ackerman calls me at the office and reports she's met with Colonel Webster, the commanding officer of the Central Identification Lab. He was clearly intrigued by the case and will put it in the works when he returns to Honolulu. I'm finally able to put the Memorial out of my mind and concentrate fully on business, family, and friends.

One morning about a week later, I'm dressing for work when Nancy, who always leaves before I do, kisses me good-bye and hurries from the bedroom. I hear the Range Rover drive off as I finish dressing, then I go downstairs to the den. I'm putting some files in my attaché prior to leaving when the phone rings.

"Hi, hon, it's me."

"Nance?"

"Yes, I'm at the gas station at the bottom of the hill."

"You okay?"

"Of course. Look, it's probably nothing, but as I was leaving, I noticed there's someone sitting in a car down the road from the house."

I turn to the windows that overlook a section of the road that twists down the hillside. A blue sedan, perhaps a top-of-the-line Olds or Buick—they all look alike to me—is parked on the shoulder just where the road turns. I can make out a man in sunglasses behind the wheel. He seems to be sipping coffee from a Styrofoam container. "Sort of bluish one?"

"Uh-huh."

"Yes, I can see it from here. I'm in the den. What about it?"

"Well, it doesn't look like it belongs to any of our neighbors, and after those burglaries up on Mountain View, I'm a little concerned."

"I don't know, babe. The man's driving an expensive car. You've heard the rumors about what's her name next door. I think he's coveting our neighbor's wife, not his TV and VCR. Chances are he's just cooling his heels until hubby leaves for work."

"Well, you're probably right," she says with a lascivious chuckle, "but I have a feeling the same car was there yesterday morning too."

"I rest my case."

"Cal—"

"Okay, I'll check it out when I leave. Hey, twelve thousand bucks for a security system, remember?"

"I'm sorry. You know how I get worried sometimes."

By the time I leave for work the blue car is gone. As I drive off, I imagine the sultry actress who lives up the road making it with the mysterious stranger in her spa. I have a ten o'clock meeting at a client's office downtown. So instead of taking the coast highway as I do most mornings, I head east through the canyon toward the freeway. The Mercedes glides through a series of turns, emerging onto a long straightaway. Now, I notice there's a car behind me. It could be blue; it's too far away to tell. Ten minutes later I'm on the Ventura approaching the 405 interchange where traffic always starts backing up at this hour, when the phone twitters.

"Cal Morgan—" I say in my business baritone.

"Hi, Daddy," a young woman's voice says with a little giggle. It's our oldest daughter, Laura, a twenty-one-year-old music major at Berkeley.

"Hi, Laur. You always manage to track me down somehow, don't you?"

"Well, I tried the house and the office—"

"How much you need this time?" I ask, teasing her.

"How much you got?" she fires back without missing a

beat. "Actually I'm trying to decide whether to take a class pass/fail or for a grade. I have to make up my mind today."

"Be easier if I was at my desk."

"Dad," she says knowingly. "I just want your advice."

"My best advice."

"I knew you were going to do this," she scolds, with adoring affection.

"No problem. Traffic's at a standstill. Hold on a sec." I switch the phone to hands-free, then flip open the laptop on the seat next to me and turn it on. "Okay. Ready. Which class?"

"Advanced psych."

"How'd you do in basic?"

"An A minus."

"Good," I say, letting the car roll to a stop before I encode the data. "How many students in your class?"

"Hundred-fifty, maybe two hundred."

"You're in the top ten percent?"

"Not after that C in European History."

"Ugh. Okay, now, how many—" I pause, catching sight of something in the rearview mirror that makes me look again. There's a metallic blue sedan two or three car lengths back in the right-hand lane. Olds? Buick? I can't tell. The driver is wearing sunglasses. A few uncertain seconds pass before it dawns on me that so is every other person on the freeway.

"Dad, you there?"

"Yeah, sorry. Just doing a little maneuvering here. Let's see? Oh, yeah, how many credits is it?"

"Four."

"A biggie," I say, running the final computations as traffic starts moving again.

"Which means I'll have to work a lot harder if I take it for a grade, which leaves less time for music."

I glance at the data on the screen. "Odds are still six to one you'll get another A minus."

"That sure wouldn't do my GPA any harm."

"Yeah, and I could face my friends again."

She laughs; then, doing her best to make it sound like an afterthought, she says, "By the way, Mom and I were talking about the Memorial. You doing okay?"

"Yes, I'm fine," I say, glancing at the mirror again. The metallic blue car is still there. Now I can see that it sort of resembles the one that was outside the house; but I'm not sure. The driver doesn't seem to be paying any attention to me. "I guess I got a little compulsive there for a while. But it's under control now."

"Well, if you ever want to talk—"

"Thanks, princess. I love you."

"Love you too, Daddy."

I hang up and check all three mirrors. Nothing. The car is gone. If it isn't, I can't see it. I decide I'm letting my imagination get the best of me. Something like ten percent of all cars in Los Angeles are probably some shade of blue, perhaps half of them sedans, which means there could be hundreds of them on this section of freeway right now. Besides, why would someone be following me? It's amazing how paranoid we get. Of course, the dozen or so drive-by killings that L.A. averages each week doesn't help.

Traffic finally starts moving. I look to the mirror again. Is that a patch of blue hood peeking through the windshield of the car behind mine? Come on, Morgan, I say to myself, you're being ridiculous. Get your mind back on business. If you're looking for something to worry about, try the woman in the next lane who's using the rearview mirror to put on her eye makeup at fifty miles an hour.

About a half hour later, I pull into the parking garage beneath a downtown highrise. The meeting with my client lasts through lunch. I'm not sure why, but I'm relieved that throughout the drive back to Century City my rearview mirror remains free of blue sedans. My secretary greets me with a stack of phone messages. I'm prioritizing the return order when she retrieves her steno pad.

"There's one more," she says, finding the page she wants. "A Captain Sullivan."

"Captain Sullivan?"

"He said he's with the Central Identification Lab at Fort Shafter in Hawaii."

"Oh, that's important. Get him back right away."

"No can do. He called a couple of hours ago. He said he was en route and couldn't be reached. He wanted to come by and review his findings with you."

"He say when?"

"Today. I told him you'd be out of the office until after lunch. I made it for two-thirty."

"Great." I walk to my office elated. I sensed Mrs. Ackerman had clout, I just didn't realize how much. Why else would the captain come all this way just to give me a name?

9

I'M ON THE PHONE WITH A CLIENT WHEN MY SECRETARY announces over the intercom the captain has arrived. I cut the conversation short, and moments later, their silhouettes are moving across the frosted glass partition that separates my office from the corridor. "Captain Sullivan," she says as she shows him through the door.

He's of average height, deeply tanned, with the wiry build of a track-and-field athlete, and appears to be in his late thirties. Gleaming captain's bars perch on the epaulets of his finely tailored uniform; the slacks have knife-edge creases that break slightly above mirror-polished oxfords. A thin briefcase hangs from his fist. Aviator-style sunglasses bridge his distinctively Irish nose.

We shake hands, then cross toward a sitting area at the far end of the office.

"I didn't expect you'd be coming to L.A."

"Sorry for the short notice."

"No problem. I meant I thought you'd call or write."

"Well, normally I would, but I had business at our port mortuary at Travis."

"Northeast of San Francisco, isn't it?"

"Yes. I was planning to call you today to set something up for Thursday or Friday; but my schedule cleared and—"

"I'm glad it did. You have a name for me?"

"Well, Mr. Morgan, before I get to that," he replies evasively, which worries me, "Colonel Webster asked me to tell you that your logic's very sound. If a body was identified as yours by mistake, that individual would be listed as unaccounted for."

"Process of elimination," I say, trying to conceal my impatience.

"Yes, we find it indispensable. Unfortunately in this case, it eliminated all the possibilities."

"All of them," I repeat with a sinking feeling.

"I'm afraid so. None matched your time/place parameters."

"Bolikhamsai Province, 12 May, '68," I say slowly, purposely confirming them.

"Right." He opens his briefcase and removes copies of the data I'd faxed to Kate Ackerman. "I have it all right here. We refer to it as a loss scenario. Mrs. Ackerman made sure we knew just how—I think she used the word *obsessed*—you are with resolving it."

"That's one way of putting it," I say, forcing a smile. "There's nothing even close?"

"What do you mean by close?"

"Within a few days one way or the other. I mean, someone might've recorded the wrong date."

"Oh, we always take that into account. The first thing we did was give your 'parameters' to a casualty data analyst. She plotted a circle search. That means she marked the location on a map and drew a circle with a ten-mile radius around it; then she screened every man whose last known location fell within the circle. When she came up empty, she increased the radius, and kept increasing it until she ran out of names."

"So she screened every man missing in Laos?"

"Correct."

"What about guys who went AWOL?"

"Them too. Actually, this was a relatively easy one. We spend months, sometimes years, on identification of remains cases. It's a painful and, often, very emotional process; and we do it under a lot of pressure. As a matter of fact, we've had to develop procedures to make sure we don't just give in to the pleas of a wife or family who've been waiting decades for a final answer. The bottom line is, we never release a finding until we're absolutely certain. That's policy, and it's strictly enforced."

"You know, Captain Sullivan, reading in between the lines, I get the feeling you're trying to tell me this man doesn't exist."

He nods gravely. "That's our conclusion."

I let out a long breath and tilt back in my chair, feeling as if I've been punched in the gut; then for whatever reason I notice his sunglass lenses are now perfectly clear. Corning, Photograys. I have a pair. Then I notice his eyes. Not their color but their shape, which is narrow, sloped, distinctly Asian.

He catches me staring. "Everyone has that reaction, Mr. Morgan," he says with a good-natured smile. "My mom's from the Philippines; Dad was a GI."

"Oh," I say, trying not to appear embarrassed.

"By the way," the captain says, "with regard to your name being on the Memorial, though your theory's plausible, it assumes a body was recovered and ID'd as yours by mistake."

I nod glumly, knowing exactly where he's headed.

"But a body wasn't recovered. All the records confirm it."

"I know; and so does the Memorial," I hear myself admitting as my mind suddenly starts zooming in on the wall from different angles in a series of instant replays. Over and over, from the black granite, to my name, to an extreme close-up of the little cross that has become the symbol for a perplexing riddle that defies explanation. "This body/no body snafu's been gnawing at me for weeks."

"Are you aware that there are as many as fourteen 'snafus' on the wall?"

"Yes, I am."

"Well, out of fifty-eight thousand plus chances that's a low percentage of error."

"Point zero zero zero two four one three."

"Let's get back to the body. The lack of one goes a long way to explaining why we didn't come up with a match to your scenario."

"Okay," I say, getting a little heated as I push up from the chair and circle behind it. "Where did that scenario come from? I didn't make it up. I didn't die either, did I?

And I've never set foot in Bolikhamsai Province, let alone weeks after my legs were damn near blown off."

"It's probably due to a data entry error. You've heard of people being declared dead by a computer; their bank accounts, Social Security, credit cards all canceled by a single keystroke. Besides, even if there was a body with your ID, every KIA—regardless of military ID, dog tags, or statements of recognition from buddies—was held in BTB status. In other words, believed-to-be so and so, until a positive ID was made at the mortuary. Even with your tags there's no way he could have been finally ID'd as you."

I spin the chair with frustration and cross toward the window; then, though I sense it will be futile, I decide to make one last challenge. "Even if there were no head or hands or other identifying marks?"

"Mr. Morgan," the captain replies with the patient dismay one normally uses when dealing with a stubborn child, "maybe this will satisfy you. The scientists at our lab are often given commingled bone fragments found at crash sites. Not only do they separate them into individuals but they also identify them. The level of technology in this area is truly amazing; believe me. I urge you to accept this finding. These things have a way of eating at you if you don't."

"With good reason."

"No offense, but if you were an MIA wife, coping with her husband's fate, I'd understand." He pauses and holds my eyes with his for a long moment, then more firmly says, "The man doesn't exist, Mr. Morgan. For your own good, let it go."

His words sound a little too much like a warning, though a sincere one; and despite his military bearing there's a clinical detachment in his tone and absence of compassion in his eyes that is troubling. At first I attribute it to an earlier remark. Perhaps like a doctor dealing with the terminally ill, he's protecting himself against emotional overload; but another thought occurs to me. "You know, Captain, I was just thinking that for someone as close to this issue as you are, you seem awfully distant."

"Well, I didn't mean to appear—"

"You haven't seen men die in combat, have you?"

"No, sir, I haven't."

"That makes a difference."

"Not to me. I assure you my stomach turns just like yours when somebody burns the flag."

"Really? Well, if you're lucky maybe they'll call you the next time one of those liberal pukes has to be taken out."

He flinches and stands, stung by the remark as I intended. We're face-to-face when he says, "I think that was uncalled for. My business here is finished."

"You're right, Captain, it was uncalled for. I was purposely being offensive to make a point. I've seen a lot of men die. They were protecting our rights—freedom of expression included."

He nods, seeming to accept my explanation. "Your point's well taken, Mr. Morgan." His eyes come alive with an idea, and he asks, "You into country/western?"

"No. Not really," I reply, unable to imagine why he's asking.

"Well, a couple of weeks ago I was watching a Johnny Cash concert on HBO. "Ragged Old Flag" is one of his tunes. You know what he said before he sang it?"

I shrug, still baffled.

"Well it was something like, I thank God we live in a country where we have the right to burn the flag. And I thank God we live in a country where we have the right to keep and bear arms—so I can shoot the son of a bitch who tries to burn mine."

I can't help but laugh. The captain seems pleased at having the last word and shakes my hand.

"I hope you'll take my advice, Mr. Morgan. We see families torn, tortured. Even when faced with clear evidence, some won't accept our findings."

"Sometimes it's hard to learn from others."

"I think it'd be in your best interests to try."

I accompany him to the reception area, where my secretary validates his parking stub. I don't know why; maybe because of the way he just showed up; maybe because his shrewd confidence made me feel as if I was being tested; maybe because prejudice born of combat is never fully exorcised; but as he leaves, I imagine the captain's glasses gradually darkening over his Asian eyes and picture him in the underground garage getting into a metallic blue sedan. A weird compulsion takes hold of me and I decide to do something I know I'll be sorry for. I return to my office, pull up the phone directory on my laptop, and dial.

"Capitol Real Estate," a woman answers.

"Yes, it's Cal Morgan calling for Kate Ackerman."

"Please hold."

"Hi! I've just listed a super condo in Georgetown: View, terrace, fireplace, modern kitchen," she says rapid-fire when she comes on. "It'd be a great corporate write-off. What do you say?"

"Sold. Now that we've covered your next car payment, I'm going to be meeting with someone from the CIL shortly, and—"

"They've got something for you?"

"I don't know; but it dawned on me I've never met the guy. His name's Captain Sullivan. Tall/short? Fat/skinny? What's he look like?"

"Captain Sullivan?" she repeats in a puzzled tone. "I don't know him. He must be new. By the way," she runs on, her pitch rising, "I got some good news too. It's about my husband."

"He's being repatriated?"

"We're waiting for the names to be released. It's a unilateral action by the Laotian government. The remains they're turning over were found at crash sites in the area where John was lost."

"Sounds promising."

"Yes, I'm trying not to get my hopes up. Hold on a sec, will you? I'm sorry. I've got to drop off, I've got a client on the other line. Let me know how you make out, okay?"

"Sure. Good luck."

I hang up slowly, thoughtfully. I was wrong. She's more than fanned my suspicions. Now, I'm going to confirm them. I find the number and dial.

"Central Identification Lab," a woman with what sounds like a Filipino accent answers.

"Yes, I'm going to be meeting your Captain Sullivan shortly, but I've no idea what he looks like. Would you describe him to me so I can—"

"Well, he'll be in uniform, and his name'll be above the right-hand pocket."

I expected her, wanted her, to say she'd never heard of him. I'm caught a little off guard. I want to be certain. "What if he's in civvies? I mean, is there something distinctive that—"

"Oh, you'll have no trouble picking him out of a crowd. Believe it or not, Captain Sullivan's Asian, but he has the finest Irish nose. We tease him about it all the time."

I stand at the window staring down at the people hurrying between the office towers. Had I made it all up? Given in to some sort of in-country fever or guilt because I'd put it all away? It doesn't really matter. Nothing could soften this blow. I'm at a complete dead end, and I feel empty.

I spend the next few days going through the motions at the office and at home. Early Saturday morning, Nancy lectures me about moping around and reminds me I promised to plant a jacaranda outside the dining room for her.

I grumble in protest, then halfheartedly haul a pick and shovel from the garage and get to work. The lack of rain has made the ground like concrete. The first several swings of the pick bounce off it harmlessly. Now, it becomes a challenge. I'd dug a foxhole once with nothing but a jungle knife. Of course, I was more highly motivated then. The next swing buries the pick deep in the soil. I work it loose, breaking up the surface. A few more swings like that and I'm really into it. Soon, oblivious to all else, I'm drenched with sweat, hands and face grimy, Reeboks caked with reddish soil. Before I know it, there's a huge mound of fresh earth next to the house, and I'm standing in a hole that comes up to my kneecaps. It's far deeper and wider than it needs to be for the jacaranda. The only things missing are my M-16 and the enemy. I'm flashing back to a fire fight when I hear a vehicle at the end of the long driveway that leads to our house. I toss the shovel aside and scramble out of the hole.

A blue streak zips between the rock formations.

I run to a vantage point from where I can see the road. The mailman's delivery jeep is chugging up the hill. I continue to the end of the driveway and retrieve the usual bundle of magazines, bills, and junk from the box. I'm returning to the house, thumbing through them, when my eyes dart to a return address, to the distinctive black military-style lettering that is sticking out between the edges of the other envelopes. I pull it free. It reads *U.S. Army Mortuary Affairs*. Almost a month has passed since I sent my letter. I've forgotten about it completely. The envelope contains a single sheet of paper that I imagine will state, in typically convoluted military syntax, that no records were filed under my name or serial number; but what I see makes my jaw drop and my adrenaline surge. I run toward the house, my heart pounding in my chest.

"Nance?!" I shout. "Nancy, look at this!"

She comes running through one of the floor-to-ceiling glass doors onto the deck, expecting some disaster has befallen me or the jacaranda.

"There was a body," I exclaim, pushing the copy of the field casualty report into her hands. "Look, they recovered a body. My name, my serial number."

10

THE IDENTIFICATION BLOCK ON THE COPY OF THE REPORT I'm holding reads *A. Calvert Morgan*. This document is responsible, beyond any doubt, for my name being on the Vietnam Memorial. I put it on my desk in the den and spend the weekend thinking about it, going back to it again and again, deducing whatever I can from the wealth of information it contains.

Not only does it confirm that a body with my dog tags and military ID was recovered; it also confirms the time/place parameters—12 May 1968, Bolikhamsai Province, Laos. Furthermore, it has three names and signatures that confirm, and perhaps promise, more:

Sergeant Richard A. Foster—graves registration officer, 24th Evac, which not only confirms that the body was recovered but also that the reporting process, which provided the information on the master casualty list, was initiated.

Warrant Officer Mario Farina—helicopter pilot, 1st Air Cav, which confirms graves registration carried out their procedures and released the body for shipment to the morgue.

Staff Sergeant John Bartlett—in-processing NCO at the main mortuary, Ton Son Nhut Airbase, Saigon, which confirms the body was actually delivered and accepted by mortuary personnel.

Despite them, and despite a body being identified as mine by mistake, I'm no closer to learning the man's identity, or to answering the other questions that have been confounding me.

Why the BNR entry on the master casualty list?

Why the cross, the MIA designation on the wall?

Why the failure to come up with a loss scenario that matches the parameters I'd provided? Captain Sullivan agreed that a soldier, whoever he was, had to be listed as unaccounted for if a body had been recovered and incorrectly identified as mine—and one had.

The report also contains one puzzling surprise. Contrary to what I and others have reasoned, the Cause of Casualty block reads *Killed hostile, small arms fire, torso*. It's clear that these wounds didn't obscure the man's identity, creating the potential for error. How could my dog tags and military ID, which included my photograph, be accepted as someone else's? It eventually occurs to me that just because I asked for copies of everything in my mortuary file doesn't mean I got them.

Monday morning, I'm sitting on the deck with a cup of coffee, reviewing the casualty report for the umpteenth time, when Nancy comes from the house with a refill and the newspaper. She pauses briefly as she approaches the table and looks off across the hill, then, mimicking a line from a movie about supernatural phenomenon whose name escapes me, sing-songs the words "They're back."

"What're you talking about?"

"Over there," she replies, pointing behind me to a section of road that, unlike the part visible from the den, winds around the rear of the house.

I look back over my shoulder and see a patch of blue hood and section of windshield visible between the trees. "You're right. It's the same car."

"What do you think's going on?"

"I don't know, but I'm going to find out," I say, pushing back my chair.

"Cal—"

"Don't worry. I'll be okay."

I saunter down the steps from the deck, and walk casually toward the road that is about fifty yards away on the far side of a rocky slope. The underbrush is stunted and sparse. Through a gap in the trees I can make out a figure behind the wheel. I'm fairly certain it's the same man I saw several days ago. He's staring straight ahead unaware of my approach, then he senses he's not alone and his head snaps in my direction. The reflections on the windshield tend to obscure him; but he appears to be thirtyish, his face narrow and tanned, topped by dark hair that's slicked back. I can feel his eyes boring into me from behind his sunglasses and I become a little apprehensive. Maybe Nance was right. Maybe this isn't such a good idea. I pause, then deciding that giving in to fear and apathy produces only more fear and apathy, I resume walking. I'm about halfway there when the man suddenly starts the engine and the car drives off. I stand there for a long moment watching the blue reflections vanish in the distance, then return to the house and report the incident to the County Sheriff's department, describing the car and driver as best I can.

"You didn't happen to get the license number, or maybe part of it?" the officer asks.

"No, I'm sorry. It was too far away."

"Well, as you probably know, Mr. Morgan, we've had some burglaries up in your area lately. Evidently the perpetrator waits until people leave for work, then he goes to work. We've been increasing our patrols as a deterrent."

"Well, maybe I scared him off for good."

Nancy and I secure the house, activate the alarm system, and leave. As soon as I get to the office, I call Army Mortuary Affairs in San Antonio. The line is busy. The invention of the redial button ranks third behind the wheel and computer. When I finally get through, it takes the duty clerk less than a minute to confirm that the casualty report is the only document in my file.

"Is this normal?" I wonder.

"No, sir."

"Well, what else should be in the file?"

"Hell, all kinds of stuff. I got me the list right here," he replies a little too eagerly. "There ought to be a toe tag with a mortuary processing number; an anatomical chart showing the location and nature of the wounds; an embalming statement from the mortician; a ready notice, which means the body's been prepared for shipment; shipping records, which would include a transfer case number; and a form thirteen hundred, which is the official death certificate."

"Sounds like a few things are missing."

"Sure does."

"Any idea why?"

"Well, yeah. I think it's pretty obvious a mistake was made somewhere along the line, don't you?"

"If one wasn't, the odds of us having this conversation would be pretty slim, wouldn't they?"

"Oh, yeah, right," he says, amused by his own denseness. "Of course, it's been more than twenty years, and to tell you the truth, I'm kind of new at this. I can't explain it, but I'll ask around."

"Sure. I'll check back with you," I say, knowing I'm wasting my time. I kick back in the chair and spin toward the windows, taking stock of the situation, which seems iffy at best. *If* the key to solving this exists, it lies with the men who signed the casualty report twenty-four years ago. *If* they survived. *If* they can remember. At least there's someone I can call to help track them down. I dial the NPRC in St. Louis, get Jack Collins on the line, and brief him.

"No kidding," he exclaims, clearly intrigued by the existence of a body.

"Look, Jack, I need to find these guys. Can you help me?"

A long breath hisses through the phone. "Not officially, no. But I'm curious as hell to find out what this is all about. Give me a little time to do some free-lance digging and I'll get back to you."

A couple of hours later, my secretary tells me Collins is on the line.

"I got good news and bad news," he says with enthusiasm, which makes me optimistic. "Farina, the chopper pilot, was killed in action, but the other two made it."

"You have locations on them?"

"On one of 'em. Foster. He lives in a town called Paradise just outside of Las Vegas. He's a musician, works at the Stardust Hotel."

"Nothing on Bartlett, the mortuary guy?" I ask, jotting the information down.

"Not enough. The last address we have for him is a V.A. hospital in Wyoming. That was eight years ago. He seems to have dropped out of sight after being released. It'll take a little time but I can check with veterans' organizations in the area. They might have something on him."

"Great. I'll run with what I've got for now."

I hang up smiling. Not only do I have a lead, but Vegas is less than an hour by plane from Los Angeles. Better yet, it's one of my all-time favorite getaways. Nancy and I go there at least a couple of times a year.

"So, what do you say?" I ask after briefing her over dinner. "Want to hit Vegas tomorrow?"

"Sure. I'll tell my class I'm taking the day off to go on a gambling junket with my husband."

"Come on, Nance, they can get along without you for one day."

"Why not go on the weekend?"

"Somehow I knew you'd say that."

"But that's five days away and it's driving you crazy. Right?"

"Right."

"Why don't you call him?"

"I could," I reply, breaking into a grin. "But then I wouldn't get to go to Vegas, would I?"

"Somehow I knew you'd say that."

"Besides," I explain more seriously, "there's something about this. I feel the need to meet these guys, see their eyes, you know what I mean?"

She nods thoughtfully and kisses my cheek.

Late the next morning, having taken care of some business that required my attention, I drive to LAX—mirrors free of metallic blue cars—and catch a flight to McCarran International Airport in the desert southeast of Las Vegas. I hire one of the chauffeured limos that are lined up outside the terminal and head for the Stardust.

One of the oldest and most luxurious hotels on the Strip, the Stardust is no Disneyland like the Excalibur or Mirage, but an updated fifties-style gaming palace with a dazzling neon tower and an immense, totally illuminated facade that advertises the spectacular Lido de Paris and its troupe of topless dancers.

The glitzy lobby is alive with the unmistakable cacophony of things spinning, whirring, and clacking, the throbbing pulse of the casino that never fails to raise the hair on the back of my neck when I first hear it. I ask the stunningly attractive woman in the information booth about Richard Foster. She points to a poster that proclaims *Constellation Lounge, The Piano Stylings of DICK FOSTER* and informs me he's on now. I thread my way between the gaming tables to a dimly lit cavern on the far side of the casino.

The handsome black man at the piano is playing the blues with feeling and virtuosity as much for himself as for his audience. I write CAL MORGAN G COMPANY RANGERS on the back of a Keno slip, and have the cocktail waitress deliver it to him. As he nods in acknowledgment, two tall, shapely women in elegant skintight dresses glide into the lounge. Jet-setters? Hookers? Probably both. This is Vegas. One of them catches my eye and smiles. I pretend not to notice, hoping she hasn't mistaken my curiosity for something more. A few minutes later, the piano player finishes his song and joins me.

"Morgan, G Company Rangers," Dick Foster says in a soft, deep-South accent as he folds his lanky frame into a chair and studies my face trying to remember it. "We cross paths over there somewhere?"

"Sort of. That's what I want to talk to you about."

We order drinks, and I show him the copy of the casualty report with his name and signature. His expression darkens as I shorthand my story, and ask if he remembers opening a body bag and finding my military ID and dog tags inside with the remains. When I finish, he flicks the report onto the table as if it's a piece of radioactive waste and leans back staring at me with angry eyes. An avalanche of silver dollars comes from a nearby slot machine and fills the silence.

"I don't need this, man," he finally says in a threatening whisper. "Spent half a lifetime putting it out of my head."

"I'm sorry. I explained how important it is."

"Well, that don't mean jack to me."

"Look, you signed that report. You had my tags in your hand. They were laced to my boots. You're as close as I've come to licking this. Come on, try and remember the guy."

"Hell, you know how many bags I handled? Like thousands. Besides, for three hundred and sixty-five days all I cared about was making it." He pauses and holds his long, expressive fingers in front of my face, then adds, "*All* of me making it. That's where my head was at."

"Yeah, and you pulled it off. I'm trying to do something for a guy who didn't."

"And you figure that gives you the right to walk in here off the street and put me through this fucking pain?"

"Bet your fucking ass, I do," I reply matching his tone. "This thing came my way, and I saw too many men die to let it go. Now, try and remember, will you?"

He sighs, shoulders sagging with the weight of the memory. "Oh, I remember, man, do I ever remember," he finally says, then he sees my expression brighten and, with a measure of disgust, quickly adds, "No, man, not your fucking tags. Bloody chunks of meat that used to be human beings, that's what I remember. The recovery teams shoveled 'em up and put the tags and ID in with the ones they figured they belonged to. No way they didn't make mistakes sometimes."

"Yes, but take another look at this," I plead, pushing the casualty report toward him. "Chest wound, small arms fire. This guy wasn't disfigured or dismembered. How could there be a mistake?"

He peruses it and shrugs. "Good question. Maybe some kind of fuck-up at the mortuary. Who knows?"

"But they had fingerprints, dental records."

"I don't know, man," he says, becoming frustrated. "I worked collection points. Far as we were concerned, every KIA was identified as believed-to-be."

"Yes, I know. I was just hoping you might be able to recall something that'd give me a clue to the poor bastard's identity."

He nods and glances to the copy of the casualty report again. "A. Calvert Morgan," he says rolling the syllables, his brow furrowing as he searches for a connection, then he shakes his head. "My screen's blank, man. Nothing."

My lips tighten into a thin line. I nod glumly. "Well, thanks for trying," I say, accepting that he can't give me what I want. I feel beaten and discouraged, and I realize it shows because his eyes are compassionate now, not angry.

"Sorry I popped off before," he offers, pausing thoughtfully before adding, "It's a good thing you're doing."

I smile, then nod to the piano. "You too. Got a real nice touch."

"Thanks."

"You do 'Dock of the Bay'?"

"You kidding? When I was in-country there was Otis Redding, and then there was everybody else."

"Jimi, Aretha, and B.B. King," I say, rapid-fire.

"Not necessarily in that order," he shoots back. He downs his drink, then stands and glances to the piano. "I guess I got no cause to be bitter. I mean, how many people earn a living doing what they love?"

"Not enough."

"Well," he says with a self-deprecating laugh, " 'round here the trick's making sure you don't give back more than you make."

He crosses to the piano, nods in my direction as he settles at the keyboard, and launches in to a rolling, rhythmic intro before pulling the lyrics from somewhere deep inside him.

> Sittin' in the mornin' sun,
> I'll be sittin' till the evenin' come,
> watchin' the ships roll in,
> then I watch 'em roll away again.
> Yeah, I'm sittin' on the dock of the bay,
> watchin' the tide roll away,
> sittin' on the dock of the bay, wastin' time.
> Left my home in Georgia,
> headed for the Frisco Bay.
> I have nothing to live for,
> nothing gonna come my way . . .

I've got some time before my flight. I listen for a while, finish my drink, and slip a hundred into the brandy snifter on the piano. As I turn to leave, I sway slightly, almost losing my balance. I've had only one drink. It's in-country anxiety, a rush of adrenaline from the past. I take a few deep breaths and head for the tables, mentally booting-up my blackjack program.

If games of chance are God's gift to actuaries, and they are, blackjack is *the* game because all the players reveal all their cards as each hand is played out. Despite the bank's 18 percent edge over terrible players, and an average 5.90 percent over all players, the player who can remember which cards have been played, determine the number of tens to non-tens remaining in the deck, and instantly turn the ratio into a decimal, can cut that edge considerably. The best players cut it to an advantage of 2.3 percent—not for the bank but for the player. I've been doing it since about sophomore year in high school.

I lose a few hands while observing the run of cards, then I start winning, and begin doubling up, and the comp drinks start coming. I decline all but one. About a half hour later, I'm ahead almost six hundred dollars when I realize it's time to cash out and head for the airport. As I stand to gather my chips, the stacks blur into patterns of dancing circles. My legs feel rubbery, and I'm swaying noticeably.

Several of the other players help steady me.

"You okay, buddy?" the dealer asks.

"Oh, he'll be fine," I hear a velvety female voice reply as an arm wraps around my waist. "He's with us. We've been looking all over for him."

They have? I wonder, as my head fills with the suffocating smell of heavy perfume. I've got double, maybe triple, vision. Out of the corner of my eye I catch blurred glimpses of tumbling blond hair, glistening ovals of neon-red lipstick, and curves of tawny flesh straining against a dress that looks like one of the skintights from the lounge. I realize there really are two of them, when her mirror image scoops my chips into her purse, then puts one of my arms over her shoulders to support me.

"Come on, we better get you back to the room," she announces with a giggle.

"Room? I don't have a room," I mumble, as the casino starts spinning and they lead me away.

"Bet he don't have a hard-on either, honey," someone cracks, drawing laughter from the crowd.

The women direct me across the casino into an elevator. I'm on the verge of passing out. When the elevator stops, they usher me down a long corridor to one of the hotel rooms, and push me inside. The door slams as I'm stumbling forward. They shove me facedown onto the bed, then they go to work rifling my pockets, removing my wallet, cash, watch, jewelry, and clothing. I'm struggling, trying to resist, but powerful hands grasp one of my arms and twist it behind me. What feels like a knee holds it against my back. I manage to turn my head to one side.

The entire room is reflected in the mirrored headboard. My vision is blurred, but I can make out shapes and forms. There are three figures, not two. One of them is definitely a man, a man wearing sunglasses. The man in the blue car?! I can't tell. He has something shiny in his hand. A gun? A knife?! I lunge sideways trying to roll free. He shouts an expletive. A sharp pain erupts in my upper arm, deep in the bone. What feels like a surge of electrical current goes down into my hand. The tips of my fingers crackle, then the pain races up the side of my head, making my skin crawl. Suddenly, they release me. The door slams and they're gone.

The deafening thump of my heart trying to tear open my chest is the only sound now. I crawl off the bed onto the floor then, grabbing fistfuls of carpet, drag my limp body to the door. Somehow, I manage to reach the knob, and with what little strength remains in my limbs, I get to my feet and try to open it. I'm bathed in sweat and my hand slips off the polished brass. Then the world dissolves into a series of white flashes that are followed by an oddly pleasant euphoria. I stumble backward across the room, and crash to the floor.

The last thing I remember is the reflection in the mirrored ceiling of a half-naked man sprawled on a scarlet rug. He looks just like me.

11

A STRONG, ANTISEPTIC ODOR THAT BURNS MY NOSE IS the first thing I'm aware of, then the sounds: people scurrying, rapid-fire conversation, equipment rolling. But I sense none of it has anything to do with me. I remain in this state of semiconsciousness for a while, finally awakening to the painful glare of a bank of fluorescents directly overhead. As my eyes adjust to the light, a green haze gradually sharpens into the folds of a hospital curtain. I've been here before. Only this time my legs aren't wrapped in bandages, and the world isn't painted in shades of khaki and brown camouflage. I lie here for a long time, baffled and disoriented. Occasionally a nurse or doctor comes by and takes my pulse and blood pressure. "Good," one finally says. "You're going to be fine."

I don't feel fine. As a matter of fact, I feel absolutely hideous, like I've got a hangover that's never going to go away. Shadows fall across the curtain, as some people approach and stop just outside it, carrying on a conversation. At least two, maybe three men, and a woman. Her voice sounds very familiar. If I didn't know better, I'd think it was Nancy. God, it is Nancy.

"There has to be some mistake," she says sharply. "My husband doesn't use drugs."

"I'm sure you're right, Mrs. Morgan," a man says in a gravelly voice. "But Vegas does strange things to people. They come here to gamble and end up doing all kinds of other stuff."

"That's not why he was here," Nancy protests, her voice starting to take on an edge.

"Maybe that's what he told you."

"Look, I know my husband."

"Don't take this the wrong way, Mrs. Morgan, but if I had a five-dollar chip for every time I've heard that, I could bail out the S&L crisis single-handed. People think they know their spouses, but believe me, they really don't."

"Well, I know mine," she snaps.

"I'd prefer you don't make this too long," I hear another man saying. His voice is authoritative and smoother than the others, and I assume he's my doctor. Finally the curtain slides back and Nancy is standing at the foot of the bed. She looks shaken and worried as she crosses toward me, followed by two men in J.C. Penney ties and sports jackets.

"You okay?" she says, leaning over the bed and hugging me tentatively almost as if she's afraid I might break if she squeezed too hard.

"Yes babe, I guess. How long have I been here? How long have you been here?"

"About a half hour. They called me at school. I got the first flight I could. I was so worried."

"Jesus, I'm sorry," I say, my temples throbbing with pain. "I don't know what happened."

"According to the police," she says, indicating the two men behind her, "a maid at the Stardust went to make up a room and found you on the floor, unconscious."

I shiver at the thought. My mind is a tangle of fractured images. "I don't know, I kind of remember stumbling and falling . . ." I pause, and finish it with a confused shrug. "What's this drug stuff?"

"I don't know. They want to know if you use them."

"They what?"

"I told them you didn't. They still want to talk to you about it."

I shrug resignedly. "Okay."

She steps back from the bed and nods to the two detectives. They exchange looks before the short, tired-looking one with the moustache leans to Nancy. "You might want to wait outside, Mrs. Morgan," he says in a tone that suggests he's trying to spare her some kind of embarrassment.

"I'll stay with my husband," she replies without hesitation.

The detective's head bobs in a "suit yourself" gesture as he fetches the remote control for the articulated bed. "I like to be able to look people in the eye when I talk to them, Mr. Morgan," he explains as the motor whirrs, slowly raising me into a sitting position. "I'm Sergeant Figueroa, this is Detective Wallach," he continues, gesturing to his younger, clean-shaven colleague. "We're with the Las Vegas Police Department. Before you say anything, I want to advise you of your rights."

"Why?" I ask, bewildered. "Am I under arrest?"

"No, sir. Just a precaution."

Out of the corner of my eye, I notice Nancy sigh with relief. "I know my rights," I grumble, starting to feel a little annoyed.

"Good," he says, going on to read them to me anyway. "Now, do you know what happened to you?"

I shrug and splay my hands. "I was sort of hoping you could tell me."

"Sure," he says, swinging an amused look to his colleague.

"Well, for openers," the clean-shaven one says, with an apologetic nod to Nancy, "several people at the hotel said they saw you leave the blackjack table with a couple of hot-looking young women. That refresh your memory any?"

"God," I groan, nodding as it starts coming back. I glance to Nancy, wishing I could disappear. "Yes, yes, it does," I reply, going on to tell them about almost passing out in the casino and the two women coming to my rescue. "They pretended to know me. I'm not sure, but I think they sized me up in the lounge. I figured they probably slipped something into my drink so they could, you know, rip me off or something, but I was too weak to stop them."

The two detectives exchange skeptical looks. They told me their names but I can't remember them. They're just moustache and clean-shaven to me.

"What does that mean?" I challenge angrily.

"Mr. Morgan, we handle a couple dozen of these a week," moustache says, taking over. "People come here looking to party, sometimes they get a little more than they bargained for. Now, if you'll cooperate there's a chance we might be able to—"

"Party?!" I explode, infuriated by what he's insinuating. The exertion and anger fill my head with pain. I lean back against the pillows until it subsides. "I wasn't partying," I explain, calmly, deliberately. "I told you these two women drugged me and took me to a room; then they—"

"We know," he interrupts, smugly. "It was registered to you."

"To me?"

"Yes. We found your clothes scattered all over the place; lines of cocaine on the coffee table, bottles of booze, porno tapes, video camera, all the standard good-time Charlie toys."

"That's ridiculous. Besides, I wasn't in that room for more than a couple of minutes."

"From the time you left the tables until the maid found you?" he scoffs. "Try a couple of hundred."

"Three hours?" I say in disbelief.

"Damn near." A thin smile raises the corners of his moustache. "You tested positive for both cocaine and heroin, among other things, so we know you weren't in there taking a nap."

I'm angry and stunned, and the words are sticking in my throat. "That's, that's even more ridiculous. I don't use drugs. I had two drinks. One with the piano player in the lounge, the other at the blackjack table. Ask the cocktail waitresses, they'll—"

"Come on, Mr. Morgan, the doc says you were higher than a kite when they brought you in."

"How many times do I have to tell you, I was drugged and robbed? I don't know what they gave me, but I remember them going through my pockets. They took my watch, my wallet—"

"They always do."

"I'm telling you I came here on personal business. I wasn't looking to party."

"Somehow these hookers got the idea you were."

"Wait, wait, hold it," I say, starting to see hazy flashes of the mirrored headboard, followed by reflections of shapes and figures. "I think there was a man. Yes, yes," I continue as the image clarifies. "Two women and a man."

"You're sure about that?"

"Positive. He was the one holding me down. Really hurt my arm."

They exchange looks again, uncertain looks, which suggests they're reconsidering their initial verdict.

"Well, that might change things a little," clean-shaven says grudgingly, circling to the other side of the bed. "I mean, the guy might've been their pimp; but flesh peddlers rarely set foot on the playing field, so there's a chance you're right. There are a number of Rolex rings working the city. If that's the case, the guy was probably their Fagin."

"Yeah, sometimes they make it look like a kink-and-coke bash," the moustache chimes in. "So the mark doesn't report the theft. We see a lot of that."

"You sure could've fooled me," I say angrily.

"Can you describe them?" he asks coolly, ignoring the insult.

"Well, sort of," I reply, taking a moment to regain my composure. "Everything was pretty hazy. I remember the guy was wearing glasses and . . ." I pause, drawing a blank, and shrug. "That's it. Like I said, I really didn't get a very good look at him."

"What about the ladies?"

"Tall, blond, sexy," I reply, splaying my hands. "Very sexy."

Moustache emits an amused chortle. "I'm sure we'll have no trouble finding them," he says in as sarcastic a tone as he can manage.

I realize I've just described half the women in Las Vegas. "What happens now?"

"That's up to the prosecutors. Go home. Get some rest. We'll file our report and send you a copy." He slips a business card from a shirt pocket and flicks it onto the bedding in front of me. "If you have any questions, that's where you'll find us." He hitches up his pants, nods to Nancy, and shoulders his way through the opening in the curtain, then he pauses, turns back to me and adds, "Of course, if it goes any further, we know where to find you."

12

I AWAKEN IN EXCRUCIATING PAIN. IT'S STILL DARK, AND very quiet, and I can hear the surf surging in the distance. It was well after midnight by the time we got home from Vegas, and I've been sleeping fitfully, if at all.

"What's going on?" Nancy asks groggily, finally responding to my restlessness. "God, it's not even five-thirty."

"My arm. It's killing me." I sit up, turn on my reading light and begin unbuttoning my pajama top to get a look at it.

She pushes up onto an elbow and squints at me through sleepy eyes. "Well, you know what they say, tiger," she teases in a voice dripping with sarcasm and sexuality, "every party has its price."

"It's not funny," I protest, wincing in pain as I slip my arm out of the pajama sleeve. "It hurts like hell. Look."

"Oh-oh," she says, frowning at the sight of it.

On the outside of my left arm, midway between the shoulder and elbow, is a swollen blue-purple mass with pinkish yellow accents that resembles an early Rothko. Nancy's expression becomes progressively more serious as she examines it, gently pressing here and there.

"Ow! take it easy."

"I don't like that at all."

"Me neither."

It's midmorning before I can get in to see our internist. Dr. Marcel Koppel is a lanky, methodical man of Belgian descent with an easygoing manner and intelligent eyes that take on a mischievous glint when I brief him on the incident in Las Vegas. Then he examines the bruise, which he calls a hematoma.

"They x-ray this when you were in the hospital?"

"No. It wasn't bruised. Felt a little sore when I went to bed last night. Then this morning—"

"Delayed bleeding of some kind."

"What causes that?"

"Usually a blood vessel weakened by trauma. It hangs in there for a while, then gives way and starts leaking." He sends me down the hall to a radiology lab. About a half hour later, I return with the X rays and he slips them into the light panel on the wall of the examining room.

His brows raise slowly. "Never seen that before," he muses, intrigued by what the X rays reveal.

"Seen what?"

"That right there," he replies, using the point of a pencil to indicate a tiny, hard-edged, and totally black line. It's about three quarters of an inch long. One end is cut at an angle.

"Know what that is?"

I shake my head no.

"A hypodermic needle."

"Jesus."

"You know, I've seen them bend in my day, but I can't recall ever seeing one break. Whoever did that must operate a jackhammer for a living." He continues studying the X rays and zeroes in on something, then nods with understanding. "That tends to explain it. See?" He uses the pencil to trace the path of a pale, squiggly line that ends in a microscopic crater. "The needle hit the bone, went scraping along it, then dug in right there and broke."

I nod sagely; then it dawns on me that that's my arm on the X ray, my arm that has the needle embedded in it. "What do we do about that?"

"Well, as they say, what goes in . . ." He pauses, takes hold of my arm, and presses down gently with his thumbs. It hurts like hell, but the tip of the needle soon emerges from beneath the bruised area of skin. He fetches a pair of forceps, grasps it, and slowly pulls the needle from my biceps. ". . . Must come out."

I'm staring at my arm.

A tiny drop of blood seeps from the pinhole.

He's holding the forceps to the light, staring at the needle, puzzled. "Wrong gauge."

"What do you mean?"

"Well, needles used to give subcutaneous or intramuscular shots are usually in the twenty to twenty-three range. The larger the gauge the finer the needle. This can't be more than an eighteen, something you'd use to take blood."

"You told me to stay out of hospitals once, remember?"

"Yes, I do," he replies with a little smile. "But no professional would make that kind of mistake."

"A guy in a hotel room might," I say, as the once-hazy scenario starts to clarify. "I remember he had something shiny in his hand; I was struggling and this sharp pain ran down my arm. The sudden movement must've broken the needle."

He nods in agreement, then as he disinfects and bandages the tiny wound, speculates, "I imagine they knew what they'd put in your drink wouldn't last long enough to stop you from calling for help or perhaps even going after them. So they tried to inject you with something else to make sure you were out."

"Try heroin and cocaine."

The doctor questions me with a look.

"The hospital said I tested positive for both."

His expression darkens. "I worked ER in an inner-city hospital when I was a resident. We handled a lot of drug overdoses. It sounds like they injected you with what in the vernacular is called a speedball."

"A speedball," I repeat slowly as a horrid memory dawns on me. "Isn't that what killed John Belushi?"

The doctor nods gravely. "Might've killed you too, but I suspect you didn't get the full dose."

"Why not?"

He fetches something from a drawer, peels off the paper wrapper, and removes a hypodermic needle. "This is a three-quarter-inch eighteen."

"Same as that."

"Right." He matches the fresh needle to the piece he removed. They're the same length. He touches the point of the pencil to the plastic collar, the part that's cast around the needle's shaft, and screws into the syringe. "See? It broke right at the hub. Which means it broke above the surface of the skin."

A chill goes through me at the thought of how close I came to being killed.

"It's probably going to look worse before it gets better." He prescribes an antibiotic and a mild painkiller, and sends me home. Before leaving, I ask him to send a copy of his findings to Sergeant Figueroa at Las Vegas Police Department headquarters.

Over the next couple of days, I go to work late and leave early, getting home just after Nancy returns from school. She's in the family room, playing the piano, which she does every day for a half hour or so. Cole Porter, Gershwin, and the classics are all part of her repertoire. Today, what sounds like a Mozart sonata fills the house, though I'm a musical illiterate and am never certain. She plays for relaxation, for me, and occasionally for others when coaxed. She's enormously talented and humble to a fault, which is part of her charm.

"Hi, hon," she says brightly, finishing with a lovely, delicate run. She leaves the piano, kissing me on the move as she fetches the afternoon paper from the coffee table. "They got that burglar."

"The one working the neighborhood?"

"Uh-huh. Caught him red-handed in a garage on Alta Vista."

I scan the article, then drift off in thought.

"What's the matter?"

"Hang in there with me a minute."

I cross to the phone and press the button that auto-dials the sheriff's substation at the Malibu Civic Center. "Yes, this is Mr. Morgan up on Sea View. Oh, no, no problem. I just heard you caught that burglar. Yes, congratulations. If you don't mind me asking, what was he driving?" There's a pause. I hear some papers shuffling before he comes up with the answer. "Oh, okay, thanks."

I hang up.

Nancy questions me with a look.

"Toyota van."

Suddenly, I'm seeing flashes of the blue sedan, and the driver with the sunglasses, and the guy in the hotel room with the sunglasses, and the excruciating pain in my arm, and the tiny piece of needle, and I'm hearing the words *heroin, cocaine—speedball*—might've killed you . . . killed you . . . killed you—and then suddenly I hear myself saying, "Maybe they wanted to kill me."

Nancy's head jerks around as if I've just shouted an obscenity. "Wanted to kill *you*?" she asks, incredulously.

"Yes. What were those buzzwords that detective used?"

"Rolex ring?"

"No, the other ones."

"Oh, kink-and-coke party."

"That's it. A kink-and-coke party gone wrong. A businessman goes to Vegas, buys himself that double header he's always wanted, does a little coke, decides to go a little further, agrees to let one of the little girls put a needle in his arm . . ."

"I thought you said the idea was to make sure you were knocked out?"

"So did I, until now. But if you really think about it, why didn't they just hit me over the head?"

She shrugs. "That's like asking why you in the first place?"

"That was my next question."

"A stroke of bad luck."

"No, no way. There was a guy next to me at the blackjack table who had a cowboy hat in his lap filled with black chips; he was up over ten thousand bucks. Why not him? Why take the risk for a crummy five or six hundred?"

"I don't know. Besides, no one knew you were going to Vegas."

"They could've followed me."

"And had the time to set up such an elaborate charade?"

"I don't have all the answers. But if money wasn't the target, you're looking at all that's left."

"Okay, just assuming they were out to kill you, why go to all that trouble to make it look like an accident?"

"To keep the police from looking for a motive. So they wouldn't ask 'Why would somebody kill Cal Morgan?' "

She shakes her head, dismayed. "I'll ask it. Why?"

"I don't know. Why was that guy in the blue car watching the house?"

"What does that have to do with this? Come on, Cal, he could still be a burglar, or what's her face's lover, for that matter. You're starting to see conspiracies everywhere."

"Don't start psychoanalyzing me, okay?"

"Hey, this is me, remember?" she says gently, stung by my tone. "I'm concerned. I don't like what this is doing to you. You haven't been yourself since we were in Washington. You're letting your imagination run away with you. I mean, you don't have an enemy in the world, yet you—"

"That I know of."

"Honey, it doesn't make sense. People don't go around committing murder without a reason."

"Chrissakes, Nance," I snap, interrupting her. "You've got an answer for everything, just like those cops. Next you'll be telling me you think I was partying."

"That's ridiculous."

"At least we agree on something."

We stare at each other in silence. The electronic twitter of the phone breaks it. Nancy scoops up the receiver, then hands it to me. "Mr. Collins," she says coolly.

"Jack?"

"Hi, I tracked down Bartlett, the mortuary guy."

"Thanks, that's great."

"Not really. He's at a VA hospital in Denver. They said he's in pretty bad shape."

"How bad?"

"He's in the AIDS unit."

I groan.

"Yes, I wouldn't waste too much time. They said it could be a matter of weeks or even days."

"Days?"

"Uh-huh. By the way, you have any luck with that guy Foster?"

"No. To make a long story short, nice man, good musician, no information, painful experience. I'll tell you about it someday. You have an address on that hospital for me?"

I jot it down, then hang up and head into the kitchen to get a beer. When I close the fridge, I notice Nancy standing in the doorway behind me. I pause and hold up the bottle. "Want one?"

She shakes no and folds her arms. "What's going on?" she asks suspiciously.

I shrug nonchalantly, fetch an opener from a drawer, and methodically remove the cap, then take a long swallow. I'm stalling. I've been stalling since I hung up the phone. Nancy knows it, which is why she followed me. "I've got to go to Denver," I finally reply apprehensively.

She lets out a long breath. "When?"

"Tomorrow."

"We're going to see *Phantom* tomorrow."

"I know. I'm sorry."

"Really?" she responds facetiously.

"Come on, Nance," I say calmly. "The guy's dying. He's my only link to the past. Probably the last chance I've got to identify that soldier."

"You know," she says wearily. "I really don't think I care anymore."

"You know what I think?" I shoot back sharply, heightening the tension. "I think you've misplaced your priorities."

"No. You're my priority. Can't you see what this is doing to you?"

"Maybe it wouldn't be so bad if you gave me a little support instead of fighting me every step of the way."

"God," she exclaims in a throaty growl, her tone a mixture of disappointment and disbelief. "You sound just like you used to."

"What the hell do you mean by that?"

"Paranoid, compulsive. You know what I mean. Look at yourself. One minute you're telling me you think people are trying to kill you, the next you're talking about dashing off to Denver tomorrow. You think that's rational behavior?"

"Ohhhh," I say, my eyes widening in a spooky stare. I can feel myself starting to lose control, feel the need to lash out coming over me like a long-dormant plague surging to life. "You know those wacko Vietnam vets. If they aren't having nightmares about fire fights and nape, they're stalking our cities and towns, blowing people away just for kicks."

"Please, Cal," Nancy pleads vulnerably, her eyes starting to glisten. "We haven't done this in twenty years. I hated it then and I hate it now."

I take a long swallow of beer, then another, trying to wash down the lump of in-country anger that's rising in my throat. "Can't hate it without hating me, babe," I say, punctuating the remark with a flick of my forefinger that sends the cap from the beer bottle rocketing off the counter and across the kitchen like a miniature hockey puck. "Go ahead, Nance," I taunt, knowing it will hurt her. I don't want to but I can't help myself and do it anyway. "Go ahead, say it, if it'll make you feel better. I can handle it."

"I don't hate you, you know that. Seeing you like this is torture." She sighs defeatedly, then, tears rolling down her cheeks, she comes around the counter and gently, comfortingly puts her arm around my shoulders.

My body is rigid and ungiving. I ignore her presence as I drain the bottle, then step away. "Yeah, well it's torture for me too."

"Don't do this, Cal. I've been through it once, but as much as I love you, I don't think I could handle it again."

"Well, neither do I, dammit!" I shout, tossing the bottle across the room. It smashes into the stone wall that encloses the fireplace and bursts, showering us with beer and shards of glass.

13

I'M STANDING IN FRONT OF A MIRROR IN OUR BEDROOM knotting my tie. It's pure silk, elegant and expensive, but I rarely wear it on weekdays because the avocado, black, and cream print with red accents is a bit loud for business. Nancy bought it for me; and I'm wearing it today as a subtle signal, an apology for behavior that was, at the least, inexcusable. I feel guilty and remorseful. I was out of control, I had turned back the clock, I did lapse into one of the paranoid rages that marked my return from Vietnam. Nancy was right about all of that. However, after a night of soul-searching, I've decided she was more right about it's being irrational to imagine that people are trying to kill me than about going to Denver. Despite recent events, my commitment to learning the soldier's identity remains unshaken.

Nancy comes out of the shower. She hasn't said a word to me since yesterday's incident and continues to ignore me as she towels off and dresses for school. The tie isn't working.

"Come on, babe. I don't want to leave like this."

"Taking your car again?" she asks curtly.

"What do you mean?"

"I was planning to have the Rover serviced when you went to Vegas, but you drove yourself to the airport."

"Stop trying to pick a fight, okay? You know I had to leave from the office."

"You still could've used a company driver."

"I didn't think of it. I told you I arranged for one this morning."

"You tell me a lot of things," she snaps as she brushes her hair, using short, quick strokes to communicate her anger.

"Look, I'm sorry. I said I was out of line. I really don't want to leave like this."

"Then don't go."

"Nance . . . You know I have to. I get in tonight at seven-fifty-five. Will you be at the airport?"

"I'll be at the theater with the Grants."

"Yes, well, I guess I should've mentioned the bottle wasn't the only thing I broke yesterday."

Her brows go up.

"I called Gil and cancelled."

"You what?"

"I made an excuse about Laura coming down unexpectedly. I'm having the driver deliver the tickets to his office."

"All of them?"

I nod contritely. "He's taking an associate and his wife. I'm sorry. I wasn't myself when I did it. I can't take them back now."

She glares at me, fuming. "You've got a lot of gall, Morgan."

"A is for acid indigestion," I quip in a last-ditch effort to loosen her up.

"Not the phrase I have in mind."

"Besides, I know how much picking me up at the airport means to you."

Her eyes are burning with rage. Finally, they cool, slightly, and she emits an exasperated groan.

"Well, what do you say?"

"You've been doing this to me since high school, haven't you?"

"A is for always," I reply, grinning.

"All right," she snarls grudgingly. "I'll be there."

"Thanks. Maybe we can talk this out."

"Maybe."

I want her to smile but she doesn't.

United's 9:15 flight to Denver is scheduled at two hours, eighteen minutes. Due to the change in time zones, I arrive at Stapleton Airport just after 12:45 P.M. It takes a half hour to pick up a rental car and twice that long to make my way through the downtown area to Fort Logan just off Route 285 near Sheridan, a picturesque rural area near Lake Marston, fifty miles southwest of the city.

The road that leads to the VA hospital is lined with budding trees and manicured landscaping. At first glance it looks more like a resort than a government facility. But once inside, I'm quickly reminded this is a place where once-proud men, crack combat troops who stormed enemy positions, fighter jocks who flew supersonic jets, now shuffle aimlessly about corridors—if they have legs that function, if they have legs at all. The thought of how close I came to being one of them sends a chill through me. I feel more than a little conspicuous in my Armani suit and doeskin wingtips. I've certainly worn the wrong tie.

A woman at the reception desk directs me to the Immunodeficiency Unit. I'm stunned by this confrontation with the walking dead. The blank, sunken eyes. The skin drawn like parchment over bones. The ghastly sense of hopelessness. These aren't concentration camp inmates, but they could be.

A nurse shows me to a room where a man in a wheelchair is sitting in front of a window. His back is to the door, his head is tilting slightly to one side. An oxygen bottle rides in a holder beneath the chair. An IV stand, affixed to one of the armrests, towers over him like the grim reaper's scythe.

Though it's not an airborne virus and I've never been homophobic, I stand there for a long moment, anxious about approaching a man who's dying, anxious about *it*, about AIDS.

"Mr. Bartlett?" I finally say.

A few seconds pass before his hands lower to the chair's push rims in response, then his fingers slowly grasp them and he wheels himself around to face me.

I introduce myself, explaining I'm a Vietnam vet, and ask if we can talk for a few minutes.

He nods imperceptibly, without looking up, and motions to a chair against the wall. I slide it closer to him and sit down. A clear plastic tube carries the steady drip of dextrose and sodium chloride to a vein just above his wrist.

Another snakes over his shoulder to his upper lip, where bluish prongs dart up into his nostrils. His freshly shaven face has a waxy sheen that intensifies its hollowness. As he lifts his head and looks at me, his eyes narrow with what appears to be uncertainty, then they widen in shock, and he lurches backward in the wheelchair.

"What's wrong?" I ask, assuming he's having an attack or seizure of some kind. "You want me to call a nurse?"

He shakes no emphatically and cocks his head to one side, studying me out of the corner of his eye.

"You sure you're all right?"

He nods warily, then reaches out and touches my face with a skeletal hand as if confirming I exist. I want to pull away but don't, afraid I'll offend him.

"You," he says in a hoarse whisper, expelling a stream of stale breath, which nauseates me. "You're—you're dead."

Is he invoking a curse, making a macabre prophecy? "What do you mean?" I ask with a nervous laugh.

"I saw you dead."

"Obviously I'm not. I don't understand."

"Were you a twin?"

"No."

"Well, then a grunt who looked a lot like you died in Nam," he explains, in a voice illness has reduced to an eerie rasp. "I debagged him."

"You remember the face of every GI you processed?"

"Of course not, but there's no way in hell I'll ever forget this one."

"Why?"

"Because it was weird, real weird." He pauses, taking a deep breath, which gives me hope that there is more to come. "It was—April? No, no, May. First or second week May of '68. I was just starting my shift, we did twelve on/twelve off. This one morning, I come into the morgue and find bodies everywhere. On the tables, in piles on the floor, stuffed into the big walk-in reefer; they were in bags, wrapped in ponchos, even rolled up in tent flaps. Worst I'd ever seen it. I'm waist-deep in bodies. I start debagging this guy . . ." He gasps and pauses to catch his breath, using the time to study my face again. "Hell, if it wasn't you," he resumes, shaking his head in disbelief, "it sure was damn near your double."

"I think I understand," I say, my mind racing, as it begins to dawn on me that this case of mistaken identity may not have been a mistake at all. "You remember what killed him?"

"Shot in the chest."

I remove the casualty report with Bartlett's name and signature from my briefcase and show it to him. "Is this the man?"

He holds it with frail, trembling fingers and stares at it for what feels like an eternity. I'm starting to wonder if he hasn't just quietly expired when he rasps, "A. Calvert Morgan." Then he shrugs, tucking his head down between bony shoulders that come up to the bottoms of his ears. "Could be. I don't remember his name."

"My double," I say, gently probing, "he was never processed, was he?"

"That's right," Bartlett replies, clearly surprised by my certainty.

"Why not?"

He pushes against the armrests with his elbows, leaning back to get a better look at me. I sense he's measuring me, measuring the significance of the moment as if he didn't want to waste it. Then, decision made, he nods several times. "I guess it's now or never, isn't it?" he asks, as if he's about to reveal a long-locked secret and is tremendously relieved. "Like I said, I'm getting this body out of the bag to log it in when the out-processing NCO who's coming on duty walks by. He takes one look at the corpse and freezes, then gets this look on his face like he's just been jabbed in the butt with a cattle prod. At first I figure it's a close buddy or something like that because I sort of recall seeing the guy around. Then the NCO takes me aside and tells me to rebag him."

"That why you remember what he looked like?"

He nods emphatically. "Like it was yesterday."

"Why'd he want you to rebag him?"

"Good question."

"You didn't ask?"

Bartlett shakes his head no.

"It was an improper order. Wasn't it?"

He nods.

"And you just went ahead and did it?"

"Uh-huh."

"How come?"

"No choice."

"You mean this NCO who was calling the shots out-ranked you?"

"No. The other way round."

"Then why didn't you refuse and report it?"

"The man had leverage, he didn't need rank."

"What kind of leverage?"

"This," he replies, gesturing to his emaciated body. "This thing that's killing me. But he got his. Somebody fragged the son of a bitch."

"You?"

"Wish to hell I had." He grins wickedly at the memory. "You see *Murder on the Orient Express?*"

"Uh-huh. You saying the man had a lot of enemies?"

Bartlett nods emphatically. "Everybody hated his fuck-ing guts. CID gave up trying to figure out who killed him."

"You recall his name?"

He shakes his head no. "It was unusual, I remember that. Been a long time. I'm sorry."

"He was blackmailing you because you were gay?"

Bartlett stiffens momentarily, then his expression softens with amusement. He rolls his wheelchair a short distance to a dresser in front of the window, takes his wallet from a drawer and returns. His fingers pull a snapshot from a yellowed sleeve and offer it to me. It's a picture of a woman, three young children, and a robust man, whom I barely recognize as Bartlett. His long sideburns and clothes are right out of the seventies. They're all smiling from be-hind a crack in the emulsion.

"Your family?"

"Uh-huh. I haven't seen them in years."

"I'm sorry, I shouldn't have assumed you were homosexual."

"Hey some of my best friends are gay," he jokes, gestur-ing to the corridor with an ironic laugh that turns into a loud, hacking cough as he continues. "Try as they might

. . . they haven't . . . cornered . . . the AIDS market . . . yet." He waits until it subsides, then wipes some spittle from his chin with the sleeve of his hospital gown. His eyes lock onto mine and, with the matter-of-fact openness of someone who has spent time in chemical dependency programs, he rasps, "I'm a heroin addict."

I nod with understanding born of firsthand observation. "Got hooked in-country."

His eyes fall as he nods. "A person can take just so much carnage. Some guys handled it like it was nothing, just removed themselves from it. Most of us drank, fucked our brains out, and got into drugs."

"You weren't alone. We all did whatever it took to get through another day."

"Trouble is, I couldn't get off the shit after I came back," he explains, biting his lip to control his emotions. "My marriage went to hell, lost my kids, my home, my job, started living in the streets, ended up on the business end of a dirty needle."

An uncomfortable silence follows.

I stand and cross to the window, taking in the fresh spring air and natural beauty of the landscape that stretches to the horizon. "You spend much time out there?"

"Not lately," he replies with a glimmer of hope.

"What do you say we go for a walk." It's a statement not a question. I remove my jacket and tie, toss them on the chair, and wheel him from the room.

Moments later, we are through the set of double doors at the end of the corridor and circling down a ramp that leads to a network of paths. I push a short distance to a grove of aspen and pine that overlooks the lake. He sets the wheel lock and I settle on a boulder opposite him.

"That noncom. He threatened to blow the whistle on your habit if you didn't cooperate?"

Bartlett's face tightens into an angry mask and he nods. "You remember the penalty for possession?"

"Sure do," I reply, hearing my CO's voice drumming it into us as if it were yesterday. "Automatic court martial, huge fine, reduction in rank, a ninety-day pass to the stockade—"

"—And a better than even shot at getting a DD," Bartlett

quickly adds, using shorthand for a dishonorable discharge to complete the litany.

"Leverage."

"Yeah, especially if you were a lifer like me. I mean, I couldn't afford to get booted out. It would've cost me my pension, my VA benefits—just try getting a job with a piece of bad paper in your file. The son of a bitch had me by the balls and he knew it. He says, 'Bartlett, that body goes.' It goes. No questions asked."

"What happened to it?"

"Vanished."

That one word explains the lack of documents in the morgue file, the body-not-recovered entry on the master casualty list, and the MIA symbol on the Memorial. The body/no body mystery has finally been solved. "Did that happen often?"

"Just that once. We had strict procedures. The bodies came in by chopper, truck, sometimes plane. As in-processing NCO, I signed for them and recorded each one in a log. It sort of looked like an old-fashioned accountant's ledger with all the columns and lines—name, rank, serial number, unit, date, whatever information I had. We used ballpoint pens. No pencils, no erasers, and no computers. Each man's remains was given a processing number and put into the reefer, a big walk-in refrigerator. No set of remains left the building until it was officially identified, embalmed, and put in a transfer case to be shipped."

"But not this body."

Bartlett shakes his head no and laughs. "Hell, poor bastard never even got a processing number. See, even if the original chopper manifest said, say, ten bodies, but I only logged in nine, then later nobody would be asking, 'We got ten bodies in and only nine out, where's that other guy?' "

"You ever find out what the problem was?"

"No, but I heard some rumors. You remember them, don't you?"

"I remember they were right on the money more often than not."

"Well the word was the dead guy was into some kind of drug-smuggling thing."

I feel myself flinch. This comes out of nowhere. A hollowness is growing in my stomach. "You sure?"

"I said it was a rumor, but I distinctly recall there was some kind of investigation in the works."

"Where? At the mortuary?"

He shrugs. "The word was he was on the lam from the DEA for transporting heroin in his bird."

"He was a pilot?"

"Uh-huh."

"Air America?"

"Air cav."

"He flew dustoffs?" I ask, using military slang for medevac helicopters.

Bartlett nods, then his eyes brighten at a memory and, like a child, he starts singing, "Pepsi-Cola hits the spot, for a nickel you get a lot—"

"What's that about?"

"Oh, a lot of the pilots who hauled bodies used to hang out in this bar on Tu Do Street. Every once in a while they'd tie one on and start singing it and laughing. Turns out the guys working the drug trade called the flights Pepsi-Cola runs."

"That's weird. You know why?"

"Hey, you know how it was in-country. They had code names and acronyms for everything. I mean, my favorite noncom even came up with one for the corpse."

"The one that vanished."

"Uh-huh," he says, frowning as he tries to remember. "Whiskey, that's what it was. One night we're working on a quart of rotgut when he starts referring to the guy as Whiskey."

"Any special reason?"

"Naw, just a nickname. Good booze though," he says, wistfully. "Calvert Reserve, that's all we ever drank. Probably consumed enough of it to embalm all the bodies we processed."

"Tell me about it. I mainlined more vodka when I was in Nam than . . ." I pause as the significance dawns on me. Calvert, Calvert Reserve. Now I'm sure, beyond doubt, that the corpse Bartlett pulled from the morgue was the one with my tags and military identification but more important, I have two new pieces of information that are significant: the man was a fugitive and a medevac pilot.

I don't need to run an analysis on my computer to deduce this means he was AWOL, was looking for a new identity, and had many wounded and dead GIs to choose from. Logic dictates he flew the chopper that evacuated me to the field hospital after I was wounded, that my dog tags and military identification weren't lost en route as I thought but were stolen, that I wasn't selected at random but due to physical resemblance, and most incredibly, that the name of the man who took them and died with them, the name I've so obsessively sought, has been in my briefcase since my meeting with Collins in St. Louis.

14

THE SEARCH IS OVER.

This sobering thought hits me during takeoff, and solidi-
fies as we circle out of Denver in a steep climb that takes
us west over snow-covered peaks.

I set out to put a man's name on a memorial, a man I
assumed had served his country honorably and was mistak-
enly denied the honor he'd earned, a man who turned out
to be a fugitive drug smuggler. It's a depressing end to a
noble effort. Aside from proving the axiom about assump-
tions, I've nothing to show for it except a painfully bruised
arm, a cut over my eye, and the possibility of criminal
charges being filed against me. The way things have been
going I'll be the first person to get AIDS from verbal
intercourse.

Nancy warned me, so did Collins and Captain Sullivan,
though I doubt they had anything like this in mind. I
should've taken their advice. The questions I've been asking were best left unanswered, and the biggest one still is.
I don't have the man's name in my briefcase as I thought.
The evac block on the medic's report, the one filled out by
the chopper pilot, is scribbled and totally illegible. I've no
doubt he did it on purpose to conceal his identity. Maybe
it's for the best.

The flight seems interminably long. I'm not busily evaluat-
ing the information Bartlett gave me. I'm not even entering
it in my laptop. None of it matters now. I'm staring out
the window into the darkness, nursing a second vodka,
when the pilot informs us of thunderstorms in the Los

Angeles area. It hasn't rained in something like eight months and the news is greeted with applause.

My spirits brighten as the plane makes its final approach and touches down on the rain-swept runway. I've put Nancy through weeks of uncertainty and turmoil. I can't wait to tell her it's over, apologize, and get on with our lives. I'm really looking forward to the drive home.

I hurry down the boarding ramp into the terminal, smiling in anticipation, knowing Nancy will be standing up front on tiptoe like she always does, but, unless I somehow missed her, she's nowhere to be seen. I step aside, scanning the area, expecting she'll suddenly emerge from the crowd, but the minutes go by and she doesn't. The knots of people gradually disperse and I'm soon the only one left.

I know she isn't at the theater. She sure was pissed off this morning, maybe she changed her mind and decided to let me fend for myself. I wouldn't blame her. Of course, three drops of rain in Los Angeles turns the freeways into a bumper-car ride. Chances are she's sitting in a traffic jam cursing me out. Chances are, she took her car to be serviced and she's sitting in my car. I call the cellular phone in the Mercedes.

"Thank you for calling," the electronic voice says, "The mobile customer you are trying to reach is away from the car or beyond our service area." I hang up, call home, and get the answering machine. "Hi, hon, it's me," I say after the beep. "I'm at the airport. Guess you're on your way."

Maybe she's driving the Range Rover. Maybe our delayed arrival caused a last-minute gate change that wasn't posted on the arrivals display.

"Let's see, flight seven three one . . ." the clerk at the check-in counter says, scanning the data on his computer. "Thirty-four B. That's its usual gate." I have him page Nancy to be sure. I wait about ten more minutes, then take a taxi.

The rain eases as the driver heads up the coast. By the time we turn into Malibu Canyon it's stopped. We're snaking along the twisting two-lane roadway just a couple of miles from the house when we come to an abrupt halt. Emergency lights strobe in the darkness ahead. Vehicles are backed up in both directions. One lane appears closed.

A motorcycle cop is directing an alternating flow of traffic through the other. As we inch forward, the *whomp* of a circling helicopter reverberates off the surrounding stone. We finally come through a sharp turn and approach a fleet of vehicles—police cars, paramedic van, wrecker, fire engine—that have responded to an accident. As we drive past, I catch a glimpse of tire marks and a broken section of guardrail. It takes almost twenty minutes to get through the bottleneck.

That sure explains it. If she's lucky, Nancy's probably just getting to the airport now. Maybe she gave up, turned around, and went home.

As the cab pulls up to the house, the driver starts grumbling about having to make the return trip. I add a generous tip to the flat rate. He's still grumbling as he drives off.

"Nance?" I call out as I come through the front door. "Nance, you here?" The sound of my voice echoing off the hard, angular surfaces is the only response.

The message light on the answering machine in the kitchen is blinking: mine, the usual friends, nothing from Nancy. I call the United terminal and have her paged again, but she doesn't respond.

Wherever she is, I've no doubt she's going to be steaming when she returns. I'll never get out of the doghouse at this rate—but I can try. I call the Galloping Gourmet, a service that picks up and delivers from restaurants in the area, and order an elegant lobster dinner for two. Then I gather linen, silver, stemware, candles and set the small table in the alcove off the dining room, the one with the romantic view of the city. I light the candles, then select a bottle of Santa Margherita Pinot Grigio—Nancy's favorite white—from the walk-in wine fridge off the kitchen. The fact that she prefers it over the trendy California chardonnays is one of the wonderful little quirks that endear her to me. She's the one who does the buying, who samples and tastes and remembers. I'm pulling the cork when I hear the car coming up the driveway. I quickly pour some into a glass with which I'll greet her. I'm crossing the kitchen to the garage entrance when the front doorbell rings.

I do an about-face, and hurry down the short staircase to the entryway. Nancy probably assumes we're going out for dinner and didn't garage the car. I open the door, wondering why she rang the bell, and am momentarily blinded by alternating bursts of colored light that come from the roof of a police car parked behind the two uniformed officers in the doorway.

"Mr. Morgan?"

"Yes, that's right."

"I'm Sergeant Downing, this is Officer Flores. We're with the L.A. County Sheriff's Department. Mind if we come in?"

"Of course not," I reply curiously.

"Are you married to a Nancy Elizabeth Morgan?"

"Yes, I am. Why? What's going on? She okay?"

The officer ignores my questions and takes something from his pocket. "Is this your wife?"

He hands me a California driver's license with Nancy's picture, signature, and our home address.

"Yes, it is," I reply, my anxiety level soaring. "Something happen to her?"

He nods solemnly. "I apologize for the suspense, Mr. Morgan. We like to make absolutely certain in these matters. I'm afraid we have some bad news. Your wife was killed in an accident this evening."

I feel the color drain from my face, then a surge of adrenaline explodes in my gut and I feel as if I'm going to vomit. I stare at them blankly, wondering: Did I hear correctly? Is this really happening? Did he actually say killed? Nancy is dead? Now I know what's meant by an out-of-body experience. I feel like I've been suddenly removed from reality, like I'm watching this taking place on a distant stage.

"It doesn't look like any other vehicles were involved," the officer continues. "She apparently lost control on one of those switchbacks and went through the guardrail. These roads get real slippery when they're wet."

"Nancy, Nancy, oh God," I hear myself saying, the words blending into an anguished wail as panic takes hold of me. I must do something. I don't know what. I bolt for the door. The officers are faster and stronger and easily restrain me. My legs feel as if they're cast of lead. "You have to take me there," I protest feebly, as they lead me to a nearby chair. "Please. I want to be with her."

"We've already retrieved her body," the other one explains. "They're still working on the car."

I nod numbly, disoriented.

"Is there someone you might want to have come by? I mean, a relative or friend we can call for you? Mr. Morgan?"

I shrug, and shake my head no.

He writes something on the back of a business card. "This is the location of the County Morgue. We'll need someone to make an identification. Any time tomorrow'll be fine. We're very sorry."

I close the door after them and lean my forehead against it as their car departs, then turn and sweep my eyes over the various levels of the house as if seeing them for the first time. Each piece of furniture, each painting and piece of sculpture appears isolated, as if spatially disconnected from everything else. I'm incapable of organized thought. The scenario races through my mind in a frenzy: The doorbell rings. I answer it. Two policemen tell me my wife is dead. Dead? She is? How do I know? Do I just accept it? My entire life changes just like that? I'm suddenly bombarded with terrifying images of what's to come: the morgue, the funeral, calling our parents, calling our daughters. How do I tell them their mother is dead?

I don't recall climbing the stairs, but now I'm slumped in the lounger outside the dining room holding an empty wine glass and staring at the piano. Nancy is sitting there playing for me. My eyes drift to the little table. Nancy is sitting there too, smiling, sipping wine, her face bathed in candlelight that compliments her beauty and goodness. Nothing could convince me she isn't coming home. I become hypnotized by the shadows dancing across the walls. I don't know how much time passes before I think I hear a car coming up the drive. The crunch of tires on gravel gets louder. It is a car! My heart leaps. I run to the entry and throw open the door.

A young man comes toward me from a delivery van, carrying two picnic baskets. "Sorry to keep you waiting, sir," he says, a little startled. "Accident down there's got everything tied up. Where you want these?"

I motion to the floor, then pull some cash from my pocket and stuff it in his hand.

"Gee thanks. Have a nice evening."

The smell of lobster is nauseating. I make my way to the kitchen, fill a tumbler with vodka and drink it, eyeing the phone warily. Finally, I force myself to make the painful calls, four traumatic, tear-filled conversations. I'm an emotional wreck. There are friends I could ask to come over but I can't handle another one of those conversations. Not now.

The sun is coming up. I haven't slept. I haven't left the house. I haven't changed my clothes.

Our daughters arrive.

Janie—moody, competitive, brunette, computer nerd and math whiz, her father's daughter, who flew in from school in Arizona.

Laura—gregarious, giving, sandy-haired; musically and artistically gifted, so much like her mother. She's driven half the night from Berkeley.

They're devastated.

We do what we can for each other, but no words will heal their wounds or mine. It's midmorning before I achieve some degree of emotional control and mental discipline, and make a list of things that have to be done.

County Morgue is at the top.

We head into the garage. It's empty. I'd forgotten. The Mercedes is wrecked. Nancy's Range Rover is being serviced. We take Laura's Jetta. I drive. The girls find a map in the glove box and navigate. We take the freeway downtown to the County-USC Medical Center, a huge complex on State Street just off the Golden State Freeway, and follow the signs to the morgue entrance at the rear of the main building.

I insist the girls stay behind in the reception area as I follow the attendant into a small, unadorned room. It smells like chemicals. The finishes are hard and reflective—chrome, stainless, granite, glass—permanent. I know what goes on here. What they do to determine how someone died. How they clinically dismantle deceased humans and analyze the parts. I'd never let them touch Nancy, but an autopsy isn't a matter of consent. Oh, God, how I wish it was.

A gurney is centered beneath a harsh light.

The attendant lifts one corner of the sheet.

I close my eyes, hoping that they've made a mistake, hoping that when I open them I'll see someone other than Nancy. God knows I've had my share of emotional torture. I've seen my best friend blown to pieces, I've killed men and women with my bare hands, I've held wounded teenagers in my arms and promised I wouldn't let them die though I knew they would. But this—this is the hardest thing I've ever had to do.

"Mr. Morgan?" the attendant prompts.

My eyes snap open. I stare uncomprehendingly at a woman's ashen face, swollen and bruised, but not beyond recognition. We've been together since we were sixteen; almost thirty years. I've never felt so grief-stricken or incomplete. I gently touch her cheek. It's rigid and cold. I vow this will not be the way I remember her.

"Is this your wife?"

I don't want to nod, but I do.

15

SEVERAL DAYS HAVE PASSED.

A Los Angeles County coroner determines by simple observation that Nancy died of injuries sustained in the accident, which means there's no need for an autopsy. I'm relieved, but still unable to accept her death. She was driving a new Mercedes, equipped with the most advanced safety systems: an air bag, anti-lock brakes, energy-absorbing body, deforming steering column, seat belts. "How?" I protest. "How could she be dead?"

The coroner gently reminds me that these features don't really come into play until impact. In Nancy's case, spinning out of control on the wet road snapped her head sideways into the window and door post with such force that fatal injuries resulted prior to any impact. Results of tests for alcohol and drugs will be forthcoming. Her body is released to a local mortuary, which arranges to have it shipped to Boston.

The funeral is tomorrow.

It's late afternoon when the girls and I arrive at Logan International. I stare at the travelers hurrying about the terminal, wondering how many are on a similar journey. I'm snapped out of it by Nancy's brother, who still lives in the South Bay area where we all grew up. It's a terribly emotional moment, and I'm glad neither her parents nor mine accompanied him. It would have been too much to handle in a crowded boarding lounge.

We take the Callahan Tunnel into Route 93 south, skirting the downtown area. Forty minutes later we arrive at my parents' house, a red brick rowhouse with a concrete stoop on Chadwick Street just across from Orchard Place.

Relatives from both families are waiting for us. It's worse than I imagined. They've aged twenty years since we were here for Thanksgiving not five months ago. I'm sure they're saying the same of me. There may be strength in numbers but these kinds of reunions go a long way to disproving it. Their well-intentioned reminiscing is anything but theraputic, and I finally put an end to it by insisting we all go out for dinner.

The girls and I return with my parents. We watch the news, a late movie, and finally try to get some sleep. Hours later, I'm still staring at the ceiling in the guest room, my old room, the one where Nancy and I listened to records, necked, did homework. I can't remember the last time I was here without her. I'm frightened and guilt-ridden. I keep thinking of that night, imagining her suddenly losing control of the car, fighting the darkness and rain, fighting to keep on the road, to stay alive, and then the awful moment when she knew she wouldn't.

I head downstairs, roaming the house. Pictures of Nancy and me and the girls are everywhere. There's no escape. I wander into the family room hoping to find an old movie on television. The next thing I know, I'm setting up my laptop on Dad's desk, a scarred wooden relic where he spent evenings figuring out how to make ends meet and underbilling clients for auto repairs. I run a line from the modem port to a phone jack in the wall, and then—doing what I always do when I want to shut everything out—I plunge headlong into a maze of statistics, into what I imagine a psychiatrist would label obsessive/compulsive denial.

I access the mainframe at my office back in Los Angeles. It takes several hours to retrieve data on all the accidents on Malibu Canyon Road for the last ten years, but once I have them it takes no more than a few milliseconds to calculate that the odds for the average driver dying in an accident on that road are 1 in 10 million.

Next, I input all of Nancy's data. Though I don't have the results of the toxicology tests, I've never seen her drunk and I know she wasn't, nor was she young and reckless, or driving a poorly maintained or rundown vehicle.

The Mercedes was brand-new. And she was driving a road she knew well, one she'd driven at least twice a day, probably a thousand times a year for five years.

When all the information is assembled, I run a comparative analysis program, working in a frenzy to evaluate the data by time, date, and weather, by the driver's age, sex, eye color, ethnic group, income level, and years of driving experience, by vehicle, number of passengers, road surface, and specific location on the road, and by the number of vehicles that traveled the road during that period.

As the glow of another empty sunrise warms the room, I finally determine that the probability of Nancy dying in such an accident is incredibly low: not 1 in 10 million, but 1 in 250 million. It should never have happened, but it did. She's gone, and, as I stare bleary-eyed at the computer screen and sink into the chair with exhaustion, I slowly realize that, no matter how many calculations, simulations, or permutations I run, nothing is going to bring Nancy back. Despite all my computing power, experience, and access to the most current data, hers was the one death I couldn't predict. The thought does little to ease the pain.

I'm just dozing off when I hear sounds in the house. My parents in the kitchen. The girls coming down the staircase in their college sweats. It's obvious they haven't slept either.

"Better start getting ready, Dad," Janie whispers as they cross to the desk and embrace me.

We wander outside for a few minutes. It's a beautiful spring morning. The air is still cool and refreshing. It smells different here. I've always attributed it to the change of seasons, the violent storms that cleanse and rejuvenate it. Now every familiar scent is laden with painful nostalgia.

The stained glass windows at St. Patrick's R.C. Church on Lagrange Avenue seem to sparkle with unusual brilliance. My mind drifts to my days as an altar boy. I'm lost in the past, numbly going through the motions of the funeral service. We're at the cemetery when I come out of it, when I'm shattered by the terrifying realization that this woman who got me through Vietnam, who put me back in touch with life, who shared my innermost secrets and fears, is gone forever. I will never see her again, never hear her voice, never hold her body against mine. Never.

When it's over, the girls and I are torn between fleeing and spending some time nestled in the family bosom. In their infinite wisdom, both Nancy's parents and mine selflessly urge us to leave, insisting that she would want us to get busy and back to our lives.

The three of us fly to Los Angeles.

Janie catches a connecting flight to Arizona.

Laura returns home with me to pick up her car. We enter the house timidly, knowing we are about to be ambushed by memories. She gravitates toward the piano, stands there trembling, then closes the lid over the keyboard. I know one day I will have to face Nancy's things, but I can't bring myself to deal with them now. I lose myself in the mail. A letter from the Army Casualty Office catches my eye.

It informs me that the Friends of the Vietnam Veterans Memorial forwarded my query to their offices. They turned it over to the CIL for processing. A search by a casualty data analyst has determined there are no personnel in their files who match the loss scenario I provided.

I feel a sardonic smile tugging at the corners of my mouth as I cross to the answering machine. Bad news doesn't always travel fast. Several of the messages are for Nancy. More than one from the local Jaguar dealer where we bought the Range Rover. It's been serviced and is ready to be picked up.

Early the next morning, Laura drops me there, then heads north to Berkeley. It's hard watching her drive off. Every good-bye has unsettling overtones now.

A half hour later, I'm heading home in the Range Rover. This is a big mistake. I'm surrounded by Nancy's things: sunglasses, notepad, felt tip pens, change for parking meters—everything neatly arranged in a console organizer. Her school parking pass is clipped to the visor next to the remote keypad for the alarm system in the house. There is also a coffee cup with a lipstick imprint, and most moving of all, the lingering scent of her perfume. I could lower the windows, but I don't. My mind drifts to that awful moment when I opened the door to greet her and found police officers instead. I try not to relive it, but I keep coming back to something they mentioned, something that when coupled with recent incidents and the analysis I ran in Boston, keeps gnawing at me.

I change direction, drive to the sheriff's substation in the Malibu Civic Center, and identify myself to the young desk officer. Short, sun-bleached hair suggests she spends her off-duty time surfing.

Her eyes flicker sadly with recognition. "Sorry about your wife, Mr. Morgan."

"Thanks. I was just wondering, the officers said they didn't think another car was involved in the accident. Any way I can find out for sure?"

"Of course. Let me pull the report." She swivels in her chair to a bank of file cabinets and retrieves a folder. "Let's see . . ." She pauses, thumbing through the contents. "No, there was nothing to indicate the presence of another vehicle."

"What would indicate it?"

"Well, for example, sometimes we'll find two sets of skid marks, but there weren't any."

"You mean none at all?"

"That's right. There's a notation here about heavy rain. She probably hydroplaned."

"But that doesn't rule out another car, does it?"

"Well," she muses, "not really, no."

"Anything else that might indicate it?"

"Yes, a P-T would. I'm sorry, that stands for paint transfer. In collisions, paint from one vehicle often ends up on the other."

"But there wasn't any."

She glances at the accident report again. "Doesn't say. The officers on the scene didn't request a follow-up."

"What do you mean?"

"If a hit-and-run or foul play is suspected, it's turned over to a team of detectives who conduct an investigation."

"But not in this case."

"No. The circumstances didn't warrant it. See, your car's been cleared for release." She turns the folder in my direction and shows me where the word RELEASE has been stamped on the report.

"I'd like to see the car."

"You sure?" she asks, her eyes softening with compassion. "I mean, it's your right. I'm just trying to spare you some pain."

"Thanks, I'm beyond it."

She nods solemnly. "Maybe I can have a follow-up team meet you there." She makes a quick call, then instructs me to be at Coastline Towing, the independent contractor for the area, at 3:30 this afternoon.

I have several hours to kill. I go home, force myself to eat some lunch, sort through the mail, and call the office, then, feeling caged-in and anxious, I drive to the auto wrecking yard, arriving about twenty minutes early. As I get out of the Range Rover, I'm greeted by the sound of crunching sheet metal and shattering glass. The deafening racket comes from one of those massive compactors. In a matter of seconds, the frightening piece of machinery turns an old Detroit gas-guzzler into a steel pancake.

"What do you need, mister?" the operator, a young Hispanic with a brightly colored headband, shouts from his perch as I approach.

"I want to see my car," I shout back.

He responds with a thumbs-up, takes a moment to finish the job, then climbs down and leads the way between junked vehicles and piles of salvaged parts to a separate, fenced-in area where a sign proclaims *Official Police Garage*.

"The black Mercedes," I say, spotting it through the heavy chain link. The damage isn't as extensive as I imagined. The front end is totaled, windshield and driver's window smashed, but from the front doors back, it's pretty much intact.

"Landed that one myself," he says unlocking the gate. "Got real lucky too. I mean, when I heard it was the canyon, I figured I was spinning my wheels. I mean, they usually end up in the bottom, you know? Takes a chopper to get 'em out."

I grunt, ignoring him.

"But not this baby," he charges on, animatedly. "Screech! Bam! Right through the guardrail, a little swan dive, no more than twenty, thirty feet, and smack into these boulders head-on. Let me tell you. Made my life a hell of a lot easier. I just dropped my hook, and reeled her in. Like boating a tuna. You ever go for tuna?"

I continue to ignore him and am slowly circling the car, wondering how anyone could be so insensitive and cruel, when I realize he probably didn't hear me over the noise of the compactor and thinks I'm a claims adjuster. As I come around to the driver's side, my eyes dart to several long streaks on the black finish. Are they scratches or paint? My pulse rate soars as I move in for a closer look. They're definitely paint. But the color puts a quick end to my euphoria. "Looks sort of like an off-white, huh?"

"Yeah. White's for wimps, man. You know what I mean? Like my cousin's got this screaming yellow Trans Am. Hottest set of wheels."

"I was really pulling for blue," I mutter forlornly. My eyes drift up to something spattered on the air bag, which hangs limply over the steering wheel. It takes a moment to register. It's dried blood. Nancy's blood. The officer at the substation was right. I'm starting to feel queasy and seriously considering getting out of there when a gray Plymouth sedan, unmarked except for the antenna on the trunk lid, pulls into the yard.

Two plainclothes officers, who identify themselves as Sergeant Daniels and Detective Molina, begin examining the Mercedes.

A few minutes later, Daniels, the one with the bad hairpiece, turns toward me and nods. "That's a paint transfer, no question about it."

"And that dull black stuff's what we call tire chatter," Molina chimes in, gesturing to a pattern of semicircular marks on the door.

"We're definitely talking hit-and-run," Daniels concludes. "It's a felony when a fatality's involved."

I nod despondently, still unnerved by the bloody air bag.

Daniels reaches into his pocket and produces one of those metal scrapers that uses a retractable razor blade to remove paint from glass. He turns back to the car, lays the blade flat against the Mercedes' slick finish, and begins slowly working the honed edge beneath a section of transferred paint.

"What are you doing?"

"Taking a sample for the lab. They run what we call a spectroscopic analysis. Sometimes they come up with nothing, sometimes they nail the other vehicle right down to make, model, year, dealer—"

"Well, at least we know the color," I say glumly as a large chip of white paint comes loose and drops into his palm.

"No, that's primer," he says matter-of-factly. Then he turns it over and shows me the other side, the side that had stuck to the Mercedes. "That's the color."

My eyes widen at the sight of it.

It's blue. Metallic blue. *The* blue.

Now I know.

I have no proof, but I know I haven't been irrational or paranoid. They were trying to kill me in Vegas. Nancy didn't have an accident. Things *do* add up. Statistics don't lie.

"With a little luck," Daniels continues, slipping the paint sample into a plastic bag, "we might be able to identify the other driver. In the meantime, we'll file a report with the coroner's office. I'm sure the official cause of your wife's death'll be changed to vehicular manslaughter."

"She was murdered," I say angrily.

"We understand how you feel, Mr. Morgan, but it's a good idea to keep an open mind in these matters," Molina advises. "Just because the other driver left the scene isn't proof he or she was at fault. It's possible, and I emphasize possible, that your wife was responsible. She may have been under the influence, or passing another vehicle illegally, or—"

"No. No, you don't understand," I interrupt sharply. "I meant she was killed on purpose."

The look that flicks between them leaves no doubt I've finally made my point.

"You mean homicide?" Daniels asks.

"I mean premeditated murder."

That really throws them. They take a moment to regroup, unsure what to make of me.

"Mr. Morgan," Molina begins somewhat skeptically, "are you saying you have reason to believe someone wanted to hurt your wife?"

"No. *Me*. They thought it was me."

Another look darts between them.

"Want to run that by us again?"

"Sure. They made a mistake. My wife's car was in the shop. She was driving mine. The windows are tinted. It was night. It was raining. She has short hair. They were watching the house, saw the Mercedes leave, assumed I was behind the wheel. Bastards!" I pause, coping with growing rage as the pieces fall into place. "They knew the rain would make it look like an accident. Did the same thing in Vegas a couple of weeks ago."

"Vegas?" Daniels wonders, mystified.

"Yes, this wasn't the first time they tried."

"Who tried?"

"I don't know, but I can tell you they wanted it to look like an accident. In Vegas it was supposed to look like I was partying and OD'd."

"You mean hookers, nose candy?"

"Exactly. I wasn't sure until now. You can check with the Las Vegas Police. A Sergeant . . ." I pause and fish the business card from my wallet ". . . Figueroa."

They glance at it, then after a short whispered exchange, return to the Mercedes and more carefully examine the circular pattern left on the door by the other vehicle's tire.

"I'd say the wheel was spinning that way," Daniels observes in a tone that suggests this detail is significant.

"Yes, both cars were definitely moving in the same direction," Molina concludes. "He might have something."

"Why?" I ask, making no effort to conceal my impatience. "Why is that important?"

Daniels stands, folds his arms, and leans against the car. "Well, on a winding, two-lane road, cars going in the same direction are much less prone to accidents than those coming toward each other."

"Which supports my contention."

"Partially. It's still possible the other driver was trying to pass your wife unsafely and cut her off to avoid an oncoming vehicle."

"That'd make a lot more sense if it happened during the day. At night, no headlights coming, you know it's safe to pass."

"Maybe, but it's still not conclusive."

"I'm telling you her car was forced off the road on purpose."

"It's possible."

"It happened. Believe me."

"Well, we've just covered an awful lot of ground, Mr. Morgan. If you don't mind, I'd like to suggest we go back to the office where you'll be more comfortable and go through it a step at a time."

Fifteen or twenty minutes later, we're sipping coffee from Styrofoam cups in an interview room at the sheriff's substation. Windowless, bright fluorescent lighting, gray metal table and chairs—it looks like the rooms where they question suspects on television cop shows.

"For openers," Daniels says, pacing the perimeter of the small space as he talks, "why do you think someone wants to kill you?"

"I'm not really sure," I reply, concerned the answer will sound totally preposterous. "I mean, it might have to do with something that happened twenty-four years ago in Vietnam."

They both nod, digesting the reply.

"Does that mean you were involved in something there?" Daniels finally wonders. "Something that might shed some light on a motive or suspect?"

"No. Whatever it was, I stumbled onto it recently. I'd say it started about a couple of months ago in Washington, D.C."

Molina sits at the table with a small spiral-bound pad and lists the events as I enumerate them:

> Finds name on memorial.
> Driven to identify the soldier.
> Time/place data from the FVVM.
> NPCR St. Louis. Jack Collins.
> National League of Families. D.C.
> Kate Ackerman. MIA wife. Laos.
> Data to Col. Webster. CIL. Fort Shafter. Hawaii.
> Blue sedan. Late model Buick/Olds.
> Driver. Sunglasses, thirty-something, dark hair.

Meeting. L.A. Captain Sullivan. CIL.
Casualty report from Army morgue.
Las Vegas. Foster. Assaulted.
Denver. Bartlett. Drug connection.
Accident. Wife killed.

A long silence follows. They both seem to be in a state of suspended animation. I'm not sure if they're overwhelmed or skeptical.

"Well, Mr. Morgan," Molina finally says philosophically, "I guess you're living proof that no good deed goes unpunished."

"I'd rather I wasn't."

"Let's go back over a few things," Daniels says. "What makes you so sure it was the same car?"

"The color. It was an exact match to that paint sample you took."

"But you didn't get a look at the license."

"No."

"One other thing I'm not clear on. The guy in Denver said this pilot was busted by the DEA?"

"No, the pilot was wanted. He was on the run."

"You don't have his name?"

"No."

They exchange frowns.

"What do you think's going on here, Mr. Morgan?" Daniels prods.

"I'm not sure. Off the top of my head, the only thing I can think of is I rubbed up against someone in the drug trade."

"Could be," Daniels says, waggling his hand.

"Everything has something to do with drugs these days," Molina chimes in wearily. He makes a few more notes, then steps aside to confer with his partner.

"One other thing, Mr. Morgan," Daniels says when they've finished. "You said you thought they wanted to make it look like an accident."

"Yes. I figure they don't want the police to be wondering why somebody would want to kill me."

"Well, they blew it, didn't they?"

"I'd say so."

"If you're right about all this, it might be a good idea to keep a low profile while we do our investigation."

"You mean, because it'd be to our advantage if they think I'm dead?"

"No, that's TV," Daniels replies, his upper lip curling with disdain. "The media's going to cover this. Not page one, most likely a little blurb buried in the Metro section. An obit at the least. Take my word for it, Mr. Morgan. We have no choice but to assume they'll know."

"Yes, I guess you're right."

He forces a smile and nods. "Point is, whoever wants you dead has just lost their incentive to make it look like an accident."

The low-key delivery doesn't blunt the chilling message: They might just as well walk up to me on the street, put a gun to my head, and blow me away in cold blood, now.

16

I'VE UNINTENTIONALLY TOUCHED A NERVE, A NERVE SO sensitive that someone was willing to commit murder to keep it from being further exposed. I've never been very susceptible to guilt, but I'm making up for it. I'm obsessed with the idea that if I'd listened to Nancy, she'd still be alive. I thought coping with her death had pushed my emotions to the limit, but it's tearing me to pieces to know that she died in my place—that she was murdered! And for what? An obscure twenty-year-old drug scam? It's so meaningless and so totally disproportionate to her worth. I can't help thinking it's more than that. It just has to be. God knows, if I'm honest with myself, I want it to be.

These are familiar feelings—deeply rooted and disturbing ones. I'd spent seven months in Vietnam watching decent men turn into violent animals and watching them die, and years trying to figure out why. I still don't have the answers. In retrospect, the day I turned the corner and began putting my life back together was the day I stopped searching for them. Now, I'm searching again. I'm not sure where to begin, but this time it's for Nancy, and I know I won't stop until I find it.

I'm crossing the parking lot outside the sheriff's substation deep in thought when a car passes within inches of me and serves as a chilling reminder that I was the target, and still am. I get into the Range Rover, lock the doors, and head for home, rolling slowly up to traffic lights, leaving room to maneuver around other vehicles, making every effort not to stop. My eyes are constantly darting from the road to the mirror and back.

As I turn into our street, I notice a car behind me. It looks familiar—probably one of the neighbors—but I'm not taking any chances. I continue past the house, going several blocks out of my way until the car angles into another street, then I circle back and turn into our driveway. I slow down to get a look at the keypad for the alarm system next to the front door. The red and amber status lights are on steady, not flashing, which would indicate it had been set off or tampered with. I use the remote on the Rover's visor to deactivate the alarm and open the garage; then, continuing directly inside, I close the door and activate the alarm as the car stops rolling.

The house is cool, still, and quiet. I'm entering the kitchen from the garage when I catch something moving out of the corner of my eye. It's a shadow, a man's shadow creeping across one of the angled walls on the level above me. I freeze in terror, my heart in my mouth, before I realize it's my shadow. Every mirror and reflective surface becomes a pulse-pounding encounter. I'm back on patrol, moving through my own home as if it were a hut in a hostile village. All my senses are heightened and operating at combat level as I settle into a tense crouch, going from one wall of windows to the next, shutting the vertical louvers, cursing the acres of glass that I love so much.

I feel trapped.

The house is too big, too open, too isolated, and due to the rocky terrain and walls that surround it, a vehicle blocking the driveway would make it impossible for me to escape, to drive out to either road, even with the Range Rover. It's a big, powerful vehicle and makes me feel secure, but it's very conspicuous and easy to follow in traffic; furthermore, it doesn't have a phone, which means I can't call for help if pursued or attacked.

I'm not sure what I'm going to do. I drift into the den and unthinkingly turn on the television, it's background noise, a presence. I'm scanning for something innocuous like the sports channel when I hit CNN. I'm captured by a report on the repatriation of the remains of MIAs from Laos. It marks the end of a twenty-year stalemate between our governments over the issue. I remember Kate Ackerman mentioning it.

I call the real estate office. I'm not sure why, maybe I'm hoping some of her gutsy courage'll rub off on me.

"I'm sorry, she's not here," a woman answers. "Is there anything I can help you with?"

"No, I'm just a friend. Will you tell her Cal Morgan called?"

"Sure. It may be a while before she gets back to you. She's taken some time off."

"Well, whenever," I say, wondering if it has to do with the repatriations. I hang up thoughtfully. I may not have reached Kate Ackerman, but the distraction has paid off. I know exactly what I'm going to do, now. Somehow, answers always seem to surface when I'm not consciously trying to find them.

I cross to my desk and open the locked file drawer. Dammit. The box I'm looking for isn't in there. I rummage through all the other drawers, then search the storage wall in the garage with the same result. I'm racking my brain trying to remember where I put it and vaguely recall it might be at the office. I call my secretary, which I was about to do anyway.

"Grace, Mr. Morgan. Hanging in there. Thanks. Just listen carefully, okay? Go into my office, open the safe, and come back on the line."

She puts me on hold. I'm treated to several minutes of rap music and make a mental note to change the station when I get there. "Okay, what do you need?" she finally asks.

"Is there a manila envelope on the bottom shelf?"

I hear the rustling of documents, the crackle of paper. "Yes, it's unmarked, kind of heavy, feels like some boxes inside."

"Great. That's the one. Make sure it's sealed, then give it to a driver and have him bring it to my home. Now write this down. I'll meet the car at the bottom of the driveway at exactly four-fifteen. That's more than enough time to get here. I don't want him to arrive early and wait, and I don't want him to come up the drive to the front door. I want him to stop down by the mailbox, keep the engine running, and open the trunk. And I want the envelope waiting on the backseat when I get in the car."

I change into jeans and a pullover, then fetch a couple of suitcases from the garage. I pack the larger one with business clothes, the other with casual, along with several bottles of wine and a quart of vodka.

At exactly 4:13 P.M., I walk briskly down the long drive, carrying the suitcases and my attaché. I'm about twenty feet from the road when I hear a vehicle approaching. A black Lincoln Town Car comes into view and stops. The trunk lid yawns open. I toss in the suitcases and close it; then hurry around to the rear door and get in, my eyes darting to the envelope that's perfectly centered on the seat.

"Let's move. We're going to the office. Don't take the usual route, and the less we stop the better."

The driver reacts to my cadence and urgent tone and takes off like a drag-racing teenager.

I open the envelope and remove the two boxes. One contains bullets, the other a .25-caliber Beretta pistol—semi-automatic, nine-shot clip, lightweight, and compact, fitting neatly in palm, pocket, or purse.

I bought it for Nancy about eight years ago. She was working at Manual Arts High School in South Central L.A. at the time. The pink art-deco building is located in a crime-ridden, drug-infested ghetto where each day dedicated teachers put their lives on the line just by showing up for class. As it turned out, permits to carry handguns in Los Angeles are issued only by the Chief of Police, and rarely so. Nancy wanted nothing to do with a gun, let alone an illegal one, and refused to carry it until a colleague was abducted, beaten, and raped by two students who were waiting in the backseat of her car. About three years later, Nancy unexpectedly came by the office, made a wisecrack about turning in her badge and gun, and announced she'd been transferred to nearby Palisades High. She was relieved to get out of the ghetto, but she never got over the feeling that she abandoned those kids. The Beretta's been in my office safe ever since.

As the Lincoln negotiates the twisting road, I remove the pistol from the box and extract the clip from the handgrip. It's empty, as I thought, as is the chamber. A release lever, located just above the trigger, allows the barrel of this elegantly designed weapon to hinge forward for cleaning and oiling, which just takes minutes.

When finished I load only eight rounds into the clip, putting the ninth in the chamber. This means I won't have to jack in a round before cocking the hammer and firing the first shot, after which the weapon will fire with each pull of the trigger. This is the first time in twenty-four years I've held a weapon with the intention of using it. I engage the safety and slip the pistol into the pocket of my jeans.

We're still ten minutes from the office when I call a private security service on the cellular phone and arrange to have an armed guard stationed twenty-four hours a day in the reception area.

Am I paranoid? Hell, no. I've been here before. This is for real. People out there are trying to kill me. I spend an uneventful, if uneasy, first night at the office. It has several entrances to fire stairs and freight elevators, and I don't feel as trapped or isolated here. For the rest of the week, I make good use of the sofa bed and shower that I had installed for all-nighters. I eat, sleep, and work, keeping the pistol within reach. I call out for most of my meals, venture out for a few, but never to the same restaurant. My secretary says I'm turning into Yasser Arafat. So far I've had his luck.

For weeks now, one of the senior associates has been running the business. I'd been grooming him to take on more of the work load so I'd have more free time. I hadn't planned on spending it as a widower hunted by an anonymous assassin. We're in my office going over the status of several projects when my secretary informs me that Sergeant Daniels and Detective Molina are in the reception area.

The uniformed guard shows them in.

Daniels takes stock of him and seems to approve but doesn't say anything. I'm probably wrong, but it looks like they're both wearing exactly the same clothes they had on last week, right down to the ties and Daniels' hairpiece.

"Sorry for the intrusion, Mr. Morgan," Molina says as my colleague gathers his paperwork and follows after the guard. "A few things we want to go over with you. It shouldn't take long."

"I'm going to be real disappointed if it takes any longer than for you to say, 'We caught this guy.' "

"Sorry. No such luck," Daniels says.

I shrug resignedly. "Get you anything? Coffee, a soft drink?"

They both shake their heads no.

Molina sits and slips his notepad from a pocket.

Daniels glances around like a tourist and crosses to the windows. "We checked wrecking yards and body shops for the car you described, came up empty," he explains on the move. "In the meantime, the lab was analyzing the paint. They came up with an '89 Buick Regal or Park Avenue. So we put that on the wire. Yesterday we got a call from the highway patrol out in Barstow. They found a metallic-blue Park Avenue abandoned in the desert. The damage on the passenger side is consistent with the accident."

"You know who owns it?"

"Hertz. The car was last rented at San Francisco International Airport three weeks ago."

"By who?"

"Man's name is Thomas Sullivan," Molina replies.

I'm stunned. A gasp sticks in my throat.

"I recall you mentioning a Captain Sullivan came to see you," Molina continues, calmly flipping the pages of his notebook, either unaware of, or unmoved by, the impact of the bomb he's just dropped.

I can feel my gut tightening in an effort to contain the rage that's building to an explosive level. Fucking bastard.

"Here it is," Molina announces, finding the page he wants. "You said, he's with the Central Identification Lab in Hawaii. I don't have a first name down here. Was it Thomas?"

"I don't know," I reply through clenched teeth. "He was *Captain* to me."

"Well the guy who rented this car was *Thomas*," Daniels says crossing behind me. "As Detective Molina said, there was no military rank given."

"You know if he was Asian?"

"Asian?" Molina replies incredulously, turning the pages of the notepad again. "We called the rental agent. He said he handles dozens of customers a day. To the best of his recollection, the customer might've been in his late thirties or early forties, was wearing sunglasses and casual civilian clothes."

"I gave you the driver's description. It sounds just like him to me."

"It sounds like a lot of men in California," Daniels says with an apologetic shrug.

"The Captain included," I add sharply.

"The point is, Mr. Morgan, that contrary to popular belief, eye-witness descriptions are generally the least reliable form of identification."

I scoop up the phone and buzz my secretary. "Grace, check your notes. See if you have Captain Sullivan's first name. You're sure? Thanks." I hang up and let out a long breath. "No. She doesn't. Believe me, it's him. He killed my wife."

"Maybe, maybe not," Daniels counters. "In case you're wondering why we're not jumping all over this, Thomas Sullivan's got an alibi."

"You've questioned him?"

"No. But according to Hertz, he reported the car stolen the day before the accident. He said he parked it in a hotel garage downtown, didn't use it for several days. Went to get it and it was gone."

"Bullshit. He was just covering his ass."

"Very possible," Molina concedes. "He could also have been telling the truth. The Captain was from Hawaii, right?"

I nod impatiently, smoldering.

"The guy who rented the car had a California DL."

"California?"

"Yes, a San Francisco address."

"Well? I told you the Captain said he does a lot of business there."

"We ran it through the DMV. It checked out. For what it's worth, he has no criminal record either."

"Come on," I plead, my voice rising a couple of octaves in indignation. "What are you saying? That someone stole the car, took it for a joy ride, and by sheer coincidence, accidentally killed my wife?"

"We've seen stranger ones. The bottom line is we're not

sure the guy who rented the car was driving it at the time of the accident, or that he's the Sullivan who came to see you."

I hear myself groan in disgust.

"And either way," Molina continues, "renting the car doesn't make him guilty of anything."

"It makes him a suspect, doesn't it?"

"Obviously," Daniels replies. He settles on the corner of my desk and begins toying with the Rolodex. "We're not saying it isn't him. We're just saying that we have to go on the assumption that anything's possible. Before we can walk through a door, so to speak, we have to know exactly where it is—San Francisco? Hawaii?—and who's on the other side."

"I know. Take my word for it."

"You have the number of this place in Hawaii?"

"The CIL?"

"Whatever you call it. The place at Fort Shafter."

"It's not in there, Sergeant. Those are clients."

"Where?"

"You're going to call Captain Sullivan?"

He shakes no. "I'm calling the CIL."

"Couldn't that tip him off?"

"Please, Mr. Morgan, we do this for a living."

I scowl, then pull up the number on my laptop, dial, and hand the phone to Daniels.

"Captain Sullivan, please?" Daniels asks as if he's called him a hundred times before.

My eyes widen in protest until I notice his finger is poised on the reset button to cut off the call if he gets an affirmative reply.

He removes it. "You're absolutely certain? Uh-huh. I see. May I have your name? Thanks. Sorry to waste your time." He hangs up and challenges me with a look. "They never heard of him."

"What?" A sinking feeling comes over me. I'd been completely taken in by a charade and I'm feeling all the more vulnerable.

"That's right. Thomas or otherwise."

"Who'd you talk to?"

"A Mrs. Oldham. She said she was the Colonel's secretary."

"Colonel Webster?"

Daniels nods.

"Yes, he's the commanding officer there. You notice if she had an accent?"

"No, no accent. Why?"

"I had a funny feeling about Sullivan after he left my office and checked him out. The woman who answered the phone verified he worked for the CIL."

"She had an accent?"

"Yes. She was Filipino."

"What makes you so sure?"

"I spent some time in Manila during the war."

"Nam?"

I nod.

"You get her name?"

"I wish."

"You're sure you called this number?"

"Positive."

"Something's fucked," Molina groans.

"Only one thing that makes any sense to me," I say, as the pieces fall into place. "Whatever game Sullivan's playing, he has this woman on the inside covering him."

Daniels and Molina nod in agreement.

"Not to change the subject, but there's something else I want to ask you guys about."

"Your show," Daniels grunts.

"I have two daughters. They're college students. They don't live at home. I've been kind of worried this guy might . . . you know . . . kidnap them or something."

"Anything's possible, I guess," Daniels offers with a skeptical frown. "Carl?"

Molina shakes his head no. "If he was going after them, he'd have done it by now. I mean, what's it get him? A hostage? Then what—a trade for you? After all that's happened, he's got to assume you've gone to the police. It's complicated and risky. Doesn't sound like how this guy does business."

Before leaving, they decide their next step will be to

contact their counterparts in San Francisco and have them check out the address on Sullivan's driver's license.

Their decision is made.

So is mine.

And, now, so are my plane reservations to Hawaii.

It all started after the CIL got involved. I'm going there to conduct a search and destroy mission for the woman with the Filipino accent. It follows that, prior to covering for Sullivan, she'd used her position to alert him to my inquiry. Now I'm going to use her, use her to find him, and find out what's going on before subjecting him to the death of a thousand cuts.

I have one knotty problem.

I've been wrestling with it all weekend.

Sunday night it occurs to me that my portable problem solver may be the solution—literally. I fetch the laptop and place it on my desk. There's an access door on the side of the case. It hinges open when I release the catch, revealing a clear plastic pull tab. I grasp it with my thumb and forefinger and slide out the battery. To my relief, the .25 caliber Beretta just fits in the deep, rectangular cavity. I'm about to close the access door when I sense a presence and look up.

Laura is standing in the doorway of my office with a shopping bag and a puzzled look on her face. She'd driven down from school on Friday. I haven't mentioned my plans, knowing she'd try to talk me out of going. Instead we've spent most of the weekend in Century City on a movie marathon. This afternoon she said she needed to buy a few things for school. I begged off, claiming I had work to do.

"What're you doing?" she asks suspiciously.

"Checking the battery."

"Daddy—I saw what you did."

I begin to explain. I'm not at all surprised to see her eyes gradually widening with concern. By the time I finish, she's bristling with opposition.

"No," she says sharply. "No, I think you should leave it to the police, and get back to work."

I can't help but smile at how much her gestures and tone

remind me of her mother. "I'm trying. I've been here twenty-four hours a day. But I'm distracted; and I'm sick and tired of being afraid to spend time in my own home."

"I don't care. I don't want you putting yourself in danger."

"Sweetheart, I already am in danger. I'm sleeping with a pistol in my hand. I take it to the bathroom for Chrissakes. You know I'm not the type to hide and let others fight my battles."

"Well, if you were," she says, a bitter edge creeping into her voice, "maybe Mommy would still be alive."

I recoil, stung by her remark.

She hurries to me, her eyes brimming with tears, and hugs me. "I'm sorry, I didn't mean it like that."

"I know. It's okay."

"I've already lost one parent. I'm afraid I'm going to lose the other."

"Don't worry, I'm not doing anything foolish."

"Daddy, the man's a killer."

I nod gravely, my head filling with violent memories, then my eyes shift from Laura's to the laptop. I close the access door over the pistol, and I hear myself say, "So am I."

17

EARLY MONDAY MORNING, THE DRIVER DROPS ME AT the United terminal at LAX. I always carry on my bags and head directly for the gate. My palms are clammy and my stomach starts churning as I approach the security check. I'm nervous as hell, though I've no reason to be. In all my departures from airports all over the world, I've never had to put the laptop through a metal detector or X-ray machine. Not even once. The mere thought of wiping out the data is intolerable. *Come on, Morgan, settle down,* I say to myself as I casually drop my two-suiter and shoulder bag on the conveyor, *you're just another weary businessman in a suit and tie.*

"This one's a computer," I explain to the security guard. "I can't chance erasing the hard drive."

He studies me stone-faced and gestures to a table off to the side. I set the computer down, then unzip the canvas carrying case, which also contains the battery and an auxiliary power cord, and fold back the top half, leaving the computer inside.

The guard runs his fingers around the inside of the case, and looks up at me. "Will you turn it on, please?"

My pulse quickens, but I'm not rattled. I expected him to ask. They always do. I raise the screen, revealing the keyboard, then connect the power cord, plug it into an outlet built into the table, and turn on the computer, which emits an electronic beep. An instant later the screen comes to life with a long list of programs.

The guard is satisfied and nods.

I pack up the computer, leave it with the guard, and walk

through the metal detector without incident. He comes around the X-ray unit and hands it to me.

A short while later, as the 767 is accelerating down the runway, my mind drifts to a flight from Rome in 1986. Terrorists had been hijacking and bombing international flights with frightening regularity. When the plane was airborne and bearded men with Uzis didn't materialize, I relaxed, but moments later it dawned on me that we had ten hours to go, ten hours for the plane to blow up in midair. Now I'm wondering just how badly Sullivan and his people want me dead?

Five anxious hours later, a string of islands appears on the horizon. Halos of glowing mist hover above patches of lush greenery that are ringed by sparkling turquoise surf. We're on final approach to Honolulu International on Oahu when the spell is broken by Waikiki's soaring towers.

After deplaning, I go directly to the nearest men's room, lock myself in a stall, remove the pistol from my laptop, and pocket it. Then I take one of the pink *wicki-wicki* buses that shuttle passengers to baggage claim and ground transportation.

The white Cadillac taxicab is immaculate and air-conditioned. Soft classical music comes from the radio. The Asian driver is neatly dressed and polite. This is paradise.

I tell him I'm going to the Central Identification Lab. He nods, repeats it, and drives off, heading east on H-1, the Lunalilo Freeway. I've been here many times on business and vacation since that rehab stint twenty years ago, and know the island fairly well. I easily locate Tripler Army Hospital perched up on the bluffs to the north and Fort Shafter spread out next to it across the foothills. As we approach the Pacific War Memorial where the freeway branches, the cab driver bears right onto the Nimitz Highway instead of left as I'm anticipating.

"Excuse me, isn't Fort Shafter up the hill?"

"Yes, that whole area there below the mountains," he replies gesturing off to the left. "The military owns everything here."

"I know, I meant I thought the Lab was located there?"

"At Fort Shafter?"

"Yes, that's what they told me."

"No, the lab's up here on the waterfront."

"The Central Identification Lab—"

"Yes. Take my word for it. I've been there lots of times."

I'm not sure whether I feel foolish or unconvinced. There's no denying I'm unnerved. Do 'they' have me already? Has Sullivan arranged for another accident? My hand slips into my pocket and finds the pistol.

The driver tromps on the gas. The taxi swiftly accelerates, throwing me back against the seat. Is he offended? Or has our conversation spurred him to get me into unfriendly hands as fast as possible? As the taxi races along waterfront streets lined with trucking yards and warehouses, I become progressively more concerned and have visions of being deep-sixed in Honolulu Harbor.

The driver finally turns right at a large sign that proclaims PIERS 38–44. A short street leads to an unmanned shack that once served as a traffic control point. We continue past it, crossing an expanse of bumpy asphalt toward distant piers where trucks, boxcars, and cargo containers sit beneath towering cranes.

My hand tightens around the pistol's handgrip. I flick the safety off with my thumb, which is poised to cock the hammer prior to firing.

The taxi bears right and drives through a gate in a chain link fence that encloses two small buildings and the surrounding parking area. To my relief, an American flag flies above a flat-roofed structure where a sign proclaims *United States Army, Honolulu, Hawaii, Central Identification Laboratory*.

Despite the brilliant sunlight and intensely blue sky, a forbidding mist hovers above the nearby mountains, and an unexpected silence prevails. As the taxi departs, it dawns on me that here, in a desolate corner of the Honolulu waterfront, in two nondescript buildings directly opposite Pier 40, is where the remains of MIAs are brought, where the scientists ply their macabre skills, where the final answers are determined.

The entrance is on the side of the building next to a

staircase that leads up to the second floor. I push through the door and find myself in a rather large clerical area.

There's nothing pristine or scientific about it. Instead of the modern suite of offices populated by technicians in white lab coats I expected, I'm in an upscale Army barracks where the personnel wear uniforms, fatigues, and civvies, and work in beige and pale green rooms with imitation wood paneling, venetian blinds, louvered windows, and harsh fluorescent lighting. Government-issue gray steel desks, office chairs, and file cabinets are mixed with an odd assortment of residential easy chairs and sofas. The all-too-familiar glow of a computer screen comes from one of the side offices.

I figure there's little chance that Captain Sullivan is here, but I've no doubt the woman with the Filipino accent is. I've no idea what she looks like or if anyone else at the CIL is involved, which is why I've borrowed the captain's tactic of not making an appointment in advance. Will they stare? Will jaws drop? Will they be surprised that I'm still alive?

I set my bags aside and cross toward a desk, centered in the area. The placard reads MRS. OLDHAM. The colonel's secretary. I recall the name. A rotund Asian woman with a friendly smile looks up from the typewriter. I identify myself, apologize for my impromptu appearance, and ask to see the colonel.

Mrs. Oldham explains he's in a staff meeting. Things have been hectic with the recent repatriations. But it shouldn't be too long. About twenty minutes later, a door behind her labeled COLONEL WEBSTER opens. A group of military and civilian personnel file out. Mrs. Oldham's intercom buzzes. It's the colonel. She jots down his instructions, then informs him I'm there and shows me into his office.

It's a large, square room with the same odd mix of furniture. The colonel's big wooden desk sits at an angle in the far corner where an American flag hangs from a pole topped with a golden eagle. MIA/POW posters and memorabilia are arranged on the walls and sideboard behind the desk. One proclaims *Fighting Quartermaster Corps.*

"I'm afraid you've picked a bad time," Colonel Webster

drawls softly as he comes around the desk to greet me. He's tall, square-shouldered, in his mid-forties with a strong military bearing and gentle handshake.

"Your secretary was telling me," I reply, trying to sound contrite as he motions me to a side chair and returns to his desk. "I just happened to have business in Hawaii and thought I'd drop by to discuss my case."

"Morgan," he says as something dawns on him. "The fellow whose name's on the Memorial."

"That's me." I have no intention of either challenging him, or taking him into my confidence until I have a fix on where he fits in all this. He doesn't seem at all shocked to see me.

"Interesting," the colonel muses, "but not a priority. Though, as you might imagine, Mrs. Ackerman suggested otherwise. I'm real sorry. We haven't had a chance to get to it yet."

I frown, feigning I'm confused. "There must be some mistake, Colonel. I mean, one of your people has already given me a response. I'd just like to discuss it with you."

"One of my people?" he wonders, his eyes clouding. "I don't see how that's possible. As you probably know, the CIL's mission is an extremely sensitive one. Nothing leaves here without my knowledge and approval, and I mean nothing."

"Well, Captain Sullivan was very specific about his findings. He came to—"

"You say Captain Sullivan?" he interrupts, becoming disconcerted.

I nod matter-of-factly, playing it out. "Thomas."

"Never heard of him."

"Well, he came to my office in Los Angeles, said he ran my loss scenario, and concluded the man didn't exist. As a matter of fact, he even mentioned Mrs. Ackerman."

"This is all very strange. I can't imagine who this Captain Sullivan is or why he'd do that."

"I've been asking myself those questions for weeks, Colonel. In retrospect, I think it was a reconnaissance mission. The Captain wanted to see who he was up against."

"I'm not sure I follow you."

"I couldn't put my finger on it at first either. But it bothered me that he didn't just call to say he'd come up empty. I think he wanted to meet face-to-face so he could gauge my reaction, and persuade me to back off if necessary—which he attempted. It was so important to him, I think he followed me to work a couple of times and picked a morning when I didn't go to the office to call my secretary and say he was coming by."

"Why would he do that?"

"To make sure he didn't get me on the phone. All I wanted was a name. He either had one or he didn't. There was no reason for a meeting."

"You have any idea what's going on?"

"A vague one. I mean, I'm not sure why, but he obviously doesn't want this case pursued any further."

"Why not?" Webster growls, annoyed. "And how the hell did he even know about it?"

I shrug. I want to hear what he has to say before I mention the woman with the Filipino accent. "I was hoping you could tell me."

The colonel shakes his head, mystified. "Let's see if the First Sergeant can shed any light on this." He picks up the phone, and dials an extension. "Top? The name Thomas Sullivan ring a bell? Uh-huh, Captain. That's what I thought." He glances up at me and shakes his head no. "Listen, grab that scenario Kate Ackerman passed on to us and come on in here, will you?" He hangs up, tilts back in his chair, hands clasped behind his head, and stares at the ceiling in thought, then he swivels in my direction and says, "She's here, you know?"

"Who?"

"Mrs. Ackerman."

"No. I didn't."

"Well, we have a policy of full and immediate disclosure now, and—"

"Yes, I'm familiar with it."

"—Soon as she got the word about her husband, she jumped on the next flight."

"Sounds just like her."

"She's not the first. Some of these next of kin are like tightly wound springs. But Kate . . ." He pauses and smiles fondly. "Kate's a real piece of work. Been camped on my doorstep for almost a week. I was just reviewing her husband's case with my staff. It's—"

He's interrupted by a knock. The door swings open and the sergeant enters empty-handed. He appears pale and soft in contrast to the colonel's leathery tan and looks like an accountant, but his eyes have the hard sparkle of gemstones. "That folder seems to have been misplaced, sir."

"Misplaced?"

"I thought it was in the active file, but it isn't. You're sure it's not in here?"

The colonel shrugs and searches through the stacks of files on his desk and sideboard to no avail. "When did you last see it?"

"Couple of weeks ago, I guess. I gave it to Carla to prioritize."

"Oh," the colonel responds flatly.

"Is there a reason why we can't ask her what she did with it?" I gently prompt.

"Yes, she's on leave," he replies.

"Mrs. O thinks it might be in the lab," the sergeant explains. "She's tracking it down."

The colonel nods resignedly, then introduces me to the sergeant. We're shaking hands when Mrs. Oldham comes into the office carrying a folder and hands it to the colonel.

"Where was it?"

"Filed under inactive," she replies, clearly puzzled. "Way in the back of the drawer."

As the colonel scowls and begins sorting through the contents, I notice a familiar document. "Looks like a copy of my casualty report."

"Yes, one of the first things we do when we get an inquiry is contact Mortuary Affairs. It's routine."

Another piece of the puzzle has fallen into place. For reasons that still aren't clear, Sullivan was being fed information from the inside, which means he got a copy of my casualty report too. That's how he knew I'd be going to Las Vegas to see Foster. He may not have known exactly when, but he knew who and had plenty of time to find out where, and he was ready. He probably didn't turn up in Denver because Bartlett was so much more difficult to locate.

"What's this Sullivan look like anyway?" the colonal asks.

My description of the captain's Irish/Asian lineage is greeted with a pregnant silence.

The colonel's eyes darken with concern.

The sergeant's flicker in recognition.

A look passes between them.

Webster finally makes his decision. "I know what you're thinking, Top. Go ahead, say it."

"It sounds just like Carla's husband to me."

The colonel nods in solemn agreement, then gets out of his chair and crosses to a bulletin board on the other side of the office.

"She your secretary?" I ask the sergeant.

He shakes his head no. "Only he has a secretary," he whispers, nodding in Webster's direction. "Carla's sort of our jack-of-all-trades. Answers the phone, keeps track of the paperwork, makes sure the files are up to snuff."

The colonel returns from the bulletin board with a snapshot and hands it to me. "Last year's Christmas party."

I easily spot Sullivan in the group gathered around a tinsel-laden tree. "That's him."

"Carla's the one right in front of him," the colonel says, indicating an attractive Asian woman who appears to be in her mid-thirties. Her jet black hair is pulled back severely, accentuating her pronounced cheekbones.

"Is she Filipino?"

"Uh-huh. Why?"

"As I said, something about Sullivan bothered me, so I checked him out. The woman who answered the phone confirmed he worked here. She had a Filipino accent."

Webster's brows go up.

"He's Filipino too," the sergeant chimes in. "Half. His name isn't Sullivan. It's Surigao."

"Suriyago?" I say, unsure of the pronunciation.

"Soor-eh-gah-oh," he corrects. "Sean Surigao. My wife and I went out to dinner with them a couple of times. Nice people."

"He in the military?"

"No. He's an actor," the sergeant answers.

I feel my jaw drop. That sure as hell explains a few things.

"Works as a stuntman most of the time. Does local theater, bit parts. A lot of movies and TV shows are made on the islands. Saw him at the Improv once. He was pretty good."

"He deserves an academy award for his performance in my office."

"He had good coaching," the colonel says bitterly. "Carla's been with us since we moved here from Bangkok in '76. Knows this operation as well as anyone. Went to Washington with us."

"Her husband wasn't acting when he tried to kill me."

"Kill you?"

"That's right. Twice. He—" I pause with calculated intent, and emotion that I don't have to manufacture. I need their support, and am about to play my trump card, the one I'm counting on to insure they're with me. "He murdered my wife by mistake."

The impact is powerful, visible. They exchange troubled looks. The colonel is stunned. In contrast to the gutsy zeal of National League of Families personnel, I sense a patient intelligence and reverence for his mission, which lead me to believe his reaction is genuine.

"I'm sorry, Mr. Morgan," he finally offers, letting out a long breath. "You have to understand, this comes out of nowhere. I can't imagine there isn't some explanation."

"Me neither. I need your help to find it."

"Before I take sides here," the colonel says, an edge creeping into his voice, "I'd like to hear what Carla has to say."

"So would I."

The colonel reaches across the desk and scoops up the phone. "Mrs. O? You have Carla's number handy?"

"I don't think it'd be very wise to call her," I caution as he jots it down.

"You may have a point there."

"You know where they live?"

"Over at the Theater Arts Complex," the sergeant replies. "I remember Carla mentioning her husband teaches in one of the acting workshops."

"It's about fifteen minutes from here," Webster explains. "Used to be an abandoned cannery. Now it's all theaters, dance studios, boutiques, condos."

"Why don't we hear what Carla has to say in person?" I suggest.

Webster thinks it over for a moment, glances to his watch, and lifts the phone again. Mrs. O? Cancel the two-thirty at Shafter for me, will you? Yes, make up an excuse. Thanks." He hangs up, then turns to the sergeant and hands him my folder. "All yours, Top, go to work. I'd like something by the end of day, if possible." He scoops his hat from a clothes tree and heads for the door.

"Colonel?" I say sharply, stopping him. I wait a few seconds for the sergeant to leave, then take my hand from my pocket and reveal the pistol that I've palmed. "We're dealing with a killer."

He responds with a troubled frown. "If you're right about all this."

"I think we ought to assume it for now, don't you?"

He nods grudgingly and crosses to a file cabinet. After several turns of the dial on the combination lock, he rolls open one of the drawers and removes a handgun. It's a standard military issue 9mm Beretta—much bigger than mine.

18

I'M IN AN ARMY VAN WITH THE COLONEL DRIVING EAST along the waterfront on the Nimitz Highway. While he skillfully maneuvers through the afternoon traffic, I slip the Beretta from my pocket to check the action.

"They die hard, don't they," Webster says.

He means what I'm doing with the pistol. It's an old incountry habit, every smart GI did it before every fire fight, and the really smart ones, especially the ones who came back, did it between fire fights too. The fact that I'm doing it instinctively surprises and pleases me. Under the circumstances a combat-level mentality might come in handy.

We're entering Chinatown where the Nimitz turns into Ala Moana Boulevard, one of the main thoroughfares between Honolulu and Waikiki.

"So, how long have you known Kate?" the colonel asks casually.

"Not very long. Couple of months," I reply as I remove the clip and eject the round from the chamber. "Actually I've only met her once."

"I thought so."

"What's that mean?"

"Well, she sort of gave me the impression you were old friends, but I had a feeling it was part of her sales pitch."

I cock the Beretta's hammer and pull the trigger. The action is smooth and silent. I thumb the round back into the chamber. The colonel doesn't strike me as a man who spends much time on idle chitchat. This is the second time he's initiated a conversation about Kate Ackerman, and I sense there's more.

"Why do you ask?"

"Oh, no special reason," he replies evasively. "Good person to have in your corner."

It sounds like Kate Ackerman really went to bat for me and, for some reason, the colonel wants to make sure I know it. My mind is elsewhere and I decide not to pursue it further now. "Guess I owe her one."

"You and me both. It's been tough holding her off like this. I mean, sometimes it gets real tempting to just give in and tell these people what they want to hear. It's important to keep some distance, so we've developed—"

"A system of safeguards," I interject, finishing his sentence. " 'Captain Sullivan' told me all about them. As I said, he was very articulate about all your policies and procedures."

"Carla—" he snarls, his expression darkening. "I still can't believe she'd be involved in anything like this."

"I have a feeling they were counting on that." I align the clip and slap it up into the pistol's handgrip.

We drive the rest of the way in silence. Shortly after crossing the Ala Wai Canal at the east end of Ala Moana Park, we pass the Hawaii Yacht Club, where sixty-foot sailing yachts bob in the surf, then turn into the Theater Arts Complex. It's a *tour de force* of prewar industrial architecture. Stalwart brick and sheet-metal buildings with sawtoothed rooftops and long rows of skylights are clustered on a large pier that juts into the harbor. They've all been sandblasted and meticulously restored.

The colonel finds a spot in the parking area and we make our way through the main entrance to a central courtyard lined with shopping arcades. An information kiosk displays a block diagram identifying the various structures and activities. He locates the housing units and leads the way across the court and between the maze of buildings to a section of condominiums.

My stomach tightens as we approach. My mind starts racing, calculating the various possibilities: Will Surigao alias Sullivan be here? If so, how will he react? Deny— that's what I'd do. Play it straight, friendly and ignorant, and deny, deny, deny. Just in case he doesn't, the element of surprise is mine and I want to keep it that way. I stay back, my hand in my pocket gripping the pistol, as the colonel climbs the steps to the entrance. Once he's in position, I follow and slip past him, working my way around to one of the windows. He waits as I lean forward cautiously and glance inside. There's no sign of the occupants or any activity. I signal Webster with a shrug and wait to see who'll respond when he rings the bell.

No one answers.

"Carla? Carla it's Colonel Webster. You in there?" He knocks on the door, then tries the bell several more times with the same result.

We're about to leave when a woman calls out, "You looking for Sean and Carla?"

The voice comes from above.

We descend the steps and crane our necks to see a lithesome, deeply tanned woman in a bikini leaning over the balcony of the adjacent unit.

"Yes, we are," the colonel replies.

"I haven't seen them in about a week. I have a feeling they moved out."

"Shit," I mutter to myself.

"Are you sure?" the colonel asks.

"No. But I remember Sean saying something about going on location."

"He say where?" I ask.

" 'Fraid not," she replies, turning her attention to me. "You in the business?"

"Sorry, we're all cast," I reply automatically. Several of my clients are in the entertainment field. I've been asked this question countless times, and have amassed an arsenal of glib replies in self-defense.

"Sure sounds like they've flown the coop," the colonel says in a dismayed drawl as we leave.

I nod gravely.

I'm still thinking film business.

The phrase THE END—set in various type styles—is racing through my mind over and over.

It's unacceptable.

We retrace our steps through the courtyard and take an elevator to the manager's office on the top floor of the main theater building, overlooking the harbor. The man behind the desk—a Hawaiian in an expensive linen suit, black silk shirt, and heavily scented cologne—confirms the Surigaos have moved.

"You know where?" I ask.

"Oh, I'm afraid they didn't say."

"They didn't leave a forwarding address?"

"Not with me. You might check with the post office."

"Can we see the place?"

"Why? Are you interested in renting it?"

"I might be," I reply, catching the colonel's eye. "That's why I was looking for the Surigaos."

"They're friends of mine," the colonel chimes in. "Sean mentioned they might be away for a while and I suggested Mr. Morgan talk to them about it."

"There must be some misunderstanding," the manager says with a trace of effeminate haughtiness that suddenly surfaces. "You see, the Surigaos were just tenants here."

"Oh. Who's the owner?" I ask.

"A Mr. Ajacier. I believe his company was one of the original investors in the complex. He retained a number of units and leases them."

"Does this Mr. Ajacier live here?"

"Oh, no, he's a citizen of the world, so to speak. Mr. Ajacier has many residences. I believe he maintains one somewhere on the mainland." He pauses, his brow furrowed in thought. "San Francisco? It's been a while. I'm afraid I'm a little hazy on that."

San Francisco? I suppress my reaction and file the name Ajacier away, noting he pronounced it Ah-jah-see-yea, like Olivier. "Well, it sounded like the perfect *pied-à-terre*," I say, handing the manager one of my cards. "Is it still available?"

"Management consulting," he muses, giving it the once-over. "I thought perhaps you were a producer like Mr. Surigao."

The colonel winces.

I sense he's been clinging to the idea that this is all some sort of misunderstanding. I don't blame him, but his hopes are fading fast. "I hope a career in theater arts isn't a prerequisite," I joke, trying to lighten the mood.

"Only an appreciation for them," the manager replies

with an amused chuckle, using a magician's flair to present me with one of his business cards. "I'll be happy to show the unit to you, Mr. Morgan."

He steps smartly to an ornately framed mirror that swings aside revealing a cabinet filled with keys hanging from labeled hooks. He finds the set he wants and leads the way out of the office. In minutes we're down the elevator, out of the theater building, and crossing the courtyard, where a group of young women in dance tights and leg warmers hurry past.

"I'm sure you'll agree, it's quite beautiful," the manager says as we arrive back at the condominium and he opens the door, gesturing we enter first.

He's right. High-tech furnishings, three levels, and right on the water, which comes as a surprise since the units ring the pier and the sea isn't visible from the courtyard. It has a lanai, hinged window walls that roll back into recessed pockets, an open kitchen, and a sunken living room with fireplace. The flue is a stainless steel shaft that pierces the roof, where skylights abound. Every room has a view of the harbor and the aquamarine Pacific beyond.

"If you're looking for paradise, Mr. Morgan, I daresay you've found it."

"I'd say so."

"I'm not sure what he'll be asking. It was twenty-five hundred a month but it might be more than that now."

The colonel winces again.

"I'd like to look around for a while if you don't mind. My wife's going to ask a million questions and I'd better have the answers."

"Why, of course," the manager says genially. "Take your time. These are decisions of the heart, not the mind or the checkbook. Just pull the door closed when you're finished. You know where to find me."

"Waste of time," the colonel drawls after the manager leaves.

"Maybe not. Maybe the Surigaos left their forwarding address here."

The colonel's eyes widen.

We split up and start searching the place; every room, closet, drawer, and cabinet. A short time later, I'm in the den going through a writing desk when the colonel comes bounding down the circular staircase from the bedrooms.

"Like I said . . ." He lets the words tail off in disgust and splays his hands.

"Ditto." I shrug resignedly and slam one of the drawers closed.

The place has been swept clean. There isn't a hanger in a closet or scrap of paper in a wastebasket, nothing. In fact, there's no evidence that Carla and Sean Surigao were ever here, let alone the slightest clue as to where they went. Equally baffling is why they split. Maybe Sergeant Daniels was wrong? Maybe Surigao does think I'm dead? Why else would he have returned to Hawaii? Come on, Morgan, I say to myself, this is no time to lower your guard. Just because he isn't here, doesn't mean he's not on the island, doesn't mean he isn't across the street watching.

"I didn't know bit actors did this well," I say as my hand goes into my pocket in search of reassurance and cradles the pistol.

"I can tell you they sure as hell weren't covering their nut on the five-sixty-five a week we're paying Carla," the colonel says, matching my sarcastic tone. "Where'd they get money for a place like this?"

I have the answer, and I've no doubt this is the time to use it, to strike boldly, powerfully, in a quick, decisive blitzkrieg. "Drugs."

The colonel reacts as if he's heard a gunshot. "Where'd the hell that come from?"

His eyes never leave mine as I go on to brief him on Bartlett. He flinches noticeably when I mention the rumors of a DEA investigation at the Ton Son Nhut mortuary. "It may have started twenty years ago in Vietnam," I conclude, "but I'm willing to bet, one way or another, something's still going on."

His eyes narrow in thought. For a long moment he is silent and still. I'm not sure if I've insulted or threatened him. Maybe he's been playing my game better than me and is involved himself. Either way, assuming he doesn't try to shoot me, I expect he'll react as if I've offended him, and ask—no, demand angrily—that I explain what it could possibly have to do with the CIL, and berate me for even daring to suggest it. Instead, he surprises me, and says, "There's somebody on my staff you should talk to."

19

THE MAN WAITING FOR ME IN THE CIL CONFERENCE ROOM
is a civilian. He's sitting alone at the far end of a long table
framed by a luminous, floor-to-ceiling projection screen
hanging against the wall behind him. Cigarette smoke curls
in front of his face. He stands as I enter, and breaks into
a cautious smile.

Tall and slender with thinning hair, he appears to be in
his mid-fifties. His shirt, worn outside his slacks Hawaiian
style, has white-on-white embroidery reminiscent of religious vestments and combines with his Scandinavian bone
structure and coloring to give him a spiritual aura. His eyes
have a fragile wariness, suggesting he had once undergone
a harrowing ordeal that left him forever shaken—and he
had.

According to the colonel, Jason Ingersoll ran the military
mortuary at Ton Son Nhut Airbase near Saigon during the
war. Each day, sometimes by truck, mostly by helicopter,
piles of body bags were deposited on his doorstep. As mortuary officer, he was responsible for their contents being
restored to as high a degree of human resemblance as possible and returned to their families. When the war ended, he
went to work for the CIL. For almost twenty years, he's
been retrieving, identifying, and returning the remains of
those men he hadn't the chance to serve in Vietnam.

We shake hands.

He takes his seat and lights another cigarette.

I settle into one of the upholstered armchairs around the
table on which pads, pencils, a thermos of coffee, and several cups are set out along with a 35mm slide projector. A

lectern and presentation easel are centered beneath the CIL seal on the far wall. After an exchange of pleasantries, I raise the question of drug smuggling in Vietnam and the DEA investigation.

Jason Ingersoll's face falls and takes on a severely pained expression.

I've wounded him.

"Why is that so disturbing?" I ask softly.

"Because it brings back bad memories." His eyes sharpen as he decides whether or not to share the past with me. "I was one of those investigated at the time."

This is a complete surprise. The colonel stole none of his colleague's thunder. "For drug smuggling?"

Ingersoll nods imperceptibly.

"I'm sorry, I didn't know."

"They said, instead of putting the viscera back in chest cavities after autopsies, we were putting in packages of heroin, which were removed by accomplices at Travis or Dover, depending on the port of entry."

I've finally found the answer. I should be elated, but I'm not. I'm angered by this violation of human dignity, and flooded with ghoulish images that turn my stomach. It takes me a moment to regain my composure. "I never heard anything about that."

"It was pretty well hushed up. There were a few articles, but the media showed admirable restraint. I guess they decided we'd taken enough of a beating over there. The accusations were nonsense anyway, made up by a few disgruntled people. I was fully exonerated."

"It never happened?"

"Never."

He giveth and taketh away in a matter of seconds. I feel like the wind's been knocked out of me. "Could it have been done without your knowledge?"

"I don't see how. We had strict procedures, paper trails that established a chain of custody. We couldn't afford to be slipshod. On the average we processed between fifty and a hundred remains a day. In the spring of '68, during the peak fighting, we must've done close to four thousand in a month."

"Well, as far as I know, '68 is about the time this drug smuggling was going on."

"Alleged smuggling," he gently corrects, oblivious to the endless stream of smoke coming from his mouth. "I was the mortuary officer, Mr. Morgan. I was always on the move, overseeing every phase of the operation."

"Certainly not twenty-four hours a day."

"No, but dozens of men worked a given shift. The embalmers were literally back to back at these rows of tables. There was a lot of talk going on: women, sports, family, and some black humor, quite frankly, anything to lighten the mood. They'd have noticed someone walking in with a big bag of white powder. I mean, this isn't a diamond or piece of microfilm we're talking about."

"In other words, it would've taken a conspiracy."

He nods and allows himself a thin smile. He's been asked all these questions before. "A massive one. The whole organization would've had to be involved."

"What happened to the remains after embalming?"

"They were transferred to out-processing. We worked two twelve-hour shifts. Remains embalmed during the day were packaged at night and vice versa."

"I recently spoke to someone in Denver who worked at the mortuary. His name's Bartlett. John Bartlett. You remember him?"

Ingersoll looks off for a moment in thought. "Yes, yes, I believe I do. Tall fellow, in-processing noncom as I recall."

"Right. He's the one who gave me the impression something was going on."

"Really? What made him think that?"

I brief him on Bartlett's heroin addiction; on how the out-processing noncom forced him to rebag the helicopter pilot's corpse, the corpse that vanished.

"Vanished?" Ingersoll repeats incredulously. "No. No, somebody would've noticed a blank in the log. Hey, this guy came in but didn't go out."

"He was never logged in."

"Oh. When was this?"

"Week of twelve May."

"Well, the investigation was over. Months. The 'smugglers' were in the clear. Why do that?"

"To make sure it stayed over. The DEA was onto this guy. Your people would've picked up on the phony identity—"

"Absolutely. Fingerprint and dental charts were routine."

"—DEA would've been notified and who knows?"

He raises a brow in acknowledgment.

"Bartlett also mentioned the term 'Pepsi-Cola runs.' Sound familiar?"

"No. Beer and pizza runs—I remember those. We weren't into soft drinks much."

"He said pilots working the drug trade used Pepsi-Cola runs as a code name for certain flights."

Ingersoll shrugs, mystified.

"The term never came up in the investigation?"

"Not to my knowledge." He takes a moment to stub out his cigarette. "That out-processing noncom—the one who pulled the chopper pilot's remains—you have any idea who he was?"

"No, I don't have his name, but Bartlett mentioned he wasn't very well liked, got himself fragged."

Ingersoll's eyes flicker. "I remember that." His brow furrows in thought, and he shakes his head no. "Been a long time. I'm sorry, his name escapes me."

"What was he in charge of?"

"The final wrapping and shipping of remains."

"Putting them in transfer cases?" I'd seen more than my share of the boxy aluminum caskets. Every GI in Vietnam had nightmares of ending up in one.

"Uh-huh. Also preparing manifests and loading the T-cases on pallets and into C-141s."

"Was he investigated?"

"Not as far as I know."

"Could he have put heroin in chest cavities?"

"You mean, gut one of those poor fellows?" Ingersoll erupts indignantly.

The sudden shift in gears surprises me. I nod, feeling guilty at having upset him.

"Right there in the middle of the out-processing building?" he charges on, his pitch rising. "And insert a big bag of heroin in his chest?"

"Look, I'm sorry if I've offended you, Mr. Ingersoll. But I've found myself in the middle of something here. People have been trying to kill me and I'm trying to figure out why."

"The colonel briefed me," he says more evenly. "I know about your wife. I'm sorry."

I nod and force a smile.

"It couldn't have been out-processing," he resumes. "You see, the mortuary had four separate buildings: in-processing and embalming, the ID lab, administration and supplies, and out-processing—where the remains were taken for final packaging and paperwork. Now—"

"Well, doesn't that support my contention? I mean, the noncom who ran out-processing had autonomy in his building. He had control, right?"

"True. But I was about to say, the work was done in a large, white room. It was spotless. Even the floor was painted white."

I sense where he's heading. My teeth dig into my lower lip, my gut starts constricting.

"I don't mean to be gruesome, Mr. Morgan, but if the corpse wasn't dismembered or badly mutilated, it was embalmed under pressure; then the wrists, ankles, and knees were gently bound with gauze to secure them. Finally, the remains were wrapped in a clean white sheet, the ends folded and tucked military style, and then sealed in plastic."

His long, slender hands—which have administered the military's last rites to so many, which came all too close to giving them to me—gesture with rhythmic grace as he goes on.

"Now, imagine undoing all that in this immaculate room, not to mention making an incision in the chest—which requires a fair degree of skill and a noisy electric saw, to be blunt—and removing the viscera. It's an elegant, compact design that God came up with, but it expands to a rather unwieldy volume. So there, in this pristine environment, the conspirator stands with all this . . . Well, you get the picture."

"Yes, I'm afraid I do," I say queasily, fighting back thoughts of the County Morgue, of Nancy lying on the stainless steel table, of my fears of her being so horribly violated.

"Could it have happened?" he wonders rhetorically, slipping another Marlboro from the pack. "Once? Maybe. Twice? I strongly doubt it."

"What about bodies that had been autopsied? Would that have made it any easier?"

"Not really." He strikes a match. A thin layer of smoke stretches between us. "We didn't autopsy that many. Only if there was no other way to determine cause of death."

"For example?"

"The crew of a plane that went down without being hit by enemy fire. We'd want to know: Did the pilot have a heart attack? Was it G-induced loss of consciousness? And so on and so forth."

"How long were the bodies kept at the mortuary?"

"Twenty-four to forty-eight hours, unless we couldn't get an identification. As a rule, a man's remains were recovered, processed, and returned to next of kin within a week. Many had difficulty accepting the loss if they couldn't actually see their loved one dead. This fast turnaround was the key to preserving what we called viewability." He inhales deeply on the cigarette, then pushes back his chair and stands.

I have more questions, but I sense he's preparing for his summation, and decide to wait.

"You see, Mr. Morgan," he resumes softly, "we were good people. Dedicated professionals with a strict code of ethics. And the stress we coped with, day in and day out, seeing the prime of American youth—" His voice breaks and he toys with his cigarette until the feelings subside. "You can't imagine what it was like to see these kids butchered like that."

"Yes, sir, I can."

"Of course," he says apologetically, emitting a steady stream of smoke. "I just can't imagine any of my people were involved in something so heinous. I didn't believe it then and I still don't."

I'm moved, and tempted to end it right here, but there is one question I have to ask. "What about now?"

He stiffens defensively. "You mean the Surigaos." It's a statement not a question.

"Yes. I know this is off the wall, but if it had been going on in Vietnam without your knowledge, could it still be going on now?"

"Via our operation here?" he asks, his voice ringing with disbelief.

I nod, expecting he'll be further outraged.

"Do you know what's being repatriated?" he challenges, bristling. "Do you have any idea what these families, some of whom have been waiting for thirty years, finally bury?"

"I can imagine."

"I'll show you," he says sharply. He turns on a heel and walks toward the other end of the table.

I'm apprehensive and about to say it's not necessary when the lights go out and the beam from the projector splits the darkness. I've forced him to share his pain with me, and if being confronted by some horrible atrocity is the price, then I must pay it. There's no way I can back out now.

He brings up the first slide.

Again, I'm flooded with thoughts of Nancy, and close my eyes, taking a moment to gather my courage. I open them to see a wall-sized blowup of a blinding white sheet. Arranged on it, in anatomical order, are parts of a human skeleton: half a lower jawbone with most of the teeth missing, a row of vertebrae, a small section of rib cage, pieces of a crushed pelvis, the digits of several fingers, and a single femur snapped like a tree limb. That's it. Eroded and discolored by time and elements, they have the look of porous, brown stone. There's nothing human about them—they could be the grotesque remains of a prehistoric animal.

"That's quite a lot," Ingersoll says matter-of-factly. "We often get far less . . ."

He pauses and advances the slide.

"That mound of bone fragments would easily fit in the palm of your hand. In case you're wondering, the remains are repatriated in these boxes."

He advances the slide again.

A group of Asians and a single American are gathered around a row of wooden boxes on a table. They are made of quarter-inch-thick mahogany. The tops, with the nails to secure them partially hammered into the wood, have been set aside. Judging by the people, each box is about 30 X 12 X 16 inches—length, width, and height respectively.

Ingersoll shuts off the projector. The tip of his cigarette traces his path through the darkness as he crosses to the light switch. "Not the sort of thing that lends itself to smuggling bags of heroin," he concludes as the fluorescents flicker back to life.

I squint at the brightness and take a moment to regroup. "Have whole cadavers ever been repatriated?"

"No."

"Not even once?"

"Never."

"What about deserters or men who chose to remain behind who subsequently died of natural causes?"

He shakes his head no. Impatiently.

"And there's never been a case where a POW died in captivity and his body was repatriated?"

"I've never seen one—despite the reports of live sightings. The Southeast Asian governments insist there are no longer any prisoners of war . . ." He pauses and raises a skeptical brow before adding, ". . . under their control. You can draw your own conclusions."

I'm exhausted.

We sit in silence for a moment.

He methodically taps the ash from his cigarette. "Anything else?"

"No, Mr. Ingersoll. I think that does it. Thanks."

He nods amiably, then crosses to the window and opens the blinds. Bands of sunlight and shadow slash across his torso. After a moment he glances in my direction and waves me over.

"See that beige wagon there?" he prompts, pointing out a dilapidated station wagon in the parking lot. The paint is dull and worn. One of the hubcaps is missing. The antenna has been bent by the wind.

"Yours?"

"Uh-huh. Seventy-eight Chevy. Needs a brake job, tires, and a major tune-up."

"I understand."

"I thought you might. In case you're wondering, I rent a small cottage in Kaimuki—no view—far from the beach."

I nod, chastised, and shake his hand. "Thanks again. I'm sorry to put you through all this."

His eyes soften and he smiles, absolving me of blame, then he lights another cigarette and turns away.

I sense he wants a few moments to himself while the memories recede. I'm heading for the door when he calls out, "Ac—I think it was Ac-something."

"Pardon me?"

"The name of that out-processing noncom who was fragged." He scratches his forehead in frustration. "I vaguely recall his family being in the mortuary business. I could be wrong. Many GR people have that background. Damn."

"Don't worry. It's not that important."

"For some reason San Francisco sticks in my mind. But I'm not sure."

San Francisco? It is important.

"Was it Acacia?" he wonders. "No that's a tree, isn't it? Well it was something like that. So aggravating. It's on the tip of my tongue."

On mine too. "Was it Ajacier?"

His eyes brighten in recognition. "Why, yes. Yes, it was. How'd you know?"

"Just happened to come across it."

20

"AJACIER?" WEBSTER REPEATS IN AN ICY WHISPER. He instantly made the connection between the out-processing noncom who was fragged and the owner of the condo where the Surigaos were living. His eyes burn more in frustration than anger as he stares across the desk at me. "You stirred all this up, Mr. Morgan. Now, I'm going to ask you again, and this time I expect an answer. What do you think's going on here?"

"I think that's a two-part question, Colonel. What was going on then? What's going on now? As far as the past's concerned, Mr. Ingersoll opened the door wide, then slammed it shut pretty hard. I imagine he was well coached by his attorneys at the time he was investigated. So he's either lying or—"

"I don't believe that for a minute."

"I was about to say, gut instinct tells me he's a decent guy who got screwed. He had no idea what Ajacier—the noncom, that is—was up to."

"Which was what? Some kind of drug smuggling operation, involving the shipment of GI remains?"

"Yes, but the investigation clearly established it wasn't being done out of the mortuary. So how the hell did they pull it off?"

"Damned good question." Webster kicks back in his chair, torturing a paper clip. "Well, regardless, it still follows that if Ajacier ran the in-country end, the family mortuary business was the stateside connection."

"They were civilians. Not easy to manipulate a military operation from the outside."

148

"Didn't have to. During the war, the remains of a lot of GIs ended up in a few Bay Area mortuaries for forwarding throughout the western states. There's always that transition from military to civilian custody. We're still dealing with it."

"For example?"

"After the CIL makes an identification, the remains are shipped to the port mortuary at Travis. We have a contract with a local mortuary to run that facility."

"They provide the personnel."

He nods. "Not unusual. Hickam Field, the local Air Force base, is eighty percent civilian. Anyway, the morticians at Travis are responsible for transferring remains from T-cases to standard coffins and working with members of the service branches to make sure decorations and awards are properly arranged on the uniforms before they're released to the family or its representative."

"Who's the contractor?"

"Golden Gate Mortuary Services. We've been dealing with them for as long as I can remember." He pauses and smiles at what he's about to say. "The owner's name isn't Ajacier."

"Okay. We've just fast forwarded from past to present. Let's stay here: We have this other Ajacier, also from San Francisco, who we assume is related—brother, father, cousin, whatever. He and the Surigaos are in cahoots on something. We're not sure what."

"We're not even sure if it's connected to the past other than in name."

"I disagree. We know it's connected, because my inquiry threatened it."

"That's right. But we don't know why. Matter of fact we don't even have a clue."

"Well, if they were in the mortuary business in San Francisco twenty years ago, maybe they still are?"

"Good a place as any to start." The colonel lifts the phone, calls San Francisco information, and is told there aren't any business or residential listings under the name Ajacier.

Something dawns on me. "That's probably the only thing 'Captain Sullivan' told me that wasn't a lie."

"What?"

"That he was in San Francisco." I go on to explain about the detectives who are investigating Nancy's accident, and their discovery that a driver's license with the name Thomas Sullivan and a San Francisco address was used to rent the car that killed her. When finished, I slip Sergeant Daniels' card from my wallet and reach for the phone.

The colonel puts his hand over it to stop me. "What're you doing?"

"I want to see what they found out."

"Let's talk about what *I* want, first."

"Shoot."

"I want to keep my own house in order if I can. The POW/MIA issue's been a political tightrope for years, and the CIL's taken its share of falls. We've been accused of everything from slipshod scientific practices to outright deception."

"Regarding identifications?"

Webster winces at the memory and nods. "Do you know there are over seventy-five thousand MIAs from World War Two?"

"Seventy-five thousand?" I echo, astounded.

He nods solemnly. "No one ever makes any noise about them."

"Times have changed."

"Sure as hell have. Anyway, the point is, we're just spinning our wheels here if we don't have the trust of the families. I've worked my butt off to prove worthy of it. The media gets hold of this, well, I've learned the hard way that the tar goes on a lot faster than it comes off."

"I understand. For what it's worth, the police have probably checked out the address. I think it might be to your advantage to know what they've turned up, if anything."

He steeples his fingers thoughtfully. "Under one condition. We play our cards close to our chest."

"Fair enough." I dial the number and get a desk sergeant. Neither Daniels nor Molina are there. I leave the number of the Halekulani, the hotel in Waikiki where I'll be staying this evening.

"You're right," Webster says as I hang up. "It's a two-part question and it's part two that's really bugging me. I mean, the thought of using the CIL to smuggle drugs . . ." he lets it trail off, visibly shaken by the specter of scandal.

"Well, Mr. Ingersoll made it pretty clear it couldn't be via remains, or the wooden boxes. What's left—transfer cases?"

The colonel shakes his head. "I don't see how. There's no place to hide anything."

"Humor me. Who's in charge of them?"

"Depends on where they are in the process: Andersen Air Force Base on Guam, here, or Travis. We're working with a number of governments in Southeast Asia, but most repatriations start with the VNOSMP, that's the Vietnamese Office for Seeking Missing Personnel. They turn over the wooden boxes containing the remains to us right on the tarmac at Noi Bai Airport in Hanoi. From there, the boxes are flown to Andersen, where they're put in transfer cases."

"One box in each case?"

"One in each case. And once assigned, a given case stays with that individual's remains. We use an alphanumeric numbering system. CIL-dash-one through however many we have on the books. I think we're somewhere in the low hundreds now."

"Okay. Then what?"

"They're flown to Hickam Field. Immediately after the arrival ceremony, they're loaded on a medevac bus and driven here."

"You accompany them?"

"Every step of the way, starting in Hanoi."

"And after the remains are removed?"

"The wooden boxes are destroyed and the transfer cases are kept here until identifications are made, then used to ship the remains to the port mortuary."

"Where they're put in standard coffins and turned over to the family."

"As I said."

"And the T-cases?"

"They're stockpiled at the port mortuary—"

"Under civilian control."

"Correct—until they have enough for a pallet, say a dozen, then they're shipped back to Clark."

"Clark?"

"I meant Andersen. Force of habit. We got blown out of the Philippines by that volcano."

"That contractor in San Francisco may have the wrong name but he's sure as hell in the right place."

Webster nods thoughtfully.

The assembled pieces quickly lead to an undeniable and intriguing conclusion. "If I'm right, I mean, if they are somehow using the T-cases to smuggle drugs, and the stuff is being removed at the port mortuary, then it follows that it'd still be in the transfer cases that are here now, wouldn't it?" I want his opinion, but I'm even more interested in his reaction. Will he be threatened? Resist? Dismiss it out of hand?

His eyes flare, not with indignation but angry agreement. "Damn. Sure would."

"But I thought you said there's no place to hide anything?"

"There really isn't—other than the doc-tube."

"The what?"

"Document tube. It's a cylinder that's built into the case. Paperwork pertaining to the remains can be rolled up and slid inside. The cap's secured with one of those wire and lead customs seals."

"Wouldn't you or one of your people have found the stuff if it was in there?"

"We don't use the doc-tubes. Never have. I can't even remember the last time I opened one."

Webster is out of his chair in an eye blink. I'm right behind him as he charges down the corridor, out the door, and across the grounds to a second chain link fence that separates the two buildings. He unlocks the gate, explaining that this is the actual laboratory where remains are stored and analyzed, where the original records of those who are unaccounted for are kept, where circle searches are plotted. We hurry past the entrance, where a sign on the door proclaims:

IN RESPECT FOR THE DECEASED
PLEASE
REMOVE HEADGEAR

I follow Webster to the rear of the laboratory, where we're confronted by a wall of aluminum transfer cases stacked three and four high. There must be twenty or thirty of them.

Unlike a traditional coffin, the halves of a T-case are separate and unhinged: the bottom a very shallow tray; the upper, deeply drawn and reinforced by V-shaped ribs that are spot-welded lengthwise along the top, sides, and ends. The two parts form an airtight seal when joined and latched. Located at one end of the top half, where the word HEAD is stenciled, is a pressure release valve and next to it, in the upper right-hand corner, a metal disc approximately two inches in diameter that resembles a small gas filler cap.

"That's what I was talking about," the colonel drawls as he unscrews one of the caps, letting it dangle from a length of braided wire that prevents it from being separated from the case. He peers into the 1½-inch diameter metal tube that extends into the interior of the case, then stabs a finger inside.

"Empty."

"How far in that go?"

"About a foot, maybe less. Give me a hand here."

We grasp the hefty U-shaped handles, lift the T-case off the stack, and set it on a tubular stand. It takes a few moments to undo all ten latches. When finished, we remove the top and set it upside down next to the bottom.

The interior is unadorned, unlined, just bare aluminum with rounded corners to facilitate cleaning. There's quite obviously no place to conceal anything. In one corner, a metal cylinder extends about nine or ten inches into the case. This end of the document tube is permanently sealed.

As we go about removing the caps from the tubes on the other transfer cases, I calculate the volume of the cylinder—$pi/r^2/h$—3.14 X .75 X .75 X 10. "For what it's worth, Colonel, we're talking seventeen point six six two five cubic inches. That's roughly a third the volume of a quart of milk."

"A kilo's what, just a little over two pounds?"

"Two point two zero four six. Just one would fill about a half dozen of those tubes."

"Not very efficient, and obvious as hell." He unscrews the last cap and shakes his head no.

All the document tubes are empty.

I return to the open case. The edges that mate to form the seal are about an inch wide. I grasp the top section—thumb on the outside, forefinger on the inside—and gauge the thickness of the aluminum wall below. It can't be more than an eighth of an inch.

We reassemble the halves and screw down the latches. "These are a lot heavier than I thought," I say, as we prepare to lift the transfer case back onto the stack.

"Hundred and twenty-one pounds empty."

I'm struck by an idea. "Exactly?"

"Exactly."

"You have a scale here?"

"Sure. We do a lot of shipping. You want to weigh one of these?"

"Uh-huh."

"Why?"

I tap one of the reinforcing ribs on the exterior of the transfer case. "How do we know it's not in there? Must be a total of thirty linear feet of that on a case. Way more than ten times the volume of one of those tubes. Enough for a couple of kilos. Easy."

"But those are welded on."

"You see *The French Connection?*"

Webster nods and quickly rounds up a couple of enlisted men, who carry one of the transfer cases around to a small shipping dock on the other side of the building. They muscle it into an upright position and lift it onto the scale.

The colonel adjusts the sliding weights, setting the large one at 100, then ticks the smaller along the beam with a fingertip. It balances at precisely 121 pounds. A half hour later, jackets off, sleeves rolled up, sweat rolling down our faces, we've weighed every T-case on the premises, twenty-six in all.

Every last one tipped the scales at 121 pounds.

"Now what?" the colonel wonders, baffled but somewhat relieved.

"Beats the hell out of me, sir."

We return to the main building and are heading down the

corridor to his office when the First Sergeant intercepts us. He's carrying a file folder.

"Pettibone, Richard M.," he announces smartly with a satisfied smile.

"The guy who took my ID?"

"Found him in the AWOL file. Loss scenario's a perfect match."

"Was he a chopper pilot?"

"Affirmative."

"Dustoffs?"

The sergeant nods.

"How'd this clown die?" the colonel asks, leading the way into his office.

"According to his file, last seen boarding a flight at Ton Son Nhut for Vientiane, Laos. The plane was forced to make an emergency landing in enemy territory due to mechanical problems. They radioed their position. By the time a Jolly Green got in there the gooks had already shot everyone aboard."

"But Pettibone's name wasn't on the manifest," I say, jumping on it. "Mine was."

"Right."

That confirms Pettibone stole my ID. The recovery team found it on his body and the casualty report ended up in my file. Pulling his corpse from the morgue kept it from going any further. "But if Pettibone was using my ID, how'd that information get in his file?"

"His commanding officer included it when he reported him missing," the sergeant explains. "Whoever saw him board that flight must've come forward when they heard it went down."

"Another thing I can't figure is, why a guy who's AWOL would go to Vientiane. Why not Bangkok or Hong Kong?"

"Beats me," the colonel sighs. "You're sure you've eliminated all other scenarios, Top?"

"Positive. When you get right down to it, sir, it's all just a formality anyway." The sergeant lays the file on the colonel's desk and opens it, revealing a photograph of Pettibone.

The colonel's jaw drops.

So does mine.

The resemblance is striking. Bartlett was right. This guy was damn near my double. As I stare transfixed at the photograph, it dawns on me that I finally have a name. It's totally meaningless now.

"Good going, Top," Webster enthuses. "Next, find out if Sean Surigao was ever in the military."

The sparkle in the sergeant's eyes intensifies. "Did his tour in '68. Crewed a dustoff chopper. Guess who he flew with?"

"Pettibone," the colonel and I say in unison.

"Pettibone," the sergeant confirms smartly.

The big pieces to the puzzle just locked into place. We have the connection to the past: Pettibone and Surigao were ferrying drugs, heroin undoubtedly, in their chopper from an unknown supplier to Ajacier at the Ton Son Nhut mortuary. He shipped it to the family funeral home in San Francisco where distribution was handled. And we have the connection to the present: Surigao, the only one who made it back, subsequently went into business with Ajacier's family.

We have a lot of answers, but not all of them. We still don't know how they were doing it then, or how they're using the CIL to do it now. Considering I've barely been here five hours, I should be elated. In a way I am, but down deep, I don't really give a damn about any of it, because I don't have the man who killed Nancy—which is the only thing I really want.

21

I'M IN THE ARMY VAN, HEADING TO MY HOTEL.

The colonel was shaken by what we'd discovered and wanted to sleep on it before deciding how he was going to proceed. We agreed to reconvene in his office in the morning. I'm a little shell-shocked myself, and it's been an usually long day with the change of time zones. I was looking forward to relaxing at the hotel. It doesn't look like I'm going to get the chance.

My driver didn't notice the car that came from the pier opposite the CIL as we departed, but I did. It's been somewhere behind us all the way into Waikiki. I'm keeping an eye on it in the side-view mirror, while she tells me about making corporal and training as a casualty data analyst. Her nose is pugged and her eyes are set a little too far apart, but in her jungle fatigues with the sleeves rolled up above her elbows, there's a dynamic "Be All You Can Be" air about her.

The car that's tailing us keeps moving in and out of the mirror. A woman is behind the wheel, an Asian woman who looks familiar. We're a few blocks from the hotel on Kalakaua Avenue—Waikiki's equivalent of New York's Fifth Avenue, or Wilshire Boulevard in Beverly Hills—when traffic slows and the car comes close enough for me to get a good look at her: attractive, pronounced cheekbones, dark hair worn back. It's the woman in the colonel's snapshot. It's Carla.

I'm not surprised Surigao has her following me. There's a far greater chance I'd spot him. But he's made a mistake.

My plan to use her to get to him had died in the starting blocks. He's just breathed new life into it.

I notice the traffic light up ahead changing from green to yellow. "Do me a favor," I say casually to my driver. "There's a shop I'd like to check out. Would you mind dropping me at the corner and taking my bags to the hotel?"

"Sure, Mr. Morgan. No problem."

"Great," I say as she maneuvers toward the curb at the intersection of Lewers. "Just have the concierge set them aside until I get there."

The light changes to red.

As traffic behind us slows, I slip out of the van and get lost in the crowd of pedestrians waiting at the crosswalk. My hand goes into my pocket for the pistol. My eyes track Carla's car. It comes to a stop in the middle lane. I step into the street and weave swiftly between a few vehicles, using a panel truck for cover so I can approach from behind without being seen. I cock the Beretta and flick the safety off as I dart forward. A quick glance to the backseat confirms Surigao isn't lurking there, confirms they haven't lured me into a trap. I yank open the passenger door, and get in next to Carla.

She whirls in surprise. "Hey?!"

"Just act like we're old friends." I ease the pistol from my pocket so she can see it, then, using our bodies to shield it from view, press it into her side. "I'll use it if I have to, you understand?"

She nods, her dark, canted eyes widening in fear, widening as I imagine Nancy's did when Carla's husband forced her off the road into Malibu Canyon. "Please don't hurt me."

I shrug, unmoved. "Why not? Your husband killed my wife."

"My husband?" she asks, her lips trembling.

"This is no time for games. Just take me to him."

"I think you've mistaken me for someone else."

"I meant what I said."

"So . . . so . . . so did I," she stammers. "I'll show you. In my bag. My driver's license." She reaches for the purse on the seat between us.

I move fast and toss the purse over my shoulder into the backseat before she gets hold of it, before she gets her hands on the gun that might be inside it. Besides, her husband had a phony license, she's probably got one too. Mrs. Captain Sullivan.

"Please, what do you want?" she whimpers.

"Your husband, dammit. I told you. Now, where the hell is he?"

"At work."

"Where?!"

"The Black Orchid. He's a waiter. He—"

"Sure."

"That's the truth. He—"

"Okay. Let's go there," I say, calling her bluff. "Come on. The light's changing. Move it."

She steels herself and drives off, continuing east on Kalakaua. I've no idea where she's going. We've traveled only a few blocks when something dawns on me, something so fundamental that I know beyond any doubt our destination no longer matters.

"You're right," I say, feeling foolish and embarrassed. "I've made a mistake. Please, pull over and I'll get out."

She glances at me in disbelief.

I nod reassuringly.

She sighs with relief, and wastes no time maneuvering through traffic to the curb.

"I'm sorry I frightened you. I hope you believe me, I really am sorry."

She nods, trembling, her eyes wide with questions.

I stare at her, hoping she'll see the sincerity in mine. "I'm not a criminal. I'm a victim, an angry one. I know this is going to sound strange, but if you possibly can, I'd appreciate it if you'd just forget this ever happened. I mean, you could make things very difficult for me if you went to the police, do you understand?"

She nods again.

"I'm very sorry. I wish there was a way I could make it up to you." I get out and close the door.

She tromps on the gas and screeches away.

I stand there shaken, trying to get hold of myself. Finally, I start walking in the direction of the hotel. She may have resembled the woman in the colonel's snapshot, but I'd let my paranoia get the best of me and overreacted. Then, having done so, I'd almost completely overlooked the obvious—the poor woman had no Filipino accent.

I bear right from Kalakaua into the Royal Hawaiian Shopping Center, a multilevel complex of department stores, tourist shops, and pricey boutiques. I emerge on the opposite side into a twisting knot of narrow streets, finally making my way to Kalia Road where the hotel is located.

The Halekulani is an oasis of tranquil luxury smack in the middle of Waikiki's frenzy of gridlocked traffic and swarming tourists. There are no doors or entrances, just a waterfall flanked by porticoed approaches that are completely open, as is the circular lobby. Once the lone hotel on Oahu's south shore, it's now one of a dozen in tight formation along the beach—about a fifteen-minute walk from where Carla and Sean Surigao were living.

While I register, the check-in clerk arranges to have my bags brought to my room, then he hands me a magnetic card key and a telephone message.

It's from Kate Ackerman.

I'm tired and unnerved and not sure if I'm up to talking to anyone. I take the elevator to the ninth floor. It's a corner room with a southeast exposure: bright white-on-white decor, tasteful prints, wide louvers, views of the Pacific and Diamond Head. It has little effect on my mood. I'm checking the place out when the bellman arrives. I unpack glumly, then decide Kate's chatty ebullience might do me some good and pick up the phone.

"Kate? Cal Morgan."

"Well hi, how're you doing?'

"Not bad. My office tell you I was here?''

"No, the colonel's secretary. She called to set up a meeting for tomorrow and said he thought I'd want to know you were in town.''

"Nice of him,'' I say, recalling Webster said the same to me about her. Now, more than ever, I suspect he has an ulterior motive. Kate's an attractive woman, but the colonel knows about Nancy. I can't imagine he's playing matchmaker. He's up to something. I don't know what. "It sounds like things're working out for you.''

"Yes. I can't believe it. It becomes official tomorrow. I'm so excited."

"That's great."

"My God!" Kate suddenly exclaims as if she'd just realized dinner was burning. "I almost forgot. The last time we talked you were meeting with someone from the CIL. A Captain—"

"Sullivan."

"Right. Well what happened? You were supposed to let me know."

"I'm sorry. It's a long story."

"I love long stories. You know the hau tree?"

"Sure."

"I'm right next door at the Sheraton. I'll meet you there in ten minutes. What do you say?"

"It's been a hell of a day. I'm kind of pooped. I don't think I'd be very good company."

"Come on. We can have a cocktail, watch the sunset, and you can tell me all about it."

"Look. I'm going to be here for a while. Why don't we—"

"Hey, this is a special day for me. You really going to let me celebrate alone?"

"I think I just went into escrow."

She laughs. "Ten minutes."

"Make it a half hour, okay? I just checked in."

I head into the shower. The high-tech fixtures deliver the therapeutic massage they promised. I stand limply, watching the water swirling down the polished drain in a perfect spiral. My mind wanders, but I know where it's headed: Laos. Champasak Province. 18 April 1968. That nurse was right. No Rockette audition for me. Not with these legs. The scars have softened and blurred over the years along with the memories, but lately, painful moments keep surfacing with the sting of hot shrapnel.

Ten minutes later, I'm toweling off and feeling refreshed when I notice the message light on the phone is flashing. Someone called while I was in the shower. I slip into one of the terry cloth robes with the decorative *H* embroidered on the pocket, then call the desk for the message: Sergeant

Daniels of the Los Angeles Police returned my call. I get him back and ask what they've found out in San Francisco.

"Let's talk about Vegas, first," Daniels counters. "We followed up with Sergeant Figueroa. Remember him?"

"Like a bad meal."

"He busted a brothel last week. One of the hookers copped a plea. Traded some information for a reduced charge. She said about a month ago some guy hired her and a girlfriend to drug a businessman at the Stardust and get him up to a room. The guy was waiting there and injected the businessman with something."

"It was Sullivan, wasn't it," I say.

"The hooker didn't know the guy's name. So we pulled a copy of Sullivan's driver's license from the DMV and faxed it to Vegas. They put it in a photo lineup with a bunch of mug shots. She picked him out right away."

"Just like on television."

"Very funny. Your turn. Anything?"

"Sullivan's an alias."

"That mean you found him?"

"Where he was living." I give Daniels the name Surigao and spell it out. That's all I give him, honoring my pledge to the colonel to keep the CIL out of it until after we meet in the morning. "What'd you find out in San Francisco?"

"Weird. The address on the driver's license turned out to be a mortuary."

"Military one?"

"No. A funeral parlor. A place over in North Beach. Golden Gate Mortuary Services."

I stifle a gasp. At least he can't see my reaction. "Who's the owner?"

"Man's name's Messina. James Messina. We went up there and talked to him. He was as baffled as we were. Claimed he didn't know anything about it. Said he never heard of Sullivan."

I resist the temptation to say this guy Messina's lying through his teeth and, instead, prompt, "Wouldn't the license have been mailed to that address?"

"I didn't say we believed him."

"My mistake."

"Let's go back to Sullivan."

"Surigao."

"I know. I got it. You saying he's there?"

"He was. Probably still is."

"Good."

"Why?"

"Last time I was in Hawaii was on my honeymoon—with my first wife."

I hang up, my mind racing: Daniels and Molina are accident investigators. They're not familiar with the intricacies of corporate structures. But I am, and I have a feeling I know what's going on. One phone call to my office and I'll know whether or not I'm right, but it's almost 8:30 P.M. in Los Angeles. Besides, I need some information from Colonel Webster before I can make it. I get into some casual clothes, slip the pistol into my pocket, and hurry from the room.

The hau tree, where I'm meeting Kate Ackerman, isn't a bar or cocktail lounge, it's a tree, a famous one on the grounds of the Halekulani. I come out of the elevator and am cutting through the porticoed shopping arcade when I spot her sitting in a lounger beneath the canopy of delicate foliage.

According to legend, this botanical rarity is more than two hundred years old. It was here when Captain Cook dropped anchor in 1778, when the Hawaiian monarchy was deposed over a hundred years later, when Pearl Harbor was attacked, and when the first casualties from Vietnam arrived. Its gnarled silver-gray trunk and branches twist skyward in an appropriately anguished gesture.

"Hi there," Kate calls out with an enthusiastic wave as I approach. She looks different. Faded jeans and T-shirt have replaced the tailored suit. Her carefully groomed hair now tumbles in soft curls to her shoulders. Designer sunglasses serve as a headband, keeping it away from her face.

"Hi," I reply, forcing a smile, as I straddle the lounger opposite her. "Good to see you."

"I'm relieved," she says with a disarming smile. "I thought maybe it was something I said."

"Sorry. A shower does wonders for my disposition."

"So? Did you get the soldier's name?"

"Yes, yes I did."

"That's great."

"Sure is."

"Sure is? That's it? You don't sound very excited."

"Well, you were right. The guy was AWOL. Turns out he was a drug smuggler who was being hunted by the DEA. He stole my ID to escape."

She cocks her head to one side with uncertainty. "Come on, you're putting me on?"

"I wish I was."

"Oh, that's just awful. I'm really sorry."

"It gets better," I say, looking around nervously. Directly beyond the hau tree is a public walkway that runs along the top of the seawall, connecting the hotels. A steady stream of pedestrians in attire ranging from wet suits and string bikinis to blazers with ascots parade in both directions. I have visions of Surigao walking right past us and calmly blowing my brains out without breaking stride. A pistol with a silencer rolled up in a large beach towel would do the job nicely. "I'm not even sure we should be sitting out here like this."

"What do you mean?"

"You know how it is when you start turning over rocks. You keep it up long enough you eventually hit one with a snake under it."

"I still don't follow you. I'm sorry, I guess I'm not very good at reading between the lines."

"Somebody's trying to kill me."

She freezes, the color draining from her face as she mouths the word Why?

"Good question." I imagine she knows Carla, maybe even her husband, and I'm curious what her reaction would be, but I keep the CIL out of it for now and go on to explain about Nancy being killed by 'people' who were out to get me.

Kate Ackerman's eyes are glistening with emotion when I finish, her expression a mixture of sadness and fear. "I don't know what to say," she whispers.

"How about, I'm pissed off because you're raining on my parade?" I suggest, trying to lighten the mood. "I'm sorry. I really shouldn't be saying any of this."

"It's okay. Really. My parade's tomorrow."

"Thanks. If you don't mind, I'd feel more secure in there." I nod in the direction of the open-air restaurant and bar behind us.

We make the move. I select a table that's against the wall. An attractive Eurasian waitress materializes. Kate orders a vodka martini. So do I.

"The colonel gave me the impression you've been a little . . . impulsive . . . for lack of a better word," I begin as the waitress glides off.

"Perfect word. But what else could I do? The names were released. My husband's was one of them. I couldn't concentrate on work. I couldn't sleep. I mean, after waiting all these years it didn't make sense to be so anxious, but I was. I realized I was wasting my time fighting it, so I went with it." It comes out in a machine-gun burst of words and thoughts, all punctuated by animated gestures. Then her eyes suddenly widen in reaction to something she sees behind me. "Look," she says, awestruck. "God, look at that."

My gut tightens. I whirl, half expecting to see Surigao coming at me with a gun. Instead I'm blown away by shafts of neon pink and yellow light exploding across the sky, turning billowing clouds into mountains of cotton candy. It's a breathtaking sunset. They all are, in paradise. East Coast sophisticates that we were, the first time Nancy and I came here, we joked about their being a cliché, but each day the sunset was more incredible than the last, and we started calling each other to see them.

Kate digs a small camera out of her purse—one of those aim and shoot types—and takes a couple of shots of the sunset. We watch in silence as the fireball slips below the horizon and the trade winds come up, gently rustling the trees.

"It's really kind of strange when you think about it," I finally say.

"What's that?"

"Where we find ourselves. I mean, you're anxious as hell to be told your husband is definitely, totally, beyond any doubt, officially dead. And me—I'm still having a hell of a time accepting that Nancy's gone, still hoping that tomorrow, or the next day, or the next, I'll wake up and find out it's all a bad dream."

She nods knowingly, achingly, then reacts to the tinkle of ice cubes as the waitress brings our drinks.

"Here's to you," Kate says, raising her glass and tapping it against mine.

"Here's to tomorrow."

"Thanks." She takes a long sip of the martini and looks off reflectively for a moment. "You know, when I was a kid, I had a dog. A big, old, dumb, clumsy mutt. Well, one day—"

"Me too. Called him Fenway."

She looks puzzled.

"I was a baseball nut."

She still looks puzzled.

"Fenway Park? Where the Red Sox play?"

She fishes the olive from her glass, pops it into her mouth, and shrugs.

"Nothing?"

"Nothing."

"You had a deprived childhood."

"Hey, all those years of 4-H competitions count for something."

"Four-H? Where'd you grow up?"

"Nebraska. Little town called Broken Bow."

"Broken Bow."

"Uh-huh. It's about twenty miles south of Victoria Springs. Anyway, getting back to my dog, we named him Hoover."

"As in President?"

"As in vacuum cleaner. I'd put down this huge bowl of food? Gone like that. Kibble, nuts and bolts—you name it he'd eat it." She pauses, and frowns sadly. "That was his undoing. Somebody poisoned him."

"No."

"Uh-huh. Found him lying out behind the corn silo. I was devastated."

"Who wouldn't be?"

"I just couldn't understand why anyone would do that to this sweet animal. I kept bugging my parents for answers. My dad kept telling me 'God works in mysterious ways.' Well, I didn't get another dog, let alone a better one, assuming that's what he meant.'' She splays her hands and breaks into a girlish giggle. "I mean, I didn't even get a date with Mick Jagger.''

"I could've told you that.''

"Right. You tell fortunes.''

"Well, this was before that. When I was growing up in Boston. People used to say the Lodges speak only to the Cabots and the Cabots speak only to God. Big family. God was a very busy guy. Didn't have time for people in Broken Bow.''

She laughs. "Well, I didn't have time for Him either, until John didn't come back from Vietnam. I mean, I didn't suddenly get religious or anything, but I caught myself saying it to my friends, to myself, even to my father—God works in mysterious ways. God works in mysterious ways.''

"Does He?''

She shrugs with uncertainty. "I don't know. Maybe. I mean, one day it dawned on me that even if my dad meant things'd get better, he didn't say when.''

"You're still waiting.''

"Sometimes you don't have a choice.''

"Maybe your time's finally come.''

"You bet,'' she says with an enthused smile. "Tomorrow.''

22

COLONEL WEBSTER SITS AT HIS DESK, HIS SHOULDERS sagging in profound disappointment.

I'm the cause of it.

I walked into his office on this bright, crystal clear morning and ruined it by reporting the address on Sullivan's driver's license turned out to be Golden Gate Mortuary Services. "Who's your contact there?" I ask, after he settles.

"I deal directly with the owner. A fellow named Jim Messina."

"That's who the police talked to. They're pretty sure he lied."

"Chrissakes," the colonel groans. "You can't trust your own mother any more. I mean, Jim and his wife have been guests in my home. We . . ." He groans again and lets it trail off in disgust.

"Maybe Messina isn't the owner." This isn't a new idea. It's the one that occurred to me during my call to Detective Daniels last night and has been simmering on the back burner since.

The colonel shrugs. He has a faraway look. This is really getting to him.

"You have any correspondence from Golden Gate handy?"

He nods thoughtfully.

"May I see it?"

"Oh, sure, sorry," he replies, coming out of it. He scoops up the phone and asks Mrs. Oldham to fetch the

Golden Gate file. He's barely hung up when she comes in with it.

"What do you need?" he asks, flopping it open.

"Anything with their letterhead."

He removes several documents and hands them to me.

I sort through them and zero in on a sheet of stationery. A graphic of the Golden Gate Bridge is centered above the company name at the top, but my attention is drawn to the bottom, to a single line of very small type that proclaims: *Golden Gate Mortuary Services, A Subsidiary of Franco-Asian Enterprises.*

"Find something?" the colonel asks, seeing my expression change.

"Maybe. Who's Franco-Asian Enterprises?"

"Never heard of them."

I hand him the letter and point it out.

He frowns, sheepishly. "I never really noticed that. Our contract is with Golden Gate."

"Not surprising."

"You think they're involved in this?"

"Just a feeling. It shouldn't take very long to see if I'm right."

"What do you think's going on?"

"What those of us in the trade call a corporate shell game. You have a fax machine?"

"Mrs. O," he replies, gesturing outside.

Now I make the call to my office that I couldn't make last night. "Grace, it's me. Making some headway. Listen, check the IRL and fax me whatever you find on a Franco-Asian Enterprises. I'm at the CIL. No, the Colonel's secretary'll give it to you."

"IRL?" Webster drawls after I hang up.

"Information Research Library. It's a corporate data base my staff's put together from 10-Ks, D-and-Bs, journals, foreign registries. It's sort of an ongoing project."

The colonel nods and drifts off in thought. "Did a lot of thinking last night . . ."

"And?"

"There's a DEA guy we've been working with. He's smart, discrete—I think I'm going to run this mess past him. See what he thinks."

GREG DINALLO

"You're already working with the DEA?" I ask, taken by surprise.

"Not how you think. A lot of MIAs were lost in opium-growing provinces in Laos. Luang Prabang and Houa Phan mostly."

"Pathet Lao country," I say, picturing the two adjoining provinces in the northeastern sector.

"Uh-huh. The farmers up there grow tons of opium every year at the expense of feeding their people. As part of their antinarcotics activities, the DEA's been working with the Lao Government to get them to switch to edible crops instead."

"In exchange for cooperation on repatriations."

"Among the other more obvious reasons. It's a subtle linkage, but it seems to be working. The entire area's of prime interest from a POW/MIA standpoint."

I'm digesting all this when Mrs. Oldham enters with the faxes from my office. As I suspected, they reveal that Franco-Asian Enterprises is a privately held corporation, and that the major stockholder, the guy at the helm, is named—Phillipe Ajacier.

"Then he does own Golden Gate Mortuaries," the colonel says.

"Since '62, when he bought it from the original owners. About fifteen years ago he sold it to Messina, immediately set-up Franco-Asian, and bought it back."

"He sold it to himself."

I nod and take a moment to study the faxes. "Along with Golden Gate and the Theater Arts Complex here, he has interests in a company called Oak Creek Springs—that's a California winery, Thonburi Film Studios in Bangkok, Trans-Asian Shipping in Manila, a Montreal-based motel chain, and a French ski wear manufacturer."

"I thought privately held companies didn't have to make that kind of stuff public."

"If they're owned by Americans. The rules for foreigners are different."

"Foreigners? Where's Ajacier from?"

"Corsica."

"As in the Island of?"

"Uh-huh."

170

"You realize what that means?"

"Sure as hell do."

Anyone who spent time in-country knew that all the bars and whorehouses in Saigon were run by Corsicans. And to most of us, it was no secret they also ran the drug trade. The colonel and I are absorbing the impact in silence when the intercom buzzes.

"Yes, Mrs. O?" the colonel answers. "Good. Show her into the conference room, will you? Yes, I'll just be a few minutes." He hangs up and takes a moment to collect his thoughts before softly announcing, "Mrs. Ackerman's here."

"Oh, that's right."

"By the way," he says casually, as he fetches an expandable manila folder from a file drawer, "she manage to reach you yesterday?"

"Yes, as a matter of fact we had dinner. I meant to thank you."

"Good. Good, I like Kate."

"So do I. Please, I know how important this is to her. I don't want to keep you."

"Frankly, Mr. Morgan, I was hoping you'd join us."

I didn't expect that. I'm caught completely off guard. "Gee, I—I mean, you sure it'd be okay?"

"Of course. I wouldn't have suggested it if I didn't. Besides, I could use a hand." He takes a box used to store files from the sideboard behind his desk and hands it to me. Then he tucks the manila folder under his arm, heads out the door and down the corridor at a brisk pace toward the conference room.

"Good to see you, Kate," Webster enthuses as we enter. He sets the folder on the long table and hugs her. "Sorry to keep you waiting."

She's glowing with expectation. "What's a couple of minutes after twenty-one years?"

"I thought you might like the idea of having Mr. Morgan here." The colonel pauses, setting up the punch line. "I mean, I may be mistaken but I'm pretty sure I remember you mentioning he's an old friend?"

"Did I say that?" Kate replies, good-naturedly. Then, the light in her eyes fades as she senses the true tenor of

171

the moment and stiffens with uncertainty. "Why? Am I going to need one?"

"I'm afraid so," Webster confesses softly, getting down to business. "We don't have John's remains. I'm sorry."

She pales, her posture slackening. The colonel directs her to the table and pulls out a chair. She literally sits on the edge, legs entwined, hands clasped tightly in her lap.

I set the file box on the table next to the folder and squeeze her shoulder reassuringly.

"How could this happen?" she finally asks in a fragile whisper, her fingers toying nervously with her MIA bracelet.

"It's a strange one, Kate," Webster replies. He opens the manila folder and begins removing the contents. "As you know, a number of weeks ago, the Lao Government released the names of nine men whose remains had been retrieved from crash sites. John's name was one of them and per policy you were notified. When the repatriations were made, we received identification for all nine. Again you were notified."

She nods numbly, her eyes riveted to the plastic bags the colonel has placed on the table. They contain a single dog tag, a military identification card, some family snapshots, and a piece of flight suit material that includes part of the breast pocket and name tag above it. I can make out the letters ACKE—the remainder have been burned and are illegible.

The colonel opens the cardboard box and lifts out a pilot's flight helmet, which he places on the table. The shell is blistered and charred, the plastic visor warped, the chin strap a blackened cinder.

Kate shudders at the sight of it.

"Unfortunately," Webster goes on, "we only received seven sets of remains." His eyes shift to mine briefly, as if alerting me to the impact of what he's about to say, then return to Kate's. "Frankly, we knew John's wouldn't be among them."

Her head jerks up toward Webster in reaction.

So does mine.

"What do you mean by that?" she asks, her voice cracking from the tension.

"As you know, his Phantom was hit by a surface-to-air missile."

Kate nods with impatience.

"Despite reports to the contrary, both crewmen ejected and survived."

"What?" she exclaims astonished.

Webster nods. "Lieutenant Fuchs, your husband's radar officer, was among the POWs released during Operation Homecoming in '73. That's how we know what happened."

Kate is rocked. It takes her a moment to recover, then her eyes flare with anger. "You've known for nineteen years that John survived? Why wasn't I told?! What the hell ever happened to full and immediate disclosure?!"

Webster knew this was coming. He absorbs the blows without taking offense, patiently waiting until she's finished and settled before explaining, "The mission was classified."

"Aw, for Godsakes," Kate groans, disgusted, burying her head in her hands momentarily before glaring at him. "And now all of a sudden, it isn't?!"

"That's right," the colonel replies evenly. "In keeping with policies designed to induce the Laos to cooperate on repatriations, more and more of these things are being acknowledged."

"I've been hanging around here for a week, getting my hopes up, thinking it was all finally coming to an—" Her voice breaks. She pauses, her lower lip quivering. "You knew all this, dammit. Why'd you make me wait?"

"I'm sorry, Kate. I couldn't say anything until all the other identifications were verified. You know the rules."

Her lips tighten, then she nods grudgingly.

The colonel's face is ashen and drawn. He looks at me uncomfortably, clearly feeling her pain.

"If I may, Colonel?" I interject gently.

"Please."

"I'm a little confused. I mean, how could Captain Ackerman's flight helmet and ID be found at a crash site if he ejected?"

"According to Lieutenant Fuchs' statement, it was a night mission—pitch black, no moon. After they bailed out and regrouped, it occurred to Captain Ackerman there was a pretty good chance their chutes hadn't been spotted. He knew the enemy would search the crash site in the morning and figured it'd be smart to make it look like the crew had perished."

"Less chance of being hunted down."

"Precisely. He and Fuchs made their way to the wreckage, tossed their flight helmets and chute harnesses into the flames, then left some pieces of clothing and ID strewn about the area."

Kate straightens with pride and smiles, then her eyes narrow thoughtfully. "They released Lieutenant Fuchs. Why not John?"

"We don't know for a fact that he was ever taken prisoner, Kate. Fuchs said they were spotted by an enemy patrol and became separated. Fuchs was captured. We don't know what happened to John."

"All these years," Kate finally whispers to no one in particular. Her fingers tremble as she takes one of the envelopes from the table and removes her husband's military identification card.

The heat-sealed plastic is partially blistered, but looking over her shoulder I can see the photo clearly. It's of a handsome young man with a thatch of dark, wavy hair, a confident smile, and sense of adventure in his eyes.

Kate studies it for a long moment. Tears roll down her cheeks as she presses it to her bosom and goes to the window, sobbing softly. After a moment, she bolts and hurries from the conference room.

Webster and I are frozen in place. Finally he nods to me and gestures to the door. "I think she's going to need a friend."

It takes a moment for it to sink in, but as I go after Kate, I suddenly understand what the colonel's been up to. I'm the safeguard, the emotional insulation, the way he's chosen to protect himself from this one. Despite the distractions, despite Carla's disappointing betrayal and the Surigao-Ajacier-Messina conspiracy, despite the threat of his reputation—as well as the CIL's—being tarnished by a drug smuggling scandal not of his doing, the colonel never lost sight of his primary mission, of the fact that he would have to deal with Kate, and that, being friends, she would expect him to comfort her. He'd be going after her if I wasn't here. But I am. And he has made a match, just not for the traditional purpose.

I come out of the main building and hurry through the gate, scanning the acres of macadam that stretch to the seawall. I spot a lone figure in the distance, silhouetted against the sky, walking with a determined stride between the piers, head thrown back in anger. There's no doubt it's Kate, and I start jogging to catch up with her. When I finally do, she glances over at me without breaking stride, then keeps walking in silence. We continue along the waterfront like this for several minutes before her pace slows.

"You sure hang in there," she finally says. "I give you that."

"That's what the A stands for."

"What?"

"Adamant."

She scowls in mock disapproval. "What are you doing here?"

"Making sure you're okay."

"That's what I was afraid of. Thanks. I'm fine."

"Didn't look that way back there."

"Hey, it's my own fault, okay? The colonel warned me. I knew better. I jumped the gun and did my thing anyway. I mean, you have any idea how many people I've counseled against doing exactly, I mean exactly, what I did? I'm disgusted with myself."

"Not always easy to practice what we—"

"Sure, and next I suppose you'll be telling me God works in mysterious ways."

"Well, things do have a way of—"

"Don't. Please don't say it, Morgan. You're starting to sound just like my father. Okay?"

"Okay."

We continue walking along the seawall. The air is ripe with the smell of salt and creosote. Kate seems deep in thought. My mind drifts to her husband's picture. The confident smile is a frightened stare now. He's trapped, desperate, being hunted in the jungle like an animal. I'm imagining an enemy patrol closing in on him . . . when a boat whistle pierces the silence, pulling me out of it.

"Is this what you usually do when you're upset? I mean walk like this."

"I'm not upset," Kate replies sharply. "I'm making a decision."

"About what?"

"Going over there."

"Over where?"

"Thailand."

"Thailand? What for?"

"Look for John. He was based there."

I'm somewhat stunned and not sure how to react. "You mean you think he's still alive?"

"I have no proof he's dead. You know there've been over fourteen hundred sightings of live Americans. Most have been resolved. But there're still about sixty or so that haven't."

"Those are pretty long odds."

"Only ones I've got."

"Well, for what it's worth, I'm not sure this is the best time to be making these decisions. Live with it awhile. Think it through. I mean you're going to be dealing with a whole other culture. The language alone is—"

"De chan hu té Kungthep khoub nung peé."

"Pardon me?"

"That's Thai," she replies with a little grin. "I said, 'I lived in Bangkok for almost a year.' "

"I walked right into that one, didn't I?"

"Khow chai na cee."

"Which means?"

"Loosely translated—'You bet your ass you did.' "

I can't help laughing.

"That was a lot of years ago," she goes on. "Nineteen seventy-five. It's hard to explain the feelings I had. I mean, the war was so, so remote. When John didn't come back I didn't have anything, no places, no images, nothing real that I could grab on to and put away. It wasn't just me. Most of the MIA wives I knew had this 'thing,' this emotional drive to be where it happened."

"You mean the exact spot?"

"If possible. Some of them pulled it off, too. I didn't, but a few who were able to find out where the crash site was hired private guides and helicopters and spent some time there."

"Did it help?"

"I think so. Yes. Of course, now the League's totally opposed to free-lance excursions."

"I picked up on that."

"Can't say I blame them. No matter how well motivated, one irresponsible act can set back negotiations for years. The Rambos, the Bo Gritzes, they're really bad news."

"What was the government's attitude?"

"Our government? In those days, they weren't doing anything on the issue except sweeping it under the rug. Even when they finally got into it, nothing really happened for a while. It was pure torture. I mean every time the phone rang, or a piece of mail with an official return address came, my heart would start racing, and then . . ." She shrugs and adds, "Back to square one."

A high-pitched whine rises in the distance. It comes from a military jet taking off from Hickam Air Force Base across the lagoon. The sleek fighter streaks down the runway and, in a matter of seconds, is soaring directly overhead, pounding us with its thundering roar. Kate stops walking and watches as it climbs into the sun, then she sits atop the seawall.

"Anyway," she resumes as I settle next to her, "I was getting sick and tired of waiting for word that never came. I get hyper. I like to be in control of things. I'm not very good at standing around while other people who are supposed to be doing something aren't. I heard about some families who had gone over there and gotten information from villagers and refugees, and I finally packed up and went."

"Make any headway?"

"Not really. I was desperate and naive. I fell prey to every crackpot scheme. There were all kinds of people working these scams. Still are. The League and the DIA, that's the Defense Intelligence Agency, spend a lot of time debunking them. There's this one guy over there, a retired Air Force colonel, who keeps sending letters to MIA families claiming he's real close to obtaining the release of live POWs, but he's running short of funds and has to raise fifty thousand dollars by tomorrow to buy their freedom or else they'll be killed. The last letter said his boat had been wrecked by a hurricane and he needs money to repair it. The League found out it hasn't been out of port in over two years and the last hurricane in that area was in '87. I never had a run-in with him, but before I made those connections I was telling you about, I bought a lot of information about crash and burial sites. Paid people to take me to them, too."

"And they turned out to be phony."

"Of course. Somebody even tried to sell me bones once."

"Bones?"

"Yes, a box of bones. Can you believe it? I didn't fall for that one." She laughs softly and emits a reflective sigh. "Going to Bangkok probably wasn't the smartest thing I ever did. But it satisfied that itch to do something."

"I understand."

"I thought you might. All John's letters came from a place called Udon Thani. It's up north near the Laotian border. I never really understood what he was doing until I got there."

"The war in Laos."

She nods solemnly. "It was a big secret at the time. Like the colonel said, we're just starting to acknowledge our involvement."

It was no secret to me. For almost thirteen years—1960 through 1973—the United States fought to save Laos from being taken over by the North Vietnamese and Pathet Lao forces who had completely ignored the Geneva Accords, which guaranteed its neutrality. For the most part, we provided air support for government troops in the northern provinces, where Vientiane, the capitol, and other major cities—Luang Prabang, Xieng Khouang, and Sam Neua among them—are located. This military action took place far from the Ho Chi Minh Trail along the South Vietnamese border—where U.S. air and ground forces were also fighting to stem the flow of North Vietnamese troops and supplies to the south, where the majority of men missing in Laos were lost, and where I was wounded.

"To make a long story short," Kate goes on, "I learned

the ropes, got to know the customs, made some contacts. All the government agencies worked out of the embassy. Still do. I got to know a lot of people."

"They were helpful even though the lid was on and you were there unofficially?"

"It was different once you got over there. It always comes down to individuals. The CIL was based there at the time. The colonel was terrific."

"You two do go way back."

"Uh-huh. I also worked with a guy in the embassy's communications section. He seemed to be more involved in getting information than any of the others. Set me up with what proved to be two very valuable contacts."

"Communications. Probably CIA."

"I don't know. Maybe. I never asked him. Really sweet guy." She pauses reflectively, deciding whether or not she'll share the rest with me. "He kept asking me to go out with him, but I couldn't get involved in a relationship. Some wives had no trouble handling it. To tell you the truth, I envied them. But I just couldn't. It's still hard." She takes a deep breath and exhales loudly. "I guess I'm kind of weird that way."

"I don't think you're weird, Kate."

Her eyes lower demurely.

A wave breaks against the seawall, showering us with spray. Another crests and comes rolling in. We scramble to safety and start walking back in the direction of the CIL.

"So, you're going to go over there and do what? Make all the same mistakes again?"

"No, I'm older and wiser now."

"Sounds like famous last words to me."

"Hey, I meant what I said about having contacts, Morgan. One of them was a guide. An American serviceman who'd stayed over there after the war ended. He helped a lot of families who came looking for men who were lost. The other was a Bangkok businessman. He did a lot of refugee work. You know, brought them out, got them jobs. In the process he asked them about things that happened in their villages during the war. We've gotten a lot of POW/MIA information that way. I'm going to start with him."

"You're really serious about this."

She nods, her jaw set, her eyes hardening with determination.

"Well, good luck, Mrs. Ackerman."

"Thanks. What're you going to do?"

That stops me. I haven't really had a chance to give it much thought, not today anyway. Now Kate's forced me to think about it. My mind has just begun working the problem when my gut tightens and I hear myself say, "What I came here to do. Find the bastard who killed my wife."

23

I'M IN THE ELEVATOR AT THE HALEKULANI.

After we returned to the CIL, Kate stayed to go over some documents with the colonel. I took a taxi back to the hotel.

I get off at nine and walk down the corridor to my room, thinking about the answer I gave her. It was bravado, no more than wishful thinking at best. If I'm honest with myself, I'd admit it's going to take much more than determination to find Sean Surigao. I've no idea where he is. I don't even know if he's on Oahu. He could easily be on one of the other islands, the mainland, or anywhere in the world for that matter.

The card key performs it's magic and the door pops open with a precise electronic click. I cross the room, toss my jacket and attaché on the bed, then roll back the floor-to-ceiling shutters. The room floods with light as I step out onto the balcony. I'm leaning against the rail, looking out across the grounds to the sea, working the problem, when I hear a voice. Distant and pleasantly haunting, it fills my head with familiar sounds and makes me smile. Nancy's voice.

Cal? Cal, I've given this situation a lot of thought, and I really think you should let the authorities handle it, she says evenly, reasoning with me as always in her calm, self-assured tone. *Really. It's time to get on with your life. Besides, you shouldn't be neglecting your business like this. Not to mention our daughters. They both need you. Depend on you. God knows, now more than ever. I know how you feel, Cal, but if you search your heart, I'm sure you'll find that A doesn't have to stand for avenge.*

It's good advice.

I'm tempted to take it, tempted to leave Surigao and the rest of this mess to the colonel, the DEA, and the police, and return to Los Angeles. Whatever I decide, it dawns on me that I haven't spoken to the girls in a couple of days. It's time to touch base and let them know what's going on.

I take the phone from the writing desk. It has a long cord, allowing it to be used on the balcony. I settle in the lounger and call Laura. Her roommate tells me she's in class. I leave a message that everything's okay, then dial Janie's number in Arizona. The line's busy. Janie's line is always busy. I spend a few minutes wrestling with my decision, to no avail. So, I try Janie again. As I hoped, the hotel phone has a last number redial button. Good thing, because her line's still busy. I try several more times and am about to press redial again when I pause, my finger hovering above the button as an idea regarding Surigao's whereabouts strikes me. It's a long shot, but I won't be able to look into it once I leave Hawaii, and I know I'll always wonder. I hang up, go down to the lobby, get in a taxi, and ask the driver to take me to the Theater Arts Complex.

Ten minutes later I'm stuck in a traffic jam, but I can see the distinctive, sawtoothed rooftops in the distance.

"That's it, isn't it?" I prompt the driver. "It can't be more than a few blocks."

"Yes, but you can't get there from here," he says resignedly, reciting what he explains is the unofficial motto of Waikiki's gridlocked drivers—taxi or otherwise.

I pay the fare and walk the rest of the way, taking the elevator to the top floor of the main theater building. The manager's on the phone when I enter his office. He waves me in with a big smile, and cuts the call short. "Well, Mr. Morgan, very good to see you again," he says effusively as he comes around the desk and shakes my hand.

"Good to see you too. Somehow I get the feeling you haven't rented the place yet."

"Well, we've had some very serious inquiries," he cautions, gravely. "Needless to say, I'll be more than happy to tell them the unit's been leased."

"I'm afraid my wife had a few questions I couldn't answer. I thought I'd take another look at it before deciding."

"Of course." He fetches the key from the cabinet behind the ornate mirror and turns toward the door.

"There's no need for you to hike all the way over there," I say, intercepting him. "I'm sure I'll have no trouble finding it."

"I'll be waiting, agreement and pen in hand," he says, dropping the key into my outstretched palm.

The elevator deposits me in the lobby. I cross the courtyard and make my way between the buildings to the waterfront condominiums, my hair blowing in the trade winds coming off the water, my hand in my pocket grasping the Beretta. I approach the entrance, looking about cautiously. In the event one or both of the Surigaos have returned for some reason, I ring the doorbell, then go to the window from where I observed the interior last time.

No one responds.

I return to the front door, unlock it, and step inside, going to the kitchen where I recall seeing a wall phone. Does it have a redial button? Is it still in service? I lift the handset apprehensively. Yes, there's a dial tone and the word redial neatly lettered beneath one of the buttons. I press it and listen to the electronic tones being replayed. Then it starts ringing, three, four, five times.

"Pizza Hut, Kalakaua," a weary voice finally growls.

"Oh. Sorry, I'm afraid I dialed the wrong number."

The guy hangs up on me.

I drop the handset onto the hook and stand there for a moment, reasonably certain the only connection the Surigaos have to Pizza Hut is hunger. I'm coping with the disappointment when I vaguely recall seeing another phone someplace. The desk. The one I'd searched. I make my way to the wall of built-ins in the den and lower the hinged writing surface. There's a phone inside, and like the other, it has a redial button. There are many more tones this time. I lose count at thirteen. This isn't a local number. The ring is a series of harsh, pulsating buzzes.

A woman answers. In a soft, lilting voice she says something that sounds like, "Deuce it than he save thee." Several more phrases in the tonal cadence of an Asian language follow. It's not Vietnamese, which I'd recognize.

"Excuse me, do you speak English?"

"Of course, sir," she replies in an Australian accent. "How may I help you?"

"Well, for openers, I'm not sure I have the right number. Who am I speaking to?"

"This is the reception desk at the Dusit Thani Hotel, sir."

"Yes, of course. I need to know where you're located, please?"

"Nine-forty-six Rama IV Road just across the canal from Sala Daeng Circle. It's a white building with a golden spire on the roof. It sort of resembles a large pagoda. I'm sure you'll have no trouble finding it."

"I'm sorry. I meant in what country?"

"Oh. Thailand, sir. Bangkok, Thailand."

I swallow hard, trying to suppress my reaction. "Ah, I thought that's where they said they were going. I was right after all. I'd like to speak with one of your guests—a Mr. Surigao?"

"Mr. Surigao? I'm sorry, I believe I saw them leaving a short time ago."

"You mean they've checked out?"

"Oh, no. We expect them to be with us for a while longer. Would you like to leave a message, sir?"

"No, thank you. That won't be necessary . . ." I hang up before adding, "I'll deliver it personally."

My fist tightens in triumph, but my pulse rate is surprisingly steady now. It's my mind that's racing, making the connections: Surigao—Actor—Bangkok—Thonburi Film Studios—Ajacier. I remain in the condo long enough to get the number of the Sheraton Waikiki from information and call Kate Ackerman. She's not in her room. I try the CIL next. Mrs. Oldham says she left about twenty minutes ago, which means she's probably en route to the hotel. I return the keys to the manager and make a beeline for the taxi stand at the entrance to the Theater Arts Complex. Then, with visions of being caught in another traffic jam, I reverse direction and start walking.

About fifteen minutes later, I'm in the Sheraton's lobby: massive dated gold-veined mirrors and glitzy chandeliers, corridors going off in every direction lined with boutiques, and airline and car rental desks. I call Kate's room from a house phone. The line's busy. I take the elevator to her floor, hurry down the corridor, and knock on the door.

"Kate? Kate, it's Cal Morgan."

I knock several more times before the door opens.

"Oh, hi," she says, a little surprised. "Sorry, I was on the phone. Come on in."

I follow her into the room. It's a clean, simply furnished tourist accommodation that faces the apartment building across the street.

She sweeps her eyes over me and frowns curiously. "You okay?"

"Couldn't be better. Why?"

"You seem a little hyper."

"I have good reason to be."

"You found the guy?"

"Sure did. In a hotel in Bangkok."

"Oh?"

"He and his wife. She works at the CIL. I think you know her. Carla Surigao?"

"Carla?" she repeats slack-jawed.

"The one and only," I reply, going on to brief Kate on the Surigao's involvement: that Carla had tipped her husband to my inquiry, that he's the one who's out to kill me, that there's some kind of drug smuggling connection.

She stares at me in stunned silence when I finish. "Gosh," she finally says. "That's really strange. I mean, I don't know him at all. But Carla's the nicest person you'd ever want to meet."

"Haven't had the pleasure. Anything else you can tell me about her?"

"Not really. We've only met a few times. Here several years ago, and on occasion at the meetings in Washington. She's very easy to get along with. The kind of person who'll go out of her way to help you."

"Yes, even to kill someone." Kate shrugs, mystified. "Do you need a visa to get into Thailand?"

"Not for a short stay."

"How short?"

"Up to fifteen days, I think."

"You give any more thought to going?"

She breaks into a wry smile and nods. "I was just talking to that businessman in Bangkok I told you about. He couldn't believe it when I told him John had survived. He said he's going to check his files for new information."

"Does that mean you're going?"

She hesitates briefly, then nods.

"When?"

She smiles and fetches a pad from the desk. "There's a flight every night at eight-thirty," she replies, referring to her notes. "Gets into Bangkok at nine-fifteen in the morning. There are also several that leave daily between eight and noon, but I'd rather not waste a day."

"I can't afford to. Mind some company?"

"No. But I'd prefer traveling with someone who wasn't being hunted by assassins."

"I gave that a lot of thought on the way over here. I wouldn't have suggested it if I didn't think it was safe."

"Want to tell me why?"

"I'm pretty sure they think I'm dead. I mean, I've been expecting them to come at me again and they haven't. It finally dawned on me that Surigao wouldn't have left Los Angeles, let alone gone to Bangkok, unless he thought he'd gotten me."

"Seems to make sense."

"I'm counting on it. It gives me an advantage. So if you don't mind traveling with a dead man—"

"I think I can handle it. By the way, do you have your passport with you?"

"Always. I've got several international clients. You never know. Get us some reservations on the eight-thirty. Make 'em first-class."

"Whoa. That's way out of my league, Morgan."

"I'll cover the difference. You have a place where you stay?"

"I know a hotel."

"It isn't the Dusit Thani, is it?

"No. Way too expensive. You want to stay there?"

"Any place but there. Long as it's first-class."

Her head tilts to one side as if something's dawned on her. "You're rich, aren't you?"

"Comfortable. I don't see you worrying about getting back to the office."

"I watch what I spend. I have some savings."

"So do I. So does Donald Trump—"

"*Did.*"

"What I make in a year still wouldn't cover his phone bill. I figure you only go around once. Why not enjoy it as much as you can?"

"Yes, why the hell not?" she says, brightening. "The Oriental's probably the best, then there's—"

"We'll stay there. See if you can get us a couple of rooms."

"Hey," she protests with a troubled frown. "I'm not your secretary, Morgan."

"Thank God."

"That cuts both ways, mister."

"Feel better now?"

"Much."

"Good. This is no time to take offense. You're the expert here, Kate. I'm acknowledging it."

She studies me, and breaks into a little smile. "That's pretty good."

"I meant it."

Kate goes to work on the phone. I return to my hotel and do the same, reviewing business projects with the office and briefing my daughters on my plans. Then I make a quick trip to a bookstore just down the street and buy a travel guide to Bangkok, spending the rest of the afternoon reading it.

Hours later, the island is shrouded in darkness as our flight takes off from Honolulu International and makes a big looping turn out over the Pacific, leaving Waikiki's glittering lights behind.

Kate and I are comfortably settled in the first-class compartment of the stretched 747. Singapore girls are rustling about the aisles in their sarongs. The laptop is at my feet, the Beretta concealed inside. The foldout map that came with the travel guide is spread over my tray table. It delineates highways, streets, canals, places of interest, train stations, and major hotels in great detail. I'm interested in the Oriental, on the Chao Phraya River, which meanders through the center of the city. The Dusit Thani is slightly more than two miles away at the far end of a nearby canal.

I'm circling these locations when Kate glances over and offhandedly asks, "By the way, how'd you leave things with the colonel?"

"Unsettled. He's going to run it past someone he's been working with before making any decisions."

"That someone wouldn't be with the DEA, would he?"

"How do you know about that?"

"The League. It was in one of our newsletters. We're hoping the crop substitution program helps when it comes to repatriations."

"Yes, the colonel mentioned that. He said a lot of MIAs were lost in opium-producing regions."

"A hundred thirty or so—less the seven that were just repatriated."

"I didn't realize they were lost up there."

"Uh-huh."

"You sure about the number?"

"I'm the unofficial expert, remember? Why?"

"Sounds like a lot. I mean, out of five hundred forty-seven that's more than twenty percent. Twenty-three point seven six six to be precise."

"I'm positive. I've always cross-referenced who was lost when and where on my mailing lists so I could connect families who wanted to share information. You know, stuff from letters home, stories from buddies, anything that might help them cope."

"This list on a computer?"

"Uh-huh, at home."

"I can think of a few calculations I wouldn't mind running."

"Why?"

"My guy was in the drug business—might be some kind of a connection."

"Then you better get that thing booted up," she challenges, taking a thin plastic case from her handbag. It contains a high-density 3½" computer diskette. "I always have a backup with me. God forbid the house burns to the ground, twenty years of work won't go up in smoke along with it."

"I know the feeling."

"What kind of software you use?"

"All of 'em. Great bridge program too. You play?"

"No. Sorry. It's WordPerfect, by the way."

"Good. I'll hang on to this, if you don't mind."

"We've more than ten hours to go. Why wait?"

I let out a long breath, then leaning close to her, I cover my mouth and explain about the Beretta.

Kate's eyes widen in surprise. All of a sudden she's not sure what to make of me. She's about to say something when a flight attendant approaches, handing out blankets and pillows in preparation for the long haul to Bangkok. My itch to get at the data is about to be satisfied. I drape the blanket over my chest and legs, then slip the computer from the carrying case and pull it onto my lap.

"What're you doing?" Kate whispers.

"Changing the battery."

She rolls her eyes and looks away.

My fingers find the access panel and open it. I remove the pistol and slip it into my pocket, then dispense with the blanket, retrieve the battery from the carrying case, and insert it.

Minutes later, I've got the probability analysis program working with Kate's diskette in the "A" drive. I extract the MIA losses by province—547 men spread over 16 provinces—and graph them. In 14 out of 16 the deviations are within the range of statistical acceptability, even in southern provinces along the Ho Chi Minh Trail where the greatest number of losses occurred. But Luang Prabang and Houa Phan approach the top of the graph. I break the losses down into the subtotals—136 for Houa Phan and Luang Prabang combined, and 411 for the remaining 14, then calculate the per province ratio—137:2 × 410:14— which works out to 68.5 to 29.285.

"Hmm . . . ," I say, making another calculation.

"Hmm?"

"We're looking at a deviation of two point three three nine between the two opium-producing provinces and all the others."

"That's important?"

"Could be. In my business anything varying from the norm that much sends up a flag. But I need more data to determine the significance."

"Like what?"

"Number of ground forces deployed; number of missions flown—"

"Don't look at me."

"The number of MIAs repatriated to date from each province would be a start."

"From each? Would you believe less then forty from all of Laos?"

"I had no idea. I'm afraid it's not much help."

She nods, then cocks her head thoughtfully. "You know, now that you mention it, there's something that's always bothered me."

"What's that?"

"Well, these guys were lost in the so-called secret war, right?"

"Right."

"The way I understand it, when it comes to secret wars, or secret missions, we always make a special effort to get our dead and wounded out."

"Yes, so they can't be used to prove we've been there. We had a hard and fast rule in Special Ops: Never, never leave any evidence behind."

"That's my point. Information on men who were lost in Laos was easy to come by because it was used in enemy propaganda campaigns."

"But nothing on the guys lost in Luang Prabang and Houa Phan," I say, sensing where she's headed.

"Nothing much. Especially in Houa Phan."

"Like they never existed."

"I know one did," she says wistfully.

I notice her eyes starting to glisten, and direct her attention to the screen to take her mind off it. "What's with these names?"

"They're next of kin."

"I know. I meant the asterisk."

"Oh, it means deceased."

"Sorry I asked."

"Hey, it's okay. Really. Parents, wives, even children sometimes, pass away. I have to keep track of it. I lost a good friend about five years ago."

"MIA wife?"

"Wrote the book. Made me look like I was standing still. I mean, always pressing, always at the CIL, always digging for information. Off to Thailand every chance she got. A real gadfly."

"What happened to her?"

"She was up north somewhere. Probably trying to get into Laos. Went off the road in a monsoon."

"She was killed in an automobile accident?"

Kate nods matter-of-factly.

"Where was her husband lost?"

"Houa Phan. Same as John. One of the reasons we became close." A moment passes before it dawns on her, before she turns to me with a spooky look in her eyes. "I've got this weird feeling all of a sudden."

"I know."

"Maybe it's the connection you're looking for."

I shrug, trying to keep it in perspective. "Then again it might be we're seeing conspiracies everywhere. Remember, my guy wasn't anywhere near those areas."

"True," she says wearily.

"It's been a long day. Let's get some rest."

She sighs, then pulls the blanket up around her shoulders and turns her head into the pillow. "Good night," she says softly.

"Good night, Kate." I shut down the laptop, and settle in for the night. The cabin lights dim. Air hisses quietly past the fuselage. A half hour later, I'm still awake, staring at the ceiling. The numbers are inconclusive, and the loss scenarios don't match, but I can't help thinking that maybe Kate's right. Maybe I'm not the first.

24

I'M ON MY SECOND CUP OF COFFEE, WATCHING THE MIST rising like incense from the dense jungle below. I was awake most of the night planning what I'm going to do when I finally catch up with Surigao. This trip came out of nowhere and this is the first chance I've had to really think it through. I can never sleep on planes anyway. Evidently, Kate didn't get much sleep either. She's uncharacteristically quiet and has a steaming courtesy towel pressed to her forehead.

According to the captain, we're on final approach to Don Muang International Airport, which is about sixteen miles north of Bangkok. We've covered 6,700 miles in just under thirteen hours, crossing the international date line before making stops in Seoul and Taipei, then continuing west across the South China Sea, along the coast of Vietnam, finally turning north into the Gulf of Thailand toward Bangkok.

I've journeyed to this part of the world before. Nearly twenty-five years ago. The accommodations were military-class, not first. My destination was Vietnam, not Thailand. And my weapon was an M-16 semiautomatic rifle, not a .25-caliber toy hidden in a computer. My mission was search and destroy—that hasn't changed.

The local time is 9:35 A.M. when we touch down and taxi up to the ultramodern terminal. The boarding ramp swings into position and several hundred travel-weary tourists straggle into the lounge.

I've put the Beretta back inside the laptop as a precaution, but passport control turns out to be a tourist-friendly, if slow-moving, formality. The pistol could've easily stayed in my pocket. I make a quick stop in the men's room to remove it, then join Kate in the line at the currency exchange. The rate is twenty-five bahts to the dollar. Once properly funded, we claim our bags and head outside, making our way through a blast of ninety-degree heat and humidity to a taxi stand. The smiling dispatcher loads us and the bags into a cramped death-trap-on-wheels made in Korea.

I notice a vital piece of equipment is missing from the dash. "There's no meter," I whisper to Kate suspiciously.

"We negotiate the price," she replies as horns sound behind us. "Oriental Hotel, please?"

"Hundred fifty baht," the driver barks, pulling away with a screech of tires before Kate can counter.

That's six dollars, I calculate. I can't get home from LAX for less than forty. Dulles to D.C. is over thirty. I'm thinking it's a pretty good deal when Kate laces into the driver in fluent Thai and proceeds to bargain the price. He finally throws up a hand and settles.

"So what's the deal?" I prompt.

"He opened at a hundred fifty. I countered with seventy five. We closed at a hundred."

"Fixed or variable rate mortgage?"

"Come on. I saved us fifty bahts."

"That's two bucks."

"Thirty-three point three three percent," she says pointedly with a grin.

"Must be a buyer's market."

The driver skillfully works his way out of the airport. We're soon hurtling at dangerously high speed down Mittaphap Road, an elevated superhighway that splits jungle, farmlands, and villages with arrow-straight indifference.

I wouldn't hire this guy as my permanent chauffeur, but he's just what I need now. I'm thinking about that vacated condo at the Theater Arts Complex and having visions of finding an empty hotel room here too. Assuming we get to the Oriental in one piece, I plan to drop Kate and our bags at the curb and make a beeline for the Dusit Thani to look up Surigao.

About a half hour later, up ahead where the lanes of the

expressway appear to converge, the silhouettes of modern skyscrapers frame the graceful gold-plated spires of centuries-old Buddhist temples. More than four hundred in Bangkok alone, according to my travel guide.

We're approaching a series of highway exit signs in English and Thai when the driver makes an abrupt lane change, cuts off several vehicles, and darts toward an exit labeled Din Daeng Road. The off-ramp deposits us smack in the middle of a massive traffic jam.

It makes Waikiki's gridlocked streets look empty. There are no lanes, no sense of order, no traffic cops, just a mass of creeping vehicles: cars, vans, trucks, taxis, three-wheeled *tuk-tuks*, and buses with passengers hanging on the steps and out the doors. All appear to be headed in different directions, as do the bikes, scooters, and fearless pedestrians, who weave between them ignoring the traffic signals. Total chaos would be a gross understatement.

The taxi inches forward. I'm squirming with impatience, looking at my watch. Twenty minutes pass, thirty, forty. We haven't gone a mile. "This normal?"

"I've seen it a lot worse."

"Okay. Change of plans. We go to the Dusit Thani first. You drop me off and continue on with the bags."

"What's the rush? I thought you said the Surigaos were going to be there for a while?"

"That's what the clerk said. The way things have been going, they're probably checking out today."

"Like hours ago."

"Maybe. I've just got this thing about coming all this way and getting there minutes after they've gone."

"The old if-game."

"Right. If the flight had gotten in five minutes earlier, if we hadn't checked our bags, if the taxi had gone a little faster, if we'd—"

"Don't tempt him," Kate jokes before informing the driver of the change, which leads to another negotiation. "It's not a buyer's market any more. He says, two stops cost twice as much."

"So do two houses. Makes perfect sense. Tell him triple, if he gets us there before eleven."

"Triple?"

"It's only twelve dollars, Kate. I think I can handle it."

"*Dai leou mai! Dai leou mai!*" the driver singsongs excitedly when she informs him of the challenge. He leans on his horn, maneuvering between the densely packed vehicles finally turning into an unpaved alley.

Suddenly we are racing headlong down the narrow *soi*, as Kate calls it, into a maze of streets behind the theater district, from which, I'm becoming more and more convinced, we may never emerge. But the frenetic zigzagging eventually pays off, leading to a relatively unclogged road just beyond the Siam Intercontinental Hotel. Huge movie posters, two and three stories high, cover some of the buildings. Their bold graphics and bright colors seem to pop up in every section of the city. We continue past a racetrack, finally turning left at a large public park. But, despite the driver's heroic efforts, it's well after eleven by the time we arrive at the Dusit Thani, where lush tropical gardens and splashing fountains greet us.

The hotel is a white, modern, twenty-five-story pagoda topped by a golden spire and overlooks a canal—just like the woman said. The cab is still rolling to a stop when I pop the door.

"Meet you in the bar of the Oriental about three?" Kate calls after me as I get out, feeling my jacket for the pistol.

"Do my damnedest."

"Take care."

The lobby's opulent decor goes past in a glittery blur as I hurry to the front desk, where the smartly uniformed staff appears to have surprisingly broad ethnic diversity.

"May I help you, sir?" an attractive blond desk clerk asks in a sharp Australian twang.

"Yes, I have a business meeting with one of your guests," I reply in an authoritative tone. "A Mr. Surigao? I seem to have misplaced the room number."

"I'll check it for you, sir." She smiles and steps to her computer.

My heart's pounding like crazy now. The thought of their being gone, of my having come all this way only to come up empty, is more than I can bear.

"Here we are, sir," she says brightly. "Fourteen twenty-three."

"Fourteen twenty-three," I repeat coolly, though I really want to shout, *"Yeah, they're still here!" Okay Morgan,* I say to myself as I move off. *Slow it down and think.* I reckon that what I do next will depend on whether or not they're in the room, and if so, who's in the room: both of them, him, her? I cross the lobby toward a bank of house phones, working out what I'm going to say should someone answer, then I dial 1423. It rings and rings. Five, six, seven times. I'm about to hang up.

"Yes?" a woman finally says. She sounds rushed, a little out of breath.

"Mr. Surigao please?"

"He's not here right now. Who's calling?"

I recognize the Filipino accent. It's Carla Surigao. No mistake this time. "This is the concierge, madam," I reply, trying to sound officious. "We have a package for him. Would it be convenient to have someone bring it up now?"

"Of course. Thank you."

I hang up and head for the elevator. It's mirrored, ornately detailed, and painfully slow. I get off on 14 and walk down a long corridor, observing that the doors to the guest rooms lack security peepholes. I reach for the Beretta, flicking off the safety and cocking the hammer without removing it from my pocket, then I knock on 1423.

A few seconds later, I hear the rustle of someone approaching. The deadbolt retracts, and the knob turns. Carla's made the obvious assumption. As the door starts to open, I catch a glimpse of her in a mirror on the entry wall. She's wearing a black silk robe and looks like she's just gotten out of the shower. I'm poised to confront her with the gun and force my way into the room, but, as the door swings fully open, she turns her back to me, preoccupied with a comb she's pulling through her wet hair, and leads the way inside.

"You can put it over there on the . . ." She pauses on hearing the door close and lock behind her, then turns curiously, recoiling when she sees me. A rapist? A burglar? She's wiry and quick, and before I have a chance to assure her she isn't in any danger, she pushes a room service cart in my path and heads for a door on the far side of the room. I sidestep the cart and pursue her into the bathroom before she can close the door. She lunges for a phone on the makeup table. I pull the Beretta and level it at her.

"Hang it up," I order sharply. "Do it. Now."

She freezes at the sight of the pistol, her perfect Asian eyes widening with fear.

I grab the phone cord and yank it from the wall.

She shudders and backs into a corner, terrified.

"Take it easy, Carla. I'm not here to hurt you. I just want to talk."

She flinches when she hears her name.

"Yes, I know who you are. Believe me, you're not in any danger. There's no need to be frightened. You understand?"

She nods, unconvinced.

"Okay, let's go back inside."

Her eyes are riveted to the pistol as we return to the room and I direct her to an armchair. She backs her way into it, clutching at the robe to prevent it from opening.

I keep the gun trained on her and look around. It's an elegant room with a small sitting alcove, views of the city, and oriental-style furniture. I notice her handbag on an antique writing desk. I go through it, making sure it doesn't contain a weapon, then turn over the bed pillows, and look inside the nightstand drawer with the same result.

"I think I liked your condo in Hawaii better," I say, purposely baiting her.

Carla's eyes narrow with curiosity. "Who are you?" she asks in a trembling voice.

"My name's Morgan. A. Calvert Morgan."

Now they flicker in recognition.

"I thought it might ring a bell."

"What do you want?"

"Revenge."

She looks puzzled.

"Your husband killed my wife."

"Sean?"

"Yes, Sean," I reply indignantly. "Come on, you know what happened. He screwed up. He thought he was killing me."

She shakes her head as if mystified.

"Where is he?"

"He went out."

"Where?"

"I don't know."

"Try again."

"I don't. He didn't tell me."

"When's he coming back?

She shrugs.

I slide a chair off to one side of the room and sit down with the pistol in my fist. This is a strategic position that puts me between Carla and the door. More important, someone entering the room can't see me, but I can see them in the mirror opposite the entry. "Okay, I'll wait."

Carla fidgets nervously, then starts to shiver and pulls her knees up under her chin, arms wrapped around her legs, wet hair hanging straight to her shoulders, looking a lot like the Vietnamese refugees who lined the roadsides during monsoon season.

"Cold?"

She nods.

"You can get dressed if you like."

Her eyes narrow warily.

I have the feeling she thinks I'm being lewd and suggesting she disrobe in front of me. "Change in the bathroom. Just leave the door open."

At this, she unknots her tiny frame, springs from the chair, and takes several quick steps to a dresser. I'm on my feet and right next to her as she pulls articles of clothing from the drawers. Then she scoops up her purse and heads for the bathroom.

A short while later she emerges in an exercise suit, settles on a sofa, and lights a cigarette.

Several minutes pass in silence.

"As long as we're sitting here, staring at each other," I finally say, "would you mind telling me why your husband was so interested in me?"

"I have no idea."

"You expect me to believe that?"

She shrugs and drags on the cigarette, appearing to have regained some of her composure. "Believe what you like, Mr. Morgan. Whatever my husband did, it was his business. He kept it to himself."

"Come on, Carla, you were involved up to your ass, and you know it."

She stands and turns her back to me, staring out the window. I grasp her arm and spin her around. Our faces are inches apart. Her breath smells of tobacco. Her eyes burn with disdain.

"Look, I'm trying to be a gentleman about this. But I'm running out of patience. Now, why me?"

"I said I don't know. Whatever it was, it's over."

"What do you mean?"

"His work is finished."

"What work? What's finished?"

"I don't know. All I can tell you is we came to Bangkok to get paid and start a new life."

"Not if I can help it."

She glares at me with hatred now. "Why did you have to come here? Why couldn't you just leave us alone?!"

I stare at her unmoved.

She stands her ground for a moment, then averts her eyes as something dawns on her. "You're going to kill him, aren't you?"

I glance to the pistol then back to her with a malevolent smirk. "I've thought about it every day since I found out he killed my wife. She was a decent, generous person. We were together for a long time and I loved her very much. I can't tell you how much. To be brutally frank, every bone in my body wants to kill him. I want to see him suffer a slow, painful death." I pause, and glance to the pistol again, letting her live with the idea for a while before adding, "But I'd be no better than he is, if I did."

Her chin lifts curiously.

"I'll get my satisfaction from catching him. A judge and jury can decide what happens after that."

She nods warily, stubs out the cigarette, and lights another. "You've called the police?"

"No. I'm turning him over to the DEA. Unless he does something stupid and forces me to kill him. I'll shoot him right here if I have to, believe me."

That was one of the decisions I made during the flight. I want nothing to do with the local police. Chances are they're corrupt. They might even be on Surigao's payroll.

Even if they're not, I don't know anything about Thai law, and I'm taking no chances they might let him go on some legal technicality. No, when Surigao walks through that door, I'll put the pistol to his head, and call the DEA at the Embassy. If he isn't already on their wanted list, their agents can verify he's a fugitive with the colonel and the Los Angeles police, then come get him. I'm going over the moves when the phone rings, a loud, harsh buzzing that cuts right through me.

Carla goes toward the desk to answer it.

"Wait," I say sharply, intercepting her as I cross to the nightstand where there's an extension. "Play it straight, like you're alone. You understand?"

She nods.

"Okay, now."

We lift the phones simultaneously on what must be the sixth or seventh ring. I've got my palm over the mouthpiece.

"Yes?" she answers.

"It's me. Where the hell were you?" It's a man's voice. A familiar voice. Captain Sullivan's voice to me. It trembles with desperation, not anger.

Carla glances at me with panicked eyes.

I point to the bathroom and mouth the word shower.

"Carla?" Surigao snarls. "Dammit, Carla, you there?"

"Yes, Sean. Yes. I'm sorry. I just got out of the shower. What is it? You sound—"

"Bastards double-crossed me."

"What?"

"It was a setup. Ajacier never showed. These guys were going to kill me. I saw it coming and got away."

"Oh, God," she gasps. "Oh God. Sean—"

"Come on, Carla, this is no time to panic. They're still out there looking for me."

"What are you going to do?"

"I'm not sure. I'm thinking, maybe I can make a deal with the other side. Rent a car. Pick me up on the northeast corner of Khlong Thom and Yaowarat. That's in Chinatown."

She grabs a pencil and scribbles hastily on a pad.

"Got it?"

"Yes, Khlong Thom and Yaowarat."

"Hurry. Soon as you can. Make sure you aren't followed."

The line goes dead.

"Sean? Sean are you all right?" She listens to the dial tone for a moment, then hangs up shaken, mouth agape. "Bastards," she curses to no one in particular. "He never should've trusted them. He did what they asked. Now when it's time to pay . . ." She bites it off in disgust.

"Sounds like old Sean's got himself into a real tight spot."

"It's not fair."

"You're breaking my heart, Carla."

She wrings her hands in frustration, convinced, as I intended, that I'm going to keep her from going to her husband's assistance.

I let her anxiety build, as I think it through. From the sound of it, Ajacier's in Bangkok too. If I play it right, chances are I can nail both of them. But Surigao's still my primary target. It's only a matter of time now. Not only do I know where he is, and what he wants, but I also control whom he trusts.

"Please," Carla says, becoming frantic. "Please, you have to let me help him."

"No, I don't," I reply in as callous a tone as I can muster.

She glares at me with hatred.

"But I might."

"Depending on what?"

"You. I asked you a question before. I didn't get an answer. I want it now—Why me?"

"I don't have the answer."

"Come on, dammit. You tipped Sean off to my case at the CIL. You just didn't pick my name out of a fucking hat. Why me?!"

"No, I didn't pick your name out of a fucking hat, Mr. Morgan," she finally replies bitterly. "There were some names that I—that I watched for."

"Why?"

"Because Sean asked me to. That's all I know."

"That's very unfortunate for Sean."

"I'd tell you if I could. Believe me, I really would." She pauses briefly, hoping for a response.

I stare at her in silence.

"Please, Mr. Morgan," she goes on, a desperate timbre in her voice. "You know what you were saying before about you and your wife? Well, Sean and I have been together a long time too. More than fifteen years. He has his faults, but he also has some very good qualities. Please, whatever you think of him, whatever he did to you, he's my husband and I love him. I really do."

Her eyes fill with tears. She looks helpless, really decent and sincere, just like Kate said, and I find myself believing her, admiring her, admiring her loyalty and spunk.

"You can't stop me," she goes on. "You can't. You'll have to kill me first." She whirls, grabs her purse, and bolts for the door. I lunge as she passes me and catch hold of her arm. She squirms trying to twist free. "Let go," she protests, her high cheekbones reddening with defiance. "I've got to help him. I've got to!"

"No, Carla," I say coolly, playing the card I've been quietly holding. "If you really want to save his life, you've got to help me."

25

"**M**AKE A LEFT OVER THAT LITTLE BRIDGE."

Carla's driving.

I'm navigating with the map.

Bangkok is a confusing city. Built on a swamp, its streets meander and crisscross like the streams they once were, devoid of any alphabetical or numerical order, and interrupted by canals that turn many of them into cul de sacs. To make matters worse, the steering wheel's on the right side of the car and they drive on the left side of the road like in Britain.

We're on Charoen Krung Road, the main boulevard that parallels the river, approaching the bridge. The car is almost too wide for the narrow span that arches across the Phadung Canal to the southeastern tip of Chinatown. The agent at the rental desk in the lobby of the Dusit Thani Hotel strongly recommended we take a compact, but I insisted on a full-size sedan instead. I have my reasons.

"I'll need your driver's license, a major credit card, and an international driver's license," the agent said, explaining the latter was an absolute necessity in Thailand—no IDL, no car. I vaguely recalled reading about that in the travel guide, but it wasn't a problem. The Surigaos had done their homework and Carla had one.

The landscape undergoes a sudden and dramatic change as we come off the bridge into the Sampheng District. Shabby and densely packed, the centuries-old enclave sits in a bend on the east bank of the Chao Phraya River. Like the rest of Bangkok, the facade of almost every building is covered with signs, but the playful brushstrokes of the Chi-

GREG DINALLO

nese alphabet are in marked contrast to the angular and
severely disciplined Thai characters. We turn right into
Song-Sawat Road and begin making our way through the
narrow streets.

"This is Yaowarat coming up. Pull over."

"You want me to park here?"

"Yes. Before the intersection. Just do it. Remember,
your husband's well-being depends on your cooperating."

Carla winces and angles to the curb.

Another car drives past just as she stops. There are two
men inside. Surigao warned Carla about being followed,
and both of us have been on the lookout, but I didn't notice
this one until now.

"Was that car tailing us?"

"I don't think so."

"It look familiar?"

Carla shakes no.

"What about the two guys?"

"I really didn't get a good look at them."

The other car crosses Yaowarat, keeps going straight
ahead, and is soon out of sight. This is no time for exces-
sive caution. Nancy's killer is waiting around the corner,
just a couple of blocks away. I'm not turning back now.

I climb between the seats into the rear of the sedan. "I'm
going to be down here where Sean can't see me," I explain,
taking up a position on the floor behind the passenger seat.
"You'll drive up and stop. He'll get in next to you. I'll put
my gun to the back of his head and explain his options. He
won't like them, but I have a feeling he'll do the smart
thing. Feel free to encourage him. After he calms down,
you'll drive us to the U.S. Embassy. It's not very far. I'll
give you directions. You understand?"

She nods.

"I mean it, Carla." I take the Beretta from my pocket.
"Don't give me a reason to kill him."

Her eyes dart to the pistol. She nods again.

"Or you, for that matter."

"Yes. Yes," she says, her teeth tugging at her lower lip,
her accent intensifying. "God. I'm so nervous."

"Good. After what Sean told you, he has every reason

204

to expect you to be nervous. Don't try to hide it. Let's go. Make a left."

Carla pulls away from the curb and turns into Yaowarat, a desolate street dotted with potholes and lined with steel-shuttered loading docks. The tightly packed buildings block out most of the light, plunging the canyons between them into shadowy darkness. We proceed west for several blocks toward a patch of daylight in the distance, passing a lone pedestrian and a couple of mongrel dogs scavenging for food.

"Okay, Khlong Thom's coming up. Nice and slow."

I lean more to the center, positioning my head in the space between the front seats, which gives me a view of the street through the windshield. The patch of light turns out to be a public square just beyond the intersection where a street market has been set up.

As we approach, I vaguely make out a figure standing in the doorway of a building on the near corner of the square. I can see it's a man. He reacts to the approaching car, but remains pressed into the shadows until it gets closer. Then, seeming to recognize Carla, he starts walking toward the street, looking about warily. His dark hair is combed straight back, his face is narrow and deeply tanned, aviator sunglasses bridge his fine Irish nose. It's him. It's Captain Sullivan. It's the guy in the metallic blue car, the guy in the hotel room, the guy in the colonel's snapshot all rolled into one.

"Remember, don't do anything foolish." I push the gun into Carla's side and duck behind the passenger seat, pressing myself into the corner it forms with the door. I'd feel a hell of a lot more secure at night. But the high headrest gives me sufficient cover and, as I anticipated, Surigao's attention isn't focused on the car. It's on the street, on the market and the alleys, the places where a threat might surface.

The car rolls to a stop.

There's a short silence. Then the sound of fast-moving footsteps gradually rises. Seconds later a shadow falls across the seats.

Carla looks to her left, expectantly.

I'm waiting for the click of the door latch. That's my

cue. My heart is pounding, mouth turning to cotton, palms becoming clammy. Perspiration rolls down my face. The humidity and heat are almost as unbearable as the anxiety.

Several seconds pass.

Several more.

Carla's just sitting there.

Still nothing. Dammit. It's been too long. Something's wrong. She's either managed to signal him, or I was wrong and Surigao spotted me. I can't wait any longer. I surface with the Beretta in my hand.

Surigao is right there, right outside the car, pulling a revolver from inside his jacket. It can't be more than a couple of feet from my head. I'm looking right down the barrel. But Surigao's attention seems to be elsewhere. He hasn't seen me. Then all of a sudden he does and recoils in shock. His reaction leaves little doubt he thought I was dead. We're face-to-face. Only the window separates us. Damn. I don't want to kill him. I want him alive. I want answers. But it's kill or be killed now. His eyes widen with terror. I'm squeezing the trigger when Carla realizes what's happening and floors the gas pedal. The tires spin wildly, emitting a piercing screech. The sudden acceleration knocks me backward, throwing the Beretta off line. The bullet punches a tiny hole in the car's headlining right above me. I hear the sharp crack of gunshots as Surigao opens fire simultaneously. Three, four, five deafening pops. The side and rear windows shatter, showering me with glass as the rounds whizz overhead.

Somewhere in the middle of it all, Carla yelps, then lurches backward and falls between the front seats. Her head comes to rest right in front of me. Blood seeps from beneath it, pooling on the floor. Her perfect face is unmarked, her perfect eyes are staring up at me blank and unmoving.

The car begins swerving right, then left, throwing me from side to side as it careens out of control. I'm wondering whether or not I've been shot too. There's no pain and no blood, but I've seen plenty of men die without much of either.

I manage to reach across Carla's body from the backseat, grab the shift lever, and slam it from Drive straight through

Reverse into Park. The transmission emits a grinding scream in protest.

The car dives to a stop.

I'm tossed forward. My shoulders slam into the back of the seats, keeping me from being propelled headlong into the dash. I clamber across the seat and slip out the door on the driver's side in a crouch, hugging the rear fender, keeping the car between me and Surigao, fully expecting him to be emptying his pistol in my direction. But I don't hear any more gunfire, only what sounds like a car driving off.

Wisps of pungent smoke are still curling from the wheel well next to me. A bluish haze hangs in thin layers overhead. The sudden acceleration burned a lot of rubber but the car covered little ground. I'm no more than twenty or thirty feet from the intersection. Surigao had plenty of time to advance and fire. But he didn't. I don't see him. I don't hear him either. Where the hell is he? Behind me? Moving up on the opposite side of the car?

I drop to the ground with the pistol. I'm flat on my belly, looking between the bottom of the car and the pavement for Surigao's shoes. Instead I see a tiny figure in the distance, running toward the street market. It's him. He's threading his way between a small number of shoppers who heard the gunfire and are hurrying, curiously, toward the street.

I get to my feet and pursue. I'm running at full tilt, wondering why Surigao's fleeing, wondering why he didn't continue firing. He had the strategic advantage. Had me pinned down. I don't get it.

I come through the space between the buildings into the square. The aisles that separate the market's rickety stalls are teeming with locals and tourists buying everything from exotic herbs to bogus antiques. Most either didn't hear, or chose to ignore, the shooting.

Surigao's gone, swallowed up by the crowd.

I'm standing there drenched in sweat, gasping for breath, scanning the shoppers to no avail. Then I notice a commotion up ahead and spot him pushing people aside, stumbling forward. The market has slowed him down. He's much closer than I thought. But I can't risk a shot with all these bystanders. I wade into the crowd, knifing sideways between the marketgoers. Some angrily stand their ground. Others glare. A few shove back.

"My wallet!" I shout, taking an elbow in the ribs. "Stop that guy. He's got my wallet!"

My plea falls on deaf ears, but finally several people step aside, allowing me to break into the clear. I start sprinting down one of the aisles after Surigao. Suddenly there's a flash of colorful fabric. A man backs into my path from one of the stalls. I try to avoid him but can't. The collision sends me sprawling. I instinctively use my hands to break my fall, losing my grip on the pistol. It goes skittering across the pavement. I can see it up ahead in a forest of legs and tramping feet. I'm crawling toward it when someone hurrying through the crowd kicks it in stride. Damn. It's gone. The pistol's gone. Out of sight.

Someone takes hold of my arm and begins helping me to my feet. It's a heavyset man in a flower-print shirt, camera around his neck, gadget bag over his shoulder. His soft, friendly face is taut with concern. "Hey, gosh, I'm really sorry. You okay?"

I ignore him, scanning the crowd frantically, and finally spot Surigao heading into an alley on the far side of the market.

"Gosh, I didn't see you coming there," the big fellow goes on. "I sure hope you're not hurt or anything?"

"No, no, I'm fine. No problem," I say, trying to get past him.

"You sure, now?" he asks sincerely, his huge girth blocking my way.

"Yeah, yeah. Guy lifted my wallet. Gotta go." I finally get around him and head after Surigao unarmed, knowing I'll never catch up to him if I take the time to look for the pistol.

The alley is narrow, unpaved, and piled with trash. I weave between the mountains of plastic bags and dented pails, ending up in a courtyard. Alleys branch off in every direction. Surigao's nowhere to be seen, but I hear the rhythmic clack of shoes running on concrete. The sound is echoing off the walls, which makes it virtually impossible to determine where it's coming from. Several seconds pass before I notice that only one of the alleys is paved, and make a beeline for it. At first it looks like a cul de sac, but soon I can see it abuts a cross alley at the far end. I pause at the last building, creep up to the corner, and peer around it cautiously.

Straight ahead is a high retaining wall.

To the right a facade of steel shutter doors.

To the left a long staircase leads up to what looks like a promenade.

Surigao is frantically taking the steps two at a time. He's only got a few to go. I've barely started after him when he reaches the top and disappears from view. I charge after him, stumbling several times. The sound of a boat horn rises as I come off the stairs onto a walkway that parallels the river. Surigao is up ahead running along the worn timbers. He turns on the move and fires a wild shot. Then another.

How many bullets does he have in that thing? It's a revolver. Six shots. But that was at least seven, if not eight, counting the ones he fired at the car. It has to be the last one.

He seems to be losing steam. No more than forty yards separate us now. I once ran it in five flat when I was in college. Nothing for the record books. But it's taking me twice as long now. Too many T-bones and not enough reps on the rowing machine. My legs are killing me, lungs screaming for mercy, heart on the verge of arrest, but I'm closing the gap.

Surigao angles to his left and heads down a short dock that juts into the river. Several cars are coming toward us. Cars? There's a ferry slip at the far end, and the ferry's in. The dockman is closing the gate behind the last vehicle and a few pedestrians who have just boarded. Surigao dashes past the ticket booth; then, almost colliding with the dockman, he grabs the top of the gate and dives over it onto the deck of the departing vessel. He lands hard, lies there for a moment, then gradually struggles to his feet, holding his side in pain.

I run up to the gate and grasp it, poised to vault after him, but the ferry is too far from the dock. I'd never make it. I stand there glaring at Surigao with hatred as it glides off into the river.

Nancy's killer is gone. He'll have no trouble vanishing in this teeming city. I'll never find him. Bystanders or no, I should've shot him in the street market when I had the chance. I'm staring numbly at the ferry's graceful wake when I feel something sticky and wet on my hand. I let go of the railing. My palm is bright red with blood—Surigao's blood.

He's wounded.

I didn't shoot him.

But someone else sure as hell did.

26

I'M NOT SURE HOW LONG I'VE BEEN WALKING ALONG THE waterfront, across the countless footbridges that span the canals, past the landings where longboats and snub-nosed ferries glide to brief stops.

Probably close to an hour.

It took that long for my brain to recover from the shock and start functioning again. As soon as it did, I realized that Surigao didn't say anything about being wounded when he called Carla at the hotel. He was frightened, not injured. No, the message was very clear: *They almost got me.* Which means it happened after that. In Chinatown. The car I thought I heard driving off must've been Ajacier's men. Despite my caution, they somehow followed us from the hotel. Carla didn't signal Surigao. He didn't see me or sense my presence, he saw the car approaching, saw Ajacier's hit men. I couldn't. I was crouching inside the car. My back was to the street. Come to think of it, so was Carla's. It all happened so fast it didn't dawn on me until now that the bullet struck the back of her head. It couldn't have been a stray round from Surigao's gun. Chances are he never fired a shot. Ajacier's men shot both of them. That's why Surigao didn't try to finish me off. That's why he ran.

This is very bad news. I wouldn't know Ajacier if I tripped over him on the street, but I've no doubt he knows me, and now he knows I'm in Bangkok, knows I'm still alive.

I've lost my advantage.

I'm going to have to be much more careful.

It takes me about ten seconds to start wondering why? And ten more to realize that caution can have it's downside, that defensive thinking would be a mistake. I should know better than to fall into that trap. How many times had I heard it in-country? Either you're hunting them or they're hunting you. This is no time to change tactics. Just targets. And I think I know how: Ajacier's in Bangkok. According to the IRL report, he has a piece of Thonburi Studios. Maybe he has an office there, too.

I make a beeline for a vendor hawking his wares at a nearby ferry stop. "Where's the nearest public phone?"

He doesn't speak any English, but a customer does. He's a slight, sprightly fellow who, like everyone else in Bangkok, listens to my question and prefaces his answer with a sympathetic smile. He shakes his head no. "Sorry. Cannot find in Bangkok."

"Are you saying there aren't any?"

He smiles again and nods. "Less than numbers on one hand. And those always broken. You try hotels. Or telephone company on New Road."

I was planning to call Thonburi Film Studios to find out whether or not Ajacier is there. I hail a taxi instead. The driver knows where it's located. As it turns out, he speaks some English and explains that any driver would know the studio. Filmmaking is big business in Bangkok. There are five major studios, evidenced by the massive billboards that advertise new releases.

The one at the entrance to Thonburi Studios is three stories high. It depicts a handsome Asian man in a tuxedo surrounded, James Bond fashion, by sexy Asian women in skintight dresses. Unlike Hollywood studios, this isn't a gated and fenced fortress. It's a modern office tower with direct access from the street. I leave the taxi, hurry into the lobby, and go straight to the directory. Listed under A is Ajacier, P., Franco-Asian Cinema 7th Floor.

The elevator leaves me in a reception area. These are sleek, high-tech offices, much like my own. The walls are lined with framed movie posters. I tell the receptionist I'm there to see Mr. Ajacier. I imagine I look somewhat disheveled, because she sweeps her eyes over me disapprovingly before asking, "Is he expecting you?"

"No, we're old friends. I happened to be in town and thought I'd say hello."

"I'm sorry. He just went into a meeting," she replies, her eyes drifting to a glass-walled room just off the reception area.

Through the narrow blinds, I can see perhaps a dozen men seated around a large conference table.

"If you'll give me your name, I'll be happy to tell Mr. Ajacier you were here."

"Thanks. I'll tell him myself."

I whirl and head for the conference room.

"Sir? Sir, you can't go in there," she calls out, coming from behind her desk to intercept me.

I blow past her without stopping, throw open the door, and stride boldly into the room, startling the group of businessmen. All heads snap in my direction. One of them is my man, but which one?

"Mr. Ajacier?" I call out.

All heads turn to a man seated on the far side of the table. He recoils slightly, then stands and measures me with wary, pale blue eyes. He's in his late fifties. Tall and well tailored, with a swarthy Corsican complexion. But his face is narrow, his features angular and refined.

"What is this? Who are you?"

"The name's Morgan." I reply evenly, fighting the surge of adrenaline.

Ajacier's surprise turns quickly to recognition. He stiffens with fear, wondering, I imagine, if I'm going to pull a gun and blow him away right there.

"But I didn't have to tell you that. You know who I am, Mr. Ajacier. And now I know who you are."

His eyes flick nervously to the others. "I'm afraid you've mistaken me for someone else."

"Afraid? Of what? That I'll embarrass you in front of your friends? In case you gentlemen are wondering, this isn't a movie we're talking about. He sent a real killer after me."

Ajacier sets his jaw and glares at me. "I think you've gone far enough, Mr. Morgan."

I'm holding his look, when several uniformed security guards enter the conference room.

"Show this gentleman out," he says, relieved.

One of the guards takes hold of my arm. I pull free and leave the room, the guards close behind. They escort me into the elevator, down to the lobby, and out to the street.

That was sweet. Really sweet. I haven't felt this good in months. I hurry off in search of a taxi, thinking about Surigao. He's probably in an emergency room somewhere. But there are undoubtedly countless hospitals in Bangkok, not to mention private physicians. It would be an impossible task to canvass them. Besides, there's an even chance he's lying dead in some rancid alley. I put my money on the latter and take a taxi to the Oriental Hotel.

Built more than a decade before the turn of the century, it's an elegantly restored mix of Art Nouveau decor and Old Viennese architecture where literary lions Somerset Maugham and Joseph Conrad, after whom suites have been named, often stayed.

Off to one side of the lobby, a string quartet in black tie is playing a piece, which, as usually happens, I recognize but can't name. I hurry past them, drawing veiled stares from some of the other guests. I'm wondering why, when I happen to catch sight of this rather unkempt fellow in a mirror. His hair is mussed and matted. His clothes look like he's slept in them—they're soiled, sweat-stained, and, on closer inspection, bloodstained.

Chrissakes. It's me.

This happened many times in Vietnam, and now it comes back in a chilling rush. After months in the jungle, I'd end up in Saigon or Manila on R and R, pass a mirror in my hotel room, and think there was someone else in there with me. It was strange how little the image I had of myself had to do with reality.

I didn't draw any stares then. That's how GIs were supposed to look. Not the case in the classy Oriental. I detour to a men's room off the lobby and spend a few minutes improving my appearance, then proceed to the infamous outdoor bar, where the literati often held court. Towering glass doors lead to a terrace that overlooks the Chao Phraya River, where traffic plying the brackish waters moves at a lazy, late-afternoon pace.

I spot Kate sitting at one of the tables reading a newspaper. She senses my approach and looks up.

"Hi, how'd it go?" she asks brightly.

"It's a long story," I reply, falling into a chair next to her. "I'm exhausted. I need to crash for a while. You get us checked in?"

"No. The rooms weren't ready. They said any time after three."

I glance to my watch. "What are we waiting for?"

"Vann Nath."

"Who?"

"The businessman I told you about."

"The one who works with the refugees?"

"Yes. I dropped the bags in the lobby and cabbed it to his office. He was out, but when I got back, there was a message that he'd meet me here. I've been waiting almost an hour. I guess he—" She pauses suddenly, and scowls. "Boy, you look awful."

"Thanks. You should see the other guy."

"Does that mean the Surigaos were still at the hotel?"

I nod solemnly, my gut constricting.

"And?"

I hesitate briefly, then, in a taut whisper, reply, "Carla's dead. I think he is too."

Kate leans back in the chair and glares at me accusingly.

"No, I didn't kill them. It was Surigao's buddies. Sounds like they said, 'Good work, Sean. Come live a life of luxury in Bangkok.' I figure Ajacier was planning to kill him all along. Carla got caught in the cross fire."

Kate nods thoughtfully. "So, now Ajacier knows you're not dead."

"Sure does."

"You don't seem very concerned."

"I'm not."

Her eyes widen curiously.

"I remembered in this game you're either the hunter or the prey. So I tracked him down and scared the shit out of him."

"I take it all back."

"Three Our Fathers, Three Hail Marys, take two aspirin, and call me in the morning."

"Pardon me?"

"You have to be Catholic."

She smiles, then her eyes brighten at something she sees behind me. "There he is. Vann?" she calls out, waving and getting to her feet. "Vann? Over here."

I look over my shoulder to see a handsome man in a business suit coming toward us. He's unusually tall for an Asian, in his late forties, with an aristocratic bearing accented by a dramatic streak of gray where his hair is sharply parted.

"Kate," he calls out effusively as she hurries to him with open arms. "I can't believe you're here."

"Neither can I," she replies, hugging him.

He removes his sunglasses and steps away to look at her. "You look wonderful. As beautiful as ever." His accent is slight. His manner almost courtly.

"Better put those back on," she jokes. Then she turns to me and introduces us, discretely explaining I'm a friend on a similar mission.

"Well, if I can be of any service," Vann Nath offers as we take seats at the table.

"Thanks. I'll keep that in mind."

"My apologies for being so late," he says, turning to Kate with a smile, "But this might just be worth waiting for."

"You have something?"

"Remember, Kate, I said might."

"Oh, my God, tell me," she says, taking his hand and squeezing it excitedly.

"After you called from Hawaii, I remembered there were several people I'd helped relocate in recent years who'd been with the Pathet Lao. They were reluctant conscripts, so to speak. Journalists and photographers pressed into service to implement propaganda compaigns. They wrote press releases, took pictures of downed American aircraft and prisoners, that sort of thing. I reviewed my records and discovered one of these men had been stationed in the area where your husband was lost."

"He has information about John?"

"He claims to. I gave him his name, and the new information you'd given me." He pauses and shakes his head with dismay. "I still can't believe they never told you he'd survived."

Kate shrugs resignedly. "They had their reasons."

"Anyway, the man called back that same afternoon and said he found something in his files."

"He say what?"

"Oh, no. He's keeping his cards very close to his chest. You know how this game is played."

"All too well. How much will you need?"

"It's hard to say. Let's see how it goes, Kate. You can reimburse me later."

"When can we talk to him?"

"Tonight. Be at this club at eight-thirty." Vann Nath takes a business card from his wallet and jots down the information on the back.

I sense a waiter hovering over us. "Excuse me?" I ask, "Would either of you like something?"

"Thank you, Mr. Morgan. Perhaps another time," Vann Nath replies, getting to his feet. "As usual, I'm running late. Very nice to meet you."

"Same here."

"You know, Kate," he says, his voice taking on a more serious tone, "things haven't changed very much when it comes to information on MIAs."

"I understand."

"Good. I just want to make sure you don't commit your heart to this."

"Thanks."

He hugs her, then turns and hurries off.

She watches him go. A tear rolls down her cheek.

"You okay?"

"Yes, I'm fine. Just a lot of old feelings all of a sudden."

"We could both use some rest."

She nods, rubs a sleeve across her eyes, and starts across the terrace.

We're entering the lobby when I unthinkingly reach into my coat pocket. It's empty. A chill goes through me. Confronting Ajacier in a room full of businessmen, unarmed, was one thing. I was in control. The element of surprise was mine. But his thugs could be standing next to me right now, and I wouldn't know it. It's a sobering thought, and

I'm feeling vulnerable. I hang back, looking about warily as Kate approaches the check-in desk and gives the room clerk our names.

He's a haughty fellow who frowns when he finds them in his computer registry. "You'll be staying in five twenty-seven," he says in a British accent. "Your luggage has already been placed in the room."

"And Mr. Morgan?"

"I'm sure you'll find his there as well, madam."

He raps his bell sharply and turns to a rack of pigeon-holes to fetch the key.

"They booked us into a double," Kate says to me with a scowl, then, as the room clerk turns to an approaching bellman, she calls out, "Excuse me? Excuse me, I think there's been a mistake."

The clerk pauses in midstep and whirls toward her challengingly. "Pardon me, madam?"

"I said, there's been a mistake," Kate replies, her tone sharpening to match his. "I didn't book a double. I booked two singles."

The clerk's brow furrows skeptically. He turns to his computer while the bellman stands by. "Why, yes, madam, so you did. I'm so sorry," he says, studying the screen, not sorry at all. "Yes, I still have several singles available, which I'm sure will be quite satisfactory. Unfortunately, the housekeepers are terribly behind today. I'm afraid neither room is prepared."

"When?" Kate asks impatiently.

"Within the hour."

Kate and I exchange exasperated looks.

The clerk gives the bellman the key and instructs him to retrieve our bags from the double room. He fetches a cart and heads off toward the elevators.

We head back toward the bar.

We've gone a few steps when the vulnerable feelings intensify and another chill goes through me. I'm flashing back again. Back to the Nam. Back to where you never knew who the enemy was. Where the gentle village girl who did your wash one day, sent it back booby-trapped the next. I haven't felt like this in twenty years. I can't get it out of my head. It's really bothering me.

"What is it?" Kate prompts, sensing my uneasiness.

"I don't know. Something isn't right."

"Mai pen rai," she says.

"What?"

"It's an old Thai expression. Loosely translated it means, 'These things happen.' Look at the bright side of it, at least they still have a couple of singles."

"That's not what I meant. I've got this really strange feeling. I used to get it when I was on patrol in Vietnam. It's sort of like a sixth sense. A lot of us developed it after a while. Especially the guys who made it back. It was as if you could almost smell danger."

"Danger?"

"Yes, danger," I reply sharply, suddenly caught up in the throes of a vivid, frightening flashback about booby traps. About the laundry girl. About climbing fences instead of going through gates. About going through windows instead of doors. I make a one-eighty and hurry back to the check-in desk.

Kate hurries after me baffled.

"Where's the bellman?" I ask the clerk.

"The bellman?" he echoes, as if I'm speaking Swahili.

"Yes, the guy who went to get our bags."

"Ah, I imagine you're referring to the porter. He's on his way to the room, sir."

"The wrong room?"

He misunderstands and stiffens indignantly. "Yes, sir. Again, I'm very sorry for the inconvenience. Is there something you require from your luggage?"

"No. No, you have to stop him."

"Stop him, sir?"

"Yes, now. You have to stop him now."

"Really, sir," he says, put off by my attitude.

"Can't you beep him or something?"

"No, I'm afraid not, sir."

I whirl and run to the elevators. One of the floor indicators is on 16. The other is moving slowly toward 3, where it stops.

"What is it? What's wrong?" Kate asks, bewildered, as she catches up.

"What room did he say?"

"Five twenty-seven, I think. Why?"

I run to the staircase that's off to one side of the elevators and start climbing. It winds upward around the shaft. I'm taking the steps two, three at a time. I can hear Kate behind me trying to keep up. Then I hear the click of the motor as the elevator starts. It ascends slowly to four, and stops. Now, I can hear the doors rolling open, then voices, and the sounds of people exiting. There's a long pause before it closes and starts ascending again toward five. The motor's whirring. I'm climbing like crazy, humping up the stairs.

I finally stumble onto the fifth floor landing and push through the fire door into the corridor. The elevator doors are rumbling open. I come around the corner. It's gone. They weren't opening. They were closing. I dash past it, rounding the next corner.

The bellman is already down the end of a long corridor with his cart. He's reached the room and is putting the key into the lock.

"Wait! Wait, come here," I call out.

He waves at me genially. "Yes, sir. One moment. I'll be right with you."

"No! Wait!" I start running down the corridor as he opens the door and pushes the empty baggage cart into the room. "Wait!!"

"What is it? What's the matter," Kate asks, hurrying after me.

"No, Kate! No, stay back!" I shout over my shoulder without breaking stride. "Stay back!"

A thunderous explosion erupts inside the room.

It blows the door to bits and sends a shock wave and blast of heat down the corridor, followed by a roaring fireball.

I instinctively wrap my arms around Kate, shielding her as we tumble to the floor.

Flaming pieces of luggage and clothing, neckties, brassieres, a sports jacket, a can of deodorant, a hair dryer, computer parts, and body parts are all blown out the doorway into the corridor. They sail through the air, landing on the floor around us in incendiary heaps.

Kate is staring in horror at a blood-spattered wall. Thick

black smoke comes billowing down the corridor. We get to our feet and make our way back to the staircase. I pull a fire alarm as we hurry through the door and begin clambering down the stairs with other guests. We reach the landing adjacent to the lobby. The place is in a frenzy. Guests and staff are hurrying in every direction, spurred on by the clanging alarm. We avoid the lobby and continue to the basement, past the hotel kitchen and laundry toward an illuminated exit sign at the far end of the corridor. A set of double doors opens onto an exterior staircase, which we climb to street level.

Dusk has fallen.

The wail of sirens rises in the distance.

We hurry down a darkened alley behind the hotel, past dozens of overflowing trash pails, into the street. Suddenly bursts of yellow and red light begin strobing across the buildings up ahead. A Metropolitan Police minibus, emergency flasher whirling atop its roof, takes a corner at high speed and roars past us. A fire engine is close behind.

"Where are we going?" Kate asks, gasping for breath.

"I don't know. Someplace where we can hide out for a while."

"I used to stay in this little hotel over on—"

"I'd rather pick one at random."

"There's a lot of small hotels and guest houses over by the train station. I used to live near there."

"That sounds more like it."

We've gone several blocks before I pause and look back at the Oriental. Smoke is spiraling high into the night sky from a window that is engulfed in flames.

"Bastard," I say under my breath.

"What?"

"That clerk. He gave us a room that faced the back."

27

A CROOKED NEON SIGN FLICKERS SOI 12 HOTEL.

It floats in the darkness deep in this knot of narrow alleys, one of the few areas in the city where the *sois* are numbered, not named.

"How about that one?" Kate wonders.

"Sold," I say numbly.

"You know, I've been thinking," she says as we approach the entrance, "Maybe a double's not such a bad idea."

"Sure," I say knowingly. "I think I'd feel more secure that way too."

For almost an hour, we've been walking through back alleys where light comes in thin shafts from an occasional window. Now, miles from the teeming tourist and business centers, we're in the Hua Lamphong district, an area adjacent to the main railway station just off Charu Muang Road where Kate used to live.

We enter the Soi 12's tiny lobby to find a lone clerk behind the desk reading a newspaper. He looks up and smiles, revealing blackened teeth. When Kate addresses him in Thai, he bows slightly, offers her a pen, and gestures to his register.

"Let's talk about this," I whisper, smiling at the clerk as I direct Kate aside. "Maybe you should tell him we'll pay extra if we don't have to do that."

She shakes her head no emphatically.

"Why not?"

"He'll know something's going on and sell the information to the police," she whispers tensely. "He will. Take my word for it. I know this city."

"Okay, make up some names."

"What if he asks to see our passports?"

She's right. They always ask for them; and, sure enough, when she returns to the desk to fill in the data, that's exactly what he does.

We pay cash for one night and climb a narrow staircase to the third floor. The room is immaculate and neat. It has twin beds, a small window that overlooks the alleys and rooftops, and not much else. There's no phone. The bathroom is down the hall.

I'm exhausted. I could sleep for a week. I fall onto one of the beds.

Kate sits on the edge of the other. The impact of what happened seems to have just hit her and hit her hard. All of a sudden, she's actually aware of just how close we came to being blown to bits. That's how it always was in-country. The realization came after a fire fight, not during it. Men who'd fought bravely, with no concern for their own safety, were often traumatized afterward when they realized how close they'd come to death, or what they'd done to their fellow man to avoid it.

"Better if you don't think about it," I counsel.

Kate's lips tighten into a thin line as she nods.

"Besides, you have a decision to make."

Her eyes widen curiously.

"I mean, you should be thinking about whether or not you want to continue this partnership."

She shrugs and splays her hands ambivalently.

"I'm the one involved in this drug thing. I'm the target. They have no reason to hurt you."

"Do they know that?" she asks in a fragile voice.

"Maybe not, now that you mention it."

A long silence follows.

Kate is staring off thoughtfully, a question forming in her eyes. "I'm confused about something."

"What's that?"

"Why did we run?"

"Why?"

She nods.

"I didn't think it would be wise to get involved with the police."

"Why not? We didn't do anything."

"For one thing, after Vegas and L.A., I've had my fill of cops. For another, I'm concerned about what the clerk might've told them. I mean, it was pretty obvious I thought something was about to happen. From his point of view, I'd say I knew something was about to happen. I'd rather not have to deal with that right now."

"You could explain."

"No. Even assuming the cops believe it, assuming they're not corrupt and up to their asses in this, they could still declare us undesirables and put us on the next flight home."

She nods resignedly, then glances at her watch and goes down the hall to the bathroom.

I'm propped up against the headboard, watching the pink and green neon flicker across the ceiling and listening to the sounds coming from the street: the din of traffic, rock music, bursts of tonal conversation and laughter. I keep seeing Carla's blank expression, and wondering about Surigao. Is he dead too? Is it over? Maybe I should be on the next flight out of here. It'd probably be the best thing for Kate. But I'll never know why Nancy died if I leave. Even if Surigao is dead, there's still Ajacier. I've no doubt he's the one who's behind it all. He has the answers. He knows why Nancy died. And I know where to find him. My mind drifts. I'm thinking about Nancy. She's playing the piano for me when Kate returns.

"I have to go," she announces, her voice a little stronger now.

I can't blame her. I'm a definite liability. A shortcut to a severely shortened lifespan. I sit up and swing my legs over the side of the bed. "I think you made the right decision."

Her eyes soften with friendly affection. "That's not what I meant. I have to meet Vann Nath."

"Oh! I forgot all about that."

"I want to ask you something. Okay?"

"Okay."

"After all this, I'm feeling a little—well, I mean, you

think maybe I could borrow your pistol? You know, take it with me?"

The fear in her eyes stops me for a moment. "I'm sorry Kate, it's gone."

"Oh, no."

"Yeah, I lost it at the street market. As they say, we're traveling light."

She nods glumly. "Tell me about it." She pulls at her blouse, reminding me that our luggage, along with our toiletries, personal items, clothing, laptop, and statistics were all destroyed. We have nothing but the clothes on our backs and our wits; and I'm not so sure about the latter.

"I wouldn't mind a shave and change of underwear myself. But we've got to get our hands on some firepower, first. And I'm not talking .25-caliber toys. I wonder if that guy downstairs has a phone book?"

"What for?"

"To look up the nearest gun shop or sporting goods store."

Kate shakes her head and smiles indulgently. "There's something you have to understand about Bangkok. You can buy everything here from knockoffs of Gucci bags to teenage sex slaves. But not guns."

"You mean, legally."

"Of course."

"Well, you lived here. You must know somebody in the black market, or a connection who could put us onto someone who has a friend who has another friend who knows someone who—"

"Vann Nath might." She pauses briefly, working up to something. "I was sort of hoping you'd offer to come with me."

"There's nothing wrong with asking, you know?"

"I think I just did."

"Where is this nightclub?"

"Patpong Road. Where else?" she replies brightly, clearly relieved she won't be going alone.

"Never heard of the place."

"Come on! It's where a half-million GIs went to get laid. You're not going to tell me you went sight-seeing."

"I went to Saigon and Manila," I explain, getting to my

feet with an exhausted groan. You have an international driver's license?''

She shakes her head no.

"Damn. Me neither.''

"Why?"

"Can't rent a car in this town without one.''

"'Yes, I know. But there's no need to. We can—''

"I don't like depending on taxis. I'd rather have a car. Come and go as I please.''

"Who said anything about taxis?''

"Then what?''

"Are you finished, Morgan?''

"I have a feeling I'd better be.''

Kate leads the way downstairs, taking us on a brisk walk though local streets to a gas station where dozens of motor scooters are neatly aligned.

"I would imagine,'' I say sheepishly, "one doesn't need an international driver's license to—''

"Nope. I used to rent them here all the time,'' she interrupts, heading toward the rental office. "The only way to travel in Bangkok.''

A few minutes later, she emerges and crosses to one of the scooters. It's a top-of-the-line maroon Honda, with a curved windscreen and elongated seat that extends atop the rear tire housing. She swings a leg over the scooter, rocks it off the kickstand, and stabs the key into the ignition, starting the engine.

"Put your feet on those pegs, grab the handles on either side of your butt, and hang on,'' Kate orders as I climb on behind her.

As soon as I'm settled she pops the clutch, and the scooter zips down the alley into the darkness. The harsh chatter of the engine echoes loudly off the buildings as she accelerates and snakes through the maze of *sois*. The sound, the movement, the cool air blowing in my face combine to give me a second wind. I'm twisting around to make sure we're not being followed when Kate takes a turn and catches me leaning the wrong way.

"Hey! Lean into it,'' she shouts over her shoulder, fighting to keep the scooter on line. She stops at the next corner, reaches back and pulls my arms around her waist. "Lean into it with me."

We make our way south along Rama IV Road toward the nightclub district. In the distance, the glow of neon turns the mist hovering above the Patpong rooftops into an ethereal rainbow. This is the heart of Bangkok's legendary nightlife, where the pleasures are carnal and the promises written in light: *Massage, Massage, Massage, Fire Cat Disco, Soul Kiss A-Go-Go, The Flesh Pot, Massage, Massage, Massage*. The signs shout in a montage of flashing, chasing, and blinking graphics that turn night into day with acerbic brilliance.

Kate skillfully maneuvers the scooter between the tourists and businessmen who meander through the streets and pulls up to a nightclub.

Above the entrance, in sync with the throbbing disco beat blaring from within, the word *Lolita* pulsates in blue-green neon, while a pair of lush, brilliant red lips part sensuously, revealing a fuschia tongue that licks a heart-shaped lollipop.

Inside, in the center of a massive room, young Thai women, very young as the sign promises, dance in mirrored cages surrounded by patrons gyrating to the driving music. Laser beams and blinding strobes pierce the infinite blackness overhead. Windows circle the room. These are really one-way mirrors through which more young women, with numbers affixed to their skimpy bikinis, can be seen posing seductively. Hostesses snake through the crowd, deftly balancing their trays and taking orders for drinks and "dates." We spot Vann Nath at a table away from the center of the action.

"Is he here yet?" Kate wonders anxiously as we join him.

Vann Nath nods. "He lives upstairs. His name is Pha Thi." He waves over a hostess, wraps a twenty-baht note around one of his business cards, and whispers some instructions before sending her off with it. Moments later she reappears and gestures we follow her. She leads the way through the club and up a flight of stairs. As we approach the landing, I detect a chemical odor, but I can't place it.

She ushers us into a loft that serves as Pha Thi's apartment and studio. The walls are papered with photo blowups of Asian girls in provocative poses. At the moment, his camera and attention are focused on a nude model who vanishes in a blinding explosion of light as we enter. By the time the spots are gone from my eyes, she's slipped into a robe and is hurrying off to a dressing room.

Pha Thi is a diminutive man with spiky jet black hair, faded jeans, T-shirt, and clogs. He sets his camera aside, presses his palms together, and bows slightly, then introduces his wife and children, who appear from their living quarters. The oldest, a girl in her teens, possesses striking beauty.

Kate says something to him in Thai.

Pha Thi responds with a puzzled smile.

Vann Nath explains he's a Meo. Though indigenous to Laos, this mountain tribe has its own language. It's akin to Tibetan, not Lao or Thai, which are dialects of the same language and mutually intelligible. "I told him you said he has a lovely family. He thanks you. He said he is very proud his daughter will soon be old enough to dance in the nightclub."

"How nice," Kate says, forcing a smile.

Formalities dispensed with, Vann Nath gets down to business. The two men converse briefly in Meo. Money changes hands. Finally Vann Nath turns to Kate and says, "He claims your husband was captured alive."

Kate's eyes brighten with hope. "Is he sure?"

Another brief exchange follows. "He says he was present at the time. He has proof."

Pha Thi nods several times in confirmation and smiles expectantly.

Vann Nath produces more cash, but holds on to it this time. Payment is contingent on whether or not the alleged proof is forthcoming.

Pha Thi goes to a row of battered file cabinets, rifles through a stuffed drawer, and returns with a black and white photograph. Stripped to the waist, hands tied behind his back, face unshaven and drawn from exhaustion, eyes pained and defiant, Captain John Ackerman stands in a jungle clearing, towering over his gloating Pathet Lao captors.

Kate gasps and looks away.

Vann Nath nods solemnly and deposits the cash in Pha Thi's palm.

I squeeze Kate's arm supportively. "Does he know what happened to Captain Ackerman after that?"

Pha Thi shakes his head no when he hears the translation, but his eyes seem to suggest otherwise.

"He knows, doesn't he?" Kate observes.

"He's probably holding out for more money."

Vann Nath nods and takes Pha Thi to task over the matter. But it's obvious from the tiny photographer's reaction that his reluctance isn't born of greed, but of compassion. When he finally gives in, what he says upsets Vann Nath, who turns to us and says, "He claims the officer in charge of the patrol that captured Captain Ackerman sold him to a farm collective."

"Sold him?" Kate echoes in an anguished wail.

Vann Nath nods grimly.

"To a bunch of farmers?" I exclaim, incensed. "Why would they do that?"

"He isn't sure. But he thinks it was because so many of the oxen and water buffalo they used to plough their fields and pull their wagons were killed in the bombing raids. Considering the circumstances at the time, I wouldn't put it past them to have bought POWs to replace their animals. Especially American pilots, whom they held responsible."

"That's inhumane, for Godsakes," I protest. "It's slavery. It's against every article of the Geneva Convention."

"Yes, but to their way of thinking no different than your migrant farm workers, for example."

"How can you say that?"

"My parents owned several plantations, Mr. Morgan. They sent me to the United States to be educated. UCLA '68. I wrote my thesis on the political impact of Caesar Chavez and the United Farm Workers. Perhaps a better analogy would be criminals who have been sentenced to hard labor. My point is that when it comes to these matters, I think it's very important to be aware of the other side's mind-set."

"Can't hurt," I reply grudgingly.

"Ask him if he knows where this collective was located," Kate suggests, fighting to maintain her composure.

"No, he doesn't," Vann Nath responds after a short exchange. "It was in Houa Phan Province, in the area around Sam Neua. That's all he remembers."

"Opium-growing country," I say.

Vann Nath nods sharply.

Pha Thi asks a question, gesturing to Kate. He lowers his eyes sadly at Vann Nath's reply, then goes on at length with heartfelt concern.

"He asked if you were the man's wife," Vann Nath explains. "He said he is very sorry to cause you such pain and unhappiness. Furthermore, though he knows it will increase the weight of your sorrow, he thinks you should know that he recalls hearing several shots fired as the patrol was leaving the area."

Kate pales and lowers her eyes.

"I don't understand. Is he saying those farmers executed Captain Ackerman?"

"He doesn't know. It's possible. It's also possible the Captain tried to escape, which was his duty. On the other hand, the gunfire may have had absolutely nothing to do with him."

Kate looks at me forlornly and shrugs. She's emotionally drained, torn by the uncertainty. I'm on the verge of exhaustion. There's no more to be said, no more questions to be asked. Vann Nath leads the way down the stairs and out a side door to the street.

"I'm sorry, Kate," he says, as we near his car.

"Don't be. It's something. It's a start."

"I'll talk to some of my contacts about locating that farm collective and give you a call."

"That's brings us to another matter," I say solemnly. "It'd be better if we call you."

"Why? What's wrong?" he asks, picking up on my tone. "What haven't you told me, Kate?"

"We're not at the Oriental anymore," she replies. "There was an incident today just after you left."

"The bombing . . . ?"

She nods gravely.

"It was all over the news tonight."

"The room they blew up was assigned to us. I was the target," I explain.

"My God. Why?"

"That's what I'm here to find out. You recall if our names were mentioned?"

"No. No, I don't believe they were."

"That's a relief. You made me an offer today, Mr. Vann Nath."

"Of course."

"We're walking around here unarmed. We have to get our hands on some firepower."

He nods and thinks for a moment, then turns to Kate. "Have you thought about contacting Timothy?"

Kate sighs. "I tried his number when I was in Hawaii, but I got a silk factory or something. There was no other listing."

"Who's Timothy?"

"Timothy Roark," Kate replies. "You remember I told you I had two contacts here? Timothy was the other. He took me to crash sites."

"I haven't seen him in years," Vann Nath resumes. "I hear he's become a bit of a recluse, taken to living on a *khlong* north of the city. I'll see if I can find out where."

"Listen, I don't want to put you to a lot of trouble. You sure it's worth looking this flake up?"

Vann Nath's eyes flare and lock onto mine like a gun turret ready to fire. "This flake, Mr. Morgan, has two silver stars, four bronze stars with additional citations, and several purple hearts. It would be your privilege to know him."

"I'm sure it would. This man—he'll know where we can get weapons?"

"No." Vann Nath replies with a dramatic pause. "Timothy will have them."

He hugs Kate, gets in his car, and drives off. We're standing in the darkness beneath a pair of neon lips sucking on a neon lollipop.

A half hour later we're back at the hotel.

Kate and I fall on our beds without undressing, the decision to sleep in our clothes prompted as much by exhaustion as modesty. But try as we might, neither of us can fall

asleep. I don't know how long we've been tossing and turning. I imagine she can't get that photograph of her husband
out of her mind. I can't. I'm finally dozing off when I think
I hear her getting up. I assume she's headed down the hall
to the bathroom, but a few seconds later, I feel her bur-
rowing in next to me. Like a child sneaking into her parents' bed during a thunderstorm, she's frightened and wants
the comfort of human contact. To be honest, so do I. It's
a strange feeling being this close to a woman again. A pleasant one. I wrap an arm around her and close my eyes. For
the first time, I'm aware of the smell of her perfume.

"Morgan? Come on, Morgan, wake up." I haven't been
asleep an hour when I hear Kate's voice and feel her shaking me. I roll over. Daylight's blasting through the window.
It's morning. I can't believe it. I slept like a rock. Over
eight hours without moving a muscle. I sit up, rubbing out
the cobwebs.

Kate is standing at the foot of my bed, smiling like she
knows something I don't. Then she hands me a toothbrush.

I glance across at the other bed. She's been shopping: A
tube of toothpaste, a razor, a can of shaving cream, sham-
poo, hair brush, and a few pieces of clothing are neatly
arranged on the cover.

"There's a street market around the corner," she explains, tossing a pair of Jockey shorts on the bed in front
of me. They're custard yellow. "I figured you were a 34/36.
Sorry about the color. It's all they had."

I grunt unintelligibly, gather a few things, and stumble
down the corridor to the bathroom. Twenty minutes or so
later, fully reconstituted and dressed, I return to the room.

"I'm starving," I announce brightly as I sweep through
the door. "What do you say we get something to eat and
figure out what we're going to do next?"

Kate nods stiffly. She has this funny expression on her
face. Then her eyes shift slightly to one side of the doorway
behind me, the side against which the door hinges open.

I'm about to turn when I hear the floor creak and feel a
gun muzzle pushed into my back.

"Don't move, Mr. Morgan," a man says sharply.

I freeze. Ajacier's thugs have found me. I'm waiting for

him to pull the trigger, waiting for the searing bullets to tear through my body, when a second man comes around in front of me. He's a Westerner in his early thirties, casually dressed with neatly combed hair and a hard professional face. He holds his gun on me while the other frisks me from behind. I'm glaring at him, frightened, my mind racing for a way to overcome them, concerned about Kate.

"He's clean," the frisker says.

"United States Drug Enforcement Agency, Mr. Morgan," the one in front says coolly, showing me his identification. "I'm going to have to ask you to come with us."

28

I'M IN AN OFFICE IN THE UNITED STATES EMBASSY ON Wireless Road, a broad boulevard where many diplomatic missions are located. In contrast to the architecture prevalent in this area, the building has severe lines. And, in keeping with this modern style, the office is cool and austere. A place for everything and everything in its place.

"Have a seat, Mr. Morgan," the DEA agent says. "It'll be a few minutes."

What will be a few minutes? I wonder. I'm prompted to ask, but I know it will be futile. These are terse, dispassionate men. The questions I asked during the drive here elicited polite replies.

"Am I under arrest?"

"No, sir."

"What's this all about?"

"I'm not at liberty to say, sir."

"Then drop me at the next corner."

"Can't do that, sir."

The chair the agent offers me is in the middle of the room in front of the desk. I've always disliked sitting with my back to the door, especially in these circumstances. I pull the chair around to the side, but before I can sit down, the agent returns it to its original position, making certain the legs match the marks in the gray carpet precisely. I take my seat, wondering why? A hidden microphone? A camera? Am I being secretly videotaped? More than a few minutes pass before a blind panel in the wall off to one side of the desk slides open.

A short, energetic man steps through it smartly and

crosses to the desk, paying me no mind. His polka-dot bow tie, brass-buttoned blazer, and crew cut combine to give him him a boyish, 1950s Ivy League quality. He lifts the phone and buzzes his secretary. "No calls," he says curtly, replacing the receiver with obsessive precision. After a pause, during which he cleans a fingernail, he cocks his head in my direction.

"Mr. A. Calvert Morgan," he says, drawing it out while he takes his measure of me. "Management consultant. Los Angeles, California."

I nod sullenly.

"My name's Tickner, Mr. Morgan. Clive M. Tickner. I'm the ranking DEA agent at this mission." He locks his eyes onto mine disapprovingly. "You're in way over your head, sir."

"Maybe. Maybe not." I hold his look, undaunted. "Either way, I don't need you to tell me that."

"Oh, yes you do. Believe me. You're involved in things you know nothing about."

"You'd be surprised how much I know. What do you want? Why am I here?"

"That's very interesting, Mr. Morgan. We both have the same questions. Guests first. Just why are you here?"

I've seen his type in corporate boardrooms and government offices: Exeter, Princeton, Wharton—no, probably the Fletcher School at Tufts in his case. Meticulous, brainy, an excess of starch, he makes no effort to hide his conceit.

"I don't have to answer that, Mr. Tickner. In case you haven't figured it out yet, I'm the victim here. I haven't done anything illegal."

Tickner folds his hands and sits very still, like a feline about to pounce. His eyes shift knowingly to one of the agents. He opens a desk drawer, and removes a small plastic bag. A red tag is affixed to the closure. He studies it for a moment, cupping it in his hands so I can't see the contents, before placing it on the desk in front of me.

My jaw slackens. The wind goes out of me. I feel like a kid caught stealing a candy bar. Despite the reflections on the plastic, I've no doubt the pistol inside the bag is a .25-caliber Beretta, nor have I any doubt that it's mine.

"Oh, yes, we were there, Mr. Morgan. We've been

watching you from the moment you and Mrs. Ackerman set foot in Bangkok. We weren't exactly sure what you were up to, so we observed for a while. When you started to interfere with our plans—"

"Someone interfered with mine," I interrupt angrily. "Up until a couple of months ago I was planning to grow old gracefully with my wife."

"Yes, I'm very sorry. Colonel Webster briefed us on your story."

I feel betrayed. It shows.

"No, the colonel isn't working with us. He merely called one of our agents in Washington to discuss your mutual concerns. Someone whose judgment he trusts."

"He said he was going to do that."

"And that's all he did. The agent had the presence of mind to call us. I'm sorry if we've inconvenienced you, but we can't very well have American citizens coming over here and settling personal vendettas with guns."

"I wasn't going to kill Surigao. I was going to—"

"Someone shot and killed his wife, Mr. Morgan," Tickner interrupts. His tone is suddenly sharper, accusatory. "You were in the car with her."

"Yes, but I didn't shoot her."

"Whoever it was shot him too."

"I know that. Check the pistol. Only one shot's been fired. If you check the car you'll see the round went through the roof. I heard him tell his wife he was being double-crossed. He said a man named Ajacier was trying to kill him."

"Yes," Tickner says matter-of-factly. "We know all about Mr. Ajacier."

"So do I. As a matter of fact he and I had a chat yesterday. But he's not my primary target. Surigao is. I would've caught him, too, if a tourist hadn't gotten in the way."

Tickner smiles in amusement, then presses one of the buttons on his communications console.

A moment later, I hear a door opening behind me. I turn to see a big man lumbering forward. He stands next to my chair, towering over me.

"Is this the gentleman?" Tickner asks.

The camera and gadget bag are gone. The flower-print

shirt has been replaced by a button-down oxford, striped tie, and sportcoat, but the friendly smile remains.

"Yes, it is."

"Agent Nash is in charge of this case. He—"

"He's with you?"

"I believe I just said that."

My outrage has been building with every word and condescending inflection. I get to my feet to confront Nash. "I don't get it. Surigao ran right past you. Why didn't you stop *him?*"

Nash clears his throat and glances to his boss.

"He was doing his job," Ticker replies. "Which, among other things, was to keep you from harassing Mr. Surigao."

"Look, I told you I wasn't out to kill him. I just wanted the satisfaction of catching the son of a bitch. I was planning to turn him over to you."

Silence. A look passes between them.

"What? What does that mean?"

"We wouldn't want you to do that either," Tickner finally replies evenly.

I'm flabbergasted. "Why the hell not?"

"Because it goes against policy."

"Against policy? The man's a killer, a drug trafficker. Call Colonel Webster. Call the Los Angeles Police. Sergeant Daniels. I have his number right here."

"We know what Mr. Surigao is."

"Well, if it isn't your policy to nail these bastards, what is?"

"That's all I can tell you."

"You're going to have to do better than that, Mr. Tickner. Much better. I lost my wife to this. Nothing's going to make me walk away from it. I'm warning you. I want answers."

"I don't have any for you."

"I think you do. And one way or another, I'm going to get them. Don't think you can ignore me. I have contacts in Congress. People I do business with all the time. You can answer my questions or you can answer theirs. Now, what the hell are you doing here if not busting these guys?"

Tickner runs his fingertips over his temples, thinking it through, then nods. "Frankly, Mr. Morgan, we wonder our-

selves on occasion. We spend a lot of time walking a tightrope. Every once in a while someone knocks us off.
Sometimes it's their side, sometimes ours. Unfortunately—
this time it was ours."

He signals Nash, who crosses to the wall and rolls back
a panel revealing diagrams of Asian drug rings. He slides
several aside until he finds the one he wants. It displays
maps, charts, and handwritten lists. Cities: Bangkok, Manila, Honolulu, San Francisco. Organizations: Golden Gate
Mortuaries, Franco-Asian Enterprises, and the CIL among
them. Photographs with names beneath: Ajacier, Messina,
Surigao, Webster, along with others that I don't recognize.

"For what it's worth," Nash explains, "We've been planning to roll up the whole damn net—growers, manufactur-
ers, distributors—I mean, the whole kit and kaboodle.
Matter of fact, your friend Surigao gave us a call yesterday.
Sounded real desperate. Claimed he had something to sell
that'd blow this whole thing sky-high."

"No wonder they want to kill him."

"That's one theory," Tickner says indulgently.

I shudder at the thought that occurs to me. All I want is
justice, but reading between the lines, I have a feeling justice is the one thing I'll be denied. "We talking a deal here?
Are you going to offer this creep immunity from prosecut-
ion in exchange for his testimony?"

"That's usually the way it works," Nash replies.

"He's getting off scot-free?"

"Oh, they all are," Tickner replies coolly.

I'm rocked. "What the hell does that mean?"

"It means, we don't want to blow it sky-high, Mr. Morgan. We wouldn't need Surigao's information if we did.
Being prudent, we suggested he come by for a chat anyway. He refused. Demanded money. Immediately. That
was the end of it. We have little incentive to make deals
with people we aren't prosecuting. As I said, he's off the
hook and we told him so."

"Just like that."

Tickner nods.

"I have a feeling we're talking policy again."

"And its implementation, to be precise."

"They both stink."

"You asked. You wish me to continue or not?"

"Please."

"Our mission is to prevent narcotics from being exported to the United States. Now, despite what you see on TV, apprehending and prosecuting drug traffickers is but one way policy is implemented. Diplomatic and financial pressures are also used to induce governments to cooperate. And successfully so. However, in this case, as Agent Nash just mentioned, the preferred method was to apprehend and prosecute."

"Now it's changed?"

"Yes, I'm afraid so." Tickner pauses to recall something. "Economics major, Cal Tech, Seventy-two. MBA, Stanford, Seventy-four," he says rapid-fire, emphasizing each with a jab of his forefinger. "I believe I have that right?"

The son of a bitch has pulled my file. Military? FBI? I wonder what they have on me. I nod warily, feeling vulnerable again.

"Then you shouldn't have any trouble understanding the dynamics of this marketplace. For starters, as you may know, opium is the cash crop in certain parts of Southeast Asia."

"The Golden Triangle."

"Correct.

"And heroin's their most important product," Nash chimes in. He steps to the panel and points to one of the photographs. A fierce-looking Asian man. "We're up against a nasty piece of work named Chen Dai. He's chief honcho of a bunch of Meo guerrillas in the Golden T. Threw in with the Pathet Lao during the war. The man sells pure heroin, Mr. Morgan. I mean, we're talking six nines pure, what we call Double U-O Globe. Chen Dai claims he uses the money to fight his miniwars and border skirmishes. He's been fighting 'em for thirty years; he'll be fighting 'em for thirty more."

"He wouldn't be fighting them in Houa Phan Province, would he?"

Tickner raises a brow in tribute. "You have done your homework, haven't you?"

"I plan on doing lots more."

"It's my job to dissuade you. Prevent you, if necessary."

"Dammit, why?"

"Your favorite word again."

"Policy."

Tickner nods. "Getting back to our economics primer, all the farmers work for Chen Dai in exchange for protection. It's like a Mafia extortion racket. He runs it out of a mountain compound. It's totally isolated. No highways, airstrips, or other effective means of transport, which means it's highly defensible. This also means the farmers can't grow crops that need to be rushed to market before they spoil." He pauses and plucks a bulbous, long-stemmed pod from a vase on his desk. "Enter the indestructible poppy seed—which makes narcotics the bedrock of Chen Dai's economy."

"See," Nash concludes, "the bottom line is the bottom line. Only thing he cares about is his GNP."

"Just a guy trying to make a buck."

Tickner nods smartly. "And despite the daunting logistics, some bored Foggy Bottom economist came up with what they call a crop substitution program."

"All you have to do is convince him he can make more money planting edible crops instead of opium."

Tickner nods and eyes me curiously.

"The colonel mentioned it."

"Understand, we're not providing seeds to grow carrots and peas here. We're talking a massive aid package. An infusion of capital sufficient to build highways, airstrips, railroads—"

"It didn't sound that grand when the colonel was talking about it."

"Well, the colonel's mission makes his view of this rather narrow." Tickner pauses, then pointedly adds, "And we've kept it that way."

He crosses to the panel of graphics, peels off the colonel's photo, then uncaps a broad-tipped marker, and goes about blacking out the name Webster.

"This is an insidious business. No one gets the benefit of the doubt. Everyone is guilty until proven innocent. In the colonel's case, these people have been using his facility for years, and we weren't sure of him." He pauses and winces as if it pains him even to think such things. "However, his forthright call to Washington, and several follow-ups, which I initiated, were sufficient grounds for acquittal. He'll be here tomorrow to review the situation."

"Then as far as you're concerned, the CIL is being used to smuggle drugs."

"Definitely. We'll come back to that. I was about to say, there are two conditions attached to this program. The first is a deficit guarantee. Opium is a very cost-effective crop. There's no way bean sprouts or snow peas will outperform it when it comes to producing income."

"And Uncle Sam's picking up the difference."

"Precisely."

"That economist wasn't bored, Mr. Tickner, he was incompetent."

"I couldn't agree more. But more important, the second condition—the one that impacts *our* relationship—guarantees there will be no black eyes in Laos. In other words, neither the government nor any of its citizens will be tainted by even the hint of a drug scandal."

"What's it got to do with Surigao, Ajacier, and all those other guys on your chart there? They aren't citizens of Laos."

"Indeed, they aren't. The problem is, arrests mean trials, testimony, congressional hearings, and that means the first-amendment folks."

"The media."

"The media. There's no way we could initiate criminal proceedings without seriously endangering that guarantee."

"So you're saying that despite identifying the players, and despite having the goods on them, nobody's going to be prosecuted."

Tickner's lips tighten. He nods imperceptibly.

I feel like I've been kicked in the groin. "Chrissakes, come on, those bastards murdered my wife. They tried to kill me. And they're still trying. They put a bomb in my hotel room yesterday."

Silence. Looks dart between them.

Nash finally leans his weight against the corner of the desk. "They pulled the rug out from under us, too, Mr. Morgan," he says with profound disappointment. "I've been busting my hump on this for years. Just when I'm ready to roll these fucks up, they cut themselves a sweet deal. And if that's not enough, we get the job of covering their asses.''

I just glare at him. How dare he equate his loss with mine, with Nancy's death.

''The bottom line,'' Tickner concludes, toying with his bow tie, ''is that prosecuting drug traffickers has never been our primary goal. Stopping the flow of drugs is. If locking these people up works, fine. If this crop-sub program works, then that's good policy too. And we're the instrument through which that policy is implemented.''

I'm seething, staring at the floor, hoping to God Surigao is dead. ''What a fucking travesty.''

Nash nods glumly.

''Call it what you like, Mr. Morgan,'' Tickner says. ''That's the way the game is played. Always has been, always will be. I hope you'll accept that.''

''Do I have a choice?''

''No. Neither do we. The man took us on and beat us. The thing that bugs me is Chen Dai played it like he always knew he would win. Even when we had his back to the wall, he seemed totally unthreatened. Too calm, too cool, too collected.'' He shakes his head, baffled. ''I've always had the feeling he had an ace in the hole or something. It's irrelevant now.''

''Would you mind answering a question for me?''

''Hard to say until I hear it.''

''I've been trying to figure out why they want to kill me. I know it has something to do with my inquiry to the CIL. But I—''

''What makes you say that?''

''Surigao had his wife on the lookout for my name. I was wondering if you had any idea why?''

Tickner's eyes cloud. He seems genuinely puzzled. ''No, none whatsoever. This is the first I've heard of that. As far as I know, he was the liaison between various way stations: Bangkok, Manila, Honolulu, San Francisco.''

''That's it?''

Tickner nods.

"Let's go back to the CIL. You said Chen Dai's people were using it to bring the stuff in."

He nods again.

"How?"

He studies me for a moment, deciding. "It's concealed in transfer cases."

That's the last thing I expected. "No. No way."

"Yes. Twenty kilos per case, as a matter of fact."

"Twenty?!"

"Twenty."

"That's more than forty pounds! The colonel and I weighed dozens of cases. Each one was right on the money. A hundred twenty-one pounds."

He smiles, pleased with himself. "I'm sure they were, Mr. Morgan. There's no need to feel inadequate. It took us years to figure it out. It's nothing short of brilliant, believe me. As I mentioned, I'll be reviewing the entire situation with the colonel tomorrow."

"What time tomorrow?"

He smiles knowingly. "He'll be here at eleven. I guess you've earned the right to join us, if you like."

"You bet your ass I like."

29

I LEAVE TICKNER'S OFFICE WITH MIXED EMOTIONS. I'M curious as hell to find out how they used the transfer cases—impossible as far as I'm concerned—and I'm fuming that those responsible for Nancy's death are not only getting off, they're being awarded a fat financial aid package. It's small comfort, but it appears the latter doesn't extend to Ajacier. On the contrary, he just had a major source of income go down the toilet. No wonder he welshed on the payoff to Surigao.

I make my way through the maze of corridors and bound down a short flight of steps to the embassy's lobby, planning to take a taxi back to the hotel.

Kate comes hurrying across the expanse of marble from one of the seating areas. "You okay?"

"Yes and no. It's a long story," I reply, taking a moment to cover the broad strokes. "I haven't the foggiest idea what I'm going to do now."

"Maybe I can help," she says, with that 'I know something you don't' smile.

"What's that mean?"

"Got something for you." She takes a fistful of pink telephone messages from her bag, and hands them to me. There must be at least a half dozen.

"Where'd you get these?"

"The Oriental. It occurred to me the rest of the world thinks we're staying there," she replies as I sift through them. Several are from my office, one from Janie, a couple from Laura. "There's one you might want to pay special attention to."

My eyes snap open in astonishment as she says it. I'm staring at a message to call Mr. Surigao. There's a phone number and, below it, the word *urgent*, which is underlined. The son of a bitch isn't decomposing in some rancid alley after all. I'm baffled.

"Why the hell is he calling me? And how did he know where we were staying?"

"Well, there are only a handful of major hotels. He probably just went down the list until he hit the Oriental. The phone booths are in that corridor over there," she prompts knowingly.

I use my eyes to warn her. "No way. Not from here," I whisper.

She nods, and leads the way from the lobby to an embassy parking area. For someone who sleeps with his car phone, the lack of public booths in this city is becoming a major pain in the ass. We set off on the scooter in search of the nearest hotel. A short distance down Wireless Road, we come upon the Hilton in a park adjacent to a canal. There's a row of booths in a lounge area off to one side of the lobby.

I anxiously thumb a coin into the slot, dial the number, and listen to that jarring, buzzerlike ring.

"*Swadee?*" A man's voice answers gruffly.

"I'm calling for Mr. Surigao."

"Who? Who I can tell?"

"My name's Morgan. He left a message at my hotel."

I hear the phone being set down and the sounds of someone walking, followed by a short, muffled conversation, and then . . .

"Morgan?" It's Surigao. I recognize the voice immediately. "What took you so long?"

"I just got your message. What's on your mind?"

"Money. I want to make a deal."

"With me?"

"Yes. I have information to sell."

That sure explains a few things. If the DEA won't play ball, maybe I will. I'm more than intrigued. "What kind of information?"

"Something that'll blow the lid off this thing."

"Why not go to the authorities?" I wonder, knowing he'd expect me to ask.

"I did, dammit," he replies, an edge creeping into his voice. "I don't have time to play their games or yours. People are trying to kill me. I have to get out of here. I need money, and I need it fast."

"How do I know you have anything of value?"

"Look, my people owed me a lot of money. They—"

"You mean Ajacier?"

"Right. He told me to go to hell. I threatened to take this stuff to the DEA. That's when he tried to cancel my ticket."

"I wish he had."

"You want to deal or not?"

"Not until you tell me why you've been trying to cancel mine."

"That's what you're buying, Morgan," he counters with a sarcastic snort. "That's what you're buying."

I swallow hard, taking a moment to collect myself. "How much do you want?"

"Fifty thousand."

"What? You can't be serious."

"In U.S. currency and I need it today."

"I don't have access to that kind of money."

"Wire it from your company."

"Not that simple. My business isn't my personal slush fund. Even if it was, it's three in the morning in L.A. The banks won't open for six hours. By then the banks here'll be long closed. It'll take at least a couple of days to wire anything."

"I'm getting out of here tonight."

"Change your plans."

"I can't. Forget it. That's not a possibility. Can you get twenty-five?"

"Not a chance."

"You better think of something fast if you want this, Morgan."

My mind races in search of an answer. I finally zero in on a vacation Nancy and I took several years ago. We were in an art gallery in Rome. She fell in love with a painting. The one that now hangs next to the piano. It was $8,500.

The dealer wouldn't take plastic and we didn't have a check-book with us. I ended up taking a hefty cash advance on a credit card.

"Okay, I've got an idea that might work."

"Today."

"Yes, it'll take a couple of hours."

"That's more like it. There's a small dock at the end of Saengkee Road."

"Yangking?"

"No," he replies, repeating it and spelling it out. "It's in the Trokchan District about a mile south of the Oriental. A water taxi will be there at six o'clock to pick you up. The driver'll wait fifteen minutes."

"I'll be there."

He hangs up.

The dial tone is buzzing in my ear. I'm not sure what I'm feeling, but I know that contrary to what Tickner said, I do have a choice. And I just made it.

"Well?" Kate prompts as I leave the booth.

"I've got till six o'clock to come up with twenty-five thousand bucks."

"Twenty-five thousand? What for?"

"Surigao wants to sell information."

"You sure it isn't a trap? I mean, he could be setting out to finish what he started."

"No, he's desperate. He wants out. He's the one taking the chance. I know I won't kill him. But he doesn't." I pause, entertaining a thought that occurs to me. "Maybe I still will."

"With what?"

I hold up my hands. "How about these? Wouldn't be the first time. Needless to say, I'm not real thrilled about going unarmed. You get a chance to check in with Vann Nath?"

"Yes, I called his office. He was out. There wasn't any message. What are you going to do?"

"You know where the American Express office is?"

"I don't think there is one."

"That doesn't sound right. You sure?"

"Come to think of it, I vaguely recall they have a repre-sentative someplace." She returns to the phone booths and starts thumbing through the Bangkok City Book. "Here it is. It's in the Sea Tours office at the Siam Intercontinental."

We leave the Hilton and head west on Phloenchit through heavy midday traffic on the scooter. About twenty minutes later, I spot the Intercontinental's roof swooping skyward, amid acres of tropical foliage. The Sea Tours office is on Level Four in the shopping arcade. I plunk a Platinum American Express Card in front of the agent and tell her I want a twenty-five-thousand-dollar cash advance.

"Twenty-five thousand," she repeats awestruck.

"Can I get that much?"

"I'm sorry, Mr. . . . Morgan," she replies, glancing to the card for my name. "There's a ten-thousand-dollar limit on advances."

"Ten?"

"Yes, sir."

"How many advances can I get?"

"Just one, I'm afraid."

I scowl, exasperated.

Kate leans her head to mine and whispers, "If I were in Surigao's shoes and someone offered me ten thousand bucks, I'd take it."

So would I. She's right.

After verifying my identity, the woman explains I can draw against an established line of credit or via personal check, which would be faster.

I make out the check.

She takes it to her supervisor.

"I was afraid of this," she says when she returns. "We don't have that much cash on hand. You see, this isn't a full service office, and—"

"Can you get it?"

"Of course. We can give you half now, which, at today's rate, works out to one hundred twenty-five thousand bahts, and the remainder tomorrow."

"Bahts?"

"Yes, sir. We can only give you local currency."

"I can't use bahts. I said dollars. I'm sorry if I didn't make that clear. It has to be United States currency. And I have to have it today."

"I'm afraid that isn't possible."

"Look. This is an emergency. You have to—"

"Did you say emergency, sir?"

"Why? Does that make a difference?"

"Absolutely. It means we can request World Wide Personal Assist get involved. They're a special unit that services Platinum Card holders in such matters: emergency medical evacuation, disaster relief, aid to travelers stranded by political events, getting dinner reservations at four-star restaurants. We even—"

"Please, just make the arrangements, okay?"

She forces a smile, dials the phone, and starts talking in Thai. I've no idea what's transpiring, but Kate does. I'm watching her face, my hopes rising and falling with every change of expression. Finally, she squeezes my hand reassuringly. "It sounds like a courier's going to pick up the money at their bank and bring it here before the end of the business day."

The woman finishes her call and confirms it. The end of the business day is four o'clock. That's plenty of time. I'm relieved and impressed. Since the advent of mileage cards, I rarely use American Express. I've even considered cancelling it. Now, as the man says, I'm glad I didn't leave home without it.

My eyes are glued to my watch. Fifteen minutes, a half hour, then an hour go by. Four o'clock comes and goes. I'm beside myself. I insist the woman call the bank. They assure her the courier is on his way. She assumes he's caught in traffic, which is very heavy at this hour. It's 5:20 when a scooter glides up to the entrance. The courier explains he stopped to wager on the kite fights and lost track of time.

"Kite fights?" I exclaim, as I scribble my signature across the advance forms.

While the woman puts the currency in a manila envelope, Kate explains that they're an annual battle of the sexes. Sleek male kites resembling jet fighters attempt to bring down their well-rounded female counterparts with a hooked prong. It involves heavy betting and is taken very seriously.

Money in hand, we dash to the scooter and head across town in heavy traffic toward the Chao Phraya River. Kate weaves between the gridlocked vehicles, swerving up on sidewalks and taking back-alley shortcuts through the darkening waterfront streets.

It's 6:10 when we turn into Saengkee Road, which follows the bends of a canal to a small landing. A water taxi waits rocking in the swells. Kate leans on the scooter's horn to announce our arrival. The driver responds with several urgent waves of his arm.

"See you back at the hotel," I say, climbing off the scooter the instant it comes to a stop.

"Wait," Kate says. She takes something from her purse and puts it in my hand. It's a black plastic canister about five inches long, and resembles a huge butane cigarette lighter.

"Mace?"

"I live and work in our nation's capital, our nation's murder capital. Just aim and fire."

"Thanks."

"Take care of yourself."

I run to the water taxi. The instant I'm aboard, the driver hits the throttle, heading south into the river. I've no idea where we're going, which makes me uneasy. My eyes begin picking up streaks of red and green in the darkness. Port and starboard running lights. There are boats everywhere. Any one of them could be following us.

A half hour later, the towering cranes of oceangoing freighters loom in the distance. We're entering Khlong Toey, Bangkok's deepwater port. Long lines of rice barges wait to unload the cargo beneath their corrugated metal roofs, which give them the look of floating Quonset huts.

Finally the driver begins angling toward one of the big piers, where a freighter sits low in the water, straining at its hausers. Smoke wafts from the single stack as the crew scurries about in the harsh glare of work lights, making ready to put to sea.

Beyond the freighter at the far end of the pier, rows of single-story rusting metal buildings sit above the river on stilts. From the looks of it, this desolate, dreary facility must be some kind of a hostel or rooming house for itinerant seamen. The driver cuts the engine and guides the water taxi to a stop against one of the floating docks.

I make him understand that I won't be long and he should wait to take me back. Then I climb onto the dock, searching the darkness for Surigao as I make my way along the rickety walkways that extend from the buildings and connect the boat slips. I'm heading for a gangway that leads up to the main pier when a voice calls out.

"Morgan?"

I turn to see a man exiting one of the ramshackle structures. Light from a window washes over his face as he comes toward me. He's an Asian with a shaved head and thin moustache. He takes several more steps before I realize it's Surigao. His wound couldn't have been very serious, because one hand holds a small travel bag, the other a pistol.

"You won't need that," I say, my voice breaking at being face-to-face with Nancy's killer.

He studies me, deciding, then nods and slips the gun into his pocket. We stand there staring at each other. My heart is racing, surging with emotion. All I can see is Nancy lying on the stainless steel table at the morgue. I vowed that's not how I'd remember her, but I can't help it now. Surigao knows what I'm thinking. He sees the hatred in my eyes.

"I tried to dissuade you," he finally says grimly. "You should've let it go."

"I did, dammit. Soon as I found out about the guy who stole my tags."

"Pettibone."

"Yes, I thought he'd died in combat. I couldn't believe I'd been breaking my ass to put some slimebag's name on the wall. It was over, Surigao. I mean over. Then you killed my wife. You bastard."

"It was a mistake."

"That doesn't change anything."

"You evened the score."

"Bullshit. That was Ajacier and you know it."

"That doesn't change anything either." He stiffens and bites a lip to maintain his composure. I notice his eyes have become watery. Is it real? Is he acting? Is he this good? "Carla wasn't involved. She didn't know."

"She knew my name."

He nods grudgingly and removes a white business envelope from his pocket. "It's all in here."

The shriek of the freighter's whistle startles us. Surigao glances anxiously over his shoulder as a cloud of smoke belches skyward from the ship's stack. "Time to go," he grunts, gesturing to the envelope tucked under my arm. "That it?"

I nod, trying to suppress my apprehension. "Ten thousand."

"Ten?" he explains as if insulted.

"That's all I could get."

He eyes me suspiciously, then with a grudging nod says, "I'll take it."

We exchange envelopes, opening them simultaneously. He smiles thinly at the sight of the U.S. currency, stuffs it into his bag, and turns toward the gangway that leads up to the pier.

"Hold it," I say, stepping in front of him. I'm about to remove the contents of the envelope he gave me when the roar of a motor rises. I glimpse the wake of a boat cutting through the water. It's coming right toward us, coming fast. I can make out a figure standing in the bow silhouetted against the distant lights of the city. Suddenly the darkness comes alive with the blue-orange flashes and ear-splitting chatter of machine-gun fire.

Surigao gets off several shots from his pistol and runs toward the gangway. I sprint across the landing toward the water taxi, stuffing the envelope into my pocket. But the driver panics and walls the throttle before I get there. I dive into the water without breaking stride and surface to see Surigao sprinting up the gangway. He's nearing the pier when the bullets tear into his body, spinning him around. He stumbles down the gangway as the gunman continues raking him with fire. The impact knocks him into the water.

The shooting stops.

Surigao is floating facedown in a widening pool of blood while the envelope with my ten thousand dollars drifts off to be netted by some lucky fisherman.

I'm treading water, keeping an eye on the boat and quietly backing my way toward the main pier, when the beam from a searchlight sweeps toward me. Suddenly, the boat's engine comes to life, the stern digs into the water, the bow swings round, and the gunman opens fire. I dive beneath the surface and start swimming toward the pier. The water is vile-tasting and nearly pitch black, but I can glimpse the splash of bullets above me. Spent rounds go spiraling past harmlessly.

I'm pulling my way through the water frantically, fighting the weight of my clothes, when I flashback to Vietnam, to the day I spent trapped by a VC patrol in a rice paddy in the Mekong Delta. They hunted me for hours. Up and down the neatly planted rows, poking, prodding, firing into the water at the slightest rustle. Each time they neared, I'd submerge and claw my way along the muddy bottom, my lungs screaming for air like they are now.

I continue swimming underwater until I brush up against a cluster of pilings that support the pier. They're easily twelve to fifteen inches in diameter. I move behind them, putting the mass of wood between me and the gunman, then surface, gasping the air. The boat cruises past a short distance away, the shooter crouching in the bow, squinting into the darkness in search of me. He finally fires an indiscriminate burst, spraying the area beneath the pier. I cower behind the pilings as chunks of wood dart through the air. He fires several more bursts before moving off. I wait until the sound of the engine fades, then begin making my way along the line of pilings toward shore. I'm halfway there when I come upon a rusting ladder and start climbing.

I walk the length of the pier, past the freighter that is sailing without Surigao, and head north along the waterfront through a vast slum. I finally come upon a cruising *tuk-tuk,* one of those three-wheeled tin cans with open sides that dart about the city at breakneck speed in search of fares. I'm still soaking wet. The driver takes one look and waves me off. I climb in anyway, offering to pay him double. He doesn't seem to understand. I hold up two fingers. He holds up three, smiles, and heads for the hotel.

I slump in the seat exhausted and check my pocket for the envelope. It's still there. I'm itching to open it, but it's wet, and I'm concerned I'll damage the contents. Besides, I have more pressing concerns: If Ajacier's people followed me, they probably know where we're staying. I'm worried about Kate.

A harrowing forty-five minutes later, the *tuk-tuk* arrives at the Soi 12. I hurry through the lobby and up the stairs to find her waiting for me.

"You swim back?" she cracks, having gotten used to my disheveled entrances.

"Damn near," I reply with urgency. "Come on. We're getting out of here."

"Why? What happened?"

"Well, you were pretty close. It was Ajacier who finished what he started."

"Surigao's dead."

"Yes, they must've followed me."

"How'd they know you were meeting him?"

"If they can booby-trap a hotel room, they shouldn't have any trouble getting their hands on telephone messages. Once they knew he was trying to make contact, they let me lead them to him."

"You mean they know we're staying here?"

"It wouldn't be real smart to assume they don't. The DEA found us. Why couldn't they?"

"Maybe they had help?"

"Hard to say. Of course, they are in business together. We have everything?"

We take a last look around, leave the room, and clamber down a set of fire stairs to an alley behind the hotel. Minutes later we're weaving through Bangkok's narrow alleys on the scooter. We head across town to a different district, pick another small hotel at random, and check in. The room is slightly larger and has its own bathroom.

I take the envelope and canister of Mace from my pocket, returning the latter to Kate.

"Better get out of those clothes," she cautions.

"Not until I see what I got for my ten thousand bucks."

The envelope is still damp, which makes the surfaces adhere to one another. My heart is pounding as I reach inside and ease out a sheet of paper that is folded in thirds like a business letter. I put it on the dresser, opening it carefully. It's a piece of standard 8½ × 11 inch bond.

Neatly typed and alphabetized in three columns is a list of names and serial numbers.

"Look, there's John," Kate exclaims, spotting her husband's name near the top of the first column.

It takes me a moment longer to find mine midway down the second. Then I start counting. The first column has thirty-five names. I don't have to count the rest to determine the total because the second column is of equal length, the third seven names shorter.

"Ninety-eight," I announce with a shrug. Not 547, not 411, not 136; neither a multiple, dividend, nor square root of any of them, nor a match to any of the statistical profiles I've drawn. It's a number without meaning. My least favorite kind. I've been disarmed. "You recognize the rest of these names?"

"Some of them."

"Any lost in Houa Phan Province?"

"It's possible."

"Possible? I thought you were the expert."

"I'm sorry, I don't have all five hundred forty-seven loss scenarios committed to memory. I do recall the guy who stole your tags wasn't lost in Houa Phan Province."

"He wasn't. He wasn't lost at all. His body was recovered and disappeared from the mortuary."

"Then what's your name doing on this list?"

"I wish I knew. Can you think of anything else they might have in common?"

She shakes her head no. "All the information you're after was blown to bits with your computer."

"You remember the names of the men who were just repatriated?"

"Yes, I do," she replies evenly.

"They on the list?"

She takes a moment to scan it. "No. They're not here."

"None. You're sure?"

"Positive."

"What about your friend who died in the accident? Her husband's name on it?"

She runs a finger down the page and stops. "Yes, right there."

"He was lost in Houa Phan, wasn't he?"

Kate nods. Her expression darkens at my reaction. "You really think they killed her, don't you?"

"Carla said mine wasn't the only name she was looking for."

"Which means there could even be others."

I nod grimly. "The question is, why? Surigao said this list would explain it, but it doesn't." I pull the wet shirt over my head and toss it across the room in disgust. "I still don't have the slightest idea why Nancy died."

Kate nods solemnly and hands me a towel.

"The only thing that makes any sense is that all these names threaten their operation."

"Well, didn't Surigao say the list would blow this whole thing sky-high?"

I nod thoughtfully. "I guess it's up to me to find a way to light the fuse."

"Up to us," she corrects resolutely. "John's name is on that list too."

30

TWENTY KILOS PER TRANSFER CASE?" COLONEL WEBSTER exclaims incredulously.

"That's what I said. I still don't believe it."

Tickner responds with one of his Cheshire smiles. "I guess I'll just have to beat you gentlemen into submission," he says, mysteriously. He opens a desk drawer and removes a hammer.

The colonel and I exchange baffled looks, neither able to imagine what the natty little DEA agent with the crew cut has in mind. If nothing else, Tickner strikes me as the kind of guy who couldn't drive a nail if his life depended on it.

He swivels his chair, stands, and pushes a button on his communications console. The blind panel in the wall behind him slides open. He leads us through it, hammer at the ready.

"By the way, I thought Mrs. Ackerman might've been here," Webster prompts as we follow.

"She sends her regards. She's on a little mission of her own at the moment."

Important mission, would be more accurate. Last night, despite changing hotels, I slept fitfully, jumping at every sound. The shooting and Surigao's mysterious list of names were part of it, but being unarmed was my primary concern. It still is. We haven't had any word from Vann Nath in almost two days. This morning, Kate and I decided she'd drop me at the embassy, then head across town to his office and remind him of our need to acquire firepower.

Tickner has led the way down a long corridor to a steel door. He pushes it open and ushers the colonel and me into a large space where Nash and one of the agents who picked me up at the hotel yesterday are waiting. It reminds me of a police evidence room. A collection of guns, knives, plastic bags bursting with drugs, and other items confiscated in raids, are stored on metal shelving that lines the walls. In the center, on stands that raise them to desktop height, are two aluminum transfer cases.

While we gather around them, Tickner contemplates his hammer, playing on our curiosity before bringing it down sharply atop one of the transfer cases. The blow leaves a pronounced ding in the brush-finished aluminum. He steps back expectantly as the two agents grip the handles at opposite ends of the T-case, lift off the top, and turn it upside down.

"Now, what's wrong with this picture?" Tickner asks like a prodding schoolmaster.

The colonel and I lean forward to examine the transfer case. A few seconds pass before it dawns on me. "There's no ding on the inside."

"That's quite good, Mr. Morgan."

"Hold it," the colonel protests, chafing at the implications. It's clear he's been clinging to the hope that the CIL hadn't been used and would be spared the stigma. Tickner appears to have destroyed it with one swing of his hammer. But the colonel isn't letting go yet. "If you're saying the cases are double-walled, we checked that."

"With all due respect, Colonel," Tickner responds, "the *cases* aren't double-walled. Only the top surface is. Did you check the top or the sides?"

"The sides," I reply grudgingly.

"Of course. That's what everyone does. The depth of the sidewalls means you can't really check the top very well, can you?"

"Not without a hammer."

Tickner smiles and steps to the adjacent transfer case. This one has been cut in two. Nash and the other agent separate the halves, revealing the double-wall construction of the top. There's about a half inch of air space between the two sheets of aluminum, which curve at the corners blending into a single thickness of sidewall.

"They knock off watches and blue jeans. Why not transfer cases?" Tickner intones. "They've made several interesting improvements."

"Yes, more than forty pounds of them," Webster counters facetiously, making the conversion from kilos.

"You recall, I told you we checked the weight," I chime in, clarifying the colonel's remark.

"It's not what they added, gentlemen. It's what they removed."

"What do you mean?"

"To compensate for the contraband, these are made from aluminum sheet that provides the same strength and rigidity at two thirds the weight. Same thickness. Different alloy. Much more expensive, of course."

"You're saying these weigh forty pounds less than the standard transfer case?" the colonel asks, baffled.

"When empty. The standard one hundred twenty-one when filled with heroin."

"A lot of people handle our cases," the colonel presses. "You expect me to believe no one noticed they were forty pounds lighter?"

"Of course I don't. Nor did Chen Dai. As soon as the heroin is removed it's replaced with silica sand. These cases always weigh the standard one hundred twenty-one pounds."

Webster bristles with frustration. "How the hell do they get the stuff in and out of there?"

"Equally ingenious," Tickner replies with a look to Nash.

In response, the big man fetches a device that resembles an industrial vacuum cleaner made of black plastic. A hose is affixed to one end, and a clear plastic container to the other. Nash stands it on the floor and plugs it into an electrical outlet. Then he turns to the dinged transfer case and unscrews the cap from the document tube. The free end of the vacuum hose has a special fitting, which he slips inside the tube, and a locking ring, which he threads onto the collar to secure it.

Tickner nods.

Nash thumbs a red button on the vacuum.

It emits a precise whine, and, with surprising speed, fills

the plastic container with white granules the consistency of fine sugar.

"One kilo of pure heroin," Tickner announces when Nash shuts it off.

"See, they modified the doc-tube," Nash explains, indicating the proximity of the document tube to the curved edge of the transfer case. "Right inside here, where you can't see it, is a little semicircular valve that makes it all happen."

I'm impressed. More than impressed. But I still find it hard to believe that little space holds twenty kilos. "How big is that case? Three by six, something like that?"

"Precisely eighty-four inches long by thirty wide," Tickner replies with an indulgent smile.

"Well, multiplying that out," I say, making the calculation in my head, "gives us two thousand five hundred and twenty square inches. Times the half inch between the double walls, gives us a volume of twelve hundred and sixty cubic inches."

"Correct. And as you can see, a kilo fits quite neatly in that one quart container. Now, if you know how many cubic inches there are in a quart container—"

"Sixty-three," I reply, retrieving this bit of trivia from a long-forgotten mathematical table.

"Well?" Tickner says in a tone that suggests any third-grader could do the next calculation.

"Sixty-three per kilo into twelve hundred sixty—twenty kilos."

"I rest my case," Tickner gloats.

"There's another problem," the colonel challenges, still unwilling to accept it. "We're always hearing about drug busts where tons of cocaine or heroin are confiscated. This is only forty pounds."

"What's your point, Colonel?"

"Well, with all the people and logistics involved, not to mention the cost of manufacturing these cases, it doesn't seem it'd be very cost-effective."

"You tell me. How many remains were repatriated over the last fifteen years?"

"A little over three hundred."

"That's an average of twenty T-cases per year or four hundred kilos," Tickner replies with a look to Nash.

"This is where the super purity comes in," Nash says, taking over. "See, Chen Dai's brought in a bunch of *chiu chau* chemists from the Hong Kong syndicates to work for him. These guys are top-notch. Came up with a system of producing this highly refined six-nines base. I mean, you have to keep in mind, ten percent base goes for sixty thousand a key."

"And this is ninety percent?"

"Ninety plus six-nines percent. In the current market, it's going in the neighborhood of a half a million or more a key. That's a two-hundred-million annual gross."

I nod knowingly. I have clients, large companies, who don't do that well.

"Of course, it didn't all go to Chen Dai," Tickner explains. "He was netting thirty percent after Ajacier and the distributors took their cut."

"That's sixty million bucks," Webster exclaims.

"Check," Nash concludes. "We figure it costs him about a million or so a month to run his army. He pockets the rest. Pretty good pay for the leader of a bunch of ragtag guerrillas."

"I know I'm not going to like the answer," Webster says apprehensively, "but I have to know. The heroin . . . they were putting it into the cases at Clark, weren't they?"

"Yeah, and they moved their operation to Andersen when you moved yours. The local authorities are totally corrupt. Our operations have been compromised, agents assassinated. DEA is all but out of business in the Pacific."

"They bring the stuff in from Laos by plane, boat—" Nash adds, disgusted. "Hell, they could be shipping it Federal Express for all we know."

The colonel seethes, trying to hold it in. "That means the people, the military people who handle those cases are in cahoots with these guys."

Tickner nods solemnly. "Some."

"So, every time I draw a T-case from stock and put a man's remains inside it, a man who died for his country, who has every right to be treated with dignity and respect, it already contains heroin."

Tickner nods again.

The colonel reddens. His outrage can no longer be contained. "Those bastards! I've been escorting that stuff into the country for fifteen years?!"

"I'm afraid so, sir," Tickner replies, a little taken aback by the outburst. "For lack of a better word, it's 'parked' at the CIL while you carry out your procedures, then goes on to the port mortuary in San Francisco, where civilian personnel remove and funnel it into the mainland pipeline."

Webster sighs and turns away, devastated.

"I'm sorry, Colonel. Tough questions have a way of producing tough answers."

"And they're going to get tougher," I say sharply.

"Pardon me?" Tickner intones.

"The colonel and I figured out early on that there were a couple aspects to this. You've covered one. We know what's going on now. But what about the other? What about the past, where it all began?"

"Much tougher . . . if, as I suspect, you're referring to the use of GI cadavers during the war."

"I don't know. Am I? I mean, I'd heard that theory. I also heard it was impossible."

"From whom?"

"From a guy who ought to know. He was the ranking officer at the Ton Son Nhut mortuary."

"Jason Ingersoll."

I nod.

"I know Jason quite well. Lovely man. Smart, too. He was right. It was impossible. But I didn't say anything about the mortuary at Ton Son Nhut. You did. Chen Dai bypassed it completely."

"I'm lost, Mr. Tickner."

"So am I," the colonel chimes in. "How the hell else could they get their hands on cadavers?"

"They bought them."

The colonel's brows go up. He's stunned.

I'm not. I'm putting pieces together: the story the photographer told us about Kate's husband and the list I bought from Surigao.

"A number of years ago while conducting refugee interviews," Tickner goes on, "we learned that Chen Dai routinely purchased the bodies of American servicemen from Pathet Lao forces."

"You ever come across a list of MIAs in those interviews?" I ask, baiting him. Will he blink? Is he threatened by it? Will it blow him sky-high?

"A list of MIAs?" he wonders, unphased. "Not as I recall. What does it have to do with this?"

"That's my question. There are indications it might have been threatening to Chen Dai for some reason."

Tickner shrugs. "I'm still drawing a blank. As far as I know, the bodies were shipped to a heroin refinery in Vientiane, where the contraband was inserted in the chest cavities. While there, they were embalmed, packaged, and put in stolen transfer cases. When the war ended and the supply of cadavers stopped, Chen Dai came up with this method."

"You say Vientiane?" Webster prompts.

Tickner nods.

The colonel and I exchange knowing looks. Now we know why Pettibone headed for Vientiane when he went AWOL.

"Anyway," Tickner resumes, "the cases were flown to Ton Son Nhut Airbase and added to a pallet of bona fide cases being shipped to the states from the mortuary."

"And the mortuary out-processing NCO took over from there," the colonel declares.

Tickner nods.

"A member of the Ajacier family," I prompt.

Tickner nods again and smiles thinly in tribute. "He prepared shipping manifests and made sure the DD thirteen-hundreds—which triggered next of kin notifications, insurance benefits, etc.—were inserted into the flow. One form, eight carbons, a relatively simple matter."

"The name Pettibone mean anything to you?" I ask.

"Not until I spoke with the colonel the other day, which prompted me to go back into our files." He turns on a heel and heads for the door. "It's well over twenty years," he goes on as we follow him down the corridor to his office. "But we've managed to piece together a scenario." He pauses long enough to find a file on his desk. "According to this, our people were hot on Pettibone's trail when he went AWOL. Lost track of him completely. They checked every flight, every passenger manifest. They concluded he was using someone else's identification."

"Yes, mine. He stole it. That's what got me into this mess in the first place. He died with it."

"Really? That's something we didn't know."

"That's because they yanked his body from the mortuary to keep you from poking around."

Tickner's brows go up. "That's two for you, Morgan."

"Let's try for three. Did you know he and Surigao flew together?"

"That's not news. They're the ones who ferried the T-cases containing the contraband from Vientiane to Ton Son Nhut."

"Very good. As I understand it, they used to call those flights Pepsi-Cola runs, didn't they?"

Tickner's chin lifts curiously. "How much do you know, Mr. Morgan?"

"Not enough yet."

"That's a matter of opinion."

"Fine. Whatever you say. Now, answer the question. Why were they called Pepsi-Cola runs?"

Uncomfortable looks dart between him and Nash.

"Come on, dammit," the colonel chimes in. "I didn't fly fourteen hours to have you holding back information."

"Well," Tickner says, still clearly uncomfortable, "Chen Dai splits his time between his compound up north in Pak Seng and a Pepsi-Cola plant in Vientiane."

"A Pepsi-Cola plant?!" the colonel exclaims.

"Yes, that's the facility I mentioned earlier."

"The heroin refinery?"

"Uh-huh. It's the perfect cover for buying ether and acetic anhydride," Nash explains. "You can't turn opium into heroin without 'em. Of course, the place never capped a bottle of Pepsi. Been a state-of-the-art junk factory from day one. When the crack craze hit, they started making what we call 'ice.' That's crystalline methamphetamine. It's as addictive as crack, but when you mix it with heroin, you get a much better high without the crash. And you smoke it. No needles. No threat of AIDS. Real big market."

"The catch is," Tickner concludes, "this Pepsi-Cola plant was built in the mid-sixties—with funds provided by the United States Agency for International Development. Needless to say, neither PepsiCo nor the USG knew anything about a heroin refinery. Unfortunately, in light of the current program, it's still a highly sensitive issue." He pauses and locks his eyes onto mine. "I'm going to have to ask you to leave this whole thing be."

"Ask Ajacier to leave me be."

"As I hinted the other day, we're not so sure it is Ajacier."

"Then who? You guys?"

"That's not funny, Mr. Morgan. We suspect Chen Dai may have decided to wipe the slate clean to make sure there aren't any black eyes."

"That means Ajacier's a target too."

"It's possible."

"And you're going to let Chen Dai do it?"

"That's his business."

"Jesus."

"To be brutally frank, Mr. Morgan, it certainly makes our job a whole lot easier."

I'm stunned. Am I supposed to be reading in between the lines here? Is he sending me a deadly message? I take a moment to settle. "One more question, Mr. Tickner, if you don't mind?"

"Would it make any difference?"

"No."

"Please."

"This crop substitution program. It's all worked out, right?"

"Yes. All but the formalities. It's a matter of scheduling and logistics now."

"And the drug smuggling is going to stop."

"Like a bug hitting a windshield." He makes a sharp, chopping motion with his hand. "Your question?"

"Why have they been trying to kill *me*?"

"That's not such a mystery. Your pursuit of Surigao provoked them."

"No, he came at me first. Months ago. Right after I made an inquiry to the CIL."

"What's your point, Mr. Morgan?" Tickner asks impatiently.

"What did I endanger? I mean, I must've threatened something for Chen Dai to sign my death warrant."

Tickner muses thoughtfully.

"It sure wasn't his drug smuggling operation."

Tickner nods.

"Then what? There must be more, Mr. Tickner. There has to be."

"I think you're overreacting."

"I always overreact. I'm a number cruncher. My friends are always teasing me about things having to add up." I pause and burn him with a look. "And I'm not letting go of this until they do."

31

IT'S POURING.

In sheets. A tropical monsoon.

The last time I saw rain like this I had to crawl out of my foxhole to keep from drowning. A half hour ago when I got into a taxi at the embassy, the sun was out. Now, I can hardly see the cars up ahead. I'm listening to the wipers slapping at the windshield, wrestling with what have become the core questions: What have I threatened? What's the significance of the list? Are they connected? If so, how? What do the names have in common? Despite my parting shot at Tickner, I'm starting to wonder if he isn't right. Maybe I am overreacting. Maybe it never will add up. Maybe the list is meaningless. Surigao was desperate, needed money, he'd have said anything.

The deluge has eased to a steady drizzle by the time the taxi pulls up in front of the hotel. A short time later, I'm prowling the tiny room still trying to sort it out when Kate arrives.

"I got it," she announces effusively, as she comes through the door spattered with rain.

"Got what?"

She fetches a towel, quickly dries her hands and face, then takes a folded sheet of paper from her handbag and tosses it to me.

It's a map of the Chao Phraya River extending well north of the city where it branches off into a complex network of *khlongs* along which are numerous neatly printed directions. A route is outlined in red marker. It reminds me of the recon maps we used to make on patrol in the jungle.

"Timothy?"

"Timothy. Vann Nath said Timothy's expecting us tomorrow."

"Great," I say, unmoved. For all my mouthing off about getting firepower, I've little enthusiasm for it at the moment.

"What's that all about? Am I picking up on something here?"

"I'm sort of at a dead end. No matter how I look at it, I still can't come up with a reason why they've been trying to kill me."

"I thought it had something to do with the list."

"It might. But what? I'm a blank. I finally get a key piece to the puzzle and I can't find where it fits. It's infuriating."

"You show it to the DEA?"

"No, I didn't."

"How come?"

"I'm not sure I trust them. If Surigao wasn't putting us on, if the list really will blow the lid off this thing—"

"It might never see the light of day if they get hold of it," Kate interjects.

I nod glumly. "I'm starting to feel like none of this is going to see the light of day."

"You're wrong."

"Give me one good reason."

"The farm collective. Vann Nath found out where it's located."

"Pak Seng," I say matter-of-factly. "Smack in the middle of Houa Phan Province."

"That's right. How'd you know?"

"DEA."

"You found a connection."

I nod apprehensively. "It looks like your husband was sold to a drug lord."

"A drug lord?"

"Yes. His name's Chen Dai. He runs the opium growers up there."

Her eyes cloud momentarily, then brighten with an idea. "Maybe that's what the list means. Maybe they were all sold to this guy."

"Crossed my mind. What if they were?"

"Then there's a chance Vann Nath was right."

"About what?"

"About John being sentenced to hard labor."

"Sold into slavery'd be more like it, but I—"

"That's not as crazy as it sounds. It's possible they've been forced to work as field hands."

"I don't think so, Kate."

"Why not?"

I hesitate as it dawns on me that despite logic, despite her protestations to the contrary, despite her years counseling other families to do otherwise, she's been clinging to the hope of finding her husband alive.

"I'm pretty sure he was killed," I say softly.

"Because that photographer remembered hearing some shots? That's not proof of anything."

"No, it's not. But, when you start factoring in other data, the probability curve gets pretty high."

"Factoring? Probability curve?" she flares. "We're talking about my husband. A person. Not some calculation on your computer."

"Occupational hazard. Sorry."

She cools, her eyes narrowing in reflection.

I see the question forming. I have no doubt what it will be. And I dread answering it.

"What other data?"

"Sit down, Kate." I direct her to the small sofa, pull up a chair for myself, and as gently as possible, explain about smuggling heroin inside GI cadavers.

She gasps, horrified, the words of condemnation catching in her throat.

"I'm sorry."

She looks off, taking a few moments to recover, then finally, still unwilling to let go, she turns to me and reasons, "But if that's what they did to him, wouldn't John's remains have been repatriated during the war? I mean this . . . this animal . . . this Chen Dai, he would have made sure of it. Wouldn't he?"

"I've thought about that."

"But they weren't. Why? Maybe John escaped. You heard Vann Nath. Maybe they shot and missed. Maybe he was able to get away and—"

"*Kate*. Kate, come on, you're not being realistic. We both know he hasn't been living on nuts and berries in the jungle for twenty years."

"Twenty-one."

"Whatever. You know better than that."

Her face reddens in protest, then she lowers her eyes and nods resignedly.

"You told me all you wanted was an answer. I'm giving you one. Accept it."

"It's not enough. I said a final answer. If I can't have John, I want his remains."

"Of course. And, God willing, one day you will. You know, Kate, somehow you gave me the idea that repatriations are victories, not defeats."

"They are."

"Don't you think it's time to start practicing what you preach?"

She nods contritely. "Down deep, I guess I know John's . . . dead. But every time there's even the slightest glimmer of hope, I just want to grab it and never let go."

"You have to let go, Kate. For yourself. It's not healthy to keep doing this."

"It's so hard sometimes. If anyone should be able to understand, it's you."

"Of course."

She drifts off in thought for a moment. "So, John was taken to Pak Seng?"

"No. That's where the stuff's grown," I reply, explaining about the Pepsi-Cola plant in Vientiane where it's refined.

"That's where he was taken?"

"The bodies of American servicemen used to smuggle drugs were taken there," I reply, driving the message home. "Yes."

"Then that's where I'm going."

"Whoa. Want to run that past me again?"

"I've been after this kind of information for twenty-one years, Morgan. You don't really think I'm going to ignore it?"

"This is Laos we're talking about. Not France or Italy. You can't just go to the airport and hop on the next flight."

"Sure you can. All you need is a visa. I used to do it all the time."

"That was fifteen years ago."

"So? We still have an embassy there."

"That doesn't mean there aren't restrictions."

"I'll call the embassy here and find out."

"No. Tickner and these guys are joined at the hip. He gets wind of this we won't stand a chance."

"Then what?"

"Let's see what the Laos have to say."

We head downstairs to the lobby. It's crowded with locals keeping out of the rain. Compared to the Soi 12, this place is a luxury resort. Not only does it have an elevator, but also a small coffee shop and public phone booth. One. Naturally, someone's in it. Kate gets us some soft drinks while I wait my turn. I finally get hold of someone in the Lao embassy who speaks English and he gives me the information.

"Well?" Kate prompts as I exit the booth.

"The good news is there are no U.S. travel advisories or restrictions."

"And the bad?"

"Visas. Two to three months to process them."

Kate scowls, disappointed.

"Of course, that's if we make the mistake of applying to their embassy in Washington."

"We can apply here?" she asks, brightening.

I break into a broad grin and nod.

"It never used to be that way. You sure?"

"That's what they said. We fill out the forms, they telex Vientiane, and we have visas."

"Then I was right."

I smile.

"But it's killing you to say it."

"You're right."

"I'm not sure which way to take that."

"I know."

She's laughing as we hurry from the hotel.

It's still raining, so we leave the scooter and take a taxi to the Lao embassy opposite a broad *khlong* on Sathon Tai Road in the business district. The application form is short, the approval process swift, the response devastating. The clerk seems embarrassed when he reports we've both been denied visas. He has no idea why. They don't give him reasons. They didn't have to. It's Tickner. I know it is. He didn't waste a minute. We ride back to the hotel in silence.

"Maybe it's for the best," I say glumly, as we enter the room.

"What kind of an attitude is that?"

"I don't know. I think I've had it with this thing."

"Had it? You saying you're throwing in the towel after all you've been through? After dropping ten thousand bucks on that list?"

"The list is useless."

"Why? Because you haven't figured it out yet?"

"It's a lot more than that. This whole thing is a bust: Surigao's dead, Ajacier's getting off, the drug lord's getting a windfall. And I don't know what's going on with my daughters or my business."

"You're the one who said we have to light the fuse. And I'm going to find a way to do it. With you or without you."

"You have to get into Laos, first."

"There has to be a way to get across the border."

"There's also a little obstacle called the Mekong River," I retort, referring to the natural border between Thailand and Laos. "It'd be a real bitch. I'm just not up to it. I'm out of gas."

"Out of gas? Whatever happened to 'A stands for adamant'?"

I shrug glumly.

"Ah, I can see, it stands for apathetic now. I spent a year doing this. A year. We haven't been at it a week. You know what your problem is, Morgan? You can't handle spontaneity. You're too used to predicting everything before it happens. Take away your computer and you fall apart."

"I am what I am, Kate. I can't change. And I'm not going to apologize for it."

"That's not what I want. Just hang in there for a while and roll with the punches."

"It's the bullets I'm worried about. I'm tired of people trying to kill me."

"You really think they'll stop?"

"Not as long as I'm provoking them. That's for sure. That goes for you too."

"Me?"

"Yes. I may not have all the answers but I do know that list is a death warrant. Your husband's name's on it, remember? You push, they're going to push back."

"How else are you going to get answers? What do you want to do? Snap your fingers and have them handed to you on a silver platter?"

"No. I want to snap my fingers and have Nancy sneaking into my bed at night instead of you."

She stiffens, clearly stung, then whirls and walks off across the room.

I flush with remorse and go after her. "I'm sorry. I didn't mean that the way it sounded."

She stares out the window ignoring me. I can see her reflection in the rain-dotted panes. She bites at her lip, then glances over her shoulder, challengingly. "How did you mean it?"

"I didn't mean it at all. I don't know what to say. I'm sorry. I guess this whole thing is just getting to me."

"It's been getting to me for a lot longer, Morgan."

"I'm aware of that. By the way, there's something I've been meaning to say. My name's Calvert. All my friends call me Cal."

"I would hope so."

"So what's with this Morgan business all the time?"

"No special reason."

"It's kind of impersonal, don't you think? I mean, sometimes I get the feeling it's your . . . your . . . It's none of my business. Forget it."

"No. Come on. Say it. It's my what?"

"Your way of keeping your distance."

"God, you sound just like this shrink I used to see. Is there a point to all this?"

"Yes, I think that's what I was doing before."

"Before?"

"When I lashed out. I—"

"Forget it. I was frightened. I wanted to be held. Don't make it into something else."

"I'm not. I wanted to be held too."

She blinks and tilts her head curiously.

"I wanted someone next to me. I mean . . ." I pause. There'll be no denying my feelings once I say it. "What I'm trying to say is, I wanted *you* next to me."

Her eyes soften and find mine.

"I'm sorry I popped off. It's only been a couple of months since Nance was killed. I guess . . . I guess, I've been feeling kind of guilty."

"I've been dealing with that for a long time too," she says softly.

"Made any progress?"

"Some."

Our eyes meet. No words are necessary. This is a special moment—surprising, illuminating, and fleeting—like a flash of light.

"So, Cal," Kate finally says with a little smile, "What do you want to do?"

"You mean other than packing it in?"

"I mean about getting into Laos."

"I haven't the foggiest idea where to start."

"Anything but what you usually do would be fine."

"Which is?"

"Calculate the odds."

"I'd be on the next flight to L.A. if I did that. This guy Timothy. You said he was your guide?"

"Uh-huh."

"He ever take you into Laos?"

"Sure. Several times."

"Maybe he's got more to sell than firepower."

32

THERE ARE NO MORE DECISIONS TO MAKE. NO MORE angles to figure. Our plan of action is set: Firepower. Laos. Pepsi-Cola.

Kate and I waste no time in making preparations. We spend the rest of the day arranging to rent a small boat at a nearby marina and shopping at Mah Boon Krong, one of the city's immense gallerias. Other than Kate's quick excursion to the street market the other morning, it's the first chance we've had to replace clothing, personal items, and luggage. When it comes to the latter, we bypass the ubiquitous designer knockoffs in favor of nylon gym bags. We also pick up a copy of the *Bangkok Post*, the city's English-language newspaper. It wasn't the headline about the presidential election that got my attention but a story at the bottom of the front page.

AJACIER BELIEVED MISSING

Businessman Phillipe Ajacier left his Thonburi Studio office several days ago and hasn't been heard from since. Associates became alarmed when he failed to attend a screening last night. A studio spokesman said Mr. Ajacier had been in Vientiane on business but was expected back in Bangkok. Authorities in both cities have been notified but have no clues as to his whereabouts. The spokesman said Ajacier is a respected and well-liked member of the Bangkok film community without an enemy in the world.

Tickner was right. Chen Dai's cleaning house. It sure took the fun out of shopping. We returned to the hotel and crashed. As Kate noted, my access to high-tech toys has been drastically reduced. I'm down to a digital wristwatch. I set the alarm for 6 A.M. We face a forty-mile river journey and I want to get an early start.

Kate's in the shower.

I'm dressing, thoroughly enjoying the feel and smell of fresh cotton as I cross to the window, buttoning a brand-new shirt.

· The sun is edging above the horizon, sending long rays streaking between the buildings. They illuminate a minivan that pulls to a stop about a half block away. Two men, who appear to be Asians, get out. One ambles down an alley next to the hotel. The other crosses to a flower shop across the street. He leans in the doorway, casually smoking a cigarette. A worker waiting for the boss to open up, I assume. I'm about to leave the window when he reaches into his jacket, brings his hand to his mouth, and starts talking. Is he DEA? Bangkok Metro Police? One of Chen Dai's thugs? After a brief exchange, he puts the walkie-talkie away and glances up at the hotel. His face is bearded and looks familiar. I'm trying to place it when Kate emerges from the bathroom. She's fully dressed, her wet hair hooked behind her ears, her movements brisk and upbeat.

"Hope you're wearing your running shoes," I prompt.

"I don't like the sound of that."

I nod grimly, and wave her over to the window. "The guy in the doorway—"

"What about him?"

"Last time I saw him he was in a speedboat with a machine gun."

We hurriedly pack our things in the gym bags and cross to the door. I open it slowly, peering into the corridor. It seems clear except for a maid's cart and some piles of laundry. We slip from the room, pausing at the elevator where a sign points the way to a fire exit. The door opens onto an exterior staircase. We clamber down four flights to a courtyard crisscrossed with clotheslines and make our way between the buildings in search of the lot where we parked the motor scooter, then turn a corner, stumbling onto it.

The other guy from the van is leaning against a car reading a newspaper. I grab Kate's hand and pull her back. It's too late. He tosses the paper aside and charges in our direction, yapping excitedly into his walkie-talkie.

Kate and I do an about-face and take off down an alley. The man pursues, exchanging the walkie-talkie for a pistol on the run. Any doubts I've had about still being a threat have just been removed. We come onto a street on the other side of the hotel. It's congested with traffic and hordes of pedestrians who spill from the narrow sidewalks. We plunge into the fast-moving crowd, glancing back anxiously as we go. The gunman pops out of the alley, his head darting left and right like a pigeon's in search of us. I'm looking frantically for a taxi. Several approach and pass. They're all occupied.

"Over there!" Kate suddenly exclaims, as one of them pulls to a stop down the street to discharge a passenger. We're dashing toward the taxi when the other gunman, the one with the beard, rounds a corner up ahead. He spots us and starts knifing his way through the crowd. Kate yanks open the door and dives into the backseat of the taxi.

"No bargaining," I exclaim as I jump in after her and slam the door.

A rapid exchange in Thai and we're moving. Really moving. Kate must've imparted our sense of urgency, because the driver maneuvers through traffic with obsessive fervor and speed, leaving the frustrated gunman behind. Our progress is short-lived. Despite the overpasses at most of the main intersections that supposedly reduce gridlock, it takes over an hour to get to the waterfront.

The boat we rented is waiting at the dock as promised. It's a twenty-foot aluminum runabout with a windshield, folding canvas top, and small inboard.

Within minutes, we're settled in the cockpit and shoving off into the river. I take the wheel and ease the throttle forward. The boat picks up speed, gliding through the water effortlessly, the motor giving off a soothing throb rather than the whine I anticipated. A sense of calm washes over me. I'm finally back in control. No longer at the mercy of frenetic cab drivers, *tuk-tuk* operators, and bus drivers who seem to have declared open season on motor scooters.

We wind our way north, beneath the Phra Pinklao Bridge, past the riverfront communities of Bang Phat and Sri Yan, and soon leave the city behind for narrow tributaries lined with villages built on stilts high above the river.

Children bathe and brush their teeth in the gray-brown water, waving to a postman who rows past making his rounds. Straw-hatted vendors in sampans sell sweetcakes, vegetables, fruits, and fish to those who hail them.

Kate pulls her camera from her handbag and starts taking snapshots of them. One vendor, equipped with a wok, makes us a breakfast of chopped peppers, pork, and eggs, all scrambled together and served in cardboard cones. Kate dispenses with the picture-taking and starts eating with gusto.

I hesitate. I eat pizza with a knife and fork, cut my waffles on the grid lines.

"Come on, it's delicious," she says, scooping some up with her fingers and feeding it to me.

I've been here only four days, but I'm light-years away from Los Angeles. It's almost as if life there never existed. I feel distant and out of touch, and strangely attached to this woman whom I hardly know, who has captured me with her gutsy determination and spunk.

"Mind if I ask you something, Kate?"

"Sounds serious."

"Sort of, I guess."

"You guess?"

"Is there someone? I mean, special, a person you're with?"

"You mean a lover," she declares.

I nod.

"No."

"Never? Not in all these years?"

"I didn't say that."

"But not now."

"Not for a long time."

"You get hurt?"

"The other way round. I was the one who screwed it up.

Just couldn't handle it. So I got out. Not very gracefully, I might add. I promised myself I wouldn't get involved again until I could. Of course by then it'll be too late."

"Why? What's the problem?"

"Gravity," she replies, with a hearty laugh. "Now why don't you ask me what you really want to know?"

"Which is?"

"What my friends are always asking me." She takes on a haughty posture and tone, mimicking a gossiper, and says, "I don't mean to be nosy, Kate, but whatever do you do for sex?"

"Well, now that you mention it . . ."

"Hard work, vigorous exercise, and a vivid imagination."

"I'll have to try it."

She's laughing again when the distant buzz of a high-speed propeller rises swiftly behind us.

I glance back over my shoulder to see a sharply veed prow cutting through the water, setting smaller boats to bouncing like corks. It conjures up visions of blue-orange tracers, of Surigao lurching as the bullets impacted, of Kate and me being blasted by the machine-gunner and left to rot in the jungle.

The boat is closing fast, very fast.

I wall the throttle and quickly angle the runabout through a sharp bend up ahead. Once out of sight of the pursuing boat, I veer into the nearest *khlong*, pulling deep into the jungle overgrowth. I cut the engine and instinctively snap off some branches from surrounding trees, draping them over the windshield and cockpit.

The harsh buzz of the engine rises again as the boat rounds the bend. It's at maximum pitch when the scream of a siren drowns it out. I peer through the leafy camouflage to see a small cabin cruiser streaking past. A red cross is painted boldly on its side.

"Kate? Kate, we're okay. It's an ambulance."

She emerges from the foliage. "An ambulance?"

"Uh-huh."

She smiles, relieved, and grabs on to me to keep from falling as the boat lurches in the ambulance's wake.

We resume our journey upriver, fighting the strong current that slows our progress, and finally arrive at a small marina. It's the local version of the bustling minimalls in the San Fernando Valley, replete with food markets, clothing boutiques, a dockside gas station, and an infinite variety of small vessels tied up in the rows of slips.

The ambulance is among them.

On the dock, where a small crowd has gathered, two paramedics are caring for an elderly woman who has evidently been overcome by the heat.

The marina is a major landmark, and from here the map becomes more detailed, the *khlongs* numbered, the route through them drawn with numerous arrows and notes. We refuel, then continue upriver, Kate counting the *khlongs,* marking them with a pen as we go.

"The next one's nine. We turn in there."

The *khlong* is twisting and narrow, the banks lined with thickets of banyan trees that march into the water. The jungle gradually closes over us. Soon, only narrow shafts of light find paths through the dense foliage. We follow the map scrupulously, checking and double-checking before making the transition from one *khlong* to the next, fearful of becoming lost in the maze of canals.

Darkness falls and the temperature along with it.

I'm chilled, less from the cold than the memories. I'd forgotten what night in the jungle was like: the absolute blackness, the scent of animals and flowers carried by the wind, the cacophony of buzzing, croaking, and chirping, which, after what seems like an eternity, is finally broken by the slowly rising drone of an electric generator.

Soon, the glow of incandescent light beckons from within the overgrowth. It steadily intensifies until we emerge into a clearing where a cluster of small pavilions perch on stilts high above us. Like all the other dwellings we've seen on the river, it's made of weathered teak and bamboo with a corrugated metal and thatch roof. This is the place. At least I think it is. It's more than possible we missed a turn twenty miles back and are on the wrong *khlong*. We secure the boat and carry the gym bags up a long wooden staircase to a cantilevered deck.

"Tim? Timothy?" Kate calls out as we cross toward the entrance.

An Asian woman comes from the house, hurrying toward us. She's barefoot, tiny, with long hair and a traditional printed sarong.

"Akamahn? Miss Akamahn?"

"Yes, yes, I'm Mrs. Ackerman," Kate replies expectantly, breaking into Thai.

The woman's face lights up. A short exchange follows. Kate turns to me and says, "Her name's Sakri. She says she's Timothy's wife."

"Of course. Who else would she be?" I joke, very relieved we aren't lost.

Sakri leads the way inside to a guest room. There's a dim light in a paper shade overhead, a double mattress on the floor, a sofa, and little else.

"So where's Timothy?" Kate asks.

"Timozy?" Sakri echoes in her thick accent.

"Yes, is he here?"

"Here. Oh, yes."

Kate smiles with relief. "Good. I can't wait to see him."

Sakri shakes no. Another exchange in Thai follows. Sakri appears adamant, Kate exasperated and confused. "She says he's here but he can't see us now."

"Why not?"

"She didn't say."

"Is he asleep?" I ask, putting my hands against the side of my head.

Sakri nods unconvincingly, then backs her way out the door and closes it.

"This is weird," Kate says uneasily.

"Yes, I don't get."

Kate's exhausted. So am I. We decide to make the best of it and see what the morning brings. We're settling in when we hear the strains of classical music. Vivaldi? Debussy? One of those guys. Nancy would know. Our curiosity gets the best of us. We slip from the room, following the music through the house to an open corridor that leads to a staircase. I pick up a scent. Sweet, and vaguely familiar. It's been twenty-four years since I last came across it. It intensifies along with the music as we climb the steps to an enclosed pavilion. The door is partially open. I'm pretty sure I know what we'll find as we push through it into a hexagon-shaped room.

The ceiling beams soar gazebo-like to a central peak. The walls are lined with books, the floor covered with them. A smoky haze hangs in the air. And sitting cross-legged in a wicker peacock chair is, I assume, Timothy Roark.

Kate nods, confirming it.

Timothy's arms rest limply at his side, head lolling against the back of the chair that frames it like a huge halo, eyelids at half-mast. He is small, rail-thin, and quite bald, with wire-frame eyeglasses, faded jeans, and a Bart Simpson T-shirt that proclaims *Yo, Dude!*

After Vann Nath's lecture about valor, I expected a long-haired, muscled wild man girdled with bandoliers. At the least, an expatriate Green Beret in jungle fatigues hunkered down amid his arsenal. Instead I'm in a library with Mr. Peepers, who's armed with an insipid smile and an opium pipe.

There's not a single weapon in sight.

33

IT'S MORNING.

Uncomfortably hot and humid like it always is in the jungle.

I'm awake, staring at the ceiling. The scent of opium still lingers in my nostrils. Last night, we left Timothy nodding in his chair and went to bed. I gave Kate the mattress and curled up on the sofa. Now, I'm getting angry again and wondering what I'm doing here when I hear the whisk of bare feet on the mats in the corridor, then a gentle knock on the door before it opens.

Sakri appears, and says something to me in Thai.

The only word I recognize is *Timozy*. I gesture she hang in there, then cross the room and shake Kate. "Kate? Kate! Come on, wake up."

Her eyes flutter open. "Hi," she says sleepily, squinting at the brilliance, then she senses the tension and pushes up onto an elbow. "What? What's going on?"

"I don't know. Sakri's trying to tell me something."

Kate twists around and questions her in Thai. "She says Timothy is waiting for us."

"Waiting for us? Where? Why?"

Kate shrugs her shoulders. "I don't know. She wants us to go with her."

We slept in our clothes, so it doesn't take long to put ourselves together and follow Sakri from the house. She leads the way down the staircase and along a well-worn path through the jungle. Minutes later, we're climbing a hill that rises above the overgrowth. A miniature gazebo perches atop the crest. As we get closer we realize there are dozens of carved wooden phalluses leaning against it. Red ones, white ones—pocket-sized to four feet long.

"What the hell is that?"

"A fertility shrine," Kate explains. "They're very common in Thailand."

"It looks like your buddy Timothy fried more than his brain."

We're not sure what's going on until Sakri ushers us around to the back of the shrine and down into a concrete bunker below. The air is thick with the pungent smell of gun oil and steel that makes the fillings in my teeth crackle. The space is about fifteen feet in diameter with a low ceiling and wooden floor. Daylight streams through encircling gun slits.

In the center, where the bands of light converge, Timothy Roark's tiny, bald head seems to float like an illuminated globe. He stands behind a felt-covered table, surrounded by racks of rifles, machine guns, pistols, knives, and crates of ammunition. His posture stiffens. His eyes dart from Kate's to mine and back.

"How are you, Kate?" he finally asks. There is more embarrassment than enthusiasm in his voice.

"I'm doing okay, what about you?"

"Don't look so worried. I'm fine. Mr. Morgan." He reaches across the table and shakes my hand. "Oh, in case you're wondering, this is my shrine. The one up top is Sakri's. Sweet lady. All she wants out of life is a bunch of kids. Unfortunately, I had a little fling with a Bouncing Betty before I met her. I keep trying to explain, but she won't hear it. Insists it's her fault."

Kate's clearly moved.

I'm not. I had a fling with one. A lot of guys in-country did. Some lost limbs. Some are scarred. Some are sterile or impotent. Too many are dead. "You have a lot of shrines, Mr. Roark," I say, sharply. "We saw another one last night."

"The library?"

I nod.

"Books are my passion."

"I was referring to the opium."

"Ah. You ought to try some. Maybe you wouldn't be so angry."

"I have good reason to be."

"Well, don't take it out on me. Everyone has their opiate. Some people watch TV, others down six-packs, I smoke a pipe."

"The guy who killed my wife wasn't working for a network or a brewery, believe me."

He studies me, adjusting his attitude. "That's a tough one. But for what it's worth, I've always thought revenge was a lousy motive. Clouds your thinking. Dangerous."

"Not what I'm looking for."

"Then what?"

"Answers."

"Same as Kate?"

"In a manner of speaking."

"And you need guns to find them."

"To even the odds."

"Well, if you're looking for an equalizer . . ." He turns and takes a weapon from a rack behind him.

It's a black sheet-metal box about 10 × 1 × 2 inches. A rectangular pistol grip, through which the magazine is inserted, extends straight down from the bottom. A stubby, cylindrical barrel protrudes from the fascia.

"Ingram Model 11. Fully automatic submachine gun," Timothy announces as he begins field-stripping it. "Nine-millimeter shorts. Box-type mag. Thirty rounds. Weight, loaded—eight-and-one-quarter pounds. Lands and grooves are right-hand twist, one turn in six inches. Maximum velocity nine-hundred-eighteen feet per second. Rate of fire, eleven-hundred-forty-five rounds per minute. Simple. Deadly. Very easily concealed. My favorite."

Vann Nath was right.

Timothy Roark does have weapons. Lots of them. And he can rattle off their nomenclature in his sleep, or, I would imagine, in an opium-induced trance if he had to. But this morning, his eyes are clear and alert, his handshake strong, his slight physique obviously still finely honed.

"All yours, Morgan," he says, gesturing to the parts neatly arrayed on the table.

I start reassembling the weapon.

Timothy fetches a pistol.

"Fabrique Nationale DA 140. Box-type mag. Eight rounds. Very little kick. Highly accurate. I like the Beretta 92 myself, but this is more compact and uses nine shorts like the Ingram." He takes Kate's hand and wraps it around the molded plastic grip. "How's that feel?"

"Kind of scary."

"No. Respect it. Don't be afraid of it."

Kate nods, balancing it in her hand.

"You get a line on John? That what this is all about?"

"On his remains," Kate replies evenly, with a little look to me. "He was killed and taken to a Pepsi-Cola plant in Vientiane. I know that sounds weird but we found out it's a—"

"No, it doesn't. I've heard about that place. Nasty business. Nasty man."

"I prefer heinous, repulsive, and disgusting," Kate says bitterly.

"You get us there?" I ask.

"No."

"Kate said that was your thing."

"It used to be. I don't do it anymore."

"How much do you want to come out of retirement?"

"Not a chance."

"That may change when you hear the offer."

He sets his jaw and shakes his head no. "Don't want to hear it."

"Why not?" Kate asks, concerned. "What's the problem, Tim? Something bad happen?"

"No. I just got tired of watching people live in hope and die in despair, that's all."

"Who're you talking about?" she wonders.

"You."

"Me?"

"Next of kin. You know what I mean. All these wives, parents, brothers, sisters. They kept coming and coming, begging me to take them to these places. We'd finally get there. It'd turn out to be a bust. And they'd look at me empty and forlorn, like I was the one who didn't deliver. I couldn't handle it."

Kate nods with understanding and puts the pistol on the table.

I finish reassembling the Ingram and offer it to Timothy for inspection.

He jacks the cocking lever and checks the action. "That's good."

"I used to be real good: I Corps, Special Forces, G Company Rangers."

"Hundred Seventy-third Airborne, Lurps," he replies smartly, using the nickname given those who served in Long Range Reconnaissance Patrol units. They were loners, skilled in fieldcraft and survival techniques, and operated in very small groups many miles from base camp for long periods of time.

"I knew guys like you when I was in-country. I admired them."

"Unfortunately, we were the exception not the rule."

"We were."

He studies me, then nods and breaks into a funny smile. "What we lacked in brawn we made up for in intelligence and guts."

"So what happened?"

"What do you mean by that?"

"It looks to me like you're wasting one and ran out of the other."

"You're out of line, Morgan."

"Why? Because it pisses me off to see someone nodding his life away in the jungle?"

"I did four tours. Four. I lived off the land for weeks, sometimes months at a time. I liked it. I liked being responsible to no one. Dependent on no one. And that's what I'm doing now." He tosses the weapon at me, hard, challengingly. "Let's see if you remember what to do with that."

He turns on a heel and strides out of the bunker. Kate and I follow at a distance with our weapons. I can feel her disapproval as we walk.

"I guess I got a little out of control there, didn't I?"

"A little."

"Sorry. But lately, I've got this thing for people who do drugs."

"I understand."

"You didn't say anything about him being so weird."

"He wasn't. He used to live in an apartment in Bangkok. What I don't understand is how he could have been so out of it last night and so sharp today."

"Well, for what it's worth, a client and his wife invited me out to dinner once. He got very drunk. Insisted on driving me back to my hotel. I needed the work. Didn't want to insult him. We ended up going the wrong way on the Jersey Turnpike. His wife is screaming. He's cursing out the other drivers like they're wrong. I'm trying to get him to turn around."

"Sounds like something out of *Cuckoo's Nest.*"

"Worse. But the next morning? Like it never happened. He was sharp, articulate, and kicked my ass in a meeting."

We arrive in a clearing where a shooting range has been set up. The Ingram is everything it's cracked up to be. Deadly accurate on single fire. Devastating on auto, taking barely a few bursts to snap a good-sized sapling in half. It takes me a few minutes to feel the rhythm of the fire and recoil, but finally the weapon is almost floating in my hands. It's more difficult to deal with the vibrations it sends coursing through my body—a long-forgotten sensation that conjures up disturbing memories.

Kate has a tough time with the pistol. It's a difficult weapon to master. Seven of nine rounds completely miss the target. She does a little better with the second clip and a two-handed stance.

"I'm hopeless," she laments.

"Don't worry," Timothy counsels smugly. "The enemy's usually a lot closer than that. Just stick it in his face and blast away."

Kate forces a smile, hands me the weapon, and walks off staring at the ground.

"What's the matter?"

"Nothing. I'm fine."

"Come on, I know you well enough by now."

"Well, this is probably going to sound silly, but I don't think I could ever kill anyone."

"Is this the same Kate Ackerman who was asking to borrow my pistol the other day?"

She shrugs. "It was just a way to get you to come with me. I mean it. I couldn't. I know it."

"Sure you could," Timothy chimes in. "And I'll tell you how. I did a lot of sniper work when I was in-country. I'd be sitting there watching some guy through my night-scope. Maybe he was eating or writing a letter home. I knew I was going to kill him. Knew at that moment he was alive. And knew, in the next, a little signal would go from my brain to my finger, and he'd be dead. I could see their faces when the bullet hit. Every time. I still see some of them."

"Are you saying you hesitated?" Kate asks.

"Sometimes. Whenever I did, I'd think about one of my buddies who had his face blown off or his guts shot out. And blam—" He makes a shooting motion with his hand. "No problem. Just like that."

"That's different," Kate protests. "You were a soldier, in a war, struggling to stay alive."

"No other reason for using this," Timothy says, taking the pistol from me and putting it in her hand.

"He's right, Kate. You get in a jam and you get one of these guys in your sights, you just keep thinking about what they did to John."

"Knowing me, I'll probably be worried he's got a wife and kids."

"Fine. Take it from me. He beats them. Daily. Mercilessly." She smiles and shakes her head in mock dismay.

A short time later, the three of us are back in the bunker cleaning and oiling the weapons. Timothy sets out boxes of ammunition, spare magazines and carrying cases, then he tosses a couple of Kevlar vests on the table. "Might want to take these along too."

"I'd feel a lot better taking you along."

Timothy shakes his head no, emphatically.

I'm about to press the issue.

Kate notices and signals me to back off. "How many trips did we make, Tim?" she prompts casually.

"You mean back then?"

"Uh-huh."

"Half dozen or so."

"Came up empty every time, didn't we?"

Timothy lets out a long breath and nods glumly.

"Did I ever make you feel it was your fault?"

He shakes no.

"Did I ever look at you like you didn't deliver?"

"No, Kate. You never did."

"And I never will. I promise."

He hesitates while thinking it over.

"Don't pressure him, Kate. He'll be more trouble than he's worth if he doesn't want to be there."

"I don't," Timothy says with finality.

"Fair enough."

"But I'll get you close. I mean right to the border, right to the Mekong. Chances are, I can even set up some transportation on the other side."

"And all we have to do is get across."

"That's the trick. Despite what Kate may have told you, walking on water never was one of my specialties. That's why I picked this up."

He pulls a black fiberboard trunk from a shelf behind him and swings it onto the table with a jarring thump— a boxy industrial case with metal-reinforced corners. He unfastens the snap latches and raises the top.

USN APV-2 ZODIAC is stenciled on the inside.

"If you don't mind me asking, Morgan, you been giving any thought to what you're going to do in Vientiane once you get there?"

"Yes. Like twenty-four hours a day."

"And?"

"We're going to look up that nasty man."

"Chen Dai?"

"Yes, and ask him some nasty questions."

"If he doesn't kill you first."

34

TWO DAYS HAVE PASSED.

Forty-eight tense, restless hours. Kate and I spent them in seclusion at Timothy's while he went into Bangkok and made the arrangements to go north.

It's just before sunrise when we load the gym bags and trunk into the runabout and set off downriver. Our spirits are high, our sense of security bolstered by the Belgian-made pistol tucked in Kate's handbag and the compact, American submachine gun in a shoulder holster beneath my windbreaker.

We're going with the current this time. The journey is swift and uneventful. It's late afternoon when we arrive in Bangkok. After returning the boat, we meet Timothy at Hua Lamphong Station, the massive main railway terminal on Krung Kasem Road. Just being here gives me a nagging uneasiness: Are the bearded gunman and his sidekick waiting for us? Have they been watching the train, bus, and air terminals?

This is rush hour.

Travelers are scurrying in every direction.

I'm anxiously scanning their faces, my hand poised to go for the Ingram, as Timothy ushers us aboard an express to Nong Khai, an agricultural and mining city on the Mekong River, which forms the border between Thailand and Laos, 385 miles from Bangkok.

We've taken three interconnecting compartments in the first-class sleeper. In the style of the classic European Pullmans, each has two entrances: one from the corridor, the other for direct access from the platform when the train is pulled into the station. I'm in the middle compartment. Timothy forward of me. Kate aft. This will be the first night, since our arrival in Bangkok, she'll have some privacy and peace of mind.

It's just after 5 P.M. when the shriek of a steam whistle announces our departure and the train suddenly lurches forward, a mechanical dinosaur sending its hot breath billowing past the windows. It snakes through the yard, emitting long, chilling screeches that soon give way to a rhythmic clacking as it hits the main spur on the outskirts of the city and begins picking up speed for the long climb into the mountains.

After settling in, the three of us gather in my compartment to review the plan to get into Laos. This only heightens the tension. It's as if we've suddenly realized just what we're doing. My gut is in a knot. Kate's fists are clenched. Timothy's talking rapid-fire like a hyperactive child.

"Nong Khai," he says, using a felt-tipped pen to circle our destination on a map that he's spread over the foldout table. "Scheduled arrival's zero-three-thirty. Chances are we'll run at least a half hour late. There'll also be a short shunting layover, before we—"

"Shunting layover? Sounds like a sex show on Patpong Road," I joke, trying to lighten the mood.

"So that's your vice," Timothy cracks.

"He's also guilty of living in Malibu," Kate chimes in with a grin.

"The man's beyond salvation."

Kate chuckles. So do I, deciding not to snatch defeat from victory by coming back at him.

"Okay," Timothy resumes. "It means the train's going to be broken down. This car will be shunted off to a local that makes stops along the river. We stay on through Hong Song and Muang Kuk, and get off *here* . . ." He pauses and circles a bend where the Mekong turns sharply north, "at Tha Bo."

"Black box time," I declare, referring to the fiberboard trunk.

"Black box time and where we part company. You'll be less than ten miles south of Vientiane, which is here." He circles a city on the opposite bank, then suggests we tackle the problem of gaining access to the Pepsi-Cola plant and getting our hands on Chen Dai.

I've been thinking about it for days, and it doesn't take us long to come up with a basic two-part strategy: arrive early morning when the plant is shut down, break in, and camp out in Chen Dai's office. Then get the drop on him, get some answers, and get out of there. Simple, direct, uncomplicated. It would give us the element of surprise. Put him on the defensive. And provide the perfect hostage if things get ugly. Unfortunately, we have no knowledge of the terrain or physical layout, and won't be able to finalize the details until we get there.

When we're finished, Timothy settles back and produces a small pipe and pouch of opium. "I've more than enough for three," he offers slyly, thumbing the oily brown powder into the bowl.

Kate holds up a hand, declining.

"I'd prefer you didn't do that," I say sharply.

"Sorry, it's the only way I can get any sleep."

"Like to try a right cross to the jaw?"

Timothy forces a smile, lights the pipe, and heads into his compartment, leaving a sweet-smelling cloud in the air. "Good night, Kate," he calls back as he closes the door.

Kate angrily waves the smoke away. "I can't believe it. Sometimes he acts like a two-year-old."

"Well, maybe since he can't have kids he's decided to become one."

"That's very good."

"Thank you. You know, it just dawned on me, you've never said anything about that."

"About what?"

"A family. You have any kids?"

She smiles wistfully and shakes her head no. "I always thought it would've been nice. You know, to have a part of him, a part of John to . . ." Her chin starts to quiver and she leaves it unfinished.

"I'm sorry. I didn't mean to upset you. I—"

"It's okay. I'm fine. I just need some rest."

"Sleep tight."

"You too, Cal."

She goes to her compartment, pauses in the doorway and

leans back, planting a soft kiss on my cheek, then closes the door without locking it.

I stand there for a moment, taken by the warmth of her gesture, then slip out of the shoulder holster and hang it on the coat hook behind the door. It's within easy reach of the pint-sized berth beneath the luggage rack where my gym bag and the trunk are stored. The Pullman cushions that serve as a mattress are lumpy and hard, the pillow about an inch thick, the bedding coarse and itchy. I pull it up to my chin anyway, listening to the rhythmic clacking, thinking about Kate, and feeling like I did when I was fifteen and had a crush on Nancy. I was emotionally immature and afraid she'd have no interest in a nerd, so I started smoking French cigarettes to impress her, which had the opposite effect. I doze off, smiling at the memory. I'm not sure exactly how long I've been asleep when I'm awakened by a knock on the door.

"Morgan? Morgan, it's Kate," she says knocking again. Harder this time. "Hey, Morgan, it's Kate. Open up."

I swing my legs over the side of the berth, rubbing the sleep from my eyes with one hand and reaching for the door with the other. As I unlatch it, it strikes me that Kate's knocking on the *corridor* door instead of the one between our compartments, and, for whatever reason, has reverted to calling me Morgan.

I'm about to grab the Ingram and cross to the other side of the compartment, which would put me behind the door when it opens, but it damn near explodes off the hinges before I have the chance.

The distinctive silhouette of a pistol with a silencer lunges into view. An eye blink later, as Kate shouts a warning and wrenches from the gunman's grasp, the bearded Asian charges through the doorway.

My brain is screaming *Go for the Ingram!* But it's sandwiched between the door and the wall. There's no way I can get to it. I go for the gunman instead, diving just below the machine pistol as it fires, emitting a wild burst of flashes and muted pops. I slam into his midsection and come up between his arms, knocking the weapon loose. We tumble to the floor of the dimly lit compartment grappling for an advantage.

He comes out on top, and with practiced speed drives a knee into my groin and a fist into the side of my head. I double up in excruciating pain, barely able to move. He's climbing off me in search of his pistol, when Kate reappears in the doorway behind him with hers. She aims, then instead of firing, freezes, her eyes wide with terror at what she's about to do.

I know what's going through her mind. *He beats them! Dammit, he beats them! Shoot! Shoot! They killed your husband!* I'm screaming to myself, not wanting to alert him to her presence by calling out. I struggle to my hands and knees and crawl to the door. I'm reaching behind it for the Ingram when the gunman finds his pistol. He scoops it up just as the door to the other compartment explodes open.

Timothy charges through it with his Beretta.

The door momentarily blocks his view of the gunman, who fires a burst from the machine pistol. The rounds hit Timothy square in the chest with tremendous force, driving him across the compartment. He slams into the exterior door, knocking it open, and tumbles out of the train and into the night.

Kate screams and pulls the trigger a split second after the gunman. He's hit, but manages to stagger around and level his gun at her. I've got the Ingram, but before I can fire, she coolly shoves her pistol into his bearded face and fires again. The round rips through his cheek just below his left eye. The life goes out of him and he drops to the floor between us. Kate lowers the pistol and stands there, staring down at him.

It seems like an eternity, but no more than ten or fifteen seconds have passed since she knocked on the door. I set the Ingram aside and quickly go through the gunman's pockets, confiscating keys, wallet, and pistol, then drag his body across the compartment and shove it out the door.

"God. God, I'm sorry," Kate says, distraught. "I was coming from . . . I was . . ." The words come in halting bursts, choked off by sobs.

"Easy. Take it easy."

"I—I was coming back from the bathroom," she stumbles on. "The guy was waiting—he was waiting for me. I didn't know what to do. I—"

"Was he alone?"

She nods, anguished.

"You sure?"

She nods again, emphatically. "He's dead, Cal. Timothy's dead. I should've—I—"

"Don't go blaming yourself. He knew better than to come blowing in here like that. His brain was on 'off,' Kate. He—"

She shakes her head inconsolably.

"Kate. Listen to me. Listen. The guy was a pro. Look what he did to me."

"I should've shot him before Timothy ever got in here." She turns away, sobbing, and curls up in the corner of the berth, head buried in her hands, knees pulled up under her chin.

I check the corridor to see if anyone heard the commotion. It's clear in both directions. Evidently the compartments on either side of mine isolated most of the noise; the train drowned out the rest.

Kate lays her head on my shoulder when I join her on the berth. I gently run a hand over her hair as the train slithers through the blackness, climbing ever steeper grades. The clack of the wheels drones on as villages go flashing past: Ban Bua, Muang Phon, Nam Phong. I think she's asleep when she looks up and softly says, "You were right."

"What about?"

"Threatening them."

"Yes. I don't know what, but there's something—something else."

The exchange prompts me to start going through the gunman's wallet. Along with the cash and credit cards are several pieces of personal ID. One, sealed in plastic, has his photograph. All the information is in an Asian alphabet.

"What's this? A driver's license?"

"Uh-huh."

"Thai?"

"No, Lao," she replies, pointing to the heading that reads *Kamphaeng Nakhon Wieng Chan*. "That says Vientiane Prefecture."

"Then you were right too."

"You mean, about going there?"

"Uh-huh. They say Pepsi-Cola hits the spot. I think we hit it dead center."

She nods uneasily. "This animal—"

"Chen Dai."

"Yes, he knows we're coming, now. Doesn't he?"

"Not yet. Not until he starts wondering why his bearded friend hasn't checked in. We should be there before then. God willing."

"Maybe we should leave Him out of it," she says with a grin. "I think I've had all the mysterious ways I can handle for a while."

"I'm going to tell your father you said that."

"I never should've told you that story."

She smiles, then reaches out and touches my cheek, letting her fingertips graze my lips. Her eyes are soft and vulnerable with a longing that I haven't seen before. She takes my face in her hands and softly presses her lips to mine. She kisses me like this again, then again, more passionately. We're staring deeply into each other's eyes when the moment is shattered by several blasts from the whistle, which announce the train is approaching the next station. Kate turns slightly and glances out the window. Signs proclaiming *Udon Thani* flash past outside. I wrap my arms around her waist from behind and kiss the nape of her neck. Her body tenses and stiffens in protest.

"Not now. Not here," she whispers. "Just hold me, Cal. Hold me. Okay?"

I hug her tightly, resting my head against hers, trying to imagine what upset her, when I recall she once mentioned her husband was stationed at the U.S. Airbase in Udon Thani during the war. I pull the blanket over us and stare out the window into the darkness. Light from distant villages flashes between the trees, providing glimpses of the rugged terrain.

It's well after 4 A.M. when the train slows and finally grinds to a stop in the Nong Khai yards. We remain in the compartment as the shunt is made and the local starts chugging west along the Mekong River past a row of rundown buildings that remind me of the French-Chinese architecture in Saigon. About forty-five minutes later, we're pulling into Tha Bo.

It's more of a siding than a station.

A cool mist hangs in the air as we disembark with several other passengers. Kate and I sling the gym bags over our shoulders and begin walking along a gravel path next to the tracks, carrying the trunk between us. We've gone a short distance when I hear footsteps crunching behind us. Kate's heard them too. She eyes me apprehensively and reaches into her purse for the pistol. I steal a glance over my shoulder. There's a man walking swiftly in our direction, hands jammed into his pockets, collar turned up against the chill. I signal Kate to stop walking, then drop to one knee as he approaches, pretending to tie a shoelace, while slipping the Ingram from its holster. The footsteps get louder. A shadow darkens the gravel next to me. The man trudges past, paying us no mind. We wait until he's a distance away, then cross the tracks, heading north toward the Mekong.

Kate navigates from another of Timothy's maps, leading the way along unpaved roads, past rice paddies and freshly tilled farmland. We walk in tense silence for about twenty minutes, finally coming over a bluff to see the river snaking across the landscape below.

Lights wink in the darkness on the opposite shore, beckoning us. Taunting us. Laos is less than a half mile away. Vientiane barely ten.

We make our way through tall reeds and bullrushes to a sandy cove below the bluff, and open the trunk. Two striped handles protrude from within. Kate and I each grab one and lift out the Zodiac.

At the moment, it's a volume of precisely folded, featherlight, and indestructible space-age fabric. But the instant I pull the inflation ring, the vessel begins taking on its distinctive shape with a steady hiss. Its sharply veed prow and cylindrical sidewalls spring forth from a rigid transom that not only connects them, but also contains a small propulsion system and tiller.

According to Timothy, who compulsively recited the nomenclature, this compact, two-man model was specially developed to enable Navy SEALs to infiltrate inland waterways after being air-dropped into the jungle. Like

Noah's ark, it has two of everything: flashlights, binoculars, nylon ponchos, packets of greasepaint, collapsible paddles, emergency rations, and first-aid kits. Due to the ingenious design and use of materials, the entire package weighs just over forty pounds.

Kate and I start by blackening each other's faces with the greasepaint. When finished, we sink the trunk in the river, then don the ponchos, more for camouflage than warmth, and push off in the Zodiac. Our supply of fuel is limited. Instead of using the motor, we paddle into the channel, letting the current take us.

This is the closest I've ever felt to being back in-country. Compared to this, the trip up the Chao Phraya to Timothy's was like a Sunday afternoon sail in Santa Monica Bay. This is the Mekong. The infamous river that not only separates Thailand and Laos, but snakes thousands of miles south through Cambodia and the southernmost part of Vietnam to the delta where it empties into the South China Sea. The infamous river in which I'd bathed, fought, and almost died.

It narrows in this short north-south leg, the sharp bends at either end slowing the current that still sweeps us along at a steady clip. We use the paddles to change direction and avoid the occasional piece of floating debris.

Soon, far ahead in the darkness, where the Mekong turns west again, the lights of Vientiane appear. All we have to do now is make it to the opposite shore before the current accelerates and takes us past our target—a small shipping canal that branches north on the outskirts of the city. Kate is huddling beneath her poncho with a flashlight, checking the map, when a powerful beam of light suddenly splits the darkness and sweeps past overhead.

An instant later, the distant outline of a boat emerges from the blackness. The gun turret in the bow eliminates any chance it might be a fishing vessel or ferry. Kate and I slouch under our ponchos to present as low a profile as possible. I begin guiding the Zodiac closer to the shoreline. She works herself into a prone position in the bow to search for the buoy that marks the mouth of the canal. The beam comes sweeping back toward us. A surge of adrenaline hits me as the circle of light races across the choppy surface, passing perilously close to the Zodiac. The patrol boat is bearing down on us when Kate spots the buoy's purple light bobbing in the darkness ahead. I fire up the Zodiac's propulsion system and jam the tiller hard left. The bow kicks sharply toward shore as the tiny vessel breaks free of the current. The sudden acceleration sends sheets of water spraying over us. I maneuver around the channel buoy into the canal moments before the onrushing boat glides past, unaware of our presence.

We continue to motor upstream against the current in search of the next landmark, a small bridge where we're to go ashore and ditch the Zodiac in favor of ground transportation. But the river valley is draped with fog. It soon becomes so dense, Kate and I can hardly see each other, let alone the passing terrain. We continue on, weaving through an area overgrown with reeds and water grasses. A short time later, we notice a ghostly form looming just ahead. The bridge emerges from the mist and is suddenly upon us. I punch the throttle and angle toward the bank, sending the Zodiac skimming across the surface onto a muddy flat directly beneath the narrow span.

For better or worse, we're in Laos.

We hide the Zodiac in a grove of bamboo next to the bridge, then shed the ponchos and use water from the canal to wash the greasepaint from our faces.

A shallow embankment leads up to the road that winds through a farming area. Kate and I hurry to a thicket of eucalyptus trees off to one side. Deep within the overgrowth, as Timothy promised, is an old left-hand drive Peugeot sedan. The paint is faded and the tires are bald, but the keys are in the ignition, and a street map of the city is on the seat. The locations of the bridge and the Pepsi-Cola plant are clearly marked, as is the most direct route between them. I uncap a marker and go to work on it.

"What are you doing?"

"Being paranoid."

"Afraid they might be waiting for us?"

"Uh-huh. A very smart lady once taught me to beware of locals who sell info to the enemy."

I quickly work out an alternate route, then turn the ignition key. To my relief, the Peugeot's engine kicks over on the first try. I maneuver it through the trees to the road, keeping the headlights off. We head west across the bridge, its aging timbers thumping loudly in protest. The road is narrow, poorly paved, and unfamiliar, and I turn the headlights on as soon as I'm certain we aren't being followed. The closer we get to the city, the more the pavement and signage, which is now in French as well as Lao, improve. We drive several miles west on Rue Tha Deua, making a right where it angles past Wat Ammon, a steepled temple encrusted with centuries of moss.

The sun is still below the horizon when we spot a large warehouse-type structure in the distance. There's nothing to suggest it's a heroin refinery, nor is there anything else distinctive about it, other than the huge, dimly illuminated bottle cap on the roof that proclaims PEPSI.

The infamous symbol of fizz, fun, and free enterprise— fully endorsed by Madonna and Michael Jackson—is a strange sight in this country where, despite the name Lao People's Democratic Republic, tyrannical Communism rules. I've consumed a lot of Pepsi in my day, but, until now, it never really dawned on me that its colors are red, white, and blue.

We continue to the top of the next hill, then leave the road and pull into a grove of trees that overlooks the plant. Kate fetches the binoculars we took from the Zodiac. Both pairs. We begin checking the place out. It reminds me of the manufacturing plants in the San Fernando Valley: painted steel, flat-roofed, surrounded by a parking lot and high chain link fence. The entrance and exit gates flank a security kiosk where a guard is posted. An electronic box, with a slot into which drivers insert a card to open the entrance gate, is atop a post adjacent to the kiosk. Probably to avoid calling attention to itself, the building is poorly maintained, the grounds unkempt.

"That guard is armed," Kate notes with concern.

"I wish he was our only problem."

Despite adhering to our plan, despite arriving at an hour when the plant should be shut down, the lights are ablaze and the parking lot is filled with cars, scooters, and bicycles.

"They get started early around here, don't they?" Kate observes glumly, getting the message.

"The upside is, they probably knock off early too. We'll just have to hang around until they do."

Kate sighs and makes a face. "It's going to be a long day."

I nod thoughtfully as a different and much more troublesome scenario occurs to me. I'll know one way or the other soon enough and decide not to alarm her. A couple of hours later, at precisely 8 A.M., my fears are confirmed when a whistle blows and the shift changes. They weren't early starters, they were the night shift. Though Tickner said the heroin operation is going to be scrapped, it's going round the clock now. It obviously never shuts down. Our plan is a bust. If getting into Laos was a bitch, getting into this place is going to make it look like a piece of cake.

35

IME AND TIME AGAIN, I DRUMMED IT INTO MY SQUAD, my staff, my daughters, and myself: If something can possibly go wrong, it will.

And it has.

Twice.

Not only hasn't the plant shut down, but also, despite being parked at this vantage point for almost eight hours, we've seen no sign whatsoever of Chen Dai. Considering his occupation and hefty profit margin, I figure he wouldn't arrive in anything less than an armored limo. So, unless he's driving a dusty compact, he isn't here.

I've been watching the comings and goings and thinking about those cop shows I've seen where weary detectives spend days in their cars, living on cold coffee and stale donuts. Right about now, I'd give anything for a Winchell's maple-glazed, not to mention a way to get inside the plant. I'm staring at the huge bottle cap on the roof and working the problem for the umpteenth time, when Kate returns from a visit to some nearby bushes.

"Anything?" she prompts, sliding into the seat.

I shake my head no.

She tears open a bar of survival rations from the Zodiac, takes a bite, and scowls. "I thought the DEA said Chen Dai spends most of his time here."

"When he isn't at his compound in Pak Seng."

"Well, we can't wait forever. Sooner or later somebody's going to spot us."

I nod grimly, a hollow sense of defeat growing in my

stomach. I can't believe we've come this far, come so close, only to come up empty.

"Besides," Kate goes on with a grin, "I may be a farm girl, but peeing in the woods has never been my idea of a good time."

"Thanks."

"For what?"

"Making me laugh. Got any ideas?"

"I'm in real estate, remember? The closest I get to anything like this is an open house where nobody comes."

"Vietnam."

"What about it?"

"That was the closest I got. Engaging the enemy was always a problem. Charlie'd hit and run, hit and run. Drove us crazy."

"How'd you flush him out?"

"Took something that was important to him. Then he'd come running to try and take it back."

"I don't think it applies."

"If we took over Chen Dai's office, it might."

"I'm sure that'd get his attention. But we can't even get through the gate, let alone—"

"Maybe we can," I interrupt, reflecting on the shift change, on cars pulling up to the gate, on the hands pushing cards into the slot to open it. I get my gym bag from the backseat and start rummaging through it. "I hadn't thought about going through the gate."

"What are you looking for?"

"The wallet I took off that gunman." I find it and begin sorting through the contents. "He was working for Chen Dai. Maybe he had a gate card."

"And if he did?"

"Not if, Kate," I reply, holding it up to her. I've no doubt that's what it is. It's almost identical to the one I use to get into the underground parking garage at my office.

"I don't see what it gives us. I mean, we can't just go driving in there."

"Not at the moment. But if we wait till four . . ."

"The next shift change," Kate says, seeing where I'm headed.

"Uh-huh. All that coming and going, I'd say there's a pretty good chance one more car won't be noticed."

"Maybe not, but *we* will."

"I don't know. Chances are we won't be the first Westerners to tour this place. The trick is not to go sneaking around. If we look like we belong, they'll think we do."

Restless and tense, we spend the next few hours in the Peugeot clock-watching. At precisely 4 P.M., the blast of a whistle announces our wait is over. As soon as the shift change is in full swing, we head down the hill toward the refinery. My window is open, and, as we approach the entrance, I ease the Ingram from its holster and tuck the snub-nosed muzzle in the corner formed by the sill and doorpost. My right hand is on the grip and trigger, my left on the steering wheel, elbow bent and resting casually on the sill to conceal the weapon.

I let the car in front of us proceed completely through before advancing toward the gate. The less time the guard has to scrutinize us the better. He waves to one of the departing cars, then glances in our direction. I tighten my grip on the Ingram with one hand, then reach out the window with the other and push the card into the slot. Kate stiffens apprehensively, then sighs with relief as the gate arm rises. I remove the card and slowly drive through into the parking lot, holstering the Ingram beneath my windbreaker. We cross the grounds unnoticed by the arriving and departing workers, who wear ID badges and use a secured personnel entrance. I park at the opposite end of the building where some broad steps, double doors, and a row of windows suggest the lobby and administrative offices are located.

An armed guard is posted at the entrance. Like the one at the gate, he has military bearing, a neatly pressed uniform with name tag above the pocket, and a walkie-talkie riding his hip along with his sidearm. Will he assume we've been cleared at the gate? Assume we have a reason to be here? Or will he challenge us? Kate and I leave the car and approach at a casual pace. The knot in my gut tightens as he blocks our way and addresses us in French.

Kate responds in Thai. As Vann Nath explained, Thai and Lao are mutually intelligible and they have no trouble communicating. From their tone and gestures, it's obvious the guard is giving her a hard time, and she's standing her ground. The give and take continues until something Kate says gives him pause. There's another brief exchange before he nods and steps aside.

"What was that all about?" I ask, as we cross toward the entrance.

"He said state your business. I made up a story about having important information for Chen Dai. He said he wasn't here and insisted we leave. I asked him what he was going to say when the DEA shows up and Chen Dai finds out he turned us away."

"You've got a lot of chutzpah, kid."

"I'm going to need lots more," she says anxiously. "We still have to get through a security check inside."

The lobby is a typical industrial space: terrazzo, fluorescents, and metal partitions that funnel us to the checkpoint dead ahead. It's more of a corridor than an office. Visitors enter at one end and, if they're cleared by the guard posted in an alcove at the midpoint, exit the other. Judging from the epaulets on his tropical tans, he's an officer. The only way into this place is through him.

"Same story and ask to see Chen Dai?" Kate prompts in a tense whisper as we approach.

"Asking's no longer an option," I reply, eyeing the airport metal detector that frames the doorway. I reach inside my windbreaker for the Ingram. "This guy's going to personally escort us right into Chen Dai's office. You understand?"

Kate nods, then reaches into her shoulder bag and grips the pistol. The instant we cross the threshold, the detector beeps, startling the guard. He looks up from some paperwork to see the Ingram pointed at his head, and freezes. While Kate closes the door, I step forward and slip the sidearm from his holster.

"Ask him if Chen Dai will be here tomorrow."

The guard responds to the translation with a defiant glare.

"Tell him we want a meeting. A peaceful one."

He smirks and shifts his eyes to the Ingram. I lower the muzzle slightly to reassure him. "Make sure he understands we won't hurt him or Chen Dai if he cooperates."

The guard studies me warily but finally responds, causing Kate to scowl in disappointment.

"He said, Chen Dai's up north this week."

"Shit. Can he be reached by phone?"

The guard nods.

"Okay, tell him we'll be setting up shop in Chen Dai's office. All three of us. He'll make the call from there."

Kate translates, eyeing me curiously as I remove the clip from the officer's sidearm and give the gun back to him. "I wouldn't want somebody wondering why he's walking around with an empty holster."

"Or wondering why he left his post."

"Hadn't thought of that. Tell him to get a subordinate to cover for him."

"I did."

The guard handles it over his walkie-talkie, then leads the way from the checkpoint. We take a staircase to the second floor and enter a large executive office. It reminds me of a skybox in the Astrodome. Except that the window wall, which usually overlooks the playing field, has a view of a heroin refinery.

It's a stunning sight.

In contrast to the rundown facade, the interior is a slick, high-tech operation. A row of huge stainless steel vats, used to distill the super-pure heroin from opium, are linked by miles of ducting and pipe chases that snake between them in perfect alignment. A network of catwalks used to service the equipment hangs overhead. One wall is a mass of dials, gauges, and electrical panels. Another is lined with fifty-gallon drums of chemicals. White, spotless, and with glass partitions between work stations where personnel toil in lab smocks, surgical masks, and gloves, the vast space resembles a cross between a brewery and one of the clean rooms at Cape Canaveral.

Kate and I exchange incredulous looks.

The guard is stone-faced.

"Okay. Tell our friend here to make the call. Points to be covered are: our names, our reason for being here, our peaceful intentions, and our location."

Kate translates, then monitors our side of the telephone conversation, nodding occasionally to indicate the guard is following instructions. After several exchanges, he pauses and offers me the phone. I'm surprised and hesitate. He nods several times, insisting I take it.

"Yes?" I say, my voice cracking with tension.

"Mr. Morgan? My apologies for not being there to extend a proper welcome," Chen Dai enthuses. "Suffice it to say, I wasn't expecting you."

"I know. It gives me great pleasure to tell you your bearded friend blew the assignment."

"Evidently so. You're an admirable and tenacious adversary. I'm more than intrigued by the prospect of meeting you and Mrs. Ackerman. Unfortunately I am, at minimum, several hours' journey from Vientiane."

"Take your time. We'll be here."

"Very well, Mr. Morgan. Please feel free to make yourselves comfortable."

His English is refined. The syntax straight out of Oxford, the accent more French than Asian, the pace measured, and, as Tickner mentioned, the attitude disturbingly confident. I hang up feeling a little disarmed and settle down to wait.

In marked contrast to the scene out the window, the office is like something out of China in the fifties. The walls are sheathed in silk and hung with ethereal landscapes. An ornate oriental rug covers the floor. All the seating is upholstered in intricate brocade.

The guard has a woman bring tea and rice cakes.

Darkness falls.

Several anxious hours pass before I hear a distant whisk. It sends a chill through me as it gets louder and segues to a haunting *whomp*. The room starts to vibrate. I cross to a window just as two parallel shafts of light come over the building and sweep across the parking area. Suddenly a helicopter appears, its purple and white strobes winking in the darkness as it circles around to the entrance, landing out of view.

Chen Dai is here.

The security officer takes up a position off to one side of the door. Kate and I take seats facing it, weapons at the ready. Several minutes pass before we detect approaching footsteps. Rather than the thumping, stormtrooper cadence

I anticipated, they fall with surprising softness, and are accompanied by an intermittent click.

The door creaks open, slowly.

An elderly man enters alone, paying no attention to the guard who closes the door after him. He's short and lean, and dressed in a gray military suit with a mandarin collar like those worn by Chinese political leaders. His posture is slightly stooped, and though he appears much older than the photograph on Tickner's board, there's no doubt it's Chen Dai. He crosses the room at a geriatric pace, using a cane to keep his balance, and slowly settles into a wing-back chair opposite us. His feet barely touch the floor. When he's comfortable, he glances to the security officer and dismisses him with a flick of his cane.

"You have me now," Chen Dai explains, reading my mind. He smiles thinly and studies us in silence.

I return his gaze, at long last face-to-face with the notorious drug lord who gave the order to kill me, who's responsible for Nancy's death, who bought—*bought*—Kate's husband and had him executed. But he looks more like Confucius than Genghis Khan. More like somebody's grandfather than the legendary nasty piece of work. His face is tired and hollow, the skin pale and translucent with age, yet his eyes are alert and without a hint of malice, or fear, for that matter. It bothers me: He knows who we are, knows we're armed, knows we have an axe to grind, yet he walked in here alone and unarmed.

Finally, Chen Dai's eyes shift slowly to the Ingram. "I was under the impression your intentions were peaceful."

"They are," I reply sharply. "We ask questions. You answer them. We leave. Agreed?"

"Agreed. You won't need that, I assure you."

"I might if I decide to tell you what I think of you and your operation."

"You're entitled to your opinion, Mr. Morgan, but I think what you're implying is unfair. This is a purely humanitarian endeavor."

"Spare us the propaganda speech, okay?"

"That's what you Americans always say when the truth doesn't suit your purpose."

"The truth?"

"Yes. For your edification, thousands of decent, hard-working people depend on this operation for their survival. Families, for the most part, who spend their days eking out livings from harsh, unforgiving land."

"I grew up on a farm," Kate says, seething. "My family struggled through droughts and blights. More than once they almost lost everything. Some of their friends did. But not one of them used their hardships to justify criminal behavior."

"Is it criminal to exploit one's sole resource?" Chen Dai challenges rhetorically. "I think not. No, Mrs. Ackerman, in Houa Phan Province, opium is the equivalent of wheat to Kansas, petroleum to Saudi Arabia." He pauses, reflecting on a thought. "The Saudis are the perfect analogy, you know? They have two things in abundance: sand and petroleum. We have rice and opium. Need I say more? If I could sell the former for the price of the latter, I would gladly be in the produce business."

"The way I hear it, you are, now."

"Will be," he corrects smartly. "Or so it seems. I'm very hopeful the new program will work out."

"And in the meantime, business as usual?" I gesture to the window and refinery beyond.

"Well, of all people, I imagine you, as a management consultant, would have a special appreciation for the concept of contingency planning."

"Come on, you're not a businessman. You're—"

"I agree," Chen Dai interrupts calmly. "To be honest, I find the term demeaning. I much prefer philanthropist."

"That's funny, I was about to say you're nothing more than a glorified dope pusher."

His eyes remain dispassionate, but I notice his bony fingers tighten around the handle of his cane in anger. "It's never been my goal to transform American teenagers into heroin addicts, if that's your point. The DEA is more than equally responsible for allowing this to go on as long as it has."

"Are you suggesting they're incompetent, or involved?"

"Neither. They're incorruptible to a fault, which, I hasten to add, was the root of the problem. More than once I've offered to sell them our annual crop of opium for a third of what they've been spending to eliminate us. Each time they turned me down."

He's caught me unawares. The perfect rejoinder comes to mind, but there's no timing or bite in it by the time I deliver it. "To their credit."

Chen Dai smiles knowingly. "My friend Mr. Tickner failed to mention that, didn't he?"

I nod grudgingly. "You're a pragmatic son of a bitch. I give you that."

"Innovative. As I said, Mr. Morgan, it isn't business, it's a matter of survival. And I find I'm all the more creative when threatened."

"I've noticed."

"Enough jousting. We have a lady here whom we're neglecting. My apologies, Mrs. Ackerman. I didn't mean to be rude."

"I find your disregard for human dignity far more offensive."

"I'm afraid you have me at a disadvantage," Chen Dai counters, feigning ignorance.

"You bought human beings. You let your—your savages defile their remains to smuggle your filth. How could you commit such atrocities? How? I've been trying to imagine what kind of a person could do that? I still can't."

"That was many years ago. We were at war. It wasn't personal." He pauses thoughtfully, then adds, "Though I sense it was for you."

Kate glares at him and nods. "Twenty-one years ago my husband was executed and brought here."

"I'm very sorry," Chen Dai says, solemnly. "I imagine you're in search of a final answer, as I believe your people call them."

"Yes."

"And you, Mr. Morgan?"

"My wife was murdered because I threatened you. I need to know why."

"Fair enough. I have the utmost respect for people who have their thoughts in order."

"We've had lots of time to think."

"Well, I'll spare you the inaccuracies of an old man's fading memory. As one of my anonymous ancestors so long ago observed, one picture is worth more than a thousand words. Come, I'll show you.''

Chen Dai inches forward in the chair and gets to his feet, pausing to secure his balance with the cane while Kate and I stand ready to follow. He takes several uncertain steps toward the door, then, as he crosses behind Kate, he pauses again, and with a lightning-fast flick of his hand, produces a small chrome-plated pistol, which he points at her head.

She gasps and recoils at the sight of it.

"Please don't move, Mrs. Ackerman," he says calmly.

I'm stunned. I can't imagine where the weapon came from. His hands went neither into a pocket nor inside his jacket. I'm wishing I'd taken his dig about contingency planning more seriously, when I notice the top of his cane is missing. The pistol's ornate grip formed the handle; the muzzle, which nested inside the hollow sleeve, is now pressed against Kate's temple.

"Place your weapon on the floor, Mr. Morgan," Chen Dai goes on in a sharper tone.

I'd like nothing better than to cut him in half with the Ingram, but he's shrewdly put Kate between us. She's right in the line of fire. Even if she wasn't, he could put a bullet in her head long before I could swing the Ingram into firing position, let alone get off a burst. I let it slip from my fingers.

Chen Dai kicks it aside and calls out in Lao.

Two bodyguards enter the office in response. These are big, powerful Asians in street clothes. One levels what looks like an Uzi submachine gun at us. The other confiscates the pistol from Kate's handbag, then scoops up the Ingram and frisks us.

"Don't look so betrayed," Chen Dai says, a sly grin tugging at one corner of his mouth. "I didn't promise you would leave here alive. I promised you answers. And, before you die, you shall have them."

36

IT IS COLD AND DARK, AND THE CLANG OF THE THICK STEEL door, which slammed shut behind us with terrifying finality, is still ringing in my ears.

We're in a room somewhere in the bowels of the plant, having been marched at gunpoint down several flights of stairs and through a storage area where drums of chemicals and sacks of raw opium are stored. Chen Dai's thugs shoved us inside with such force we went sprawling across the concrete floor. It's hard and cold like a Boston sidewalk in the dead of winter.

I get to my feet slowly, rubbing an elbow and searching the darkness for Kate, but the absence of light is total.

"Cal?" she calls out in a shaky voice.

"Kate? Kate, you okay?"

"I think so. I can't see a thing. Where are you?"

"Here. Over here. I'll stay put and keep talking. Come to my voice. Just keep coming toward the sound. Walk slowly, keep your hands out in front of you, and come in the direction of my voice."

I hear her shoes shuffling on the floor, then the rustle of clothes as she approaches. I keep talking and extend my arms, groping for her gently until our hands meet and we clutch at each other.

"That bastard," she says bitterly.

"Easy. Take it easy."

"I'm freezing. What is this place?"

"Don't know."

"Maybe a wine cellar or something."

Our voices echo as if we're in a large space. We move

313

cautiously until my hand finds a wall. The surface has a metallic feel and is so cold my fingertips almost stick to it. We pause, waiting for our eyes to become accustomed to the darkness. After a few minutes, I make out a ghostly form rising above us along the opposite wall. It appears to be some kind of scaffold or lattice-type structure. Maybe it is a wine cellar. I hope so. I could handle a bottle or two of a robust Bordeaux about now. I try to determine where we are in relation to the door but to no avail. I've turned around too many times. It's a fifty-fifty proposition. We start moving to the right, feeling our way along the wall. We've gone a short distance when I stumble over something and grab onto Kate to keep from falling.

"You okay?"

"Yes. Hang on a sec."

I drop into a crouch and find a body at my feet. A man's body as best I can determine. It feels rigid, as if it's frozen stiff. I'm about to stand when I hear a number of sharp clicks behind me, then a buzzing sound overhead, which is followed by the flickering of bluish light.

Kate's found a bank of light switches.

There's a slight pause before the place is bathed in harsh fluorescent brilliance, before I'm stunned to find myself face-to-face with Ajacier's corpse. I don't see any blood, bruises, or wounds. He evidently froze to death. I'm staring at him, thinking the slate is really clean now, when Kate, who's facing away from me, screams in total horror. She screams and screams, and screams again. I've never heard anyone scream like that. Not even in combat. It's a primal wail of anguish that comes from deep inside her. I look up and gasp, recoiling at a gruesome sight. Chen Dai has kept his promise, kept it with characteristic viciousness. The final answers have been suddenly and shockingly revealed—dozens and dozens of them.

There, so close I can almost reach out and touch it, is a wall of boots—pairs of boots—military boots. Dusted with light frost, their heavily textured soles confront me just as they did at collection points in Vietnam where the bodies of dead GIs were processed. But these corpses are neither covered with ponchos nor hastily stacked like firewood. No. Feet together, toes pointing skyward, these are neatly stored on metal racks—four high, perhaps fifty or more wide with aisles between them—half of which are empty. They go from floor to ceiling along one wall of the long, narrow room, which I realize is a massive, walk-in freezer. The system of lightweight poles and brackets make the cadavers appear to be floating eerily in space. Each is encased in a plastic bag that is tied about the ankles; each has a plastic identification sleeve hanging beneath the boots, which contains a pair of dog tags; each offers a chilling glimpse of hands, face, uniform, flight suit.

Traumatized, unable to move or speak, Kate and I stare at each other in total disbelief until she emits an anguished cry and lunges into my arms. We're shaking from fear and subfreezing cold, trying to keep from retching, our hearts pounding in our chests. We stay like this, bodies pressed together, arms wrapped around torsos, providing comfort and minimizing heat loss. It's a few minutes before my head clears and I begin thinking about finding a way out of here.

"Feeling a little better?"

She doesn't respond.

"Kate? You okay?"

She nods imperceptibly, without looking at me. Her attention is fixed on the corpses, her eyes wide, piercing, staring at them obsessively, despite the unnerving details revealed by the wash of cold light.

"Just take it easy for a couple of minutes. I'm going to have a look around."

She nods again.

"It might be a good idea if I put out some of these lights."

"No," she replies firmly, without the slightest hint of uncertainty in her voice. She lets go of me, then turns and walks toward the wall of boots.

"Kate. Kate, don't." I catch up and step around in front of her.

"I have to, Cal. I have to know he's here."

She resumes the long walk to the far end of the racks. Her steps are halting, but her head is thrown back in angry defiance, just like it was that day on the pier. She pauses briefly at the first pair of boots, steeling herself to the task, then gently rubs the frost from the plastic sleeve to read the name on the dog tags. She moves to the next sleeve, and then the next, her pace quickening, gradually building into a frenzied search. I'm soon doing the same, trying, with little success, to keep from putting faces to the names: Lucas, Carlucci, Nugent, Horowitz, Garcia, Abney, White, Rosenthal, Jackson, Smith, Perez. Each time I brush the frost from one of the plastic sleeves, I flash back to that day in Washington, to that chilling moment when I brushed the snow from the black granite and found my name. I don't know how long we've been at it when I sense the silence and glance over at Kate.

She's deathly still, clutching a single dog tag on a chain. Her hand is trembling uncontrollably as I approach. I gently take it in mine, steadying it, and read the name—Ackerman, John W. She wipes away some tears, then raises her eyes. They reveal emotions I've never seen before in one person at the same time: devastation at the absolute horror of our discovery, and delight at the incredible relief that the decades of uncertainty are finally over. It's as if our present circumstances are meaningless, as if she could die happily with her newfound peace.

She slips the chain around her neck and clutches the dog tag in a fist. I've no doubt that I'd find mine if I keep searching, no doubt that these are the ninety-eight men on the list—ninety-seven plus Pettibone's corpse with my tags. It didn't vanish. It was taken here to make certain it would never be found. Like Ajacier. Like us.

I touch her face. The tears have frozen on her cheeks. We're both shivering from the cold. I don't know how long we can last, but I remember from survival school that a naked human exposed to forty below zero and thirty-mile-an-hour winds would have a life expectancy of about fifteen minutes. Kate and I are clothed, it's probably just below freezing in here, and there's no wind—so I know we'll last a lot longer than that.

I begin with the steel door. As I feared, there is no handle on the inside, only a keyhole. As I also feared, a quick survey confirms there aren't any other exits, hatches, windows, gratings, or ducts. The room is hermetically sealed. I'm at a loss until the buzz of the fluorescents gets my attention. My eyes drift to the bank of light switches next to the door. An idea is starting to take shape, when Kate calls me.

In one of the rows of empty racks, she's found several boxes of plastic bags, balls of twine, and a stack of Army ponchos. They're probably twenty-five years old, but the ones in the middle are still pliable. I throw several over Kate's shoulders, then one over mine. She's helping me fasten it when she suddenly grabs the collar in her fists, pulls my face close to hers, and says, "We have to get out of here."

"Yes, Kate, I know. I'm working on it."

"No. I mean, we have to, Cal. We *have* to. You don't understand."

At first I think she's panicking, but her voice is even, her eyes focused and clear, then it dawns on me what she means, what's driving her. "For them."

She brightens and nods emphatically.

"I understand. I was trying to tell you I might have a way." I brief her while sorting through the contents of her handbag for some things I'll need and come across the camera. I'd forgotten all about it. "Any shots left in that?"

She checks the frame counter and nods. "Why?"

"You heard what the man said about pictures. You think you can take some while I work on getting us out of here?"

Kate nods with determination and goes to work.

I go to the electrical box and use her nail file to unscrew the cover plate, exposing the six switches along with a jumble of multicolored wires. I carefully begin pulling them from the box. Closer inspection reveals they're the three standard color-coded groups of black, white, and green—positive, negative, and ground respectively. Those of like color are twisted together and capped with a self-threading plastic insulator.

I pirate two short lengths of green ground wire, then remove the insulator cap from the black group, twist one of the pirated wires around them, and screw the cap back on. I do the same with the white group, taking care to keep the two leads, which I've just wired in, far apart. Next, I remove one of the switches from the box and disconnect the wires. A bank of fluorescents at the opposite end of the freezer goes out. I make sure the switch is in the off position, then twist the lead from the black group around one terminal, the lead from the white group around the other, and tighten down the screws. I'm installing the switch back in the box when Kate finishes taking the pictures and joins me.

"What're you doing?"

"Wiring all the positives to one side of the switch and all the negatives to the other. When I throw it, well, it'll be sort of like tossing a hair drier in a bucket of water while it's plugged in."

The switch is the industrial type with a hard click-point and will require a strong upward pull to throw it. Considering what I expect to happen, it's not something I want to do with my fingers. While I tighten the connections, Kate fetches the twine she'd found earlier. I tie the end tightly around the switch, then throw the ball over the top bracket on the pole nearest the wall. It takes me several tries, but it finally loops over and goes rolling across the floor. I pay out the line as far away as possible from the panel. Then I gently reel it in until it's taut.

"Ready?"

Kate nods and winces in anticipation.

I jerk the line sharply.

The switch emits a loud click.

An instant later, all the lights in the freezer go out as the electrical panel explodes with the sharp crack of lightning, sending a shower of sparks and flames shooting outward. The pyrotechnics are short-lived, but the box continues to glow in the darkness, giving off hissing sounds and acrid smoke that curls lazily into the air.

I don't know what else was wired into those circuits, but judging from the number of conduits and connections and the high-tech nature of the plant, chances are pretty good that some equipment is down or, at the least, a technician is staring at a panel with a lot of flashing caution lights. In either event I'm counting on someone coming down here to investigate.

Waiting in total darkness makes it seem like an eternity, but it isn't long before we hear the harsh metallic *thwack* of the latch. Since the door opens out, eliminating the possibility of hiding behind it, I curl up on the floor beneath the electrical panel to create the impression I was injured while toying with it. Kate crouches in a corner concealed by the blackness.

The door to the freezer creaks open.

A shaft of light widens as the guard enters, letting the door clang shut behind him. He has a flashlight in one hand and a pistol in the other. He sweeps the beam around the space, then crosses toward the still-smoldering electrical panel.

I hear his footsteps, then see his shoes coming toward me. They stop within inches of my face as he pauses to examine the panel and length of burnt twine hanging from above. I moan weakly to get his attention. He crouches to investigate. I wait until the last possible instant before blasting him with Kate's canister of Mace. He shrieks in agony and recoils, dropping the flashlight and pistol as his hands claw wildly at his eyes. Kate scoops up the flashlight, I grab the pistol and descend on him, confiscating his walkie-talkie and keys, which I give to Kate. While I keep an eye on the guard, she hurries to the door with the flashlight, trying several keys before finding the one that unlocks it. We slip out of the freezer, looking about warily. There's no one else in the area.

It feels like we stepped into an oven. We shed the ponchos and take a moment to get our circulation going, letting the warmth penetrate deep into our nearly frozen bodies. We're making our way through the storage area—between the drums, sacks, and crates, all labeled in Lao—when Kate suddenly detours to some boxes and begins tearing one of them open.

"What're you doing?"

She points to the markings on the boxes. "These are lab smocks. Those are surgical masks."

Moments later, we're hurrying down a corridor appropriately attired, searching for the staircase. We push through a set of doors into a large room and stop dead in our tracks. We're staring at rows of stainless steel autopsy tables, trays of embalming instruments, and transfer cases. Dusty, untouched for over twenty years, the air still reeks of chemicals and death, of the heinous practice of inserting packages of heroin in the chest cavities of dead GIs.

We waste no time getting out of there, finally finding the staircase that takes us up into the plant. The landing opens into a corridor. One side is a glass partition beyond which workers in smocks and masks busily tend their stations. Up ahead a group turns a corner, startling us. We keep walking as they approach making small talk. One says something to Kate in passing. She mutters a short reply in Thai. We quicken our pace and make our way to the personnel exit, discarding the lab smocks and masks in a trash receptacle before exiting into the parking area.

"That was close," Kate says, relieved.

"What do you mean?"

"That guy commented on my Reeboks. They're very hard to get here. I said I have a friend in Bangkok."

There's no sign of Chen Dai's helicopter as we walk to the Peugeot. We drive across the grounds slowly, passing the security kiosk, and through the exit gate, which opens automatically on approach. I swing onto the road and, suppressing my impulse to put the pedal to the floor, head south toward the Mekong at a normal speed.

Kate is stretched out next to me, her head thrown back against the seat, a serene expression on her face. We drive in silence through the darkened countryside. Finally she sits up and turns to me with a little smile. "So, tell me. Does A stand for answers, or doesn't it?"

"Sure does," I reply, telling her what I'd figured out about the list, concluding, "Tickner said he thought Chen Dai had an ace in the hole. He didn't have one. He had damn near a hundred of 'em."

"The MIAs were bargaining chips if things ever went wrong."

"Why else keep them all these years? They were useless for smuggling, but they'd make dandy hostages. The threat wouldn't have been, 'Back off or they die,' but, 'Back off or they'll never be repatriated.' "

"Yes, but he can kiss his aid package good-bye if this gets out now."

"That's what he's been worried about all along."

"He could've gotten rid of them."

"He will. Soon as the deal with Uncle Sam is finalized and the money starts rolling in."

"But we're going to make sure it doesn't." Kate removes the camera from her bag and begins rewinding the film.

We continue south until we reach Thanon Fa Ngum, the main boulevard that snakes along the river, then heads west into the heart of Vientiane. A short time later, we turn into Rue Bartholini—a short street between Chantha Kumman and Lan Xang—and are relieved to see another well-known symbol of free enterprise aglow in the darkness up ahead. It's red, white, and blue, just like the Pepsi sign, but this one is rippling in a light breeze and has a field of stars. Embassies are sovereign territory and, as the Marine guard checks our passports and opens the gate, I can't help thinking, it sure feels good to be back in the United States.

37

A COMFORTABLE BED, A GOOD NIGHT'S SLEEP, A COUPLE of great meals, and hot, hot showers. Kate and I are fulfilled and at peace with the world. The champion of evil will be crushed, the good and just shall prevail.

But something is wrong.

In my euphoria, I've made an uncharacteristic error of omission when writing the equation. I've totally forgotten about other forces and factors—powerful and determined ones—which might have an impact on it. In fact, I haven't even considered the possibility, let alone calculated the odds. I've been away from my laptop too long.

The uneasy feeling surfaces just after breakfast when we are informed by an embassy staffer that Tickner and Colonel Webster have arrived from Bangkok and are waiting for us in a conference room.

The film has been processed, and, when we join them, color prints of the photos Kate took in the walk-in freezer cover the table. They elicit genuine and heartfelt exclamations of surprise and horror, as does our story. In the course of telling it, we are gently chastised by Tickner and praised by the colonel, and then, after a pregnant pause and conspiratorial glance between them, Tickner locks his eyes onto mine, shifts them to Kate's, and utters some stunning words.

"I'm sure you're both pleased to be finished with this. Unfortunately, the Colonel and I aren't. And it's important to know we'll be able to count on your continued cooperation."

Continued cooperation? I don't like the sound of that at

all. Kate flicks me a puzzled glance. I shrug and am about to challenge him, when a staffer slips a form onto the table in front of me and hands me a pen. He does the same with Kate.

"It's standard USG boilerplate," Tickner explains. "Basically you're agreeing that these photos and your stories will never see the light of day."

"Or what?" I challenge indignantly.

"My apologies, Mr. Morgan. I didn't mean it to have such a coercive ring."

"I'm sorry, I don't understand," Kate protests.

Webster puts a comforting hand on her shoulder. "There are still over two thousand MIAs, Kate," he explains, softening the blow as best he can.

She nods, a little chagrined.

So do I.

"Try not to lose sight of the big picture," Tickner counsels. "We'll get what we want out of this, I promise you. But not at the expense of upsetting the diplomatic balances that years of painstaking work have achieved. Nor can we afford to ignore the need to send positive signals to other drug lords and guerrilla groups in Southeast Asia, not to mention governments."

Kate and I sign the documents.

Within hours the diplomats are at work, and within days the media is heralding the outcome. So are we.

LAOS TO REPATRIATE REMAINS OF 98 MIAS

The evidence of improving relations between the United States and Laos continues to mount. Along with the recently announced aid package for impoverished Houa Phan Province, and the related Drug Enforcement Agency crop substitution program that will have a powerful impact on eliminating the production of opium and heroin, an agreement to repatriate the remains of 98 MIAs, lost in Laos during the Vietnam war, has been reached. The bodies—inadvertently discovered by a team of Laotian geologists who were exploring a subterranean cave—had evidently been hidden there during the so-called secret war by Meo partisans.

Fiercely proud mountain warriors, they risked their lives to retrieve dead Americans, preventing Pathet Lao and North Vietnamese forces from using them to prove that the U.S. military was illegally involved in the war in Laos. Apparently all members of the partisan group who were involved were killed during the conflict and the cache of MIAs went unreported. U.S. diplomats have roundly praised the Lao government for this humanitarian gesture.

38

KATE AND I GO BACK TO OUR LIVES.

She's been living for this moment and has a much easier time of it than I. I love the house in Malibu, but there are just too many memories. After a few months, I sell it and move into a waterfront condominium in Marina Del Rey. It's close to my clients on the west side, near the freeway, and literally minutes from the airport. I've been seeing a lot of Kate, and my daughters have been teasing me about getting a discount for the Friday-night red-eye to Dulles. But this trip is special and they've accompanied me.

It's a crisp autumn morning in Washington, D.C. Several hundred people have assembled at the Vietnam Veterans Memorial. Slow-moving clouds are reflecting in the black granite as a military band launches into the National Anthem.

Kate and I and my daughters are in a group that includes Colonel Webster, Tickner, piano-player Dick Foster, Jack Collins from the NPRC, and Vann Nath, who came from Bangkok. Representatives from all the service branches, both houses of Congress, veterans organizations, the Friends of the Vietnam Veterans Memorial, and the National League of Families are also present, as are the next of kin of the ninety-eight men whose remains were repatriated. Along with the names that have had their symbol changed to signify their fate has been resolved, are a number of replacement panels from which fourteen names have been removed. Mine was one of them.

The last strains of the anthem segue to the rising whine

of jet engines. The sound builds to a thundering roar as we look skyward to see three Air Force F-15s in a missing man formation come streaking out of the clouds. They pass directly over the Washington Monument and continue straight down the center of the Mall. The ensuing silence is soon broken by sharp military commands and the crisp reports of a twenty-one-gun salute. As the volley of gun-shots reverberates, an Army sergeant in dress blues steps forward, raises a bugle to his lips, and begins to blow taps.

The first haunting note sends a chill through me. My eyes well, then tears go rolling down my cheeks as I flash back to those brave men I'd fought with so many years ago, to all those kids who died in my arms.

When the ceremony is over, Kate and I make our way through the crowd to the panel that contains her husband's name. She runs her fingertips over the letters, stopping when she gets to the symbol that separates it from the next.

"Look," she says, beaming, pointing to the diamond that has been inscribed around the cross, signifying his fate has been resolved. She slips the MIA bracelet from her wrist and places it at the base of the panel.

We turn from the wall and look back across the grounds to see hundreds of people hugging and crying, pointing to names on the wall, the years of uncertainty and pain finally resolved, the final answers at last known. Nothing will ever deaden the pain of losing Nancy, but seeing their joy certainly helps. I'll leave here knowing that her death wasn't in vain. That in the end, somehow, the numbers do add up. That there is some purpose, some reason, some grand design.

"He does, you know?" I whisper, taking Kate's hand. "I really believe He does."

She looks at me curiously for a moment before it dawns on her and she smiles with understanding. "Yes," she says, softly. "Yes. My father was right."